ISHMAEL'S ORANGES

ISHMAEL'S
ORANGES

Claire Hajaj

ONEWORLD

A Oneworld Book

First published in Great Britain and the Commonwealth by
Oneworld Publications 2014

Copyright © Claire Hajaj 2014

The moral right of Claire Hajaj to be identified as the Author
of this work has been asserted by her in accordance with the
Copyright, Designs, and Patents Act 1988

ISBN 978-1-78074-494-0
ISBN 978-1-78074-495-7 (eBook)

Text designed and typeset by Tetragon, London
Printed and bound by CPI Group (UK) Ltd, Croydon, CR0 4YY

This is a work of fiction. While, as in all fiction, the literary
perceptions and insights are based on experience, all names,
characters, places, and incidents either are products of the
author's imagination or are used fictitiously.

Oneworld Publications
10 Bloomsbury Street
London WC1B 3SR
England

For my family, near and far,
with admiration and love.

Darling Sophie,

I don't expect you to forgive me and I don't expect you to understand. You were always the good one from the very first. The peacemaker.

But it makes perfect sense to me, now that I'm here and seeing it, really seeing it, Sophie, after imagining it all these years. It's just like the picture. White. White as a bone. There are trees behind the gate and dust everywhere like gold.

I should hate it, shouldn't I? But it's so beautiful out here on its own. Quiet as a dream. Like the home movies we made in the desert when we were children. You remember, with light but no sound, where we were all laughing and waving and he was behind the camera cheering us on. Those were the only times we weren't pretending, when we were almost like a family.

You know the thing that hurts the most? All those bedtimes when Mum read to us – you know, once upon a time and now that's the end of the story. Remember how we used to love that? Well, it was all a lie. Stories don't have any beginnings and endings. They just go on and on. You, me, them, all the people before, just dancing to the same old bloody tune. And I'm tired, so fucking tired. But I can't see how we'll ever stop.

The worst thing is – maybe we really would have been happy in this house. Wouldn't that be the joke? If the old fool was right after all, if this was truly where we belonged? All our best memories hanging on the wall. My first performance. You and me holding hands at the beach. Mum in her wedding dress. Even one of him, maybe playing football right here, in the dust with bare feet and the sea all around. All the things

I could have loved about him, that I kept loving even after he threw me away.

I wish I could explain this better, Sophie. I want to find some way to make sense of it, so you can understand me without any word like we always used to. I know you'll try because you love me, but sometimes that isn't enough, is it?

But, you know, I have this idea that we'll all be here together one day. The two tribes, hers and his. Wouldn't that be the perfect ending? We could walk down this little track, right here, until we reach the sea. I can hear it over the hill just out of sight. It's talking to me. I swear, it's whispering in a hundred voices. I bet it could tell the truth of what happened here – if anyone was listening. But no one ever is. We're all just stumbling around blind in this world. We look straight through each other like strangers, even the people in our own homes.

Remember I love you always.

Marc. Jaffa, December 1988

Even as he finished he knew he'd left too much unsaid. But time was running – the moments flooding together, an exquisite sensation of drowning. He was riding the flood now, carried towards his purpose by the brilliance of the reflecting sea, by the warmth of white stone under his hand as he slipped across the high wall, by the trembling arms of leaves and shadow helping him down into the silent garden.

At last his feet touched the earth. And he saw it – there, cut into the tree's trunk, a child's uneven letters curling into the bark. His fingers touched its faint lines. *Salim.* The circle of the *m* was half-finished, swallowed by the swelling wood. For a moment it confounded him; the long-forgotten script became a face, and in it a pair of eyes asking a question to which he had no answer. He laid one hand over them, blotting them out. Then, with a knife in the other, he dug his own signature underneath.

The glass in the kitchen door was made of water; it parted when his hand went through and he felt nothing. And then at last he saw the house open up to him, welcoming him inside.

By the time he returned to the kitchen with his empty bag he could hear them gathering beyond the gates, high and insistent as the whine of a bee. It was nearly time, and for an instant he felt the beat of fear. But then he reminded himself; his work was done and he was ready. And between him and those voices stood the whispering trees, the weight of earth and the guarding lattice of branches.

He could hear them as he closed his eyes, the distant song of voices drifting through the boughs like bubbles of the past, freed by the same wind that lifted the leaves, that carried the smell of oranges into the house.

It was laughter he heard through the trees, or something like it – the bright, high call of boys playing. And from somewhere behind him, deep behind the closed doors, a woman could have been singing.

Suddenly he was seized with a moment's desire: to answer those voices, to stand up and throw open the door and be recognized. But then, in that instant, the light came roaring in. It came with a fury, passing through the door and over him, rushing on and on into the heart of the house. And it filled him with peace as it went, sweeping everything away before it like a returning tide.

*Each man's life involves the
life of all men, each tale is but
the fragment of a tale.*

STEPHEN VIZINCZEY

1

JOURNEYS

*An 'absentee' is a Palestinian citizen [who]
left his place of residence before 1 September
1948 for a place… held by forces seeking
to prevent the establishment of the State of
Israel… Every right an absentee had in
any property shall pass automatically to the
Custodian Council for Absentee Property.*

ISRAEL ABSENTEES
PROPERTY LAW, 1950

*No doubt Jews aren't a loveable people; I
don't care about them myself; but that is
not sufficient to explain the pogrom.*

NEVILLE CHAMBERLAIN,
LETTER, 1938

1948

'*Yallah*, Salim! Farm-boy! The Jews are coming for you! They're going to kick you out and break your skinny arse like a donkey.'

Two boys stood opposite each other on the dirt road between Jaffa's orange groves and the sea.

One was older, burly and black haired. His chin, arms and belly rolled in chubby folds, like a lamb ready for the oven. Some day those folds would smooth into the coveted fat of the *ay'an* – one of the rich, the coffee drinkers with their white mansions and expensive wives. But today the excess weight was only good for bullying and sweating his way through the warm spring air.

The younger boy stood facing the darkening water with a football in his hand. He wore laced black school shoes and neat brown shorts. His white shirt was tucked carefully around his waist and buttoned up to the chin; his small, pale face was an open book, the Frères liked to tease, a page that anyone could write on.

'Don't call me a *fellah*,' he said cautiously, turning the football around in his hands. It was never a good idea to argue with Mazen, who at nearly ten was brutishly heavy-handed.

'Why not? You live on a farm. Your father makes you go and pick fruit, like the *fellahin*.'

An angry retort filled Salim's mouth, but he swallowed it, suddenly uncertain. Hadn't he begged to go to the groves last week? The harvest was ending, and his father's labourers had picked the family farm – all fifteen full *dunams* of good orange land. Joining the harvest was supposed to be a birthday treat; he was seven now, and one day he would share the groves with Hassan and Rafan. *Let me go*, he'd asked, but his father said no, and to his shame Salim had wept.

'My father pays *fellahin* to work, yours puts them in prison,' he said, changing tack. Mazen's father was one of Jaffa's top judges, a *qadi*; Hassan said he stank of money. 'If the Jews come and live in your house your father can help them lock us all up.' Mazen grinned.

'Don't worry about it,' he said. 'If you ask nicely I'll take care of you and your pretty mama. But that stupid Hassan will have to look after himself.'

He grabbed the football from Salim and turned down the path towards the sea. The younger boy followed him instinctively, empty arms swinging by his side in the falling sun.

'The Jews aren't coming, anyway, not while the British are here,' Salim said, remembering suddenly what Frère Philippe had told him at St Joseph's that morning. A scuffle broke out between two boys in the yard at playtime: one had called the other's father a traitor for selling his *dunams* to the Jews. The other shouted that at least *he* hadn't fled his home like a coward. They were dragged off by their ears, still hitting each other. Salim had stood by transfixed, while Mazen laughed and cheered them on. Afterwards, Frère Philippe had patted him gently on the face. 'Don't worry, *habibi*,' he'd said over the wet *thwack* of the whip as the boys took their lashes. 'All this talk of Jews and armies… not everyone is crazy for fighting, not while the British are still here and God watches over his flock.'

'God helps those who help themselves,' said one of the nearby Frères, darkly. 'God better had,' said another, 'because the British surely won't.'

'You're such a donkey, Salim,' sneered Mazen, bringing him back to the present. 'The British don't care if we live or die. They want to slice this place up like an orange and give the Jews the biggest piece. But we'll be ready for them, by God. Let them test the *Najjada*. I can't wait to shoot a Jew.'

Salim could not imagine shooting anyone. He had once seen a British policeman shoot a sick dog – a stray; the sad noise it made as the bullet went in had made Salim kneel on the ground and vomit. And then there was what happened last month – the blood that ran over the bricks onto his shoes – but he would not think about that.

'You can't join the *Najjada*,' he said, pushing his hands into his pockets and squaring his shoulders. 'You're just a boy. Mama says they only take men.' Boy scouts with guns, she'd called them at the parade last week; but Salim had stretched up on his toes behind Hassan's back to see them standing to attention in Clock Tower Square. They had tall rifles and fine grey uniforms. He knew one; Mazen's gang called him cat's arse because he had a deep brown pimple in the middle of his chin. They'd teased him to crying about it, but that day his eyes were bright and proud. Hassan would have joined them too – but Mohammad Nimir al-Hawari accepted no boy under fifteen.

'Your mama has a woman's brains,' Mazen scoffed. 'Al-Hawari is a friend of my father's. Anyway, why would I tell you if I joined? They don't take little donkeys like you.'

'I'm not a donkey,' Salim whispered, as Mazen ran ahead. Sometimes, in his wildest moments of courage, Salim imagined knocking Mazen to the ground like a fat football. But with his big fists and blistering scorn, Mazen was more terrifying than even the Jews. *I hope the Jews get Mazen when they come.*

The Jews are coming. That's what the Frères whispered to each other at school. The countryside was emptying as the fighting drew near, bringing refugees to Jaffa with their dirty bags and clinging

children. Salim's father had complained to the Mayor about them –
but his mother had sent packages of food for the women with babies.
Salim could not understand what would make people want to sleep
in Jaffa's mosques and churches instead of in their own homes.

But today, with the sun high and the air filled with salt and
oranges, it was hard to feel afraid. They chased each other along the
path, racing through the scrubland and yelling into the warm rush
of sea air. The ball flew towards the sea and Salim streaked ahead,
breathless and exultant, scooping it before the surf could claim it.
Spinning around to cheer his victory, he suddenly realized he was
alone. His cheeks turned red as he spotted Mazen, grinning down
at him from the top of the embankment.

'You always fall for that one,' he laughed. Salim hung his head to
hide the shaming flush. *Why do you always let him trick you, stupid?*
the stones on the ground seemed to say.

'Come on, *fellah*,' Mazen said, pointing to Salim's dirty knees and
sweaty face. 'I'm hungry. Let's go to the souk.'

There were two ways to get from Al-Ajami to the souks of Jaffa's
Clock Tower Square.

The route from Salim's house led straight through the silent inland.
It passed the sun-bleached whiteness of the seaside villas, their walled
gardens spilling glorious streams of red bougainvillea and the dusty
tang of oranges. It turned left onto old Al-Ajami Street, where new
motorcars whined past donkeys trundling loads of pomegranates and
lemons. The door of Abulafia's bakery was always open, even in the
bracing winter months. Salim had waited there a hundred times, his
senses scorched by the smell of pastries rising in clouds of cinnamon
and allspice. His mother liked *manquish*, a flatbread sprinkled with
thyme and sesame. He used to eat it from her hands, a little piece at
a time, as they walked out into Jaffa's old city, with its coffee shops
and yellow plumes of nargile smoke.

The *other* way to the Square belonged to Jaffa's boys; it was a rite of passage. As soon as a boy was old enough to walk, another would dare him to try it – crossing down over the wild beaches, braving the slippery rocks and then inching out step by step under the ancient port wall.

Today, the sun beat down on the great crescent of the Mediterranean; the water shone gold against the black land like a ring in an African ear. Salim and Mazen jumped across the tide pools, splashing the bare-armed boys fishing for crabs. They picked their way across the jagged rocks until the port of Jaffa emerged in white, sea-stained stone.

'Jaffa's harbour is as old as the sea,' Frère Philippe had taught them. 'It was here before the Arabs or the Jews. God Himself led Japhet here, Noah's son, in the times before time. The bones of twenty-two armies rest here. The pagans of Thebes chained their maiden sacrifice just there,' his wrinkled hand pointed and a dozen pairs of eyes followed it. 'There, out on the rocks that we call Andromeda, waiting for the sea monster to devour them. The Crusader king, Richard the Lionheart, lay in his sickbed on the port just there, begging Salah Al-Din for peace. The godless Emperor Napoleon camped by the lighthouse, while the plague destroyed his army and his righteous prisoners rose against him. He learned a lesson that I tell you now, *mes enfants*: that Jaffa is God's beloved place, and they are cursed who come to harm it.'

Salim cherished a guilty love for the English king with the lion on his chest, even though most of the boys liked Napoleon and Salah Al-Din, champion of the faith. He imagined Richard now as he edged carefully under the yellowing harbour wall. It might have been the same for him: the sour slap of shallow waters and the bloody scent of feluccas bringing in the catch. Only the great steamships on the horizon marked the passage of centuries.

By the time he pulled himself up onto the harbour floor, Mazen had already found a loose orange. He was dropping the pith on the ground, the yellow juice running down his chin. 'There it is,' he said, a chubby finger pointing north. 'There they are.' Across the bay, the gleaming high-rises of Tel Aviv curved up the coast as far as the eye could see.

Salim barely noticed Tel Aviv most of the time. Only the very old, the grandmothers and grandfathers of his friends, sometimes talked of a time when Jaffa was surrounded by circling dunes and Tel Aviv was just a few shells in the blowing sand. To Salim it had always been here. It was the same with the British. They had always been here too, the Commissioners and Commanders, those starched, pink-faced men. The boys called them *schwee schwees*, the noise that pigs make. But they were fond of the Jaffa garrison. A private called Jonno used to give Mazen and Hassan cigarettes. He'd promised that Salim could have one too, once he turned eight.

Only these days Salim felt he was seeing more of Tel Aviv and less of the British. *British rule in mother Palestine ends next month*, the Frères said. *And then a new place called Israel will burst out of her belly, and split her in two forever*. Salim had overheard Mazen's father putting it more simply. 'The next time you see the British will be from the deck of a ship, waving goodbye.'

'It's late,' Mazen said, frowning as the call for the early evening prayer started to rise. 'If you weren't so slow, we'd be there by now.'

'Let's not go,' Salim said suddenly. The fear that had crept up while he climbed under the wall now swept over him in a bitter wave. In the evening light his feet looked red again, red as the blood on the stones, as the sound of screaming. But Mazen just laughed and said, 'Chickenshit baby boy.' He wiped his mouth and grabbed Salim along by the arm into Jaffa's narrow alleyways, as the words of the muezzins flooded the city, dissonant keening, rolling down from every quarter.

They burst into Clock Tower Square as the songs faded. Salim was panting and his arm was sore. Mazen let go, and he stood for a moment to catch his breath and calm his pounding heart. His eyes ran automatically up the Tower's severe angles. A plaque on the wall read *Sultan Abd Al-Hamdi II*. They had learned about him, the great Ottoman emperor who was short of money – or perhaps of patience – and asked Jaffa's leaders to pay for the Tower themselves. Today, there was hardly a rich man in Jaffa – Muslim, Christian or Jew – who didn't claim to have bankrolled it.

But all that was over now. At the other end of the Square, like an ugly tumour, the ruins of the New Seray Government House lay in a shattered pile. The building itself had been blown completely open, gaping over the Square like a toothless mouth.

He crept over to the rubble. Mazen was watching a man wrapped in a *keffiyeh* pulling stones out of the pile.

'I bet there are still bodies under there.' Mazen pointed to dark red stains. 'Or maybe arms, or legs or something. If my father had been voted Mayor instead of that idiot Heikal, he would have cleaned all this up by now. Smell that stink! Or maybe you can't, because Hassan smells like this all the time.'

Salim felt his stomach heave. The bomb had been hiding in a truck of oranges, they'd said. The man who drove it must have looked like an Arab, but he was really one of the Irgun, the most dreaded Jews of all.

They'd heard the *boom* on their way to the schoolroom, and afterwards the screaming. Hassan had turned to run back, his schoolbag bouncing across his shoulders. Salim had run too, terrified to be left behind. He'd clutched at Hassan's bag until it vanished ahead of him into a thick yellow cloud. And then the cloud was on him too, choking him with dirt, while under his feet shards of glass and stone crunched and broke, sending him sprawling to the floor. Through the ringing of his ears he'd heard sirens. Someone was screaming over and over again. *Omar! Omar!* He was lost in a dark well – he was drowning, he tried to call Hassan's name but dust filled his mouth. Something large and soft was lying near his legs, leaking in slow pulses, turning his canvas shoes red under the faint returning sun. The colour had blossomed around him as he lay transfixed. Until Hassan suddenly appeared overhead, grey dust spattered over his face, his eyes white as a beaten horse. He'd hauled Salim up by his filthy shirt and dragged him home.

The next day Jaffa's mothers howled while the British soldiers crawled over the ruins. He'd watched paralysed as Mazen pulled a strip of someone's shirt from under a piece of masonry. It was white cloth, wet and stained black with blood and caked brown dirt. The smell on it was foul, and it stayed with him even when the police came to chase them away.

Salim pulled at Mazen's shirt. 'Please can we go? I don't like it here.' Mazen shook Salim's hand off, but he turned away all the same. *They'll become ghosts*, Mazen had told him as they carried the bodies away. *The dead can't rest without vengeance.*

They made their way to Souk El Attarin, to buy sweets. The mounds of pistachio, lemon, rose and gold smelt as delicious as ever, but Salim's mouth was dry. The boys were used to fighting through the crowds to get their share. Not today, though. The souk was almost empty. The old shopkeeper looked at them with hungry eyes as they handed over pocket money.

'Hey, Salim!'

Salim looked around in alarm; they were not supposed to be out so close to curfew.

'Shit,' said Mazen loudly, 'it's the *Yehuda* boy.'

'Hi, Elia,' said Salim. 'How's life?' He shifted, grateful the Square was empty. It was not so good to be seen with a Jew, even a local one.

Elia was older than Mazen, fair skinned like Salim with thin arms. He shrugged his narrow shoulders and said '*Yani*,' the universal Arabic expression for that grey place between good and bad. 'I was going to see my father,' he said, pointing in the direction of Souk

10

Balasbeh, the clothes market. 'We close early now. He doesn't like me to walk alone, with all the troubles.'

'Who's causing the troubles?' said Mazen. 'Your father and his friends, that's who.'

'He's not one of those people, Mazen,' Salim protested. He dimly remembered a time when they had been allowed to be friends. Elia's father, Isak Yashuv, was nearly an Arab. You could never tell him apart from any other Palestinian, with his dark Iraqi skin and hawk eyes above the coals of his nargile, bubbling away all day long. But Elia's mother came from outside Palestine, with the white Jews.

This had been endlessly and furiously debated in Salim's house when a final halt was called to Elia and Salim's friendship.

'A Jew is not a Palestinian and a Jew is not an Arab,' Abu Hassan had yelled at him, his hand hitting the table. 'They are all bastards who came here for nothing but to rob us. You want to shame me?'

'For God's sake, calm down,' said his mother coldly, her high forehead smooth as glass. 'Isak's family was fitting buttons in Souk Balasbeh before you were born. And as for his foreign wife – what about me, eh? Didn't you drag me to this forsaken country, like a cow in a cart?'

Salim knew that his mother and the pale Lili Yashuv had a strange kind of friendship too; when they went to collect her finest clothes from Isak's shop, Lili would talk to her in halting Arabic with a heavy accent. And his mother would smile in a way she rarely did even with the wives of the other *ay'an*.

Today, Elia looked even more miserable than usual. His family was among the tiny handful that still kept a foothold in Jaffa; the rest had moved to Tel Aviv. Their shop in the textile souk had become an open target, but Isak refused to move. 'I won't give in to this madness,' he'd said, doggedly coming into work every day while his small stock of business dwindled.

11

'My family don't want any trouble,' said Elia to Mazen. 'We just want to work. But it's not just the Irgun causing the problems.' He jerked his head over to the south, where the *Najjada* and the Arab Liberation Army headquartered.

'Look, Elia, I'll take you to your father now,' said Salim quickly. Mazen had a look Salim knew well, his beating face. 'We have to get back before the curfew.'

'Okay, *Yehuda* boys,' said Mazen, the words smeared with contempt. 'Enjoy your walk. I'll see you when the Arab armies come.' He moved across to Elia, and bent his head towards the other boy's ear. 'There are thousands of us, Jew. You'll see.' And he turned his back on them and ran across the Square.

'You don't have to walk with me, Salim,' Elia said. The sky was turning dark now, slate grey clouds rolling in with the night.

'I won't walk all the way. Maybe just a little bit. Is your mama okay?'

'Yes, she's okay. She's afraid now. She and Papa fight a lot.'

'Mine too.' Salim kicked the ground in front of him. 'Is she frightened that the Arab armies are coming to save us?' These days, the radio and Friday sermons were full of nothing else.

Elia didn't reply, and they walked along in silence. Salim started to feel sorry for him. If he were Elia, wouldn't he fear the great Arab armies? He imagined them, rows and rows of men with their flags streaming and guns waving, just like the bedouin from the old stories.

'You can come to our house,' he said in a rush of feeling. 'Mama will hide you. We won't tell anyone you're Jewish. You'll be safe with us.'

Elia raised his head sharply and Salim was suddenly frightened by his expression. '*Ya* Salim, I don't think we can live like we used to,' he said, slowly. 'Mama says your people hate the Jews and will never let there be peace. So we'll fight each other, no matter what.' He shrugged his shoulders again. 'Only God knows who will win.'

'The Arabs will win,' said Salim firmly. He had little affection for his father, or Abu Mazen, or for any of the other heavy men who came and went from his house. But his world was built around the smell of their cigarettes and the low hum of their conversation. It was impossible to believe that their authority might ever cease to be there, quietly ordering the universe.

'You're just like Mazen, if you think that,' said Elia, stopping dead beside him. 'Why didn't you go with him? He'll teach you how to shoot at my family and trash our shop, like his terrorist friends.'

Salim laughed before he could stop it; the thought of fat Mazen screaming with a pistol in his hand was too funny. But the sound seemed to hurt Elia somehow; his thin shoulders recoiled into his body like a jack-in-the-box ready to spring. Yelling, '*Yallah*, go on then! Go!' his arm shot out in a half-punch, half-shove, hitting Salim in the chest and pushing him against the stone wall.

It felt like the time he was stung by a bee – numbness, followed by a sharp, rising pain that made Salim want to howl. Hot tears sprang to his eyes.

'*You* should go!' he shouted back, bunching his hands into fists. 'Go away. This is Palestine, where the Arabs live. Go back to your own place.'

'Jaffa *is* my place!' Elia sounded tearful. 'But that bastard Mazen wants to throw a bomb through my window. What are we supposed to do?'

Salim thought of the terror of Clock Tower Square, the bloody pile of broken stone and the raw screams filling the air like smoke. Mayor Heikal had spoken on the radio that night and called the Jews murderers of children, as savage as bears. Mazen and his gang had sworn revenge. On that day, across the whole of Jaffa, it was heresy to think that Jews were not devils.

But despite this, Salim still believed the world of Jews must surely be divided into the bad and the good. The bad ones lived in Tel Aviv and those vast farmlands where Arabs did not go. People said they had driven families out of their homes, invaded Haifa, Jerusalem and other Arab villages and killed in their hundreds while the British just stood by. Salim had never seen one of these nightmare Jews. But at night, they stood dark and faceless on the borders of his sleep.

But Elia's family looked much the same as everyone else in Jaffa. They worked and lived just as his family did. So how could they be enemies?

He wanted to explain some of this to Elia, but confusion tied his tongue. Instead he just stood there, eyes cast down, twisting his foot on the gravel. They were still some distance from the gates of El-Balasbeh, and it was already closing time. Elia sighed, a sound that seemed to say: *Well?* But if it was an invitation, Salim did not understand it.

'I have to go home now,' Salim said finally. Tomorrow, perhaps, they could put it all right. Elia nodded.

'Okay, Salim,' he said. '*Ma salameh*' – go in peace.

As Elia walked away, Salim's stomach felt heavy – like small stones of worry knocking together. And then there was nothing left to do but run, past the ruin of the Square and through the shuttered streets, back towards the safety of home.

The Al-Ishmaeli house was known as *Beit Al-Shamouti*, the Orange House. A thick wall of shamouti orange trees flickered darkly behind the bars of its iron gate, spring blossoms swelling on their boughs. Over summer, they would turn from small lemon buds into globes of Jaffa's gold. Then the air would fill with a bruised sweetness as they were crushed into juices or sliced and sprinkled with sugar and rosewater. Across Jaffa, others would be wrapped in paper and packed into steamships, destined for lands Salim had only dreamed of.

The neighbours whispered, too, that without his fifteen *dunams* of orange land south of the city the thick-lipped Saeed Al-Ishmaeli – Abu

Hassan to his friends – would be lucky to afford a shed in his own back garden. That was the other reason for the house's nickname.

As he walked back home through the darkening streets, Salim brooded over Elia and Mazen. They'd all been friends once. But last year everything changed.

Frère Philippe had tried to explain it at school. Palestine was to be divided up between the Jews and the Arabs. The Jews would get the northern coast, the Galilee and the southern desert. The Palestinians got the fertile west bank of the Jordan and the green hills before Lebanon, as well as the southern port of Gaza. Jerusalem was given to the whole world. Because Jaffa was in the Palestinian part, by law, the Jews could not take it. Salim had looked at his teacher in amazement. Who were the people doing all this giving and taking of homes?

The thought of anyone taking his own trees made his skin prickle. *Fellah!* How dare Mazen call him a peasant? Peasants were dirty and poor, with rough hands and bad teeth. They worked the land, but never owned it. *I am a landowner's son. It's my right to pick the harvest.*

When he visited the fields last week, he'd not been allowed to take any fruit. Salim was too young, Abu Hassan said – by which he meant *too disobedient.* Harvest is a job for a man, not a child, he'd proclaimed.

Instead it was always Hassan who went. It suited Abu Hassan to parade his eldest boy up and down the lanes of trees like a real *effendi* – 'As if he was heir to something important and not just a few acres of dirt,' his mother had said. Salim was too complicated a case for a man who loved income, idleness and coffee in that order, who bought Jaffa's newspaper *Filastin* just to keep folded by the living room table.

This is why Mazen's jibe hurt so. It was his way of saying 'My father is a clever and important man who understands things. Your father may have a bit of money, but he has the brains of a *fellah.* So when the fighting comes your family will be out in the cold.'

15

Turning the handle of the back gate, Salim slipped inside the garden. The trees looked sleepy in the dusk, the air between them still flushed with the sun's warmth.

He liked to count them as he walked the path towards the porch. Each had a story: this lopsided one lost its branches in a famous winter storm and now stood like a beggar at the gate, reaching out to guests with one plaintive arm. This one was a bully, pushing its branches into all the others while its roots bubbled up out of the earth like a sea monster.

Then there were the three smallest trees planted for the three sons: Hassan's first, then Salim's and then Rafan's just last year.

Hassan's tree was a good height for its age, tall enough to shelter under, with thick roots. It had matured early and Hassan was only five when he started taking its fruit. Salim could not recall a year without the ritual of holding his elder brother's woven basket and breathing in the bitterness of freshly plucked oranges.

Salim's tree had been fruiting for a year now. But his father had not let him take the fruit during this harvest, to teach him a lesson in obedience. Orange farmers plant trees when their sons are born, the *fellahin* said. But they only grow sweet when the boys are ready to become men.

Perhaps that was why you're so little, he thought sadly, stroking its bark. It was only three years younger than Hassan's but less than half the height. The tree leaned westwards into the sunset, its branches like hands clambering up the wall to escape.

The stunting of Salim's tree was a kitchen joke in the Al-Ishmaeli household. Hassan found it particularly funny. 'I hope your balls grow bigger than your oranges, Salim,' he used to say. 'Or you might turn into a woman after all.' His mother blamed it on the wrong ground. It was stony by the gate and lacked the morning sunshine. But she never mocked him for loving it. He touched the fresh cut on the trunk made that week, the memory of tiptoeing into the garden by candlelight together, to mark his seventh-year height on the tree and eat sweets under the stars.

She was sitting on the porch as he reached it, Rafan at her breast. Behind her the sky was emptying, and the blue shadows made her red hair look black. Her head was bent to the baby and the hushed sound of her song was swallowed by the sea breezes.

Noor Al-Ishmaeli was a breathtaking woman. Even Salim knew it, from the whispers of the boys, and the deference of the Frères when she took him and Hassan to school. It was her remoteness – as still and melancholy as a sculpture, as scornful as Andromeda tied to her rock. Her white forehead and olive-green eyes were the legacy of a noble Lebanese family, fallen on hard times, who bargained away their fifteen-year-old daughter's virginity to Saeed Al-Ishmaeli for the equivalent of two new cars and her father's retirement fund.

Now, despite fifteen years in Palestine, with three children born and raised there, she still lived like a stranger. But to Salim she was the source of all wonder and love. He had always been her favourite – until the new baby came.

He put his chin over her shoulder, suddenly desperately tired. She tipped her head to rest her forehead on his, and he closed his eyes for a moment in peace.

'Where have you been, *ya'eini*?' she asked. Salim was the only child who ever won that endearment from her, the mother's blessing that says 'you are more precious to me than my eyes'. She chose to say it the old way, in the formal Arabic of imams and singers – words that distanced, that said *foreigner*. But to Salim it sounded noble; it stirred his daydreams of knights and queens.

'Out with Mazen, Mama.'

She laughed, as Rafan snorted on her lap. 'I don't know what you see in that son of a pig.' Salim felt guilt itch up his back.

'I don't like him either, but there's no one else still here,' he said defensively. It was true – many people had left Jaffa, saying they would be back when the 'troubles' were over. Salim hesitated and then said, 'He called Baba a peasant.'

'*Aya*, maybe he's cleverer than I thought.' She lifted her head into the dying light and turned those vivid, searching eyes on him. 'Did it bother you, *habibi*?' Salim hung his head, afraid to answer.

'My beautiful boy,' she said, and he heard amusement in her voice. 'So sad, a mosquito stung him. There are so many here, buzzing all over the place. But when morning comes, *ya'eini*, what happens to mosquitoes?' She opened her empty hand, and Salim imagined tiny puffs of shadow disappearing into the air. 'One day, all these Mazens will mean less to you than that. You're going to be a bigger man than them.'

Then, just as quickly, she dropped her hand and turned back towards the horizon, where the pale darkness had settled over the sea.

'If you want to see what kind of big man Mazen is going to become, go inside,' she said, carelessly. 'Abu Mazen is there, talking shop with your father.'

The kitchen was dark, with the evening meal prepared and covered on the table; warm smells of rice, lamb, hummus and little parcels of steamed cabbage leaves. The kitchen door opened directly into Abu Hassan's domain with its plush leather seats surrounding a coffee table of tortoiseshell lacquer.

From behind the door, Salim could hear his father's low, complaining rumble and Abu Mazen's smooth replies. Hearing the word *Jews*, he pushed the door open just enough to listen.

'You can think what you like, my friend,' Abu Mazen was saying, 'but these guys leaving now have their heads screwed on. Look at Heikal and Al-Hawari! Heikal is Jaffa's first politician and Al-Hawari is its first soldier. But are they here? No. They're waiting it out in Beirut and Cairo. They know the British have already dropped us like a rag. The Jews took Haifa and Jerusalem without the *Angleezi* firing a single shot. They're coming here next. And when they do, it will be like Deir Yassin all over again.'

Deir Yassin. The words made Salim go cold. He'd seen the pictures of the bodies in that village, after the Irgun came. They said Jews had put whole families in front of the walls and filled them with bullets.

'The Jews are cowards.' Abu Hassan's voice, a wheezy bass. 'Haifa and Deir Yassin had no defences. We have the Arab Liberation Army here, more than two thousand men.'

'They don't care about that rabble. They have the *Americani* at their right hand, and the United Nations. They have guns and artillery coming from Europe. In three weeks Palestine is facing a death sentence. When the British leave, the Jews will raise their flag and defend it. You think Ben-Gurion is going to wait while we hit his convoys and kibbutzim? For the Egyptians and Jordanians to invade his new Israel, to bed down in our cities then cross to Jerusalem and destroy him? No, the Jews won't risk it, I promise you. They're attacking first, and they'll take all they can get. Haifa's gone. We're next. Remember Clock Tower Square? They don't care what they have to do to us. Maybe we should all clear out, until our friends come across the border to help us.'

Clear out? thought Salim, just as his father said, 'Why should I leave my own house because of the *Yehud?* Let the Arab armies fight around me.'

And then suddenly Salim yelled in shock; a hand had clapped over his eyes and another over his mouth.

A giggle from behind him told him it was Hassan. He felt a hard pinch on his cheek as Hassan said, 'What's this, *ya* Salimo? Listening at the door again? Shall I tell Baba or can you pay me not to?'

Salim wrenched himself around in panic, trying to break from Hassan's grip. One flailing arm caught Hassan on the cheek. The older boy stopped laughing and started yelping 'Baba, Baba!'

The conversation halted; footsteps approached and then the kitchen door swung open. Stuck in Hassan's furious arm-lock, Salim could just see his father's round cheeks and sunken eyes glaring at him over his white shirt and neck-cloth.

'He hit me, Baba,' panted Hassan. 'He was listening at the door and when I tried to stop him, he hit me.'

The injustice made Salim choke; the words surged up before he could stop them. 'You liar!' he screamed. 'You're a lying son of a pig!'

Hassan's eyes widened in shock and Salim realized what he'd said. Then Abu Hassan's ringed hand came sweeping out of the air, slapping him hard enough to drive his teeth into his lips. Saliva and the tang of blood mingled with tears running down his face.

Looking up at his father's face he saw the lip thrust out, the same immovable lip that last week said no to the harvest, no to his orange tree, no to his mother's idea for a birthday party like the ones the British children had. He heard himself saying: 'I hope the Jews do come to kick you out.' Then he ran past them, sobbing as he hurtled up the stairs into his bedroom and slammed the door shut.

Gradually his tears gave way to stillness. Sounds beyond the door became audible once again; the evening meal went ahead without him, his mother's and father's voices raised in their nightly argument. Today it was about the pearls Rafan had broken, that Baba said were too expensive to replace. 'Do you think you married a rich man?' he was yelling, in his fractured bass. 'Wasn't it enough those Lebanese thieves beggared me when I took you, now you want to finish the job?' Then, 'You want to dress like a Beiruti whore, go back there, I won't stop you,' before her cold reply, 'In Beirut even the whores live better than I do.' Salim pulled the pillow over his head.

After dinner, the door creaked open and he heard soft footsteps. A voice whispered, 'Hey Salim, Baba said you were to stay here without any food – but I brought you a plate.' It was Hassan, contrite. Salim turned on his side to look at him, but did not speak.

'By God, it was just a joke, Salim. You take everything so seriously, you ninny. But why did you have to go and upset the old man? You know what he's like.' He reached out and ruffled Salim's hair, a shamefaced touch.

After Hassan left, Salim tried to ignore the food. But his tummy rumbled so badly that he ended up pulling it towards him and cramming it into his mouth, gulping each furious bite.

Thoughts twisted through his mind like snakes. The burning unfairness of it, of Hassan's proud day at the harvest, of Rafan arriving to occupy their mother's arms and time. And him, Salim – not a man to be respected nor a baby to be loved. Then came Abu Mazen's words, slipping down his hot throat with the taste of ice and fear. Why were the Jews coming here next? Why would they need to leave their home? *It will be like Deir Yassin all over again.* The story of that massacre had blown through Palestine like a red wind – fifty dead, one hundred, two hundred. The rice in his mouth was gritty as dust and he heard the woman screaming – *Omar! Omar!*

He pushed the plate away and lay down again, pulling the blanket over his head. Another hour went by before he heard another click of the doorknob. This time, Salim felt a cool hand come to rest on his forehead, and breathed in the reassuring smell of his mother's perfume. He lay still as he could, afraid that if he spoke a word, he would make her want to leave again.

A long silence passed. Finally he could hold back no longer. 'It's not my fault, Mama,' he whispered. 'Baba hates me.'

'Hate?' Her face was a white wall in the darkness. 'You don't know about hate yet, *ya'eini.*'

'Why should Hassan go again to the fields and not me? It's so unfair.'

'What's fair in this life?' she said, her voice low. 'Not even God is fair. Only fools say different – but you'll learn, Salim. If a man wants something, he must find his own way.'

21

'*I* want to take the harvest,' he said, pulling himself upright. 'It's my right. My turn.'

She laughed softly. 'So you want to be a *fellah* too, my clever boy?' The words pricked him into shame, just like Mazen's.

'I'm not a *fellah*,' he said hotly. 'But they're my trees as much as Hassan's. And now I'm seven, it's my turn. You and Baba promised.'

She took his chin in her hand, fingers smooth as marble. 'Well, *effendi*. There's one thing we can thank God for. He gave you a clever mother – *w'Allahi*, just as clever as her son. Too clever for your Baba, anyway. We spoke tonight, after the shisha calmed him down a bit. Go downstairs tomorrow morning and kiss his hand – and you'll have your harvest. There – that's your birthday present, *ya'eini*.'

He clutched the edge of the pillow. The surge of joy was so unexpected, seizing his breath like the slap of cold surf on the beach. His arms were around her neck, and the words *Mama, Mama* came into his throat but he swallowed them in case they brought tears too, like a baby.

She held him against her. 'Never worry, *ya'eini*,' she said softly, her breath warm against his hair. But then something shifted – she disengaged his arms, pushing him back to the bed. '*Bookra, Insha'Allah*,' she said to him, her face turning towards the door. Tomorrow, if God wills it. 'Tomorrow,' he said in reply, feeling the old tug in his chest.

She leaned over to kiss his cheek, and he remembered at the last minute, in a rush of anxiety.

'Mama,' he said urgently. 'What about the Jews coming?'

She stopped in the doorway, framed softly against the light in the hall. 'What about them?'

'Abu Mazen was talking about it. And Mazen, and the Frères. Will it be like Deir Yassin? Why did they do that?'

At first she did not answer, and he feared he'd angered her. When she spoke at last, the words were slow, as if she drew each one from a well.

'They are all dreamers here, Salim,' she said. 'The Jews dream of a homeland, the Arabs of the way things were. Your father dreams of being rich. Even me.' She sighed and looked away. 'When dreams become more important than life, you don't care what you have to do to grasp them.'

He lay motionless, the pillow still tight in his hand, his chest still light with happiness. When she spoke of dreams, all he could think of was the trees in the garden.

She turned to go, but he saw her hesitate – and her hand reached down to touch his face.

'Salim, if someone calls you a farmer, don't deny it,' she said. 'The *fellahin* are the only honest men in Palestine. They truly own this land – not the Jews and not the *ay'an*. They built it with their hands and sweat. They would have saved it if they could. But they were betrayed. Do you understand?'

Salim nodded, determined not to disappoint her. In truth, her words were as bewildering as a song. They left him confused, tired and entranced.

Her hand left his cheek and she said, 'Sleep now.' But Salim lay awake long after she left. Then, the day slipped from him into the well of exhaustion and his eyes fell shut.

⁂

'Every Jew has a foundation story,' Rebecca used to tell her. 'Where they were when Israel was born. And you, Judit, are your mother's.'

'But I don't want to be a war story.'

'You are your own story, *mommellah*. To yourself. You can't help what you are to other people.'

'It took me *days* to get her out,' Dora would say whenever the Ryhope Road *Shul* would start worrying over the war for the Homeland, like dogs over a bone. Her finger would shake in the air, conducting a personal symphony of woe. 'She was late, because I was so worried sick with her uncle in the army, you know, in Jaffa and Haifa. *Glued* to the BBC day and night we were, with all those *meshuganas*, those bloody Arabs threatening to push us into the sea.'

This was how it went on: they'd just closed up Gold's Fashions and were driving home when Dora felt the first wave of true pain kick her like a horse. She'd grabbed Jack's steering arm and shouted, 'Stop you idiot, it's coming!'

Thirty minutes later they were staggering into the Sunderland Royal, where Dora was annotated on the obstetrician's chart: *D. Gold, elderly primigravida – NB DIFFICULT*. The midwife made sure the doctor on call was sober, changed her apron and readied herself to be soothing.

But it was all for nothing. Dora's pains lingered, the doctor poked and prodded, but her waters did not break. Two days passed under the unflinching hospital lights before they finally decided to pull the baby out for better or worse.

Jack called Judith's arrival 'the Miracle of Steady Driving'. Dora, on the other hand, blamed it on an act of God – a sign that her daughter's birth was, in some way, a catastrophe narrowly avoided. It was the price of her middle-class entry into the great theatre of Jewish suffering – a forty-eight-hour labour that reduced her to yelling 'For God's sake, get it out of me!' There was enough blood and ripped flesh for a battlefield and at the end a tiny, limp girl born struggling for oxygen just as the new State of Israel was drawing its first breath.

Judith was installed in a bedroom already occupied by Gertie, a shadowy presence of sixteen. 'Not your blood sister,' Grandma Rebecca explained once, 'but one of God's people all the same.' Her first memories were of Gertie, lying beside her at night and weeping. The music of that crying spread over her childhood like a pale blue stream, creeping into her dreams and filling them with sorrow. Then one day she found a picture under Gertie's pillow: a different family – two stiff girls with the same solemn look, holding a baby boy in their arms. A note on the back read: *Gertrude, Esther und Daniel Kraus, Wien 1939.*

Judith's birth certificate, filled out in Jack's shaky hand, read: *Judit Rebecca Gold.* Dora had insisted on the *Judit.* This was her own mother's name, an early war death in Budapest still violently mourned. Dora's youth had been filled with Judits; it never occurred to her how the name might wear outside the clannish walls of Sunderland Judaism, in a sturdy English classroom filled with Charlottes and Victorias. And she would have been horrified to learn of the treacherous *h* her daughter stealthily added to the end soon after her fifth birthday.

'It sounds funny, Bubby,' Judith said to Rebecca during the walk back from kindergarten, hanging her pale blonde head. 'They laugh at me. Why can't I have another one? Will you ask Mummy for me?'

'Oh *mommellah*,' Rebecca said, her freckled hand stroking the white, chubby one. 'One day when you're older, you can choose your own name, just like Papa did, and I did too. But when we're little we have to have the names our parents give us. They're our baby names, they show that our mamas and papas love us so much and hold us close to their hearts.'

'But why did she choose such a funny name? Your name isn't funny. Tony doesn't have a funny name either.' Anthony, her wealthy teenage cousin, was much envied and talked about in the Gold household.

'*Your* mama called you after *her* mama, because she loves *you* as much as her mama loved *her*. That's how we remember the people we love, by keeping them alive in our children. That's why your papa gave you my name too, so that when I'm gone you can remember me and keep a little piece of me alive.'

Judith shivered and drew her grandmother's warm hand next to her cheek. A pet budgie had died in their class the week before. She had watched in tears while the teacher scooped up the tiny bright body, its red legs curled into withered little stalks on the soiled cage floor.

'Don't die, Bubby,' she said very seriously. 'I want you here.' How would life be without her grandmother's easy voice, her warm red hair and soft lap to sit on?

Rebecca was as much a part of her as her name. Rebecca was the shriek of the gulls above Ryhope Road, the air scrubbed and raw as a kitchen sink, the distant moan of the shipyards. She was the grimy churn of the sea at Roker beach, the roar and grind of the docks – the sounds she called the heartbeat of the north. Sometimes, when the great tankers sailed up the Wear and stirred the waters into foamy life, Rebecca would take her down to the banks. And Judith would be lifted, safe in her arms, to hear the cheers of the crowds and wave her pocket handkerchief at the shining vastness of steel.

Sometimes Judith wondered why their family seemed so thin and small compared to the other Jewish clans at *Shul* every Saturday. They never felt like a clan even together – even on the family days out at Roker beach. There, Dora would sit motionless on the deck-chair behind her sunglasses, while Jack fanned himself with the *Sunderland Echo and Shipping Gazette*. Gertie stayed under the umbrella, fully clothed, and Judith would sit alone with her bucket and spade – desperate to paddle but afraid of the waves.

Rebecca explained it like this.

'You come from a family of *mensches*,' she said, using the Yiddish word that means a worthy and righteous man. Her fingers traced the gold Star of David always hanging around her neck – a wedding gift. 'That's not true for everyone round here, *mommellah*. Your grandpa and I, God rest him, had three wonderful boys. Each of them did something good with his life. Your Uncle Max is fighting to build our homeland in Israel. Uncle Alex is giving some of all the money he makes to help poor and sick people. And Jacob, your papa, well – he and your mama thought they could not have children, so they took

Gertrude in when she was a little girl just like you, saving her from the Camps. And they are keeping me in my old age, too.

'So you see, God sent them you as a reward. And He sent work for each of my other sons – more important than raising big families. Don't be sad about it. It's a *mitzvah*, a blessing for us.'

Her cousin Tony had a different perspective.

'Dad says that Max is crazy,' he said, through a mouthful of rum and raisin ice-cream, during a visit up from London. 'Mad as a fruitbat, living in the desert, growing melons and shooting at the natives. St Max of Zion, we call him. As for my Dad, maybe old Grandma has to tell herself that he's some Jewish Robin Hood, stealing from the rich to give to the *schmucks*.' He grinned and ruffled Judith's yellow hair. 'Frankly I think your Pop is the only normal one in the family. So cheer up, *bubbellah*. You'll probably be normal as normal too.'

War children shouldn't grow up to be normal, Judith remembered thinking. They're supposed to be heroes. *Mensches*. That was how the story ended for Dora, the Sunderland version of the great Foundation of Israel and Judit Gold. St Max came back from the fighting after the Yishuv was safe, when the five foreign Arab armies had been routed and half the local Arabs had vanished with them. 'He told me that at the minute, the *very minute* she was born, Ben-Gurion was raising the flag.' Max had presented Dora with a dirty blue patch of fabric embroidered with a six-pointed star, as a birth gift. 'He wore it when he signed up, and it went with him from Jaffa to Yerushalayem,' she'd say. 'Something to remind Judit of all the sacrifices our generation made.' But Judith had only seen Max's star once in her lifetime. She'd spied it, a ragged square hidden away in Dora's make-up case like an old *schmatter*. 'Your brother might be dining with the righteous,' she heard her mother say to Jack in an unguarded moment, 'but he's not exactly money in the bank.'

Judith had touched it lightly, as if it might hurt. It was torn around the edges and it smelt strange, a hot, red smell like dust.

It was nothing like the sky-blue flag she'd seen on television; this blue was wounded, grey as the Wear at high tide, and the stains on it were dark as blood.

⚸

Salim awoke to the sound of an explosion.

It was a deep, piercing *boom* that dragged him up from the depths of sleep like a loud knock on the door. He sat up, confused; his room was dark and he could still smell his mother's perfume.

Outside the inky sky was fading into dawn. Hassan's bed was unmade and empty. In the silence he could hear his own breath.

Then it came again, a giant crash that rocked the walls and sent dust spiralling from the ceiling.

He leapt up in terror. *What's happening? Where is everyone? Have they left me?* He clutched the blanket to himself, as the tears started to come.

The open bedroom door suddenly looked threatening, a black hole leading out into the unknown. Then another explosion hit. This time instinct drove him to his feet.

As he raced down the stairs he felt a third *boom* nearly knock him off his feet. The front door was open and a grey light streamed into the house.

Then he saw them – his mother, father and Hassan standing outside in the orange garden. They were still in their nightclothes, and Hassan was barefoot. Rafan cried in his mother's arms, his face red as a bruise over her shoulder.

Above them the pre-dawn sky was split with white shocks, like lightning strikes. Each blast sent bright needles of light through the leaves of the orange trees. Thick flags of smoke drifted out to sea.

'What's happening?' he pleaded, ashes in his mouth. Even Hassan looked terrified, clutching his father's hand like a baby.

'Mortars,' Abu Hassan replied, without looking down. A high whistling followed his words, before an explosion made the ground tremble. 'They want to drive us out with bombs and then kill what's left.'

Salim looked at his mother. She stood still as stone, eyes fixed on the sea. Behind their heads, a hint of milky light warned of an imminent sunrise.

The thuds of the mortars were still a little way distant. They were east and north, up towards Clock Tower Square and the town centre – its hospitals, the Al-Hambra cinema with its red seats, the Mahmoudiya Mosque and the churches of St Peter and St George. But between the crashes, Salim heard other sounds closer to home: shouts and sirens, the excited barking of dogs and the squeal of tyres.

Suddenly someone was banging on the gate; the whole Al-Ishmaeli family jumped. In her shock, his mother even did the unthinkable – grabbed Abu Hassan's arm and clung to it. She hissed 'Get inside' to Hassan and Salim. Neither could move, rooted to the spot like cats watching a hound.

'Abu Hassan!' An urgent voice, a man's voice, spoke through the metal grill. 'Open up, for God's sake.'

Salim recognized the voice at once; his mother did too. 'It's Isak Yashuv,' she told Abu Hassan. 'Quick, let him in.'

Gates were rarely locked in Jaffa, even in those days of fear. But that night Abu Hassan had decided to close the rusty bolt for the first time in years; it creaked and juddered as he fumbled to pull it open. His family stayed behind, huddled into an anxious knot.

Isak Yashuv's black eyes were wide with haste; his beaten old Austin was behind him, its engine running. Lili stood in the embrace of its open door, her light brown hair covered by a yellow cloth patterned with flowers. In the back seat, Elia sat bundled up beside piles of bags and clothes. His eyes caught Salim's, and he looked away again in confusion.

Isak was talking quickly to his parents. 'This is the Irgun, Abu Hassan. They're going to take Jaffa today or tomorrow. I'm worried they'll come through our neighbourhood, so I'm taking the family out.' Isak lived in Manshiyya, on the flimsy border between Jaffa and Tel Aviv. 'You should lock the door and don't let any fighters use your house. Stay out of the fighting and the Irgun will stay away from you.'

'So where are you going?' asked his mother, coming up to stand by her husband.

Isak gave her a strangely apologetic look. 'To Tel Aviv,' he said. 'Whatever dream we have been living is over now. Either the Irgun will get us in their attack or the Arabs will, in revenge.'

Abu Hassan turned his head from side to side, as if the answer might materialize suddenly out of the orange trees. While he hesitated, Salim's mother said coldly, 'We will not run. This is our house. There are soldiers here too, let them protect us.'

Isak raised his hands. 'Don't put your faith in soldiers, Umm Hassan. Thousands are already making for the port and onto ships. Arab fighters are among them. I thought Jaffa must be empty and you would be alone here. But if no one stays, who will be left to claim Jaffa after this madness is over?' He shook his head, unable to say more. Salim was astonished to see wetness on his cheek.

Lili came up now, touching Isak lightly on the arm. In her weak Arabic she said, 'Don't frighten them so, Isak.' Turning to Salim's mother, she said, 'Stay, if you want to keep your home. Go into the cellar and stay. I know what you think, but these people are not monsters. They just want…' She made a gesture with her hands, before falling silent and dropping her eyes. Salim stared at her. What was she saying? What did these Jews want? There was nothing for them here. Everything here belonged to him.

Then Lili was tugging on Isak's sleeve and speaking to him quickly in Hebrew. He turned his head back towards the car and Elia.

'We have to go now,' he said. 'God bless you and your family, Abu Hassan. I hope…' but whatever he hoped was lost in another crash and rumble.

With a last look at Salim, he urged his wife back into the car. Elia's eyes held his as the engine roared into action and the Austin sped off towards the coast road.

His mother turned to Abu Hassan. 'We're not going anywhere,' she said to him. 'Lili is right. If we go, who knows what could happen to this house? The British are still in charge here, aren't they? Call Michael Issa!' The Christian was hailed as one of the heroes leading the Arab Liberation Army. 'Go to see the British. Make them do something!' She clenched her fists in rage, Rafan wedged hiccupping under her arm, as the sky flickered and shook behind them.

Back in their house, the long, slow Sunday morning dawned – and gradually the noise of the shelling stopped. A dull silence fell. No mosque called the morning or the noon prayers. As the heat of the day rose, so did the sound of car horns, the rumble of engines and the babble of frightened voices. Salim thought they were coming from the port. Isak Yashuv was right. The whole of Jaffa was in flight.

Salim sat with his mother and brothers in the kitchen listening to the radio. Michael Issa was talking; he said that the shelling had killed hundreds of Arabs near the town centre and port. The Jews were advancing from the north, spilling from Tel Aviv's steel bowels. People were fleeing ahead of them. Northern Jaffa was almost empty. He begged people to stay calm and stay in their homes. He would defend Jaffa to his last drop of blood.

The heat of the afternoon became too much for Salim, and he went to pace around the garden. A yellow haze filled the sky. It seemed to him that the trees themselves were trembling, their leaves shuddering in the still air. Did trees feel frightened? He rubbed his hand on the bark of his tree, feeling the notches marking his growth. 'Don't worry,' he whispered into the wood. 'It will be over soon. Just keep growing, until the next harvest.' He stood there into the uncertain afternoon, saying it again and again under his breath. *Don't be afraid. Don't be afraid.*

After a restless night, his father put on his best suit of brown wool from Jerusalem to go to beg the British Police Commissioner for help. His stomach strained against the belt loops and sweat coloured his armpits dark. Salim stood by the door as he walked past, out of the kitchen and through the back gate. Outside, Abu Mazen's new car was waiting, its engine whining gently like a dragonfly over a pond. Mazen was in the back, dressed in his boy scout uniform. His face was pale against the tight buttons, and when he turned Salim saw his eyes were red and swollen. But as soon as he saw Salim staring, he raised his hand into the shape of a gun, aiming at Salim through the window; Salim saw his hand jerk back as the car roared to life and made off through the silent streets.

Abu Hassan returned that night with good news. 'The British have given the Jews an ultimatum,' he told them. 'If they don't pull back, the *Angleezi* will blow those rats out of their holes.'

Salim took a deep breath and Hassan, beside him, clapped his hands and said, '*Al-hamdullilah*' – thank God!

'Don't be so sure,' their mother replied darkly. 'The British have made plenty of promises before. They leave in three weeks. Why would they want any more of their soldiers to die? Better to let us kill each other.'

But this time, not even his mother's words could quell Salim's relief. They had been rescued from the brink. It was like when that little girl slipped into the sea from the pier last summer, while her mother screamed. Everyone had leapt to the dark water's edge, but then a wave from nowhere had washed her right back onto solid ground.

That night they all slept. But the next morning, fear crept back. It was nearly three days since the mortars started falling. Three days, with no water or power. The house reeked of sweat and fumes from the toilet, and the air was oily with smoke.

Where were the British? The streets remained empty. Sporadic radio broadcasts said the fighting was still going on to the east and outside of Manshiyya. Villages close to Jaffa, and the outermost suburbs, had been taken. Where was the Arab Liberation Army? They felt utterly alone.

In the afternoon, Salim's mother asked Hassan to start bringing in their stocks of food from the garden shed. 'We have to hide them,' she said. 'Who knows how long it will be like this?'

He helped his brother heave the hessian sacks of flour inside. They looked like the bags the refugees carried, the ones the *fellahin* used to take fruit to the market; now they were all that stood between him and an aching belly. *You're just another stupid fellah now, you donkey.*

As evening fell, the hairs on the back of Salim's neck rose. The sound of mortar fire returned to the north. In the gathering darkness he rushed into his parents' room. His mother was there, filling a suitcase with trembling hands.

'What are you doing, Mama?' he said, dry fear swelling in his throat.

'I won't let them take our things, if they come here,' she said, not looking up. 'You need to get ready too. Put some clothes in a bag and bring it to me. Tell Hassan.' Her voice was calm but her hands fluttered over her dresses and jewels.

Salim ran from her, stumbling down the stairs in panic. His heart was pulling him like a desperate animal. *Out, out*, it urged. *Run! Hide!* He tried to calm himself. His mother needed him to be a man.

He walked slowly over to the family mantelpiece. It was packed with carefully arranged pictures – grandparents he had never met, and one sad, yellowed image of a young girl at her wedding. His eyes searched desperately for the one he wanted.

There it was: a small, rectangular photograph of a wide-eyed baby propped up against a tree. The baby was looking up in placid bewilderment at some distraction behind the camera. In the background, the white Al-Ishmaeli villa rose like a ghost, flowers curling around its façade.

It had been taken at Rafan's tree planting ceremony, one year ago in the garden. The baby, his tree and the little shovel pushed into the earth, to mark the start of two new lives. Only Rafan's tree had been too small to lean against. So they'd propped him up against Salim's.

'Don't be such a baby,' Hassan had said, when Salim complained it wasn't fair. 'It's just a picture. What does it matter to you?' But he'd always pretended it really was him in the picture, there in his rightful place.

He touched the trunk of his tree in the image, and courage came back to him. Pulling it down from the shelf he ran into his bedroom. He packed his schoolbag with his pyjamas, two pairs of underpants and a change of shirt, laying the picture in the middle. Then he went outside, to wait for what would come.

On that final night, Salim kept vigil in the garden under his tree, a penknife in his pocket. His mother twice tried to bring him inside, but he refused. Finally she brought him a blanket.

He lay huddled with his backpack against the bark. Jaffa's lights were out, and it was the deepest night he'd ever seen. Through the dark, flickering leaves, the sky was seeded with fiery pricks of starlight. As he closed his eyes, they blurred into a brilliant river.

In the milky air of dawn, he got to his feet. The world was wrapped in stillness, empty but for the birds and dogs. For a moment he wondered if he was still asleep – if he might yet wake up in his own bed, with the light streaming in through the window.

Then he saw them – the dark clouds rising into the air over the port. A burning stench crept over the sleeping houses. Nearer than before he could hear gunshots and shouting – a wild mix of whoops and shrieks. His stomach clenched. The back gate clanged; he turned in a heartbeat and saw his father scurrying back into the house. A second later his mother rushed out, her face drawn and blank. She grabbed him by the arm and began pulling him inside.

'The Jews are here,' she said, her voice thick. 'Manshiyya has gone and they've reached the sea; they'll come here next. The British have failed us. Come now, it's time. Your father says we must go.'

Salim looked up to see his father hefting two large suitcases down the stairs. Hassan followed with a duffel bag from their bedroom. Tears were running down his brother's cheeks, and the sight of them sent more surging into Salim's eyes.

'I don't want to go,' he wept, feeling as helpless as a leaf in a storm. 'We live here. I want to stay here.'

'Don't be stupid,' said his father, his round face pocked with beads of sweat, his clothes stinking of terror. 'Jaffa is gone, the Jews are coming. Don't you remember Deir Yassin? We'll all be dead if we stay.' At that moment Salim did not care.

'We're going to your sister's,' Abu Hassan continued, as he lugged the heavy bags out to their car. Abu Hassan meant his grown-up daughter by his first, long dead wife. They'd once visited Nadia and her husband, Tareq, sipping sweet tea and eating dates in the hill country of Nazareth.

In the background, Salim could hear his mother's gramophone – a woman, singing sadly about love. *They can't make me go.* The words hammered in him, louder than the lament, louder than the *boom boom boom* coming from the port. He ran out to the patio, ignoring Hassan's shout of 'Hey, Salim!' and Rafan's wailing.

He couldn't go. They didn't understand. The air was thick, and the branches of the trees drooped wearily as he raced towards them.

The penknife bumped heavy in his pocket, sneaked from Hassan's wardrobe weeks ago. He pulled it out and dug it into the yielding bark, carving the word out one letter at a time. *If anyone comes here, they'll know you're mine.* His hand was shaking and the marks were weak, and before he could finish he felt his mother's hand close on his arm.

'Come on, Salim, don't make it worse,' she gasped, pulling him back inside. 'Your father has made up his mind, and please God it won't be for long.'

Over the years to come, Salim would try to replay those last minutes in the Orange House, scraps of memory dancing away like embers from the flames. The fluttering of the yellow curtain in his bedroom as he pulled his socks on and the dim reflections of his mother's mirror as she gathered the last of her jewellery. The sudden spring wind that set the orange trees whispering as they bundled him into the back seat. The squeal of the gate as the bolt slid shut. And the final slam of the car door. That last sound seemed to ricochet inside his heart, as they tore from the gates of the house, speeding him away.

1956

'S tretch, pet, stretch. Stretch those arms out! For God's sake, Judith. Give it some heft, girl! How do you expect to get anywhere if you don't bloody fight for it?'

Every Thursday afternoon of her eighth year, Judith would put her head under the water at Wearside Swimming Club to escape preparations for the Tercentenary Celebration of Jews in Britain. Mr Hicks at the Wearside Pool didn't care that the Prime Minister himself – and the Duke of Edinburgh too! – would attend a dinner with 'every Jew that matters'. Dora's temper was righteously inflamed: Alex Gold was one of the event's organizers – and his family didn't get an invitation!

Judith knew that they were not rich, because Dora mentioned it at least once a day. She referred to Uncle Alex as 'that rich *pishaker* in London', and seemed determined to punish Jack and Judith for conning her out of her rightful place in society.

Jack blamed the war. Gold's Fashions had been a hit in the thirties. But when the bombs fell on Sunderland's shipyards, blowing them to smithereens, half of its customers left. 'Between your mother's clothes and those bastards at the bank, even Moses couldn't find a pot to piss in,' Judith would hear him grumble as he went through the accounts.

'He's ashamed of you,' Dora raged at Jack, the day before Judith's eighth birthday. 'We're just the poor relations from the north while your brother's *machering* around in Regent's Park.'

'Don't be ridiculous,' Jack said, edging towards the back door. 'There are four hundred thousand Jews in Britain, we can't all have dinner with the Prime Minister. Calm down and organize a dinner here with the *Shul* if you want to. Now I have to pop out to the shop, Gertie's having some trouble with the books. Bye, pet.' He kissed Judith on the top of her head, and slipped away.

Dora swept past Judith into the kitchen in a blur of blue heels, and started setting the table with a furious clattering of china on wood. Judith tiptoed in.

'See what your father's family are like?' Her mother's chin gave a bitter jerk. 'They don't even know they're Jewish. Gold by name but coal by nature, that's all they're bloody worth. After all we've been through, Jews should stick together. But not these fine fellows, oh no. It's self self self all the time, and the rest of us can go *shtup* ourselves. Don't you take after them, young lady.' She shook a warning finger at Judith's reflection in the kitchen tap. 'It's no *naches* to raise an ungrateful child, you know.'

Judith nodded solemnly. It made her queasy, the idea of people sticking together – the Jewish people as a great stuck-together mass like so many pieces of the grey papier mâché they used at school.

As she lay in bed that night she imagined that they were all standing outside Uncle Alex's famous party in London in their finest clothes. But for some reason, as she slipped into sleep, it had become a wedding, and hundreds of feet were swirling round in the *hora* – a din so furious that Judith covered her ears. Then Dora snatched her hand yelling, 'Come on, we're all waiting for you, madam!' But something was wrong – she couldn't move, and when she looked down she saw her feet sinking into wet pieces of paper, clinging to her, gluing her to the spot.

*

The Jewish girls at Hillview Junior School might not have minded being stuck together; neither Judith nor any of the others knew what it was to have a non-Jewish friend. But in their second year the girls found themselves arranged in the classroom not by tribe but by pure alphabetical populism. Judith was seated next to a new girl called Kathleen, a mass of black curls, gappy teeth and pink leggings under her school skirt.

At break time, when the *Shul* club (as Tony called them) went into their usual corner, Kathleen asked blithely to see where the swings and the toilets were. As they walked around the playground in the cool morning sun, Judith felt Kathleen's thin hand slip into hers, as she chatted away in a happy lisp.

'You're not like *them* at all,' she said, kicking one of the boys off the swing and hitching her skirt up to sit on it. 'They're just like the ones at my old school – keeping themselves to themselves, you know. You're nice, though.'

Judith blushed and shrugged. 'They're not so bad,' she said, uncertain. She looked nervously over her shoulder and saw the little group she knew so well – Minnie, Blanche, Ethel and Rachel – staring back in frank astonishment.

Kathleen pushed herself off the ground and swung her legs to the marbled sky. Judith sat down next to her and did the same, a swooping feeling filling her stomach with the fall of the wind.

'So why are you playing with me and not them?' the stranger asked, as they flew past each other.

Judith had no idea how to answer. She didn't dislike her other friends. But she didn't like them much either. 'Just because,' she said at last, feeling a perverse rush of courage as she imagined what Dora would say. 'I like you. Why shouldn't I like you?'

Kathleen giggled and jumped off the swing onto the ground. 'You're a rebel,' she hooted. 'Mamma says rebels are the best kind of people.' She started skipping around Judith, waving her arms in the air. 'I LOVE it!' she said. 'It's so romantic, like a song.' And then she started singing 'Tutti frutti, oh Judy' again and again, until both girls leaned on the school wall and laughed until they cried. From that day, Judith became *Judy* and she and Kathleen were inseparable.

Kathleen was a swimmer. 'Mam says it's all I'm good for.' Wearside was on their way home, and Judith stood rapt as she watched the girls flying through the pool, their white caps cresting against the clean blue like the sea from Uncle Max's postcards. There were no Jews under the water. That's what Mr Hicks said in so many words when Kath nudged Judith to ask what it took to join the swim team. 'Just strong legs and a bit of old-fashioned brass, pet,' he answered.

Life was different from that moment on. It was a rush of bubbles of water and air, the bursting exhilaration of the first breath at the surface, the cooling pressure in her ears that blocked out Dora's irritation, and the feeling of weakness in her arms turning slowly to strength. After Wearside every Thursday, she'd walk with Kathleen to her house and listen to Pat Boone and Little Richard on her mother's record player.

Kathleen's home smelt of fried sausages and chips. Her mother wore bright, tight trousers that showed her ankles and stripy tops that made her look like a doll. She had Kathleen's black curly hair, she smoked and laughed like a teenage girl and told Judith to call her Molly. Judith once asked where Kathleen's father was and got nothing more than a shrug from Kath and a 'gone and good riddance' from Molly. But she loved the fun they had together; the endless hints from Molly around making your own rules and living your own life. Judith was too young to see that Kathleen had trouble reading, that Molly sometimes cried and drank and Kath's clothes were dirty behind their splashes of colour.

On the last Friday afternoon of the summer holiday, Kath knocked on Judith's door. From her bedroom she heard Gertie's voice and Kath's pipe, and tumbled downstairs. Mind yourself, Judit,' Gertie grumbled, her lingering German accent soft against the northern vowels. Judith wriggled past her sister, rolling her eyes. Kath giggled, her shoulders squeezing up into her black curls.

'Guess what, mon?' she said, when Gertie had vanished. 'I'm off to Wearside for a splash. Mam went out with some fella. She won't mind. You coming?'

Judith looked instinctively back over her shoulder. Gertie and Rebecca were in the kitchen, and the sour smell of gefilte fish was filtering through the hall. 'I can't,' she said, frustration filling her. 'It's Sabbath.'

Kath shrugged. 'Judy-Rudy, you're no rebel.' But she smiled, a wicked freckled grin. 'We're doing Roker this Sunday. Last one of the summer! Mam says come too, why not?'

The *Shabbas* prayers that night made Judith itch. Over Dora's song, all she could hear was Kath yelling 'Don't get wet, pet' as she skipped down the street.

At the table she stirred her spoon morosely round the bowl, watching uneven balls of dumplings float to the surface. Earlier she'd watched Rebecca roll them up out of matzo-meal and egg, and drop them so tenderly into the pot, the sour wheat smell of them filling the kitchen. But now they floated heavily around her spoon, dreary and lumpen. Her stomach turned at the very thought of putting one into her mouth.

Stealth in her fingers, she lifted one out and rolled it under the soup bowl. Gertie was concentrating hard on her own bowl, and Dora was telling Jack about a woman at *Shul* who was *shtupping* some *goy* from London.

Judith lifted another one out and hid it. She was just trying for a third, when Rebecca suddenly said, '*Mommellah*, what on earth are you doing with those *knedlach*?'

Dora's head snapped up and her beady eyes saw the treacherous dumplings peeking out from under the plate rim. 'What's this, young lady?' she said. 'Hiding your food again?'

'They make my tummy ache,' Judith said, stubbornly. Dora raised her eyebrows and Jack pointed his spoon at her.

'After all the work your grandma did for us today, pet,' he said. 'Don't you know there are hungry children in the world?'

'I don't know what's come over her recently,' said Dora, lips pressed together and the candlelight glinting off her earrings. 'I never heard of a girl not eating what her parents gave her. Gertie was just as old as you, madam, when she came to us – and she'd been *starving*,' she pointed a thin finger at Gertie's round frame, 'starving in the ghetto and millions of Jews along with her. Hunger took almost as many as the Camps in the *Shoah*. It's an insult to their memory not to eat when there's plenty, isn't that right, Gertie?'

'God commands us to eat at *Shabbas*,' said Gertie earnestly to Judith, poking her in the elbow. 'It's a holy commandment, Judit.' Judith jerked her arm away.

'Stop telling me about God all the time,' she said, miserably. 'It's not normal.' Gertie wrinkled up her face in wounded astonishment, and Dora threw her hands in the air.

'Normal?' she said, her voice swelling with scorn. 'Normal? What's normal about a girl talking back to her parents? What's normal disrespecting your traditions? Well?' Judith stared at the table, trying to pretend she was under the water, and Dora's voice was dim and faint like a song through the waves.

'You'd best go to your room then, if you're not hungry.' Dora started scooping *knedlach* into her mouth and nodding in exaggerated thanks to Rebecca. 'Go on then! You're starting to give me indigestion.'

Judith stood up from the table, her legs wobbling as if lead weights were strung to the end of them. She walked slowly out of the kitchen, feeling as she went the soft, consoling brush of Rebecca's finger on her arm.

As she lay on her bed upstairs, hunger was an exciting empti-ness inside her. A low hum of conversation drifted upstairs from the kitchen. *They're talking about me*. The idea gave her pangs of guilt and queasy delight.

She swung her legs off the bed and opened her schoolbag, pulling out a red notebook and a chewed pencil. Tearing out a page she drew a small heart at the top of the page and wrote:

Dear Kath, ive been sent to my room without dinner. Im really a rebel now! Hope you have fun at Roker this weekend. See you at school, love Judy.

She folded up the paper and wrote *Kath* on the front. She wondered if she could persuade Gertie to pass by Kath's house on Sunday during the weekly trek to Hebrew class.

A week after the *Knedlach* Incident, as Tony called it, Max came home from his kibbutz in Israel for Yom Kippur. 'It's a day of atonement for all our wickedness,' the Rebbe told Judith in Torah class. He stressed there was to be no eating or drinking from sunset to sunset, no wearing of leather shoes, no washing, no anointments with oils or perfumes and no marital relations. These last two confused Judith; she had never known Dora to miss a day of perfume. As for *relations* – it was several years before she understood what was supposed to happen in Jack and Dora's separate single beds, and then felt furious for having been fooled for so long.

It was hot for September, and Jack had spent all month lamenting poor sales of autumn stock. Judith crept into Gertie's bed one night while the sound of Dora wailing at her husband pierced the floorboards. 'What was the point of more coats in August?' she thundered, while Jack's reply was lost in a shamefaced mumble. 'Do they hate each other?' Judith whispered to Gertie, wrapped in her pale, soft arms. 'No,' Gertie whispered back. 'But they've come a long way up, they're frightened to fall back down again.' And Judith found herself wondering if Gertie ever wanted to go back where she came from – ever wished that Judith was an *Esther* or a *Daniel* from Wien rather than a pretend sister who pushed her away.

It was the tradition to keep Judith home from school on Yom Kippur, even though she was too young to observe the fast. 'Your little belly is too small to be empty so long,' Rebecca said to her gently when she asked why she had to mope around the house all day. 'Our Law puts the safety of human life above all other holy obligations. That means your health comes first, *mommellah*, but you can still sit and think and pray like the rest of us.'

During Yom Kippur, Dora, Jack and Gertie went to synagogue. Rebecca, nursing a weak heart, stayed quietly at home with Judith to make the festival supper – baking chollah bread, chopping boiled eggs and preparing sweet kugel cakes. She didn't try to go to Wearside, so Kath went without her again.

At sunset, Uncle Max lit candles he'd brought all the way from the kibbutz, kissed and blessed his mother and hugged Jack and Dora. He shook hands with Uncle Alex, up from Regent's Park. Cousin Tony had come down from university, and as the sun slipped behind the horizon, he blew a loud blast through his cupped hands in a parody of the *shofar*, winking at Judith as he did it.

Judith enjoyed the family coming together; the two uncles felt like adventure and drama. Alex was a snappier version of her father, with tailored suits and pinkie rings and an accent filed into London smoothness. When he spoke, Judith thought of a chocolate milkshake flowing into a cold glass. Uncle Max, on the other hand, was like someone you'd see at the pictures, tanned and lean. Rebecca glowed with pride and happiness to see all her sons gathered around the table; she sat holding Max's hand and wiping away silent tears.

'So Max,' said Alex, helping himself to a cake, 'how are the melons of Zion coming along?'

'Come and see for yourself,' Max said with half a smile. 'Donate your labour instead of your money.'

Alex grinned and chucked Judith in the ribs. 'Your Uncle Max thinks I'm one of the moneylenders in the Temple,' he said. 'He doesn't realize that without scoundrels like me funding pure-hearted idealists like him, Israel would have sunk into the marshes decades ago.' Rebecca tsk-ed and waved her hand at Alex, and Jack said, 'Come on, now.'

'No, no, no,' Max said, leaning forward and widening his fierce blue eyes. 'Speak your mind, Alex.' But then he turned to Judith and Tony saying, 'Uncle Alex here knows that when the war finished we had nothing at the kibbutz – not even water. I don't remember any calls offering me tools and irrigation systems. We had to build them all with our bare hands.'

'Good for you,' Jack said, nodding, as Alex laughed. Max went on.

'I was younger than our Tony here, and I thought I knew about hard work. What did I know?' He smiled ruefully at Judith and shook his head. 'After the first week my hands were so full of blisters I couldn't hold my spoon to eat. They had to feed me like a baby. And then there were the Arabs, sending in grenades, shooting at us in the dark. So don't listen to your uncle, Judit. Your papa here, he knows. Money can't buy everything. And it didn't buy the Jews a homeland.'

Alex cut in. 'For God's sake,' he said. 'Why does every Jewish dinner party have to end up mired in Israel or the *Shoah*? Don't we have anything else to talk about?'

Max pointed his fork at Judith. 'Look at these kids here. They should know that Israel didn't just appear like one of the miracles. Jews were slaughtered there too, to make a safe place for all of us.'

Rebecca stroked Max's face and said, 'I know, my love.'

Alex sipped his wine. 'You take it so seriously, Max.'

'Because it's a serious thing. Every day I have to look after three hundred people, dozens of acres, more than a hundred cows and sheep and several tons of farm machinery, plus a well that needs reinforcement and drainage every year.'

'No wonder you're looking so old.'

'Alex, ten years I've been asking you for money, Papa's money, by the way, which he meant for all of us. What, aren't I important enough for you to give your pennies to? You can't believe a man might not be wealthy and still be a *mensch*.' Alex rolled his eyes.

'Jack, you remember? Gold's Fashions was supposed to be our investment together after Papa died, some security for the family. But our little brother had a different idea – no sacrifices for him, right? No, it all went on that big-shot university, those nice suits we couldn't afford and a Golders Green accent. Should I have to beg my own family for a little money? Should Israel ever have to beg a Jew, I ask you?'

Alex's face darkened, and Judith saw his hand clench beside her, under the table.

'You want me to thank you for your sacrifice? Max Gold's personal sacrifice, leaving his mother and family to indulge in socialist collective agriculture and shoot at Arabs? Jews like me have already paid enough for Israel. Who do you think bought your machinery and your precious cows? It wasn't the Soviets, that I can promise you.'

'It wasn't the bankers either.'

'Oh really? Who was it – Moses? Papa lost everything running from one war, Max – he never wanted his money to be spent on another. Safe!' he snorted, as Jack tried to interrupt. 'High walls and barbed wire don't mean *safe*, they mean siege.'

'And whose fault is that?' Max threw back, paler now under his tan. 'We tried it your way. We tried living together with the Arabs, but they're savages. No education, no civilization – and they all hate us. For fifty years they shot and bombed us and tried to drive us off our land. They called us monsters! And the partition – it would have meant peace – well, they refused to even discuss it. They'd rather wipe us out!' He pushed himself away from the table, the screech of the chair making Judith jump.

'The Arabs weren't the only ones with the guns and the bombs,' said Alex calmly. 'What about the Irgun? What about that UN man they blew up – Bernadotte? And – more to the point – what about the rest of us who don't live behind your barbed wire fence? Sorry to tell you, Max, but Israel hasn't made a single Jew safer. Too many people hate us for it, right or wrong. They've been putting anti-Semitic mail through Tony's door at university!' Max shot a glance at Tony, who returned his gaze evenly. 'What's the solution? We all pack up and move "next year to Jerusalem"?' He raised his glass like the sacred Passover prayer. 'No. Thank you for the favour you're doing us, but I think I'll stay here in London and keep paying my taxes, while you dig your wells in the desert to make life safer for me.'

Something made Judith turn her head to look at Rebecca, sitting quietly on the other side of Max – Rebecca, the gentle stream that carried them all along.

Her grandmother's face was turned slightly to one side, towards the mantelpiece where pictures of their lives lay in dusty frames. Judith knew them by heart, although she could never remember, if pressed, what it was each one showed. Rebecca's eyes were unfocused, 'a thousand miles away', as she might say. In the half-light of the candles, she looked like she was swimming in some private sorrow. The shadows seemed to be clambering up her body to grasp her. Something leapt in Judith's throat, and she put her hand out saying, 'Bubby.' Alex looked sharply up and said, 'Mama, are you okay?' Jack leaned over to take her shoulder, and she suddenly came back from wherever her mind had been walking, putting her hand to her eyes in confusion.

'Mama, sorry for the racket,' Jack said. 'You want to lie down?' Max breathed out slowly, Alex sat back in his chair, and Dora reached past Jack to take hold of Rebecca's hand.

'It's all right, darling,' Rebecca said, although it wasn't clear whom she was talking to. 'Don't worry about me, your mama's just getting old.' She looked around the table, her eyes still wet and somehow hazy. 'Eat, eat, children,' she said, a little breathless. 'It's a blessing to be together. Our home is with each other, wherever we are. So many families have been lost.'

She shook her head and began to eat again. Alex and Max picked up their knives and forks and began to talk about something called the Suez Canal, which Judith vaguely understood was a waterway like the Wear that had recently been stolen by an Arab man called Nasser, which all three brothers agreed was a very bad piece of work and would lead to trouble.

In the darkness of her room after dinner, Judith fell asleep thinking of melons in the desert that grew and burst. Hundreds of little people came streaming out of them, scattering this way and that as heavy boots stamped down on them, while Judith screamed 'Over here! Over here!' and wept bitter tears.

At the end of September Mr Hicks gave Judith permission to try for the Junior Team. 'You're less than completely hopeless,' he told her. Later in the changing rooms, she wondered why she didn't feel more excited.

'Kath?' she asked, as they dried themselves, goggles dripping on the bench.

'Yes, Judy-Rudy?'

'What do you think about us?'

'You and me?'

'No.' Judith felt her cheeks flush. 'You know. Us. Jews.'

Kath stood up and gave this question the consideration it deserved. 'Don't know. Why, what do *you* think about them?'

'I don't know either.' There was no similarity between Max, Dora, Alex and Rebecca. They were more likely to be invaders from Mars than members of the same family.

Kath rubbed her hair until it stuck out from her head like wire.

'My mum says that people don't like Jews much,' she offered, pulling on her damp leggings. 'They're too rich and they control everything.'

'*We're* not rich,' said Judith. 'I don't really know anyone rich, except my Uncle Alex.'

Kath shrugged and grinned. 'Well, you're okay then.' Judith nodded uncertainly. How could Kathleen tell? She herself did not know.

Over the next few weeks, Judith made a point of coming home and watching the six o'clock news on their brand new television. She lost interest in *Crackerjack* and was half-hearted about spinning records in Kathleen's mother's living room.

On the twenty-ninth of October, bombs started falling in the Sinai. Judith listened to the BBC presenter explaining that Britain and France were helping little Israel to punish Egypt for closing the Suez Canal. The Israeli soldiers waved cheerfully to the camera before climbing into fighter jets. And then they cut to the blast of the bombs, and howling hordes in London with anti-Israeli banners chanting anti-Jewish slogans.

The year rushed towards its end; everyone else was preparing for Christmas and Kathleen headed to Ireland. In the Gold household, Judith and Gertie lit the Hanukkah candles for the Jewish Festival of Lights.

Looking into the menorah's flames in the early darkness of winter, Judith heard them again – the explosions and screams. The match light wavered at the tip of the candlewick as the last candle burst into glorious bloom. She thought of Uncle Max's star, lying lightless in Dora's cupboard. And she wondered what life would be like if everyone was doing the same thing at this exact moment – and if no person had to feel different from another.

The day of his betrayal came out of the cheerful blue sky, at the height of Nazareth's midsummer.

It was a school day; the bells rang at noon, ending the first shift. Dozens of books snapped shut, bags were hoisted onto shoulders and shoes pounded the dusty concrete floor. An excited hum of teenage chatter headed out into the stifling air of downtown Nazareth – away from lessons in mathematics, English and Hebrew, ready for the gruelling trudge uphill.

He was one of the few boys walking alone. A recent growth spurt had added sharp cheekbones, pale skin and bony arms to the other indignities of being nearly fifteen.

In the fierce heat, Nazareth turned from sandy yellow to blazing white. Salim's eyes ached as he walked up the winding main road. He passed rows of street stalls, children selling soap, car parts and badly made clothes.

The truth was, the Al-Ishmaelis were lucky. They'd come to Nazareth like everyone else, running ahead of the *Nakba* – the great Catastrophe. Thousands had arrived with them, the *fellahin* and the *ay'an* flocking together in a shared disaster.

Eight years later, Salim had a bed in his half-sister's flat, a school and an Israeli passport. They lived on Tareq's wages and his mother's jewels. Most of all, they still had the deeds to Jaffa's orange groves. But these children had nothing. Their fathers had worked the land, and now the land was gone. Today, work meant scraping a hollow living in the car repair shops or handing out tomatoes at the market.

In the block of flats where his family now measured out the days, Salim climbed slowly, counting the floors. The stairwell was wide, but dirty and rancid with the smells of daily life – washing, cooking, sweat and the sewers somewhere beneath.

His half-sister Nadia was in the kitchen leaning out of the window to hang their washing on the narrow balcony. 'Hi,' she called out. 'Did you have a good day at school?'

Seconds later, she appeared around the kitchen door, wiping her hands. Her brown face was round like Abu Hassan's, but without the thickness. It was lined beyond its twenty-five years – like so many Arab women deserving a greater serving of happiness than life had seen fit to allot them.

'Lovely,' he said, smiling up at her. 'Did they all go out and leave you in peace again?'

'Oh yes, there's a lot happening today,' she said breathlessly. 'My goodness, you must be hot, let me get you some water.' And she was off again, scurrying into the kitchen like a mouse through sacks of grain.

The apartment of Tareq and Nadia Al-Ghanem was a perfect reflection of its owners – neat, ordered and conservative. A kind home, stretched beyond its tiny limits to accommodate five more people than it was ever meant to hold. The shameful fact of Nadia's childlessness – one dead infant and three miscarriages – had become cause for celebration. Had her own children been here, where could the family have gone?

Nadia returned with a glass of water, and sat down next to Salim. He saw that her hands were nervous, fidgeting in her lap.

'What's up?' he said. 'Do you have a boyfriend hiding in here somewhere?' She didn't slap the back of his neck as he expected. The absence of her touch sent a warning chill through him.

'Listen, Salim,' she said and then stopped. Her hand reached over to touch his arm. 'Please, Salim, promise me you won't get all crazy.' That word, *majnoon*, was his father's favourite insult. That Nadia used it now told him there was some problem, something to do with Abu Hassan.

A door opened behind them with a click. Salim turned to see Rafan emerge from the bedroom. His small face was sleepy and white, his mother's green eyes hiding under pale eyelids.

'What are you doing home?' asked Salim, opening his arms for the boy.

'I was sick so Mama let me stay home from school.' Rafan came slowly, trailing his fingers along the chair backs. When he reached Salim, he curled his thin body into his brother's side and looked up into his face.

'Did Nadia tell you?' he said, small fingers tapping Salim's arm. 'Baba is going back to Jaffa, to sell the house.'

'What?' Salim went rigid, panic rushing through him like ice water. 'That's impossible. Baba would never do that, never.' He turned to Nadia, who spread helpless hands. She slapped Rafan on his forehead, half-loving, half-scolding.

'Rafan, you're a real troublemaker,' she said. 'What do you know about anything, you monkey?' Then to Salim, '*Habibi*, don't get upset. Nothing is decided. Your father is at the office with Tareq, talking to Abu Mazen.' Tareq was a family lawyer, making a little living piecing together the broken parts of Arab lives.

'But he can't sell,' Salim said. He felt seven years old again, pleading. 'It's the last thing we have, now all the money's gone.'

'That's just it, Salim. The money has gone. Your father and mother want you to have something to live on, not just dreams.' Nadia's eyes were sympathetic, but life had taught her that sentimentality does not feed you, or keep you warm at night.

'Where's Mama?' Salim asked. She would never let this happen.

'She went to Al-Jameela's for a haircut,' said Rafan. 'She knows about it, though. She told me.' Salim stared at his brother in disbelief. Rafan was only eight, a baby still – what right did he have to her secrets?

Nadia took Salim's hand. 'I know how important that place is to you, *habibi*, believe me,' she said gently. 'But please, don't worry yourself sick. They'll all be home soon. We'll talk it through.'

He nodded and detached himself from her. Hoisting his schoolbag onto his shoulder, he walked into their little bedroom.

It was close and hot, the air motionless. He lay down on his mattress underneath the window.

The boys had all shared a room until Hassan left for England two years ago, to live with Tareq's relatives. Hassan's bed was still just as he'd left it, his blanket patterned with little black footballs. Rafan's mattress was on the floor beside it, filling the room with a sour stink. At first the little boy had tried to climb in with Hassan, who had no time for him. 'He pisses every fucking night,' he'd complained. 'Pissing or crying is all he ever does.' So Rafan had started crawling onto Salim's mattress in the dark, whenever his own bed became too wet or full of pursuing dreams. Sometimes Salim woke up damp and smelling of urine, but he couldn't find it in him to deny his brother's need.

Something to live on, not just dreams. It was all very well for them to say. But what was life worth, once all the dreams have become dust?

After a while a key turned in the front door, and he heard Rafan's shrill voice crying out 'Mama, Mama!'

Swinging his legs off the bed, Salim moved towards the door, opening it a crack. His mother passed him by, her copper hair shining in the sunlight as she leaned forward to scoop Rafan up in her arms. She looked fresh and even happy – perfumed and coiffured, wearing a light red dress with flowers stitched along the hem.

He opened the door and said, 'Hi, Mama.' She turned, Rafan with his arm around her legs.

'Salim, *habibi*. How was school today?' She smiled, reaching out her hand for him. Surely, surely, this nonsense about the house could not be true?

'Not bad. They think I'm doing well.'

'So they should, that clever brain of yours. If only I had half of your brain, I'd be rich by now.'

Salim shrugged to hide his pleasure. Nadia, standing in the kitchen door, came to put her hand on Salim's shoulder.

'He's a very smart young man, for sure,' she said, almost defensively. It irritated him; sometimes Nadia acted as if she didn't trust his mother.

'Mama,' Salim said, as his mother turned to walk into her bedroom, 'the house – our house in Jaffa.'

'What about it?'

'Are we selling it?' The words came out in a higher pitch than he'd wanted. His mother's face smoothed into a blank.

'It's more complicated than that, Salim,' she said – but then the sound of the door stopped whatever she had been planning to say. Abu Hassan and Tareq were home.

Nadia hurried over to kiss her husband and help her sweating father to his armchair. Casting a glance over at Salim she said, 'I think the boys are keen to hear what's been happening, Baba. Can you tell us anything?' Salim realized she wanted to keep him out of trouble, by asking the first question herself.

Abu Hassan shook his head. 'These *Yehudin* make it all so difficult,' he said. 'First it's my house, then it's not my house. Shit on these new laws! By God, what right do they have to say it's not my house?'

He reached for the salted sunflower seeds and began crunching. Salim had never seen him so flustered. He remembered that day, long ago in Jaffa, when Mazen had joked about their fathers. For all their money, he could see that Abu Hassan was drowning, like a flounder in the net.

'Baba, why would you try to sell the house?' Salim asked, trying to keep his voice steady. 'We always said we would go back one day, didn't we?' He'd dreamed of it; the misery of the past eight years wiped out by the turn of their key in the lock.

His mother answered. 'It's not a question of wanting or not wanting, Salim,' she said. 'We must think of our future. Who do you think can pay for that school uniform of yours, or that university you say you want to go to?'

Salim looked from Tareq to Abu Hassan, his heart still racing and his fingers numb.

Tareq said to Abu Hassan, 'Maybe we should take Salim with us tomorrow?'

'What's happening tomorrow?' Salim asked.

'We're going to the municipal offices in Tel Aviv,' Tareq said, setting his briefcase down on the coffee table. 'There is some dispute about the house, it seems. We've been on the telephone all day, to Abu Mazen and the Israeli authorities.'

He gave Salim a wink and nodded towards the kitchen. 'Let's go and help your sister, *habibi*, and I'll tell you all about it.'

The kitchen was just big enough, Nadia used to say, for one person not to step on a cat's tail. Nadia busied herself on the balcony hanging out the washing. Tareq put on a pot of thick, black Turkish coffee, adding four teaspoons of sugar and stirring. Salim waited, impatient. Finally Tareq sighed.

'Okay, so here it is. When the war ended, the Israelis started planning how to claim all the land left empty by the Arabs. So they passed some laws saying the people who fled – well, they had no right to come back again. The State took their homes and gave them some money, to say it was fairness. Do you understand me?'

Salim nodded, desperate to show he could follow it all.

'To stop the Jews taking your father's house under these laws, his friend Abu Mazen moved in and pretended to be his cousin. And now your father is thinking to sell up,' this, very gently, 'to get the money he needs for your education and your future. But, it seems there are some problems. So we will meet Abu Mazen tomorrow at the City Hall in Tel Aviv, to speak to him and the Israelis together. Then we'll see.'

'OK, *habibi*?' His uncle squeezed his shoulder and Salim forced a smile. 'Things will work out, don't worry.' Then suddenly Nadia was between them, complaining to Tareq about another problem with the stove, cutting off Salim's questions before they'd been formed.

A strange atmosphere filled the flat as evening fell, like a thunderstorm brewing in the far distance. Supper was cleared and the men relaxed in front of the radio listening to General Nasser of Egypt rant about the Suez Canal. Rafan had his ear to the box, bewitched by its tinny sounds, his small fingers tapping and twisting. Nadia stayed in her room, mending clothes.

Salim sat alone with his bubbling thoughts. A great desire to see his mother filled him. Rafan was distracted for once, and she would be alone.

Finally he found her sitting out on the balcony. As he hurried towards her, her head twisted away and he faltered in sudden unease. *Is she crying?* There were lines on the sharp planes of her cheeks and her eyes were in shadow. A piece of paper lay open in her hand, yellow with black type. Salim thought it was a telegram. When she saw him, her hand closed over it, covering the sender's name.

'What's that?' he asked.

'Nothing.' She turned away from him, out towards the north. 'A letter from an old friend.'

'From Lebanon?' he said, half-joking. Away to the north, the hills of the Lebanese border were split into red and black chasms.

She stiffened. 'Why ask me that, *ya'eini?*'

'No reason,' he said, surprised. 'You just say sometimes that you miss it. I guess you miss it just as much as Jaffa. Do you?'

Salim saw her glance at his face, a questioning look, hard to read. 'I do,' she said at last, her voice slow. 'I was so young.' A laugh came from her, scornful. 'A young fool. My father used to call me the prize of the house. I was so proud, so special, and I thought he meant my life ahead was going to be the prize. But really he meant it was me. That I would be his gift to the highest bidder.' Her eyes were almost black, looking past him to the empty horizon. 'And now look what has happened to us.' She reached out her hand, palm facing forward to the setting sun, a gesture of denial. Then she dropped it to her side. 'No one understands,' she said quietly. 'I hope one day you can understand it, Salim. Why things had to be this way.'

'What things, Mama?' A torrent of love streamed through him and he went to hug her. Her arms were about him and all wondering left him. He was perfectly content.

After a time, he asked her, 'Why did Baba never go back to Jaffa?'

'He did – once,' she replied. 'During the second truce. He went to see Abu Mazen, to give him a copy of the title deeds for the house. He was gone for three days,' she laughed suddenly, 'and you boys, you didn't even notice. Then after that,' she sighed, gesturing out at the deepening skies, 'we were all in this *Israel* and it was very difficult to make sense of it. Things moved on – you were in school, Hassan left us for England… it needed an energetic man to sort it out. And your father is not an energetic man.'

'But *you* want to go back, don't you, Mama? It's your home too, more than Lebanon.'

She laughed again.

'Ah, Salim, you know better. It's not how long you live somewhere that makes it a home. Home is a feeling *here*,' she tapped his chest, 'that you belong somewhere and somewhere belongs to you. But, I'll tell you a secret, *habibi*. Some people don't feel they belong anywhere. No matter where they are, they are always unhappy.' Her voice shook. 'They go from place to place trying to find peace. And usually they find themselves back where they started. It's the greatest curse under heaven.' She took a breath, wiped her forehead and took Salim's chin in her hands. 'I pray you escape it, my clever son.'

'But we know where our home is,' he said, disturbed. 'We were happy there. *You* were.'

'Were we?' She shrugged her shoulders. 'Even in Jaffa, you and me, we had restless feet.'

She stood up in a sudden, fierce movement, her body turning northwards like a needle towards the deepening shadows.

'Let your father dream of Palestine,' she said. 'He's the one who really knows where he belongs – with all the other useless *ay'an*, eating nuts and drinking coffee. Their time has passed for ever now. That's why he's selling up. But you, Salim. You're made for better things. Don't forget it.'

'Okay, Mama,' he said, softly. Then he watched her walk into the dark kitchen, the tall line of her back disappearing, the telegram clutched tightly in one elegant fist. And he suddenly thought of a felucca he'd once seen drifting on the sea, cut loose from its moorings, its white sail tall and straight against the falling sun.

Later, Salim sat in his bedroom trying to concentrate on his maths homework. He was good at sums. They comforted him, hinting at a universe where rules right and wrong were clear and dependable, obedient to fundamental laws.

But today the numbers swam before his eyes. What did it matter if one and one made two? The Israelis didn't care about any laws but their own. They could claim one and one makes ten as easily as they said *what's yours is mine*.

Pushing his books to one side, he reached under his pillow. The hard edges of the picture frame met his fingers, cool and reassuring. For eight years it had lain with him while he slept, blending into his dreams.

Now his fingers traced the pale tree under the glass, a dark sliver against ghostly white walls. It was a lifetime ago that they had left it, so sure that they would return one day in triumph.

When he closed his eyes, he could still feel the terror of that day. Jaffa's familiar streets had transformed into a locked labyrinth, threatening to trap them forever until they followed the thousands of others into the churning sea. The Al-Ishmaeli car had frantically hurled itself around, turning countless times, until at last they found their way into the quiet hills and Nadia's waiting arms.

Since then he'd never given up hope. When they heard Mayor Heikal on the radio saying that Jaffa had fallen, he wouldn't believe it. *Heikal's an idiot*, he'd shouted, like Mazen in the Square that day. Even when he heard Jews had rounded up all the Arabs behind barbed wire fences in Al-Ajami, he trusted Abu Mazen to keep their home safe.

As the summer burned and the smell of dried sweat filled every corner, he'd begun to understand that the *Najjada* and the Arab Liberation Army and the five nations who'd promised to save them were all failing. And when the green-shirted Jewish army finally came marching into Nazareth, Salim had climbed onto the balcony and screamed *Come on! Drive us out! Send us back!* But Tareq came to tell them that the kindly Jewish commander had refused to expel them – and he'd wept in disappointment.

Now he remembered the worst moment, how Hassan had been parroting something about driving all the Jews into the sea as revenge for Jaffa – for Clock Tower Square and Deir Yassin. Tareq had shaken his head, saying, 'Talk like this will give us more Deir Yassins. Maybe it's time for peace, before we lose the little we have left.' Abu Hassan had slammed his fist on the table, making everyone jump. '*Abadan!*' he'd shouted. Never!

His voice sent a spear through Salim's heart; at that very instant he'd been looking at his picture, planning his day of return. *Abadan!* Never! The word came back to him now, ringing through long years of waiting.

He'd heard it in his dreams, seen it in the new world around him and the Star of David flying in their streets and schools. He would not believe it.

Putting his hand on the fading image he whispered his promise: *I will come back. It's not too late. I'll come back to you, and we'll have our harvest.*

*

The great Tel Aviv adventure – as Nadia deemed it – dawned on a bright and scorching Thursday. Salim had the day off school; Tareq loaned him a smart pair of trousers and a clean, white shirt.

In the gloomy basement, Salim, Abu Hassan and Tareq squeezed into the faithful old Austin. The deeds to the Orange House and lands were tucked safely away in Tareq's briefcase. The two women and Rafan came downstairs to wish them all good luck. For the first time in his life, Salim felt like a man.

He leaned his head out of the back window and smiled at his mother. Her clothes were so plain that day – a long black dress and clumpy black shoes – not her usual style at all. Salim thought it must mean she was going to miss them. She'd be spending the day in the flat on her own; Thursday was Nadia's turn for coffee and chat at the market.

He wished they were all going together, for a family trip somewhere wild and fun like the old carnivals in the desert of Nabi Ruben. Maybe they would do things like that again, once the business in Tel Aviv was done.

'Goodbye, Mama!' he called. 'We'll come back with good news, I promise!'

She crouched down beside him. 'I know you will, *ya'eini*,' she said. 'You're such a man all of a sudden.' She touched his cheek for a second. 'Take care of him, Tareq,' she said.

'For sure I will!' Tareq replied cheerfully, leaning back from the driver's seat to slap Salim's shoulder. Rafan pushed past his mother to press his gap-toothed mouth to Salim's cheek. As they pulled away Salim saw the little boy waving, one half of his face alive with smiles, the other hidden in shadow. And then they all dwindled away, lost in the blackness of the garage.

The drive from Nazareth to Tel Aviv was a journey from the old world into the new. At the edge of the Galilean hill country, ancient Arab towns and villages balanced precariously on the land's broken bones. Heading south-west and downwards, these dark green, rocky slopes smoothed into the undulating yellows of the Jezreel Valley.

At school they'd learned about the centuries of Turkish rule, when great Palestinian granaries were sown here in the Vale of Esdraelon. But that was before the Sursuk family from Lebanon sold out to the Jewish National Fund. They reached out their arms from Beirut, Nadia told him on one of their sad evenings, and cleared nearly seven hundred *fellahin* out of their farms. The Jews paid the peasants for their trouble – a pittance of silver for an easy conscience. And that's why they came, she said, the *fellahin* – flooding into Haifa, and Jaffa and Nazareth, with nothing but their names and a handful of coins. Their fields were handed over to the Jews, empty but for birds and mice.

As the Jezreel Valley ended Salim began to sense the tang of the sea. The wide coastal plain stretched out before him – a bare and hard world where Arab and Jew had once worked side by side, draining swamps and raising great plantations from Jaffa to Acre. But then the Zionists came, Nadia said. And soon no Arabs were working on the colonies springing up along the plains. Nadia told him that foreign landlords and even the *ay'an*, men like his father, had sold *dunam* after *dunam* to the Jews, transforming tenant farms and pastures into mountains of fodder for the Jewish dream. 'They let the land slip away from us,' she said. 'It slipped away until only stones and bitterness were left.'

On the intersection of the Plain of Sharon and the Philistine Plain stood Tel Aviv. Salim saw it rising out of the haze less than an hour after leaving Nazareth, the sun glinting sharply off its razor-thin edges and smooth, eyeless façades.

It was blisteringly bright and, as they got nearer, snarled in traffic and smoke. As they slowed to a crawl, Salim began to worry that they would not make their appointment at noon. Tareq was tapping anxiously on the steering wheel as the horns blared all around them. '*Insha'Allah* we'll make it,' he said.

Salim pressed his nose to the window, his breath coming back to warm his cheeks. The roads were wide and full of expensive-looking cars, surrounded by a world of angles, glass and glare.

By the time Tareq parked the car across the road from the City Hall it was already five minutes to noon. Salim jumped out of the back seat and opened the door for Abu Hassan.

The building was a quaint old hotel, sadly dilapidated next to its newer neighbours. It was thronged with a mass of motorbikes and people pushing past them. Salim and Tareq both had to elbow their way through, pulling Abu Hassan behind them, until they reached the cool of the lobby.

Tareq started looking around for Abu Mazen. 'We're on time,' he said, shaking his watch to his ear. 'So where is he, by God?' Then, something made him catch his breath.

Standing at the receptionist's desk was a tall figure, almost as shabby as the building itself. On seeing the Al-Ishmaelis coming up the steps, he walked towards them, speaking the Arabic greeting: '*Ahlan wa sahlan*, Abu Hassan' – you're as welcome as my family. Salim could not believe his eyes. It was Isak Yashuv.

Abu Hassan looked dumbstruck too. He took Isak's hand in a daze and stuttered the traditional return, '*Ahlaeen.*'

Isak then turned to Salim and said, 'How's life, Salim? How's your mama? Elia wanted me to say hello to you. He misses you.' Salim nodded and tried to smile. It was wonderful and painful to see him again. But what in the world could bring him here?

'Forgive me for coming here without an invitation,' Isak said, spreading his hands to Abu Hassan and Tareq. 'I am working now, as a... liaison, you might say, between this municipality and the Arabs in Jaffa. I guess because I speak Arabic and, frankly,' he ducked his head, looking embarrassed, 'I'm not much use for anything else these days, with my eyes too bad for sewing. Anyway, I saw your name on the appointment list and I wanted to ask if I could help you at all. I know the man you're seeing – he's not a bad one, but young.'

He looked from Abu Hassan to Tareq, his dark eyes narrow as ever but more clouded now. With his dusty and deeply lined face, Isak looked more like a *fellah* than anyone else Salim knew.

Abu Hassan shrugged his shoulders. 'You're welcome to help if you can, Abu Elia,' he said. 'My son-in-law here,' he motioned to Tareq, 'is a lawyer, and he tells me he understands *your* laws.' His emphasis was clearly deliberate but Isak didn't blink.

'Help would be wonderful.' Tareq's reply was instant and firm. 'Thank you for your kindness.'

'All right then,' said Isak. 'Well, let's go up. I'll show you the way.'

The sign on the door of their appointment read: *Office of the Custodian, Tel Aviv Municipality.* A young, pale man sat at a cluttered desk inside, wire-rimmed glasses over his blue eyes and sweat beaded on his receding hairline.

'Come in, come in,' he said, in Hebrew. 'You're on time, that's a good start.' Hebrew was now compulsory in school; Salim was now reasonably fluent but he had yet to hear Abu Hassan utter a single word. It put them at a disadvantage now. Doing business in Hebrew was like trying to do arithmetic while balancing on a log.

Isak gestured for Abu Hassan to take the seat in front of the desk, while Tareq and Salim stood behind. 'Saeed Al-Ishmaeli, this is Mr Gideon Livnor,' he said.

Mr Livnor reached out his hand to Abu Hassan; it was a second before the old man took it, and then dropped it quickly.

'Thank you,' said Livnor, briskly. 'You're welcome, Mr Al-Ishmaeli. I hope we can sort this issue out for you today. I have some records here,' he indicated a folder in front of him, 'and I believe you have some with you? The deeds to the properties?'

Tareq translated quickly for Abu Hassan, who replied, 'Yes, yes,' and held out the papers from Tareq's briefcase. Livnor took them, and looked them over, occasionally rubbing the steam off his glasses. Opening the file in front of him, Salim saw he was comparing another set of papers inside. It confused him for a moment before he realized – these must be the papers Abu Mazen protected for them all these years.

At last Livnor sighed and took his glasses off again. Salim began to wish he would leave them alone. Grimy and misted, they seemed to bode ill.

'I want to be sure I understand things properly here,' he said. 'Mr Al-Ishmaeli, you claim to own two pieces of land in Jaffa – a house in Al-Ajami district and fifteen *dunams* of citrus farm outside of Jaffa. Correct? And now you want to sell these lands to the State?' Abu Hassan simply stared, but Tareq answered in Hebrew: 'That's right.' Livnor looked from one to the other before turning back to his papers.

'Well, there are two problems, Mr Al-Ishmaeli. First, our records show that you left your property here in Jaffa in May of 'forty-eight. This house and your other *dunams* have been vacant since then. Which classifies you under our national legislation as a "present absentee".' The words *nifkadim nohahim* sounded almost funny in Hebrew, like a child's skipping rhyme.

'I never left,' interrupted Abu Hassan. 'My family has been there the whole time.'

'You may not have left the country, but you left your farmlands,' Livnor said. 'As a present absentee, your land defaults to the Custodianship Council. Our records show that your orange groves outside Jaffa have already been appropriated, Mr Al-Ishmaeli.' His voice was flat, mechanical, and Salim found himself wondering how many people he'd delivered this bitter news to, and whether he wept for them later in his bed at night.

'It is morally, legally and in all ways wrong, this thing you are doing,' said Tareq, his voice thick and furious.

'It's the law. Many people left their homes. Hundreds of villages and farms were standing empty. They could have been fallow for generations. Now they are being put to good use, for all Israeli citizens.'

'Did you take the homes that the Jews left?' Salim asked, his voice shaking in his throat. Tareq shot him a warning look, but Livnor ignored him completely.

'The State will give you the compensation to which the law entitles you,' he said, eyes fixed on Abu Hassan. 'Our taxation records,' he brandished another paper from the file, 'show that your orange groves were valued at four hundred and fifty Israeli pounds in 'forty-eight. Unfortunately,' and here he glanced up at Tareq, 'our records also show a large tax debt to Mandate authorities, which remains valid. Taking this debt into account,' he scribbled on the ledger in front of him, 'you can claim three hundred Israeli pounds in compensation for these abandoned lands.'

He tore the paper from the ledger and passed it to Abu Hassan. Salim was reeling from shock. From wealth and independence to three hundred pounds! He clutched the back of his father's chair.

'This is a joke,' Tareq protested. 'Even if these were your lands, which they are not by the way, the market value would be considerably higher today than four hundred and fifty pounds. I don't know where you get these numbers from.'

Livnor made a small gesture with his shoulders and hands, between a shrug and a dismissal. 'I'm sorry. This is the law. If you want to appeal the amount it's up to you. Or you could take the money and save your family more difficulties.'

Abu Hassan was holding the paper without comment and looking at it through unfocused eyes. He was silent so long that eventually Tareq said gently, 'Baba?'

The word seemed to jerk him out of a stupor. Abu Hassan's head snapped up and he said, 'What about the house?'

Livnor looked back at his papers, this time more thoughtfully, and drew two identical-looking deeds out of the file.

'I'm seeing this deed today for the first time, Mr Al-Ishmaeli,' he said, waving the yellowing document that Abu Hassan had just given him. 'It says that you are the freeholder of the house in Al-Ajami district.

'But I have another document here, lodged with us many years ago, before my time,' he pointed to his file. 'It tells me that you were just a tenant in the house. The legal freeholder, according to this paper, was Hamza Abu Mazen Al-Khalili.'

This time Abu Hassan sat up straight. Salim gasped.

Livnor took his glasses off again, leaned forward on the table and tried to catch Abu Hassan's eye. 'I'm sorry, sir,' he said, with a trace of sympathy. 'This house is no longer yours.'

Isak reached over and took the paper out of Livnor's hand.

'Mr Livnor, I don't know about these papers,' he said, 'but I can promise you that Abu Hassan here was the rightful owner of the property. I have known his family for many years.' His voice was wheezy and cracked in distress. 'I can personally vouch for him.'

Abu Hassan put his hand out across the desk in what looked strangely like supplication. 'I gave copies of my deeds to Abu Mazen, before the war ended,' he said. 'There has been some mistake. The house is mine. My family built it. There has been some mistake,' he said again, putting his palm on his forehead and rocking his head back and forth under the glare of the strip light.

'This document is damaged,' said Tareq. 'It's been forged or altered. Your people must have seen that. You can't make out the proper names clearly. And everyone would have known the house belonged to Abu Hassan.'

Livnor shook his head. 'As I said, it was before my time.' His hands tapped the desk. 'There was a lot of confusion after the war. Arabs were still making trouble in Jaffa. Perhaps the checks were not as vigorous as they should have been.'

Salim felt his breath coming in shallow pants. He willed his father to speak. But Abu Hassan's arms were slumped in defeat. His eyes seemed fixed on Livnor's paper, the only sign of emotion a sudden heave of his chest.

Livnor sat back in his chair and wiped the sweat off his forehead, like a doctor delivering terminal news. 'I'm sorry,' he said again. 'There's nothing to be done.'

'So what does this mean?' Salim said, light-headed and dry-mouthed. 'What does it mean for us now?'

'It means,' said Livnor, 'that the house has already been sold to the State. By Mr Al-Khalili. The money has been handed over.' He took off his glasses and spoke directly to Abu Hassan. 'You must take it up with him yourself, sir. Because this is now out of our hands.'

Salim could not remember getting back down the stairs. The lobby was now grey and oppressive, the air outside fierce and hostile. There was still no sign of Abu Mazen. Abu Hassan walked off to the nearest payphone, leaving the others standing wordless in the shadow of the City Hall.

Tareq stood straight with his hand on Salim's shoulder. Isak spoke hesitantly, his eyes on the ground.

'I'm no lawyer,' he said, 'but surely there must have been collusion somewhere. That document Livnor had was not right. The government probably just wanted to take the house and be done with it.'

Abu Hassan came back ten minutes later, and told them they would meet Abu Mazen at a coffee shop by the beach boardwalk. Salim did not ask why they were not meeting in Jaffa. Suddenly, he did not want to go near the place. Jaffa had betrayed him.

The Tel Aviv beach boardwalk was the light of western modernity turned up to full flood. Men and women laughed arm in arm and raced along the beach together, playing with balls or sunning themselves in a great tangle of limbs. Sheltered from the glare by the shop awnings, Salim felt a confused mix of emotions as he watched them – creatures from another world, the noon light glistening on their skin.

In the distance, Jaffa rose up from the coast in a jagged row of yellow teeth. He searched inside for a hint of desire, and found nothing. *That is not Jaffa.* That was somewhere else, a defeated, dirty place where all the gardens were dead and the orange trees cut down.

The worst had already happened to him, and yet he was beginning to feel lighter, like a bird on the wing. He could almost see his possible futures separating, like two bubbles waiting to be freed. There was this broken cart of Palestine, and a life hitched to it with men like his father. And then there were other dreams, worlds not yet in focus.

'Looks like fun, eh?' Isak's voice broke into his thoughts. 'I take Lili to the beach on Sundays sometimes. She likes to get a tan.' He shook his head and smiled. 'Tel Aviv is always moving and changing, while old Jaffa has changed so little. Lili says time stands still for us Arabs, no matter what our religion.'

Before Salim could reply, he heard a boy's voice shouting in Arabic. 'Salim!' Turning, he saw a young man coming towards him – paler than Isak with an earnest expression and Lili Yashuv's long nose.

A smile surged onto Salim's face in spite of himself and he shook the hand that Elia offered.

'Dad told me you were coming, I could hardly believe it,' said Elia, breathless. 'I got out from school and ran all the way. How are you? What's up? Are you coming back to Jaffa?'

The question pierced Salim, bringing him back to the moment; he dropped Elia's hand, suddenly noticing the pinkness of his skin, like the cold Eastern Jews. 'Maybe,' he said, turning away. He sensed Elia standing behind him, felt his hurt even as he tried to wound. He remembered their last day together at the souk. *Elia was right after all. Things can never be as they were.*

Elia was clearing his throat to say something, but then Abu Hassan looked up sharply and said in Arabic, 'Enough, you boys.'

Abu Mazen was walking towards their table. Behind him came Mazen. The plump child had disappeared completely behind walls of rolling muscle and a tight, modern suit. Only the tight fleece of black hair was the same, curling down his neck.

As they drew near, Mazen lifted his head; when he saw Salim he recoiled with something that looked like guilt.

'*Ya* Salim,' he said – an indeterminate greeting that merely acknowledged his presence. 'Still hanging out with the *Yehuda*, I see.' His voice touched memories that made Salim shiver. But he saw the older boy was quick to look away.

Abu Mazen had taken a seat at the table and ordered a coffee. Salim waited impatiently for someone to begin the discussion, to accuse Abu Mazen of his crime, but this was not the Arab way. First coffee needed to be drunk and pleasantries exchanged. Only then could something real be said.

Finally, Abu Mazen stretched his arms over his head and said, 'So, tell me how it went today at the City Hall.'

'You were supposed to meet us there, I thought?' Tareq said, his voice cold.

'But it looks like you had good help already.' Abu Mazen favoured Isak with a smooth smile. 'I would have been one big body too many.'

Salim's father was toying with his coffee cup, swirling the thick, sweet liquid round and round. Without lifting his eyes from the table, his voice came in a hoarse whisper. 'Why did you sell my house, Hamza? What right did you have?'

Abu Mazen's face turned a shade darker, and he leaned forward in his chair. 'Do I understand you, *Saeed*?' He stressed Abu Hassan's forename, a gesture of disrespect. 'Are you feeling someone has wronged you?'

'You wronged me,' said Abu Hassan. 'You made a forgery with the Jews. You pretended the house was yours. You sold it to them.' His voice shook, but he still could not look Abu Mazen in the face.

He's afraid of him, Salim realized. All Abu Hassan's bluster was reserved for his family.

Abu Mazen gave a short, barking laugh. 'Wronged you?' he snorted. 'You should be thanking me on your knees, Abu Hassan. The Jews would have taken that house from under your feet and given you nothing. You can hardly even read a piece of paper – did you ever tell your boy here that? How could you have fought them? So I saved you, out of my goodness. I took all the trouble on myself. I sold it to them for what they would give – a good price, actually.'

Salim felt a surge of fury. 'This was our family's decision to make, not yours,' he shouted.

Abu Mazen turned to smile at him. 'Ah, the clever Salim! Maybe there are some things you should know about your family. They never did a business deal in their lives. Everything your father had, he inherited. You think you're a man, now? All I see here is a big mouth and a small purse.' Salim sprang to his feet, stopped by Tareq's firm hand.

'But don't worry, Abu Hassan,' he went on. 'I've got the money here for you. It's not so much, but it was the best we could get. I would take it now, if I were you. Take it back to your beautiful wife and buy her something to cheer her up.'

He slid a packet of notes over the table. To Salim it looked soiled and flimsy, like their dreams of a homecoming. He held his breath.

Abu Hassan was still for a moment. His hand jerked towards the envelope, as if it were hot to the touch. And then he grasped it, his head bowed low. Salim's heart wrenched. He could not bear to see him exposed so brutally, like a beggar without his clothes.

'*Yallah*,' said Abu Mazen, standing up. 'I'll see you, then. Next time you come, come for coffee in Jaffa. My very best regards to Umm Hassan. A beautiful wife is the only luck a man needs, eh?' And with that, he turned and strolled away.

'*Yallah*, Mazen,' he called back over his shoulder, and Salim saw his old friend flinch at the command.

Mazen paused for an instant, turning around towards the huddled Al-Ishmaelis. Salim saw his hand move outwards towards him, the fleshy palm open. And the thought came that the boy he'd known was still there, trying to reach beyond all this with an apology.

But the hand kept rising, and as Mazen touched his finger to his forehead Salim recognized the salute at once. It was the obeisance that a worker gives his master, the grateful thanks when the wages were handed over. And as Mazen's smile broke out, more confident now, Salim knew that the boyhood jokes had finally become real. He was the *fellah* with his hand out, and his masters had just given him his last payment.

The envelope and its pitiful contents nestled in Tareq's briefcase on the long, slow journey home, along with the now useless title deeds. Tareq talked during their weary drive, working hard against the persistent silence in the car. He came up with solutions and strategies, court battles and cases they could put.

Abu Hassan grunted and nodded his assent. But Salim knew it was just for show. His father had acquiesced to fate. The world would have to go on, and Salim would have to find a new place in it.

As they pulled up into the little, dark garage Salim was overwhelmed with a desire to see his mother, to feel her soothing hand on his forehead. He raced up the dim flights of stairs, through the sweaty heaps of dust, and burst into the flat calling, 'Mama! We're home!'

Nadia came rushing out of the kitchen, a wet cloth in her hands. She was holding it in a strange way. 'Hey,' he said. 'Where's Mama?' She did not reply. A disconnected part of his brain realized that she held a wet tissue, and not a dishcloth at all. Her body and face seemed wrong too. Her eyes were red and her face bloated. She reached out her hands to him but he backed away, suddenly terrified.

Turning around, he ran into his mother's bedroom shouting, 'Mama! Mama!' The room was dark, with the curtains closed. But even in the dim light Salim could see the gaping holes of open, empty cupboards where once clothes had hung.

He pushed past Nadia's reaching hand, tearing into the bedroom he shared with Rafan. The small box of Rafan's clothes was gone. The blanket they'd shared for all these years was missing too, along with the old duffel bag that Salim had brought from Jaffa.

His legs gave way and he fell onto Rafan's stinking mattress, nausea filling his throat. *Now I understand you, Mama.* She had known how it would go. She had known they would fail. After years of pretending to belong to them, she had left at last.

1959

Returning from *Shul* one afternoon, Dora called her husband and daughters together to make a grand announcement.

'Judit's going to have a Batmitzvah!' she said triumphantly, one manicured hand reaching down to pinch Judith's chin. 'I talked to the Rebbe and he agrees completely. Hymie and Martha's girl had one last week, and there are at least three more planned this year.'

Gertie clapped her hands, and Jack said, 'Okay, well, if you think so, why not? She has a year to get ready, after all.'

Judith stood stock still in horror. Her eleventh birthday had come and gone almost unnoticed, to her great relief. The thought of reading the Torah in front of dozens – maybe hundreds – of Doras and their yarmulked husbands sent a chill of fear down her spine.

'But Mummy, everyone will be looking at me,' she said. 'I can't read in front of all those people.'

'Of course everyone will look at you,' was Dora's breezy reply. 'And why shouldn't they look, a smart young lady like you? Think of your Bubby, how proud she'll be! And your sister too, who never got to do such a thing.'

She swept away into the kitchen. 'We can make all the arrangements later, Jack,' she called cheerfully. 'It won't be a big thing, nothing like the shindig that brother of yours put on for Tony. Just family and a few friends, you know.'

Judith looked helplessly at her father and Gertie, who gave her a kind smile and a 'what can you do?' shrug.

'Do I have to?' she whispered.

'Oh Judit, love, it's a wonderful thing.' Her sister was beaming through the dark-rimmed glasses pressed around her round face like a cage. She straightened them with one hand and touched Judith's cheek with the other, fingers soft as warm bread. Outside of Dora's hearing range, Jack leaned over to whisper, 'These Batmitzvahs – I don't know why girls should bother, to be honest. But it's an innovation, and your mother's a real innovator, God bless her.'

Rebecca also thought it was a fine idea.

'In my day, people would have laughed at a coming-of-age for girls,' she said, rubbing the back of Judith's neck. 'All we knew is that when you got your bleeding, you were old enough to marry.' Judith blushed – Dora had sat her down for the excruciating 'talk' just a week or so before. 'Barmitzvahs were only for the boys. I never had this privilege, nor did Gertie, nor did your mama. So times have changed for the better, *mommellah*.'

'I don't see why it's better,' pleaded Judith. 'What if I can't learn all the verses, and I get it wrong?'

Rebecca smiled. Her faded red hair peeped out of her blue scarf and her deep green eyes were full of life.

'Don't worry, my little love,' she said. 'Every child is frightened of growing up somehow. Even the *goyim* children are afraid. But you are luckier than them, because now you know exactly on which day you can stop being afraid – the day you put down the Torah scrolls and the Rebbe blesses you as an adult.' She leaned forward and took Judith's face in her hand, as frail as a butterfly, and squeezed gently.

'This is a special honour, my Judit. It means you take your place as a woman among your people. So chin up, little one, and be brave. Be a *mensch*!'

Kath was all disbelief at Wearside. 'It sounds mad, Judy-Rudy!' she said as they lined up for Mr Hick's whistle, against the echoing clamour and splash of the pool. 'I'd be wetting me pants. But why didn't you tell your mam about the bloomin' Tryouts? You're the best in the Club, you'll make the Juniors for sure.'

Being chosen for Sunderland's North-East Junior Swim Team seemed a far higher honour to Judith than being chosen by God. Wearside's Tryouts were coming up fast and Judith was practising to exhaustion, coming home late with wet hair and sore eyes to avoid Gertie's questions; she was burning through the Club's target times. The Junior Team was her secret hope, a desire so fierce it frightened her. After her last race Mr Hicks had nodded as she emerged gasping from the water, saying, 'You'll do.'

She squeezed Kath's arm, sad to think that after this summer they would never sit in the same classroom again. The Eleven-Plus was looming; Jack and Dora had their hearts set on Bede's Grammar School. Kathleen's mother had never even heard of it, and Kath was as likely to qualify as to fly to the moon. But they'd promised to stay friends. Blood pact, Kath said, as they'd cut the tips of their forefingers with Molly's razor and pressed the red beads together.

'Stop gassing, you two,' Mr Hicks yelled. 'First time trial for Group One. On my mark. Remember, I want flying fish, not beached bloody whales.'

Judith stepped forward, her toes curling over the slick tiles of the pool edge, feeling the pull of the water below. Out of the corner of her eye she saw Kath blush and wave at someone. She just had time to see a tall red swimming cap and ice blue eyes a head above her, before the whistle sent her into the water.

Instantly the world faded into the silence of blue bubbles, the blissful cool flying past against her skin, the extraordinary rush linking her disconnected limbs, heart and legs and breath pounding out the same rhythm. *Go on!* someone was shouting, and between the beats of breath she felt the words rather than heard them. *Go on, Judith! Fight for it!* The wall loomed ahead and she reached with all her heart; her fingers touched the edge and she burst to the surface – but as she gulped in her first full breath she saw blue eyes smiling down at her, and realized the tall girl was already taking off her red cap. As Judith floated there, flushed and swallowing down air, the girl leaned over to whisper, 'Sorry, dolly,' before pulling her long body out of the pool and setting off towards the changing rooms.

'Never mind,' said Kath as they dried themselves later. 'You'll still be in the first Tryout group. They're taking two from the first.' Judith looked down. She had expected to win the first group; she'd been depending on it.

Kath nudged her arm. 'Look, Judy – she's coming. She's so cool, I promise.'

Without the cap, Judith recognized her instantly: Margaret Smailes – or Peggy S as she called herself, like the Buddy song. An outbreak of tonsillitis at school had made Peggy Kath's new deskmate two weeks ago, and Kath was already smitten.

Peggy was a head taller than the rest of the class, with straight, strong legs under a shorter than regulation skirt. At school she was always trailed like a comet by giggling girls. Now her white ponytail hung long and wet down her back and her fingers glowed with varnish. Judith could see gold draped in a chain around her neck.

Peggy pointed a white finger at her. 'So Kitty K, this is your other friend, right?'

Kathleen grinned and said, 'Right, this is Judy.'

Judith shifted awkwardly, hotly aware of her bunches and brown socks.

'Who's Kitty K?' she asked.

Peggy laughed. 'Can't you guess? It's Kitty Kallen, from the *movies.*' Peggy reached out to Kathleen's wild hair. 'She's sooo gorgeous with all those lovely brown curls. My mother says that she can't be a great actress because she's just a cheap American. But *I* think who cares if you're that glamorous, right?' Her white shirt was open revealing damp patches on a budding cleavage and a heart-shaped pendant sticking to her skin. Judith thought she saw the lace of a bra, and found she was nodding her head along with Kathleen.

'So you're Judy, right?' Peggy peppered her sentences with 'rights' like bullets; it was impossible to do anything other than agree with her. 'Judy's not your real name, though, right? I saw it on the register. You're Judith, aren't you? You're one of the Jewish girls. It's okay, you can tell me.' Her voice was warm and friendly but Judith felt a cold wind. No one had ever called her a Jewish girl before, except for Dora. She glanced at Kathleen, who smiled and said, 'She is, but she's super cool. My best friend, aren't you, Judy?'

'All right then. Well, I think we can do better than *Judith*, for such a cutie, right, Kitty K? I don't think you look like a Judy. What about Jude? You could be a Jude, right?'

'That's a boy's name,' said Judith automatically.

'What, that's so hip. Don't you want to be hip, Jude? You're already such a dolly with those blonde little bunches.' Peggy was looking at her, head on one side with a perfect, white smile. Suddenly Judith's spirits lifted, her nerves ebbing away like a kite taking to the air.

'Okay, I like it,' she said.

'Great!' Peggy gyrated her hips like she was doing the twist on *Crackerjack*, her head up to the sky and eyes closed. 'Kitty K and Jude, super swimming pals!' And she squeezed Judith's arm affectionately, as Judith blushed and giggled back.

For the next few weeks, Judith felt like she'd fallen in love. Peggy was the single most fascinating person Judith had ever met. At twelve she was already the kind of person Judith dreamed of becoming when she grew up. She knew how to wear their school uniform to make boys turn their heads when she walked by – how to be sweet and mean in just the right balance. She knew other things too, things they hadn't yet imagined. She knew 'all about' men; she had a boyfriend, a secret she whispered to them, who was *sophisticated* and gave her beautiful presents like the diamond pendant lying over a red mark on her throat. A *hickie*, she said. Her only flaw was on her nails – red, bitten cuticles that she covered with varnish.

Under the bright glare of Peggy's self-assurance, the shadow of Judith's own anxiety began to retreat. Peggy taught her not to care about anything, not even the Eleven-Plus. She was going to private school next year regardless of her results – and promised to write a letter every week for them to read. 'I told Daddy that I wanted to go to one for debutantes in London, but he said he just can't *bear* to be so far away from me,' she sighed, fingering her necklace. When Judith suggested they might go to visit her, Peggy doubled over with laughter, her skirt riding up her legs.

'Oh, Jude, what a card! You're going to come to my school! I'll leave a note on the door to make sure they let you in, right? Ha ha ha.' And she howled again, Judith joining in with the rest even through a little pain inside. Peggy was funny like that; when Judith had slipped at the poolside yesterday and fallen splayed into the water Peggy had started calling her Jude the Jellyfish.

She talked to cousin Tony about it when he came up for Passover dinner. 'She's my best friend,' Judith told him. 'She's pretty and lots of fun.'

'Is this the one your mother calls a *shiksa* goddess-in-waiting?'

'They only saw her once at parents' evening, so she doesn't know what she's talking about.'

'And have you met her family?'

'No,' Judith hesitated. 'They're rich, I think, like you.'

Tony laughed. 'Listen, being rich doesn't make you one of the fellas, particularly if you're a *jay ee double-you*. They don't let our sort into country clubs, you know. I got my share of grief at school too.'

You don't understand, Jude thought. None of them did. To them she was just a little Jewish dumpling, shaped by Mama and Papa to be swallowed up one day by Jewish mouths. But to Peggy she was someone else. Someone in her own right.

The week before the Junior Tryouts, Judith finally got Dora's grudging go-ahead to miss half an hour of Hebrew class. Peggy was excited, Kath oddly morose. Peggy had taken to hugging Judith and saying, 'I'm SO thrilled we'll be swim teammates next year, little Jude.' She knew they were the first and second place in the class, that Kath must be jealous, but still she couldn't help her own triumph shining through. She was on the cusp of something sweetly, truly hers – an evolution of her half-formed self into a fullness she couldn't explain but longed for with all her heart.

The Tryouts were on Monday. Judith was prepared for her world to change forever. Even the threat of the Batmitzvah faded in the brightness of her excitement.

On Friday Peggy S gathered them all by the school fence at lunchtime and told them she would be hosting a pre-Tryout party for her special friends.

'I'm going to miss you all soooo much next year!' she said, putting her chin into her hand like a movie star, her mouth pink and open. 'Daddy's printing special invitations for all of you. There's only one rule – everyone has to come as someone glamorous. Kitty K, that should be no problem for you, right?' Kathleen grinned and squirmed as Peggy reached out and stroked her wild black hair. Her other hand took hold of Judith's, her palm as smooth as a china plate.

'And what about my little Jude? Can you come as someone glamorous too?'

'Who should I come as?' asked Judith anxiously. She was the only one without a Peggy name from the world of music or film.

'Goodness, Jude, it's not for me to say. Just make it up! Right? Be your own person!' She squeezed Judith's hand and turned to her other acolytes, leaving Judith to worry about who her own person could be.

Peggy's father drove to the school in a silver Jaguar to drop off invitations for all the girls, and Peggy distributed them on Friday at school. Judith's had *Jude* written on the front of the card, with a dark swirl of balloons and hearts underneath.

Inside it read: *Sunday 12 noon*. Judith's Hebrew class was at noon too, she remembered. She was struggling with the readings and the Rebbe had said she needed extra help. Could Dora be persuaded to let her skip it just this once?

At the end of class, Peggy was packing up her desk with Kathleen's help. She flashed Judith a bright smile as she approached, hesitant. 'What's up, little Jude?'

'Peggy, can I come late to the party?'

'Why on earth would you do that?'

'It's at the same time as my Hebrew class. My mother already said yes to the Tryouts, she'll never agree to this too.' Judith heard a couple of giggles behind her. Peggy looked aslant at Kathleen and Judith thought she saw Kath give a small, secretive smile back.

Peggy was looking at her now with the half-smile still on her face.

'Hebrew class! Wow. Exciting. We wouldn't want you to miss *that*, right? If you'd rather go to that, I don't mind at all.'

'No, no,' said Judith. 'I want to come to yours, but...' she tailed off as Peggy slung her bag onto her shoulder and started walking out of the door. The tall, sharp line of her back was like an exclamation mark. In the doorway, she paused, the ponytail bobbing by itself for a second, before she turned to look over her shoulder.

'If you want to come, then come, *Jude*,' she said. 'Be your own person. I *so* hope you do.'

Judith watched Peggy leave the room. Kath was still pushing books into her bag. Judith tried to catch her eye, but Kath's blue ones seemed determinedly downcast. 'They're a posh crowd, Judith,' she said all of a sudden, squaring her shoulders as she yanked up her bag. 'Maybe it's for the best if you've got other things on.'

At Sabbath dinner Judith broached the subject of missing Hebrew school for Peggy's party.

'Absolutely not,' Dora said. 'Twice in one week, forget it. Don't you know your Batmitzvah is coming up? Rebbe Geshen says you're already behind with your reading. First this swimming and now partying – what's got into you?'

'I'll do even more next week, I promise,' Judith begged. 'Please, Dad?' But Jack just shook his head and said, 'Listen to your mother, pet.'

'God help us, what are you thinking, Judit?' Dora said. 'Are you in love with this *shiksa* goddess? Are you converting? There'll be plenty of parties, young lady, but only one Batmitzvah. So let's hear no more about it.'

But the argument went on and on, into Saturday until Dora stamped off in frustration to *Shul* and Judith retreated to her bedroom. On Sunday morning, she toyed with the idea of just slipping out. But in an unusual streak of foresight, Dora had called Gertie to come and hang around outside Judith's bedroom.

Gertie was terrible at hovering; her large breasts and round hips made her awkward on the cramped landing. Judith sat in her room hating even the thought of Gertie, her disapproving glasses and her sanctimonious brown stockings.

Eventually, Gertie opened Judith's door herself and said, blinking rapidly, 'Judit, it's nearly time for school. Shall we go together?' Judith glared at her, but did not have the courage to refuse. Despising herself, she stood up and hoisted her schoolbag onto her shoulder.

In just a few minutes, Kathleen would be knocking on Peggy's door dressed in her best clothes, and Judith would be sitting with a sweating Rebbe, trying to make sense of ancient scrolls.

Suddenly, she heard an odd sound from Gertie, like a puzzled cry. Her sister was looking at something on Judith's bed, and quicker than Judith had ever seen her move she crossed the room to snatch it up. It was Peggy's invitation, in all its embossed glory.

'Give that back,' Judith said fiercely, but Gertie ignored her. She turned around to face Judith, her chest rising heavily, the invitation held out like a pistol in her hand.

'What's this?' she asked, in a whisper. 'Who wrote this to you? Judit, why didn't you tell us about this?'

'It's nothing,' Judith said warily. 'It's the invitation to my friend's party. What's the big deal?'

'But what's this?' Gertie said again, whiter still, one finger pointing to the name on the front.

'That's my name. Jude. That's what they call me at school.' She saw Gertie step backwards, her brow furrowing in horrified disbelief.

'You *want* them to call you that? Don't you know what that name means?' She had started sweating, pale beads on her broad forehead shining under the bedroom light. 'That's the word they called us. *Jude. Juden.* That's what they called us in the ghettos and the Camps.'

She walked towards Judith, who backed away. 'How can you let someone call you that?' She shook the invitation in Judith's startled face. 'How could you?' she said again.

Judith had a flicker of shame; but it was snuffed out the next moment by a quick, cruel pinch of self-pity. *Godly Gertie*, she thought, resentful. *Always some way to make me wrong.*

'I didn't *let* them call me it,' she said, with affected nonchalance. 'I called myself that name. I like it. It's cool.'

Before the words were even out of her mouth, Gertie reached out and slapped her – a blow that burned like hot bread from the oven.

Judith cried out in shock and Gertie covered her mouth with her fist, tears running between her fingers. From behind her hand, she whispered, 'How can you say such a thing, Judit? You don't understand anything, nothing at all about who we are and what happened to us.'

Judith's face itched and stung. She couldn't believe Gertie had hit her. Her sister's fingers, round and unpainted, looked so gauche holding the delicate white card. For an instant it faded and transformed into another picture – *Gertrude, Esther und Daniel Kraus, Wien 1939* – and hot anger at Gertie, at the endless guilt, rose scalding into her throat.

'No, *you* don't understand anything,' she screamed, feeling her cheeks turn red. 'I'm sick of you people always telling me what to do and how to be. I *hate* being Jewish. You just leave me alone.'

As she spoke she felt her legs propel her past Gertie, who called out her name, carrying her pounding heart down the stairs, racing across the hall and through the front door, slamming it hard behind her. The rush of the cold sea wind tasted of exhilaration and pain, like the first surge of oxygen into burning lungs at the end of the race.

She caught the bus to Peggy's house. As it rattled from Ryhope Road to the smarter part of town, Judith clutched her bag to her chest. She felt dizzy with anticipation, watching the solemn rows of semi-detached houses reel by her as the road swept away from the dockyards. *They'll be so happy to see me. They'll laugh when they know how much trouble I'm in.*

The bus stopped at the edge of the town, where the houses had back gardens as well as front ones, and the sky was a smokeless blue. Judith climbed off and watched it roar away, standing on a silent pavement.

Walking up the street to the Smailes' detached house, Judith felt as tall and straight as Peggy herself. She pulled down her skirt and pushed back her hair. A brief worry passed through her mind like a shadow: she hadn't obeyed the party rules – she wasn't in the least *glamorous*. But after pinching her cheeks and biting her lips she hoped she might pass if she made a good story of it.

She opened the front gate cautiously and saw a flicker of movement in one large, curtained window. There were roses in the garden, pink as schoolgirls hanging their heavy heads. Smiling, she jumped up the steps and reached out to knock on the door.

Then something stopped her. Stepping back, she saw it: at the entrance to the porch someone had stuck a large, yellow sign on the wall.

Written there, in capital letters, were the words *NO JEWDES ALLOWED.*

At first Judith's eyes could not take it in. The words swam in front of her; her legs wobbled until she had to hold onto the porch pillars to stay upright. Her chest tightened and her throat felt full of stones.

She heard a click and looked up. The front door had opened, and standing in the bright hallway behind it was Kathleen. At her back stood Peggy. The blonde girl was grinning, a fox in bright red lipstick, one hand on Kathleen's shoulder. Kathleen stared at the ground, red under her freckles.

Judith stood up straight, wondering if she was expected to smile or to cry. If she reacted the right way, would it all be all right? Was it a test? *It's all a joke*, she thought desperately, *and they're going to ask me in.* But she saw with brutal clarity the hand on Kathleen's shoulder, its pale pink varnish shining lightly in the gloom of the porch.

The hand tightened, and Kathleen's head jerked upwards to look at her. There was such genuine misery in her face that tears came to Judith's eyes, and with them a sick certainty of abandonment. *Still*, she thought, *she wouldn't go inside. She won't go.*

For a second no one moved. Judith took a deep, hopeful breath. Then Kathleen closed the door, the slow groan of polished oak shutting her outside.

*

By the time Judith got back to Ryhope Road, the world was a very different place. The first thing she heard when she opened the front door was the sound of weeping. It seemed to come straight from her own heart and she imagined it must be herself crying. Next she thought of Gertie. Then, quick as a snake, the realization struck her. It was Rebecca. *She knows*, Judith thought. *She's crying because of me.*

Suddenly, Gertie appeared in the living room doorway. Her face was blotched and red, and she reached out to clutch Judith's hand.

'Oh Judit, thank goodness. There's been bad news. Your Uncle Max – well, Father will tell you.'

Judith was trembling as she walked into the sitting room. Rebecca was on the green sofa, rocking and wailing against Jack's awkward shoulder. Dora was on the other side, her hand tight on Rebecca's arm.

Rebecca's eyes opened as Judith approached; she reached out to pull her granddaughter towards her. Judith instinctively resisted, shame lying like a stench on her skin.

'What's happened?' she said, her throat thick and sore.

Dora answered from Rebecca's side, her voice low as if confiding a secret.

'Your Uncle Max is hurt, Judit. He was on a bus, and it was attacked. They shot him.' Judith took a moment to comprehend this, to remind herself of other lives she was still connected to. While she was mocking Gertie and running away from home, people who hated Jews were trying to hurt her family.

Dora looked at Jack, who clutched his mother tighter than ever and said, 'He'll be okay, Mama. Max is a fighter. He has the best care.'

Rebecca shook her head. 'Oh my boy, my poor boy.' Her voice was hoarse – it seemed to tear from her throat as she raised one open hand towards the ceiling. 'Are we never finished with all of this? The Russians come and then the Germans and now my son gets shot on a bus. When will it stop?'

They put Rebecca to bed and Jack explained things quietly to Judith. Max was in a serious condition in hospital in Tel Aviv. Jack and Alex were going to take the first available flight to Israel they could.

Judith received Jack's injunction to be a good girl with silent thankfulness. When he looked at her and shook his head, she thought for an instant he was going to tell her of his deep disappointment. But instead he only said, 'It's such a shame, Judith. He was just a farmer, growing and building things. Where's the wrong in that?'

Later, she crept upstairs to Rebecca's room. The house was eerily still. Dora and Gertie were sitting in the kitchen over cold cups of tea. Jack was out at the shop, scouring the books for the price of an airfare. Rebecca's door was ajar, and Judith could see her propped up on her thin pillows. She tapped lightly on the doorframe and saw Rebecca's head rise slightly.

'Come in, *mommellah*,' she said, her voice so frail it made Judith ache. She knelt down and took Rebecca's hand in hers. 'I'm so sorry, Bubby,' she said. Rebecca nodded, turning her head towards the window and the white summer sky sailing past them. Judith sat in silence for a minute, feeling Rebecca's gentle pulse. But eventually the weight of unsaid things tipped her mouth open and she found herself blurting, 'I had a fight with Gertie today.'

Rebecca turned back to look at her with tired eyes. 'Oh yes, she told me. About the name.' Judith's face went red and she waited for Rebecca's verdict. But instead, Rebecca laid her head back on the pillow and sighed.

'I'll never forget the day she came to us.' Her eyes turned to the window, looking far away. 'Just a little girl, even smaller than you – and thin too, although you'd never guess it now. She came on the rescue trains, the *Kindertransport* from Austria. Your mother and I went down to Liverpool Street station to meet her. Gertie had a sister with her, and she held that girl's hand so tight I thought she'd never let go. They looked like two peas in a pod and it broke my heart to separate them, but we couldn't take both. Gertie cried all the way home and for weeks afterwards. She didn't speak any English at all, so I had to try in Yiddish. Don't tell your mother, but Gertie is the reason her Yiddish is still so good.' She paused to cough into her hand.

'Gertie didn't want to talk about her mama or papa or the brothers she'd left behind. She didn't want to eat or sleep. She just wanted to see that sister of hers. I thought it was a strange thing to rescue a child from murder only to have her die of sorrow in a safe place. Then I found out that her sister was living just a few miles away, so Dora and I took turns to walk Gertie there every Friday before prayers. It took us four hours there and back but we never missed a Friday. I'd listen to her and her sister talking away in German and Yiddish, and it did my heart good. But that was before the war. Her family went to the Camps, and they never came out again. Then the sister moved away because their house was bombed. And that was the last Gertie saw of her, apart from letters.' Tears were running down Judith's face, and she didn't dare wipe them away. *Gertrude, Esther und Daniel*, she remembered. Rebecca's voice was running on.

'You don't know how hard it was for Jews when the war came. The Nazis had plenty of friends here who thought they had the right way with us. When the dockyards were bombed I saw it in people's faces. They thought we'd brought a plague on them. Maybe they were right. Wherever we go, hate follows. We always dream the next generation will shake the curse.' She sighed and squeezed Judith's hand.

'I said something terrible to Gertie.' Her confession was a relief. 'She didn't like my nickname and I was angry, so I told her I wished I wasn't a Jew.'

Rebecca smiled and tapped Judith on the cheek. 'You and that name of yours!' she said. 'Let me tell you something. Your name has a very impressive history. When Nebuchadnezzar sent a wicked general to destroy the Jews, young Judith came sneaking inside his tent. And then do you know what she did? She got him drunk and cut his head off. His army ran away. So Judith saved her people. A modern woman, my Judit. Not a bad name to have, don't you think?'

Judith forced a smile. From inside the haze of exhaustion, Peggy, Kathleen, Gertie and the faceless children of the *Kindertransport* all seemed to be calling her. She wanted to lie down and block them out.

'You're tired, Bubby,' she said, standing up. 'Let me get you a cup of tea.' Rebecca nodded and said, 'Let me give you something first, *mommellah*.' A pale arm was pulling open the bedside drawer, and Judith saw an envelope with her name on it, in Rebecca's slanting scrawl. 'I was saving it for your Batmitzvah, but I've finished it already so you should have it. Don't read it until the day, though. It's bad luck.' Judith took it carefully and her grandmother settled back down onto the bed and closed her eyes. 'What is it?' Judith whispered, feeling the weight of paper inside.

'Nothing special,' came the answer, even softer. 'But promise you'll read it when the time comes.'

Judith said, 'I promise,' but this time Rebecca showed no sign of hearing. She stepped quietly from the room, stopping at the door to look back at the sunken form in the bed. 'I love you, Bubby,' she heard herself saying. But her grandmother was already breathing gently, lost in the beguiling sleep of old age.

She set the letter down on the bed, which still bore the imprint of Peggy's invitation. After a moment of hesitation, her hand eased under the envelope flap. Several sheets of paper fell out, crossed with Rebecca's writing. She read the first line:

Judit, my darling girl,
    Today is your Batmitzvah – such a special day for you, to become a grown woman. I know that you will do everything so beautifully, and that you will make us proud.

Her eyes blurred and she rubbed them, pressing fierce hands down until they ached. As her room came into focus again, she saw her swimming bag hanging over the doorknob. Pulling it down, she clutched it to her chest. The bright red canvas was still musty with friendly smells, the sharpness of chlorine and damp rubber. Kath had drawn a yellow heart on the fraying corner, on her first day at Wearside. She felt the hard outline of tomorrow's Junior Tryouts schedule pressing against her shirt.

Shame and revulsion rose inside her; pulling out the schedule she ripped it up and thrust the pieces under the bed. Then she opened her cupboard door and pushed the bag into the depths at the back, heaping shoes on top of it until it was buried, until she could pretend it had never existed. Then she curled back under the blanket, Rebecca's letter falling to the floor. *Make us proud.* How could she, with only a hole inside her where certainty should live? *I'm not a mensch, Bubby,* she whispered to the pillow. *I'm not, and I never will be.*

ℑ

There was no frantic scurrying to get Salim's mother back, no threats or phone calls or demands. She was gone as completely and irrevocably as if she had just lifted herself out of the sea.

Even in his anger at being left, at being cast on the scrapheap of her life, Salim could not find it in his heart to hate her. Pain pulled the needle of blame towards the Jews, towards fate, and most of all to his father. He came running out of his room that day and pulled Abu Hassan's hand; clutching it to his chest he begged him to find her. 'She can't be far,' he sobbed, feeling his stomach twist and the shame of water leaking down his leg in a child's grief. But Abu Hassan just stood there, his mouth gaping, his eyes muddy pools. Something came out of his throat that sounded like 'No, no,' and then he turned away from his son, as Salim screamed, 'It's your fault!

You made her miserable! You did everything wrong! Now we have nothing.' Tareq pulled him roughly into his arms, half a restraint, half a hug. He whispered into his hair that he should never blame his father, who loved him despite everything. 'He only can't tell you because he's old, and life has buried his words.' But at that moment Salim knew only rage and despair; so much that if Abu Hassan had still owned the Orange House, Salim felt he could have burned it down himself.

At night there was a cold space beside him where Rafan used to sleep, an empty room where all three brothers had once lain and plotted their return. And his dreams were full of his mother, of opening the door of strange houses he did not recognize, and finding her there.

The ache in his heart refused to fade with the months. Most of all he grieved that she had taken Rafan and not him, hooks of jealousy and sorrow catching him whenever he tried to rest.

But despite himself he spent hours picturing where she might be, a flutter of excitement in his throat. Maybe the tall boulevards of Europe, or the bright streets of Beirut. And then the pain of her escape became somehow animating – cutting through his ties to Palestine, letting his imagination float upwards into the sky, over Nazareth's crowded tenements into the great unknown.

In one concrete way, his mother's flight did set him free. Buoyed up by Abu Mazen's blood money, and with two fewer mouths to feed, Abu Hassan became more persuadable on the matter of how to dispose of his remaining son.

Nadia and Tareq truly loved Salim, and worried for his future. Sensing trouble ahead if he stayed in Nazareth, they began to concoct a plan. Suppose, Tareq said to Abu Hassan one night, Salim were to improve his English and learn a proper trade? If he were to go and stay with Hassan in England, he might be able to send money back here and be a better support to his father.

Abu Hassan was quick to acquiesce. After all, he was too old to be looking after a teenage boy. Visas these days were not hard to come by if a sponsor could be found.

Salim was elated when Tareq broke the news to him. He agreed to work hard, get good grades, stay out of trouble and not to upset his father. He longed to leave the dusty powerlessness of Arab life and remake himself. Every speck of desire to stay in this new land of Israel had been extinguished.

On his last night in Israel, he gathered together his clothes, books and flimsy photographs. The clothes went into a small black bag. He laid the pictures carefully in the bin on the floor. Reaching into the back of his cupboard, he lifted out a shoebox and opened the lid.

The photograph of the Orange House had yellowed after so many years. It was the first time he'd looked since coming back from Tel Aviv. What was the point of it now? He tipped it into the bin, hearing the sad little thud as it hit the bottom. Then he sat down on the bed, breathing hard.

After a moment, he bent down slowly and retrieved it. The baby boy's eyes stared at him from the frame, accusing. Salim answered: *I have new dreams now*. But he pushed it quickly into his suitcase.

In the autumn after his seventeenth birthday, as the orange harvest season approached, Salim stood at Lod Airport in Tel Aviv to catch the El-Al flight to London. In his pocket he carried a one-way airline ticket, his Israeli passport, his national identity document and his Palestinian birth certificate. His father had given him the equivalent of one hundred British pounds to start him in a new life. This was his total legacy from the past, the last gift of the Orange House.

Tareq and Abu Hassan walked him to passport control. Nadia had been unable to contemplate coming too, overcome with grief. Salim had felt tears welling up when he hugged her goodbye, aware that in some ways she too was losing a son.

Tareq leaned over to give Salim a rough embrace, pulling the young man tight to his chest. 'God bless you, God bless you,' he repeated, tears wetting his cheeks. 'Take care of yourself. You know that you always have a home with us – always.'

'I know,' said Salim, deeply moved. He wanted to tell Tareq how much he loved him, that he had been brother and father to Salim all at once. But with his own father standing nearby, he could not bring himself to say it. All he said was, 'Tell Nadia goodbye. Tell her I'll eat, and study – and I'll miss her yelling at me.' Tareq nodded and turned away, to allow Abu Hassan the last farewell.

The two stared at each other slowly. In the harsh light of the departure hall, Salim saw more clearly than ever how old his father had become. He remembered they were Abu Hassan's second family, the last gasp of a long life. He saw the weakness in his body and legs, and the greyness of the old lips, and a tenderness came over him that he could not explain.

He reached over and put his arm around Abu Hassan's shoulder.

'Goodbye, Baba,' he said softly, searching for words that were both true and kind. 'I'll… I'll write to you often. Take care of yourself.'

Abu Hassan brought up a shaking arm and let it lie for a moment around his son's back. He pulled Salim to his chest quickly, and Salim felt the old heart hammering against his ribs like a woodpecker's beak. Then Abu Hassan let go and said, '*Ma salameh*' – go in peace. Salim stood for a moment, then hoisted his rucksack on his shoulder and turned towards the gates.

It was all too quick, the jump from one life to another. Within the hour, Salim sat strapped to his seat while the El-Al plane rose out of the clouds of yellow dust sent skywards by the summer heat.

They crossed Israel's narrow waist before the jet had risen. Looking out of the window, Salim saw the strip of land so many had fought over, as it slipped out of view. It was so small that it took his breath away.

As they reached into the radiant blue sky, he felt as if he was entering a void inside himself as profound as the one outside his window – a terrifying, exhilarating emptiness ready to be filled.

Four hours later, they touched down at London Airport. The grey and gloomy skies and great green expanses were oddly refreshing. Salim was ready to welcome the differences between the world he'd left and the one he would soon belong to.

As he stood in line to show his passport and visa, he watched the other faces standing next to him – some dark, some fair, all with the same contained expression. He wondered how many were like him – starting over again. He looked across at the fast moving line of British passport holders. He promised himself that next time he would be standing in that line.

Waiting in the arrivals hall was one familiar face. Hassan – still broad, fleshy and jolly – was standing waving frantically, a smile smothering his face. 'My God, Salim!' he said, rushing over to give his brother a hug. He was bundled up in a bulky jumper and a black leather coat. 'You look just the same. What a mug you have! Like a movie star! I'm going to take you out, and maybe I'll have better luck with the girls!'

'Not if you wear that sweater, you idiot,' Salim laughed. He was genuinely happy to see him, relieved to find something familiar here to cling to. Hassan slapped him on the back and said, 'Come on. Let's go home.'

Outside, the air was wetter and heavier than Salim had ever experienced. *How do people live here?* It was all so disorienting – the oppressive sky, the vastness of the airport, the rows and rows of cars shining in the gloom and the howl of traffic from the dozens of roads spinning off in every direction. It was nearly half an hour before they found the car and could be on their way.

Driving through the rainy, busy streets, Salim listened with half an ear to Hassan's stories about his car repair shop, the exciting new projects they could start together and the girls they'd meet. When Hassan asked him what his plan was, he fingered the money in his pocket and said, without thinking, 'Take a course in English, and try to get into university.'

'University? What do you want to do that for? Believe me, Salim, you don't need all this studying rubbish. There's plenty of money to be made with me in the garage.'

Salim didn't answer. He watched the grey, endless concrete roll by outside the window and wondered how he was going to make his mark on it, make this alien country work for him.

Eventually, they pulled up in a dirty little side-road under a railway bridge. By the crumbling buildings lining the road and the darkness of the faces walking down the street, Salim assumed they were in a poorer district, reserved for foreigners like him. Hassan heaved Salim's bag out of the trunk and dragged it over to a little brown door. It stood next to a shop selling Indian food, with a green and yellow illuminated sign blinking cheerlessly in the drizzle.

'This is it!' Hassan said, as they reached the top of a dim, brown stairwell. 'Not a palace, but cheap and very convenient. You'll see.'

He pushed open the facing door and they entered a place smaller even than Tareq and Nadia's, with one bedroom and a small kitchen off the main living area with its spiral orange carpet. 'You'll have to sleep on the sofa at first,' Hassan said. 'But with the money you bring in, soon we'll be able to move to a bigger place! Right? You want a beer?'

Salim nodded, cold and tired to his bones. As Hassan went into the kitchen, he sat down on the brown sofa. It creaked and wobbled with his weight. Looking through tiny windows across the street, he saw a small, green park. A children's playground was at its centre, a striking patch of colours against the grey.

Hassan brought him a can of beer and he cracked it open. It tasted strangely sweet and sharp against his throat. Children were playing in the park outside. He could see them, a misty blur of waving arms and bright clothes. They seemed a world away from him, there in that dirty little room. As he sipped his beer he had the strangest feeling of disconnection – as if he were not really there but just a character in an old film, sad and soundless, painted in the vivid colours of loss.

Later Hassan sent Salim down to buy groceries – 'to get the hang of things'. He took Hassan's wallet, heavy with coins, and headed out under the drizzle. The streets were nearly empty, and the few people out walking passed quickly by him, heads down. There was nothing there, no flicker of recognition – they were all strangers caught in their own troubles, looking straight through each other. Homesickness swelled in his throat, trickling into him with the watery cold.

The sign on the cornershop Hassan had directed him to said *Freddy's*. The shopkeeper looked up as Salim walked in to the jangle of warning bells, white bearded under a dull orange turban. Salim walked up and down the aisles, looking at the brands. He picked up the ones he recognized from the days of the British in Palestine, when Private Jonno would sneak him cigarettes. When his basket was filled it struck him as ludicrous that his English kitchen might be the closest he'd been in years to their pantry in Jaffa, to his mother and the English tea she used to drink, the imported biscuits she'd prized.

At the counter, he fumbled with the strange silver and bronze money, turning over coins in desperation as the queue behind him grew restless. A man behind him called out, but Salim couldn't understand the words. Perhaps it wasn't even English. Irritated, the shopkeeper pushed Salim's hand away and gathered coins and notes together himself, beckoning the next customer. Salim picked up his bags and went outside.

The rain was lifting, and the rolling clouds had changed from iron to shining steel and marble, brilliant at their edges. The bags weighed him down – but it was a start, just a start, he told himself. Everything else would come in time.

As he walked down the brightening street, he heard the children again, high voices drifting above the sound of the traffic. They reached into Salim, pushing past his sorrow with their small song of delight.

As he saw them, just a touch away, he thought – *there may be harvests to be reaped here too.* He stood there for a time, watching them while London moved past and around him in a blur of faces and car horns. And all the while the children chased each other with oblivious laughter, defying gravity as they swung round and round deliriously in the light rain.

On the morning of Judith's Batmitzvah, she stood beside the Rebbe with her parents, dazed and resigned. Her portion of the Torah was committed to memory. Pieces of it had been flitting through her dreams for weeks, like bats under a dark sky.

She was dressed for the part: a new skirt, heeled shoes, a smart blue shirt and a woollen waistcoat. Her nails and hair had been done the day before. She looked like a mini-Dora, or a doll that Dora might have picked out as a child. *It's all a game, dressing up and pretending*, she thought. *I'm not really a grown-up today and I won't be tomorrow either.*

Without warning, the door opened in the Rebbe's office; urgent voices were raised in the corridor and Judith saw Jack grip Dora's arm. The gesture was chilling, a stone falling from the dam around her heart, letting in a flood of sudden fear.

A man in a yarmulke was saying, 'Come quickly, she's just outside.' As if in a dream she trailed behind her parents as they raced to the front door. A wailing noise poured in from outside, a distorted, inexplicable sound. When the door opened and the light came in, she saw Gertie standing there, red with hysterics.

They ran the five hundred yards back to their little home, Jack and Dora ahead, Judith behind them, holding tight to Gertie's hand.

From halfway there she could see the ambulance, its siren flashing without a sound. The silence was a terrible omen as she pounded the pavement in new heels, pain shooting up her legs.

The front door was wide open and she stumbled in. A man stood in Rebecca's doorway, talking to Jack. Dora's mascara had run, and Judith heard the words *pneumonia* and *congestive heart failure*. Jack shook his head like a dog with water in its ears and Dora put her hand to her mouth.

Judith walked slowly up the stairs to stand beside her father. Jack's face was grey, tears pooling in the hollows of his cheekbones.

'What's happening to Bubby?' she whispered.

It was Dora who spoke, her voice steady and kind.

'Your Bubby is leaving us, Judit. There's nothing we can do. She had a wonderful life. They want to take her to the hospital but your father thinks,' she reached out and took Jack's hand, 'that she should stay here. It's what she would want.'

Judith nodded. *Be brave. Be a mensch.* 'How long will she stay?' she asked.

'Maybe a day or two, pet,' Jack said, hoarse. He was holding the top of his balding scalp, his hand clapped to the thin black yarmulke as if it pained him. Judith's starched hairdo itched at the sight. 'Not more. She'll go to sleep soon and have her rest.'

'Can I see her?'

Jack looked at Dora. Her mother nodded. 'It's right you should see her, Judit. She loves you most of all, you know.'

Judith walked into the little room as she had done hundreds of times, seeking comfort. Now she would have to give it.

Rebecca was lying on her pillows with an oxygen mask over her mouth. Her eyes were half-open and her mouth slack. The only colour on her body came from her Star of David necklace, still bright against the grey skin.

In Judith's Torah lessons the Rebbe has said all kinds of things about the dignity of death. But there was no dignity here. Her grandmother looked defeated, life beaten out of her. The anger inside Judith frightened her; she felt fooled by them all. They told her she would grow up today, and everything would be better afterwards. *You know the day you can stop being afraid*, her grandmother had said. *The day you put down the Torah scrolls and the Rebbe blesses you as an adult.* But what was the point of it all, if Rebecca would not see it?

Leaning forward, she took Rebecca's motionless hand in her own. It felt strange, empty somehow, as if a fire was burning Rebecca away from the inside, leaving nothing but heated bones and skin that crinkled like paper. 'I'm here, Bubby,' she said. 'Don't be afraid. We're all here.' Rebecca's eyes opened. Her pale red head turned towards Judith and she made a small noise, from deep inside her throat. The bony hand clenched and gently squeezed Judith's, the faint pressure of a feather landing on the ground. Then a doctor came between them, pushing Judith back and leaning over Rebecca until she vanished behind a wall of white coats.

Jack met her at the doorway. 'Pet, we have to decide about the service and reception. We think we should cancel it. Your mother agrees. Everyone will understand.' Judith stood for an uncertain moment. Part of her wanted to cry with relief, to take off her coat and new shoes and be a child again. She closed her hand in a fist, her fingers curling around the memory of Rebecca's touch.

'Can we wait?' she asked, finally. 'I need to pray for Bubby.' It was a lie. If a God created such a world, one that stole so much from people, then Judith wanted no part of Him. But it was good enough for Jack. He passed his hand over his brow and said, 'Of course. We have a little time.'

In the silence of her bedroom, Judith reached under the bed and pulled out the crumpled papers hidden there, beside the ripped pieces of the Junior Team Tryout schedule. Rebecca's writing leaned across the page like falling branches. Judith's eyes could not focus and she wiped them in frustration. *Be brave. Be a mensch.* She'd made a promise. Taking a deep breath, she felt the rest of the house fade away. Judith started to read.

Later she came out onto the landing where Dora and Jack were talking in low, heavy voices. Gertie stood beside them, her arms wrapped around her waist.

'Don't cancel the Batmitzvah,' she said. 'I can do it. I want to do it.'

'Are you sure?' Jack said, astonished. Dora clapped her hand to her chest as if to calm her heart.

'I'm sure,' said Judith, steady and without a trace of doubt. Her back was to Rebecca's room, and the light that came streaming in through its open door traced the determined lines of her face.

Afterwards Judith remembered that coming-of-age day as a whirlwind of frantic phone calls, a blur of sympathetic handshakes at the reception and a dull sense of grief growing inside her like a young tree.

She could not recall anyone familiar in the sea of people in front of her, even though Jack must have smiled at her from the front row and Dora and Gertie would have been wiping away tears beside him. The only clear memory, the single lasting picture in her mind, was woven of sound not sight. It was the sound of her own voice as she picked up the scrolls – the sound of singing as if other voices had sprung up inside her, singing her way out of fear and into the adult world.

Judit, my darling girl,

Today is your Batmitzvah – such a special day for you, to become a grown woman. I know that you will do everything so beautifully, and that you will make us proud. All this past year I have watched you work so hard to prepare – sometimes it felt like I was preparing too. I was not blessed with daughters until you came. So forgive me if I think of you as myself, my daughter and my granddaughter too. When you are old, you can't remember the when's and who's of life. But the real nature of things becomes much clearer. The truth is that you are all of this to me, and more.

When I was a child, it was traditional to give a boy a gift on his Barmitzvah, a piece of his inheritance. This way his family acknowledged he was no longer a child, but a pillar of his community, of our whole faith. I thought about what to give you, my Judit. There is only one piece of your inheritance that I hold for you. It's just this – the tale of my life, which is a part of your life too. I'm sorry if it's a poor gift. I hope one day you will feel that it was worthy of you.

You know my real name is not Rebecca at all. It is Rivka, in Hebrew. My papa chose it from the Torah. Rivka was the girl that Isaac married, who gave Abraham's servant water from the well. The Torah says that Abraham wanted to find the right wife for Isaac, but could not find any girl good enough. So he sent his servant further and further away until he and his camels were hot and tired. When he stopped to rest by a well, a girl came to him, even younger than you, to give him water for his thirst. She said if his camels were thirsty she would draw water for them too. She was so kind that she even had time to think about a thirsty camel.

I think that is why God chose her to be the mother of all the Jews. She was kind in her heart, which is what a mother must be. She also had to be brave, to leave her home and journey so far to find her place in life. So our stories are the same in some way. When I was on the ship coming here, and I cried for my mama and papa and my sister Etka, I thought about Rivka and it made me feel better.

When I was your age, my home was in Kishinev, in Imperial Russia. Those names have changed now, as all names do. It was a beautiful city – grand buildings inside and pine trees and roses outside. We used to say the birds came to Kishinev in summer because it was cool and stayed in winter for the warmth. My father put out food for them, so we could hear them sing.

We lived on a farm owned by my Uncle Simeon on Kishinev's outskirts. All Jews in the Pale of Settlement lived in Shtetls. My papa told me that Catherine the Great herded all of Russia's Jews into the Pale like sheep, and told them to stay there or die. It was hard for Jews then, my Judit. The Russians would take our little boys and force them into the army for all of their lives. Some mothers would cut the index finger off a son's hand, so they couldn't hold a gun. The new Tsar had passed new laws against us – they called them the May Laws, and they said no Jew could live with Christians, own land or go to Christian schools.

My Uncle Simeon was one of the lucky ones. His farm was too small to be noticed, and close enough to Kishinev to walk there in just five minutes. It fooled the Mayor, and we were safe. But we did not go to school. We learned at home, while Mama and Papa sewed clothes.

Etka, my sister, was nine years older, and she was fierce and quick. Really, I was afraid of her. She would slap me on the head if she thought I was too slow. I had a little brother too, Moshe, born when I was nine. He was a funny boy, always in trouble like your Uncle Alex, and smiling too. If he'd been a dog, his tail would have always been wagging. And there were my cousins – Isaac and Chayah were the same age as me, Gurta not yet old enough to read, and Benjamin the baby. Did you know that whenever I smell a fire burning, I think of them? That wood smoke smell was always with us in those days, from stirring the pot on the stove. It is the greatest sadness of my life that I left them, to be taken by the terrible flood that took us all.

This is the hardest part, my darling. It came in April in the third year of this century. I remember it was Easter Sunday for the Christians. I was eleven like you, just about to come of age. We were forbidden to work on Christian holidays, so we stayed at home and waited for the day to pass.

The first word of it was from Uncle Simeon. He came back from the town centre and said the Russians had left their churches and started marching in the streets. They said we had killed a boy in a town not far from us. Jewish doctors tried to save him, but he died anyway from a poison in his belly. But now the Russians were saying we killed him for his blood to make our matzos. I can't tell you how it disgusted me to hear that, Judit. Did they think we were monsters or pigs, to eat all manner of filth?

That day my mother was supposed to go to see our friend Navtorili at his shop on Stavrisky Street. She needed Navtor's candles for the next Sabbath meal. So she waited until the evening, when the Christians were having their Sunday dinner. Then she took Moshe with her and went into the town.

Well, we waited and waited for her. After dark, one of Navtor's sons came with a note. There was trouble, and Mama was too afraid to come. She stayed there, in Navtor's house. A thousand times since I've dreamed that she risked it, and came back after all. What would our lives be like now? It's pointless to wonder such things.

We spent that night in fear, and when dawn came, we saw smoke was coming from the town, dark and dirty. Papa wanted to go fetch Mama, but Ekta kept saying 'Stay, she'll come.'

It was nearly noon when we heard the screaming. Isaac came running up the path towards the house. He said the Russians were coming up the hill with sticks and knives. When I thought of one of those knives going inside me, I went cold.

Papa and my uncle pushed us down into the cellar and locked it from the inside. I could see through the floorboards, as the men came into the house and began to break everything like mad dogs. They smashed until their sticks snapped. They tore the mezuzah off the door, broke all of our pots and threw the sewing machine on the floor. I heard the screams of the chickens outside as they killed them one by one.

I must have been afraid in that cellar, but all I remember is shame – at the stink on us, at how we hid like rats. I didn't feel like a mensch, like a human being. We had become animals, just like they said.

When we eventually came out, it took a while for us to stop being rats and have a human thought again. For a few minutes we just picked things up without any plan. Then Papa started shouting and crying for Mama. He could not wait any more to find her. I wanted to come with him. But he told us all to wait inside the house and hide. Etka stayed with us, standing inside our broken front door with an axe in her hand.

I think I knew in my heart she wasn't coming back, Judit. A daughter knows. I heard the screams and the weeping coming from far away, but I didn't know if it was real or a dream. Etka knew too. I saw the tears falling onto her axe as she stood there. Now I know what really happened was this: they came to Navtorili's shop at eleven o'clock in the morning, broke down the door and killed almost everyone inside. Mama died with Moshe behind her, and then they struck him down too. I don't want to know if Moshe smiled at them as they burst into the room, or if Mama cried. I want to remember them as I see them in my heart right now.

Nearly fifty people died that day in our beautiful Kishinev.

We buried them in fear that we would be next. Moshe and Mama lay together in the same box. Two days later, Papa took Etka and me and left our home with a donkey and a cart. The fear, Judit, the fear of those knives and sticks drove us like whips. As for me, I sat on the cart and watched my cousins getting smaller and smaller, before vanishing as if they'd never existed.

Papa told me we were going to a place called Pinsk where we had relatives. He might as well have told me we were going to the moon. Can you imagine, I had never been out of Kishinev? Just a few miles out to the river and back. Now we had more than seven hundred miles to walk, right across the Pale, taking turns resting and pulling the donkey.

After a while, walking becomes like a dream you can't stop dreaming, and your legs even twitch in your sleep. Sometimes we slept in roadhouses and sometimes we slept on the cart. Etka used to shake her fist at the sky and say thank God this happened to us in summer. If it had been winter we would have died. There were other Jews on the road too. Some of them were heading north, like us. Others were going south, to Odessa. They were trying to get back to the holy land, they said, Palestine as it was called then. Etka said they were mad. God's promise is broken, she'd tell them. Better go forward than back.

I came of age on that cart, Judit, but no one noticed. There was no Batmitzvah then for girls, just added burdens. Etka remembered only after we reached Pinsk, and then scolded me for not reminding her. She gave me a hug and bought me a bowl of stew. I was so relieved that we could finally stop walking that I forgot about my coming-of-age as I ate it, and just thanked God for our safety.

I lived in Pinsk with Papa and Etka for five long years. You would think it would have become a home to me, but in truth I hated it. These relatives of ours were long gone, and the town was filling up with Jews just as afraid and poor as we were. Etka ran Papa's house, and I was like a maid – cooking and cleaning all day long. I think she was worried we might stop still like clockwork mice unless she wound us up every day. Perhaps she was right. Sometimes we would hear of a new pogrom somewhere, or there would be some ugliness in town, and my blood would freeze like puddles in winter. If it weren't for Etka, I think I would have slowed down and never started up again.

Then Papa died. Etka couldn't keep him wound up forever and one day his heart just stopped. She went into his bedroom to wake him in the morning, and there was just silence for a few seconds. Then she came back into the workroom where we slept, and said, 'Papa's dead. Go fetch the Rebbe and let's see to his burial.' Straight away she started heating the pot of boiled dough we ate for breakfast. I don't think I cried then, to my shame. But later I cried when I remembered the smell of him, and how he used to chase Moshe and me, pretending to be a great forest bear.

After Papa was buried, Etka packed us up and said we were leaving. There's no future for us here, she told me. This is a dead place for Jews, she said, and even these rich Pinskers are just waiting around to become poor corpses. I did wonder where on earth we could go now. By then I was no longer a child. I was a woman of sixteen. Other girls of my age were married with children of their own. Etka, at twenty-five, was nearly old – and it showed in her face. I was a pretty girl and I remember thinking in my pride that Etka was a shrew. It wasn't until later, when I held my first son in my arms, that I realized she'd given up everything, every hope for herself, just to keep me safe.

We had no cart this time. So we made our way on foot nearly two hundred miles to Minsk. That was the first time I ever saw a train station, with all the Russian ladies and their fur hats. Our journey hadn't seemed real up to then, but afterwards I knew it was going to take us to a whole other life.

We bought a ticket to Libau on the Baltic Sea. Etka had heard bad stories about Russian guards waiting for Jews on the German border crossings. This was the easier way, but longer. The fare cost us five roubles – a lot of money in those days. Etka kept our money in a purse tucked inside her underclothes. She said she'd like to see the man brave enough to look for something there.

Our journey was standing up like cows squashed in with a lot of other cows. But it was better to have those iron wheels do the walking for us. Etka only spoke to me once that whole journey, digging my ribs with her elbow to say we had crossed into Litvak – Lithuania these days. I must have looked blank because she said, 'Don't you know what that means, you idiot? We're outside the Pale.' Outside the Pale! It was such a thrilling sound. But the world looked much the same as before, only bigger and further from home.

We changed trains at Kovno and the next day's journey took us to Libau. This is where the Jews caught their ships out of Russia to the new worlds. Those Russian port towns are nothing like our own Sunderland. Libau frightened me. It was dirty and it smelt. Everywhere there were drunken men and bad women. We took a room at a boarding house where the stench from the toilet pits was so bad I retched whenever I went inside. There was singing underneath us all the time and it was too hot to sleep.

Etka spent two days trying to find one of the Jewish relief organizations to sell us a ticket on the Danish ships leaving for England or America. On the second day she came in nearly in tears and threw two pieces of paper down on the bed. She picked up the menorah we had brought all the way from Kishinev and hurled it on the ground, shouting, 'Thieves and devils! May God sink this place like Sodom the second we get on that forsaken boat!' I guessed she had been forced to pay everything we had for those tickets, by some rogue after a good commission.

That night I dreamed that Etka had talked to me in my sleep. When I woke I saw that her sheets were wet and red. I must have become hysterical because I remember running downstairs and screaming. The woman who owned the boarding house called a doctor and he came quickly. He told us she had dysentery and it was very bad. Even then, I could see he didn't have much love for Jews. He kept calling us 'you people' when asking questions about Etka and me.

I stayed with Etka for two nights and cleaned out the bucket. On the third day of her illness, Etka woke up from the fever and grabbed my hand so hard that it hurt. She told me to go to the Winter Harbour and take the tickets. I could sell hers, she said, to get some money for the passage to England, and take the boat myself before it sailed. Of course I refused. Not because I was brave at all. It was the opposite. Etka was my shelter. What use was I without her? She twisted my hand, her face red and angry like I'd seen it so many times before. She said, 'Don't be such a bloody fool, Rivka. It's time to be a mensch. Mama and Papa will never forgive you if you miss this chance. I'll haunt you and you'll never have a moment's peace.'

Well, I did go at last, but I tell you that Etka haunted me anyway. I made her promise to keep the second ticket and come on the next boat. Of course we both knew that Etka would die in that room, but what could we say? When we made our goodbyes she was just as impatient as ever. The last thing she said to me was 'Hurry up and go, girl.' I walked down to the docks to find my ship with Papa's menorah, one rouble and some clothes. That's all I had left, after so many long miles.

The boat operator was called Det Forenede Dampskibs-Selskab. I looked at the ticket so many times I will remember the words forever. It was big as a monster and it stank of sick cows. I walked onto it like a sleepwalker, without any feeling at all in my heart. Today they say it's the way we keep away the things we can't bear to feel. If so, I'm grateful for that gift.

The person who sold Etka the tickets must have been a rich man when he finished, because every Jew in Europe was on that boat. If we'd been cows, we'd have kicked each other to death before we were halfway across. As it launched I felt everything was slipping away from me – my family, my home, my care for the future.

That was my darkest time, Judit. But then something happened that saved my life. Standing right next to me on that deck was a boy the same age as me, and his brother with him. They saw I was alone and they reached out their hands to me. We spent four days on the water together, listening to the vomiting and the prayers. If you ever talk to someone – really talk to them – for only one hour you will find out most of the truth of them. So just imagine, we talked and listened for four whole days and nights. I started that journey as alone as it was possible for a human being to be. But by the time it ended I had met the man who would be your grandpa.

Had there been just one body between us on that journey, we would not have met, and all the things that flowed from that meeting would not have been. God did that for me, so I can almost forgive Him the rest.

When we docked I had to be told where we were. The port was Hull – of course I had never heard of it. Your grandpa had family in Newcastle and said we could go together there, and marry. He would set up a shop selling buttons, and I had learned enough about sewing from Papa to help us get by.

Standing on that dock I had something like a waking dream, of the roses and pine trees in Kishinev under a blue sky. I could smell the flowers, as if they were right there on my filthy skin.

Your grandpa had family on the Jewish Board of Guardians, and when we arrived in Newcastle they came to meet us at the station. They were so happy to see him and ready to welcome me too as his betrothed. It was my last day of being sixteen, but I could not bring myself to tell anyone. It still felt sinful to celebrate life, when Etka, Mama, Papa and Moshe were all dead.

What to say next, my Judit? I married your grandpa and we were happy together, as much as two people can be. We opened our little shop in Sunderland and this place became my home. We changed our names and spoke English not Yiddish, and taught our children only the ways of the country of their birth, not the countries of their history. We shed those old lives like a caterpillar's skin, because they were no use to us any more.

Your Uncle Max came, named after Moshe. Then your papa and Uncle Alex. For some years I dreamed that a girl would come, so I could remember Etka and Mama. But it seemed they were truly at rest, and God did not want their spirits disturbed. Some lost things can never be found – at least I thought so, until you were born to us.

What a long letter I've written you, darling Judit. I hope you can forgive me. But I wanted you to understand why it is such a joy to me to see you come of age. You take this step in a new world. Here, the Jews don't need to hide or be afraid of the knock on the door. You can celebrate your life in a synagogue with family around you, not on a dirty old cart followed by ghosts. The Jews even have a homeland of their own, and a flag among all the goyim. Perhaps your generation will be the one to make it safe, to finally end the suffering for all of us.

The only sadness I feel is from knowing that I may not be with you to see you fulfil your promise. But you should not be sad, darling girl. Your journey is just beginning, but I am ready for mine to be done. You are walking ahead of me on the road – wherever it leads, it will shape the woman you become. You must think of me holding your hand as you set out. I only pray you find the courage to make your own way. And that your journey brings you joy in the end, as mine has done.

Always your loving grandmother.

Rebecca

2

SETTLEMENT

*I too was driven out by a cruel fate and
forced to seek a new home. And through
my suffering, I have learned how to
comfort others who suffer likewise.*

Virgil

1967

LONDON

T he first time he saw her it was just a glimpse of gold, yellow hair
and a long, bright chain ending in a star. The star had six points,
and for one confused moment it reminded him of home.

Then the crowd in the room closed in, and Margaret took his arm,
steering him into the corner for a kiss. Her mouth tasted of cigarettes
and sour lemons from the pink cocktail in her fist.

They leaned by the window, the rain battering the glass like tiny
hands trying to claw their way inside. His mind felt light as a balloon.
Nadia's telegram was still curled up on his desk where it had been
lying for three weeks. Hassan had sent another just that morning.
Salim had dropped it in the bin.

Margaret stirred against his chest, and pushed herself away. Her
eyes were circled with thick kohl and her mass of black hair was tied
in a purple scarf. One long leg twined around his, her skirt riding up
her thigh. Everyone wanted Margaret; she worked hard at it, chain
smoking like a movie starlet, learning the guitar and casting off her
farmyard accent for something more sullenly Soho. That first time in
bed, her mouth had torn into his like a desperate animal. But now it
was tight and petulant. *Here it comes*, he thought.

'What the hell is up with you, Sal?' Her foot tickled his, but the eyes were not friendly. 'Smoked the wrong shit? I'd have more fun with a fish tonight.'

'I'm sorry,' he said, supremely indifferent. Why did he even like Margaret, apart from the obvious things? Margaret only liked him because he was tall, exotic and – above all – older. At twenty-five, he was a man to her pretty teenage doll. 'I'm still thinking about my father.' That put a stop to Margaret nine times out of ten these days. It's hard to argue with a man whose father died less than two months ago, right in the middle of end of term exams.

'Oh, for Christ's sake. Then you should have gone to his funeral.'

'I couldn't,' he said, irritated by the effort of having to lie. 'I told you.'

'Yeah, well, you haven't got exams now. So you could still go, if you don't want to stay around here and be a full-time drag.' Margaret disengaged her legs and looked around the sweaty room. She had the most amazing eyes. They could pierce the back of a man's head and see through to the more interesting thing beyond him. *Something out there is more promising than me*, he thought. *Go find it, why don't you.* As if in answer, Margaret pinched Salim's arm with brittle fingers.

'I'm getting a proper drink,' she said pointedly, setting her pink punch down on the windowsill. 'This sweet shit is giving me a headache.'

Salim watched the crowd swallow her like a tiger disappearing into the tall grass. This was Margaret's kind of room – the dense smoke, the long-legged crowd, the music he'd never heard of sliding out of the turntable in the corner. *This is the end, my only friend*, the man sang. *Of our elaborate plans, of everything that stands.*

It had been the end of Abu Hassan, two weeks before Christmas. A stroke had taken him right in the chair where he used to sit and crack nuts all day. One minute the hand was at his mouth, and the next it lay by his side, flaccid and empty.

Abu Hassan's death had been many years in coming. But any tears he'd cried had been for an imaginary dream of a father, not the man himself. The far more powerful feeling had been a deep reluctance to return for the funeral.

He had a good excuse. It was his final year of an economics degree at University College, London. Exams were upon him. He was the only Al-Ishmaeli ever to go to university, and Nadia and Tareq assured him repeatedly that his father was very proud. Although Salim doubted it, he was happy to let Hassan take the burden of going back to Nazareth. Tradition decreed that a burial must take place within twenty-four hours. In any event, neither son could get there in time to attend to their father's body. It was left to Nadia, the oldest child, to usher her father out of the world with all the consideration he'd denied her while he was in it.

Salim stayed behind while Hassan performed the other family duties – and saw to the will. When Hassan mentioned this to Salim, he'd actually laughed out loud. 'They teach you how to count at university, you know,' he said. 'The last time I checked, nothing divided by two is still nothing.'

Margaret had not come back. But Salim was happy to stand on his own, and watch the dance of strangers. He never looked out of place in London. He was made to be here, with his attractive, pale darkness, his long, slim body and his smile that people called *easy*, as if they knew anything about him. It was a revelation to Salim how ready English women were to throw themselves at a penniless Arab who could make them laugh, and make them cry too. They imagined he would be passionate, unknowable, charming and cruel, like Omar Sharif in *Lawrence of Arabia*. And he obliged on all counts. But all those arms around him never seemed able to creep inside him – and in the end he was left preferring his own company.

After a few minutes, he decided to go and look for the blonde girl. He walked through the crowd to the drinks table, but couldn't see her. Margaret was there, though, deep in conversation with someone else. Salim walked once around the room and ended up back by the windowsill. *This is ridiculous. I should just go home.*

He saw the party host rushing by, a tall green hat falling over his eyes. Salim reached out to grab his wrist. 'Hey, Mike.'

'Sal, man! What's up?'

'I was looking for a girl.'

'Aren't we all? Where's Margaret?'

'Clawing someone else,' Salim said. 'This one was kind of small, long blonde hair, dressed like a nun.'

'Jude? You flake, she's right behind you.' Salim blushed for the first time in years as he realized his mistake and the unnoticed girl at his elbow began to turn at the sound of her name.

'Sorry, man,' Mike said. 'I'll leave you cats to get to know each other. Bathroom calls,' he said, tapping his nose.

She was small, he saw, and perhaps that's why he had missed her. Her head would barely have grazed his chin. Her blonde hair was long but somehow boyish, cut in a fringe framing a serious face. She was white as a bird, and her slightly worried blue eyes called up a fleeting memory of Lili Yashuv with a scarf over her hair.

'Am I really dressed like a nun?' she asked. She sounded curious. Salim looked again at her gawky dress, and she put up her hands unconsciously, smoothing the front of it as if to protect herself from his judgement. The gesture stirred something unexpected inside him – a kind of mirrored sympathy.

'A cute nun,' he replied with a smile. 'The kind about to break her vows.' She grinned and shook her head.

'This isn't really my kind of party,' she said, looking around the room and then at her feet. 'I only came with my roommate. And I know Mike from class – he's studying literature too. What about you?'

'This isn't my kind of party either,' he said. She looked up, sceptical.

'Oh come on,' she said. 'You came here with Margaret.'

116

'Everyone came here with Margaret, I think.' Salim grinned, trying to catch her eye. But she just looked at the ground again. Irritation bubbled up inside him. *What do I have to do to make this girl look at me?* 'I went all over the place looking for you, you know. And you were hiding here all the time.'

'I wasn't hiding,' the girl said, her blue eyes finally fixing on his, with a touch of defiance. 'Maybe you didn't really know who you were looking for.'

'Maybe I didn't,' Salim agreed, seeing for the second time the gold chain with its six-pointed Star of David lying on her chest. He pointed to it. 'So what's the story with that?' Her hand went up to it and he saw her fingers trace the edges as if it was something done many times. Years later he would wonder if it was that moment that caught him, if he had really been so jealous of a piece of jewellery and longed to be cherished in the same way.

'It was my grandmother's,' she answered, before hesitating. 'A Star of David. It's…'

'I know what it is,' he said quickly, thinking not of Abu Hassan and the flight from Jaffa but of Elia and that afternoon they said they could never be friends. There was a pause and she looked startled. He sensed he'd made her anxious. But he couldn't find the words to turn it into a joke.

'So, where are you from?' she asked him, finally. It was his turn to hesitate now.

'London.'

'Really?' She smiled, and shook her head again.

'What is it?' he said, worried she had caught him in the lie.

'It's just… well, you look like one of my uncles.'

'Oh God,' he said, laughing. 'I hope he's a handsome uncle.'

'No, not like that.' Now she was laughing too. 'You just remind me of him. You're both very… very dark and intense.'

'And where is this most excellent uncle?'

'He lives abroad.'

'Well, thank God for that.' Salim held out his hand. 'I'm Sal.'
She took it, and shook it earnestly up and down, like a child after
receiving a medal.

'I'm Jude,' she replied. 'I'm glad you finally tracked me down.'

'Me too,' he said, with a complete sincerity that matched her own.

It was only two days until they met again. Jude had agreed to a coffee
in Bloomsbury, near to her classes. She was only in her first year of
university, and London still felt terrifying. It operated on a different
speed to Sunderland – a jerky, racing world full of noise and hurry.
People thought the north was grey, but Jude used to sit under London's
endless winter sleet and dream of the sharp blues of Sunderland's
breeze-blown skies, the clouds chasing across the docks like seagulls.

When the man called Sal suggested that they see each other for
coffee, Jude had not been sure what to think. At nearly nineteen,
she'd never had a boyfriend. There'd been Stuart, a boy nearly as shy
as she was, who used to talk to her at swimming practice and once
went so far as to walk her home holding her hand. He did it again a
week later, and she'd wondered if he might kiss her, but he was the
perfect gentleman. In the end she became so irritated by that limp,
moist palm in hers that she'd run home early to avoid him, feeling a
wicked relief every step of the way.

She knew about love from the news; from stories about the war
in Vietnam and the kissing protests in America. But it was no more
real to her than a trip to the pictures. Even now, after five months
in London, love seemed fake, painted-on – like the flowers she saw
everywhere on people's clothes and in their hair, floating through
Chelsea and Soho in swirling patterns. There were no flowers around
Jude's student lodgings on Camden Lock. Only concrete and steel,
bare cracks in the pavement and row upon row of windows dirtied
by the smoky rain.

In Jude's world, it was polite to be early. She sat in the corner of Virginia's and pulled out a book. Outside, the silent drizzle of late February drifted down. The faint music in the café was nearly drowned by the keening of a harmonica outside. Buses surged past, dimly red through the cigarette smoke and fogged glass.

Sal. It was a name that told no story. Who was he, with those fierce eyes so like Uncle Max and that odd, gentle way of speaking? He had seemed even more a stranger at the party than her.

That, more than anything else, made Jude want to say yes to him, to see a real smile come to his face and wipe away the practised one. *How does he smile for Margaret?* She shook the thought away, and clutched Rebecca's chain for courage. The gold felt like warm water in her hand.

When she looked up, he was standing in front of her. His awkward smile sent a thought flashing across her mind – *he made a mistake, he doesn't want to be here.* Before she could speak, he'd pulled up a chair and sat down.

The daylight showed him paler than her memory, his hair seemed blacker and his eyes more serious. His face was soaked with rain and his thick overcoat and green scarf dripped onto the floor. Her instinct was to ask why he came without an umbrella, but she stopped herself. *Just because, that's why,* as Dora used to say. *Why* was a habit Jude had trained herself out of, along with all the other Jews of the world.

There was a moment of silence and then he asked, 'What are you reading?'

She held up the book for him and he squinted at the title. '*The Brothers Karamazov.* Dostoevsky.' His expression was a polite blank, and she stumbled on. 'One of my course options is foreign literature. I'm doing Russian and French.'

'Sounds good,' he said, although she heard a note of uncertainty. 'Why did you go for those two?'

She had to think for a moment, to find the true answer under the rationalizations she'd given her parents.

'I had a holiday in France once,' she said. 'It was the first time I'd been abroad.' She remembered the rich grey of the Seine as it glided along the Left Bank, the rough song of Parisian laughter, the smell of paint and the exhilarating emptiness of the sky. 'I never saw anywhere like it before. I felt so alive there. They think in a different way to us, a freer way. I wanted to...' She ran out of words to describe the longing she'd felt, and bit her lip in embarrassment. But then, to her amazement, he found the words for her.

'You wanted to take a piece of it away, so you'd never really have to leave.'

'That's right.' She flushed in the warm surprise of feeling understood. 'The French writers like Stendhal, they're so brave. They don't have limits like us. They make these characters – Fabricio or... or Candide – who get to be different people wherever they go, to live a thousand different lives.'

His eyebrows went up, in mock surprise. 'A thousand lives? Would it take you a thousand lives to find one you were happy with?'

'No,' she said, considering seriously. 'But isn't it interesting to imagine who you could be, if you didn't mind giving up everything you are now?'

'It depends.'

'On what?'

'Is it a trade worth making? Suppose you gave everything up for something or someone, and then you found it wasn't really worth it after all?'

Jude smiled and shrugged. 'I don't know the answer. That's why I read the books, to see what happens at the end of the story.'

'But these brothers of yours aren't French.' He pointed to the book still open in her hand.

'They're Russian. My grandmother was Russian too, originally.'

Jude grasped the star around her neck, feeling its points worn to reassuring smoothness. She asked again the question that had been on her mind since she first met him. 'Where is your family from?'

He looked up at her and down at the table again; his face seemed sad, almost shamed. 'My name is Salim.' He said it casually, but it sounded like a confession. 'Salim Al-Ishmaeli. We're an Arab family, not a Russian one, I'm afraid. Or a French one.' He raised his eyes to hers.

Jude said, 'That's okay,' automatically, but her heart started to race. The overwhelming urge inside her was to reassure him – of what? 'My uncle lives in Israel.' That one escaped her too, the stupid, uncontainable words stumbling off her tongue.

'I guessed it.' He nodded towards the gold star in her hand. 'That's where I'm from too. It was Palestine, we called it back then.'

Jude sat in silence. She almost forgot she was at the table, part of the story, waiting to hear what would come next from his mouth. He was hunched over, his elbows and forearms on the table and his hands clasped together. At first she thought he might be in pain, but then he looked up with a wry smile. 'You weren't expecting that one, were you?'

'No,' she said. She could not speak for fear of saying the wrong thing, of hearing Dora's voice come out of her mouth. *The bloody Arabs*. Eventually he threw his hands up and sat back in his chair.

'What a goose you are. I had Jewish friends back there and I've made Jewish friends here too. We can get along, you know.'

Jude raised her coffee to her lips. It was weak and white and bland. She put it down and pushed it away from her.

'I never met any Arabs,' she said. 'I just heard about them through Uncle Max. And to be honest, I thought you must hate us.'

'Who says I *must* do anything? You're a person. I'm a person. Why should I hate you before I get to know you?'

'I'm not worth hating,' she said. 'I'm just a girl from Sunderland who had to be forced to go to Hebrew school.'

'I guess you don't even know yourself. You're clever, and kind and honest. You're very pretty too, as it happens. Maybe you're absolutely worth hating.'

Jude put her book down on the table, and waited for her face to turn red. Blushing was the only thing that she and Gertie shared – their white faces transforming into the same beetroot colour at the slightest provocation. But the only warmth in her cheeks was from the raw wind, and now her heart beat more slowly.

'Were you born there?' she asked.

'In Jaffa, before the war.'

Jude felt a sudden deep rush of sorrow. 'I can't imagine,' she said quietly. 'I never learned much about it.'

Salim shrugged. 'I was just a boy when we left Jaffa. Seven, maybe. I don't remember it so much. Afterwards we just got on with life.'

Jude saw his hands were clasping and unclasping, and he was running one finger over his pale knuckles like a child trying to rub off a dirty mark.

'Did your family come with you?' she asked.

'No.' He looked up at her. 'My mother left us years ago. She was one of those people in the stories you talked about. She wanted a different life. My father was an old man, and not that smart. He died a couple of months ago.'

Jude nodded. She put her hand over his on the table, and he stopped moving. Suddenly she realized what she'd done. Her hand jerked away, as if from a flame, and she clenched her fist. His eyes flicked up to meet hers. 'Why did you do that?'

'I'm sorry.' She felt miserable – for him, for her clumsiness, for all the wrongs suffered and wrongs done. 'I wanted to say I was sorry.'

His eyes held hers, and he didn't smile. 'I wasn't asking why you held my hand,' he said. 'I was asking why you let go.'

*

Salim didn't understand why he'd left without making a plan to meet again. He'd just gone without a backwards glance, wrapping the sopping wet scarf around his neck.

He knew through the pounding of his feet on the pavement that he was angry. Later he left a message for Margaret. That night he spent getting drunk and listening to her pluck the guitar, lying naked between his legs.

They'd ended their coffee like guilty children caught kissing. She'd told him about the grandmother who fled the Russians and he had talked about the siege of Nazareth and the Jewish commander who'd refused to sack the city. They'd agreed that religion didn't matter, that they had a lot in common and some nonsense about peace that reminded Salim of the flower songs.

But it all meant nothing, he told himself. How could she ever understand him, this little English Jew? The words his father had shouted came back to him. *Abadan!* Never! The hand she'd placed on his was a lie. He knew that, even if she didn't.

A week later he bought *The Brothers Karamazov* from a shop on Charing Cross Road and after a brief, fumbling conversation with the bookshop owner, Stendhal's *Charterhouse of Parma*. He could make sense of neither. Books were a torment, unless full of numbers and formulae. And Hassan told him that his Arabic was now just as lamentable, no better than a child's.

He started walking past the coffee shop from his lectures in King's Cross every other day. Sometimes he'd see her inside, bundled up against the cold. She never looked up.

At night, he remembered her blue eyes fixed on his in vague bewilderment. She'd peeled him like an orange with her guileless-ness. He felt exposed and irritable. He called Nadia, pretending he wanted to hear all about her life, and tried to be soothed by the gentle, motherly voice crackling on the end of the line.

In the end, he found her waiting for him outside Virginia's. He spotted her from a hundred yards away, her yellow hair beaded with cold drops of water twinkling in the pale sun. Bloomsbury traffic swirled madly around her in steely flashes of black, red and silver. Her coat was so big she seemed huddled inside it like a baby animal. He stopped next to her and grinned ruefully. She smiled too, wiping her red nose.

'So, how did you know?' he asked her.

'I saw you so many times,' she said, blinking into the low sun. 'Maybe you thought you were so clever, but even the waitress saw you looking in and teased me about it.'

He raised his hands to the skies, laughing as weeks of worry suddenly slid from his shoulders and crashed into tiny splinters on the icy pavement. 'I should have told you I wanted to see you again,' he said. 'I wasn't sure that you would be interested, and I didn't want to be disappointed.' The half-lie felt so easy and right to tell.

'I know it's complicated,' she said, blue eyes glassy in the light, 'but I was hoping you wouldn't mind. That we could try.'

He wondered if that was the first time she'd ever told a man how she felt about him, in that oblique way of hers. He remembered how her hands had held the Star of David, and took one of them in his own.

It was the beginning of something unwritten, Salim thought later. After he walked her back to the lecture hall, on the point of saying goodbye, he stooped down to kiss her lips. As she turned her face up to his, he saw the sun blaze through the whiteness of her skin to the pulse of life inside her. *White as a canvas*, he thought. *White as a new page, a place to make a fresh start.*

For their first proper date he took her to the Finsbury Astoria to see the Walker Brothers. The tickets had been sitting in his wallet for weeks – intended as a present for Margaret, who hated the Walker Brothers but liked Cat Stevens and Hendrix, who were also on the bill. Margaret told him she'd shared digs with Cat Stevens's sister in Marylebone, and that she and Hendrix rolled their joints the same way, between the thumb and fourth finger.

Inviting Jude instead had seemed so smart. In the fever of excitement after her lips left his it had been so easy to play the cultured man, to offer to take her out to a concert. But as his front door slammed and he stepped out into the raw evening air he felt crippled by worry. He'd been too quick, too thoughtless; she wouldn't enjoy it, she'd see right through him.

He couldn't begin to afford a taxi all the way from his tiny lodging in south London to Jude's student halls in Camden, and then even further north to Finsbury Park. But he refused to make her walk, like a *fellah*'s woman. So he took the Tube to Camden Town and called a taxi from the telephone box just outside the station. When they pulled up outside Jude's building a few minutes later, he smoothed his hair back to dry his nervous palms.

Her door swung open the instant he knocked on it – and there she was, smiling up at him. Her hair was pulled into high yellow bunches, her face upturned above a long dress falling in light green circles. In the dimness of the narrow corridor, as people pushed past him and dormitory doors banged shut, she reminded him of a pale, hopeful flower on a slender stalk.

'Hi,' he said, leaning in to give her a swift kiss. 'You're very beautiful.' He saw her flush, and felt his own cheeks redden in sympathy. It was ridiculous; he wanted to shake himself. *You've been with a hundred women, idiot. What's the matter with you?*

'And you're very handsome,' she replied, taking his hand. 'Dashing, my grandmother would have said.' He felt her fingers squeeze his, the lightest pressure, but it lifted the cloud of anxiety a few inches.

He opened the taxi door for her, and they made small talk for half an hour through the darkening north London traffic to Finsbury

Park. When they pulled up outside the Astoria on Seven Sisters, the cabbie said, 'A quid, mate,' and Salim handed it over with a careless smile. He'd saved the same amount for their journey back and that was the last of his monthly budget. For the next few days he'd be living on boiled rice.

He hurried round to open Jude's door, and she looked up as she pushed herself to her feet. 'Wow. Look at it.' His eyes followed hers. The Astoria rose up grey and enormous in front of him, on an island circled in pandemonium, a swirling centrifuge of horns and headlamps sending cars plunging back into the London night. Its notched brick façade was dark with smoke and dust, and red posters glared bright from its supporting pillars. His mind twisted and it was Jaffa's Al-Hambra cinema in front of him, or its ghost, its white walls and red flags turned grey and pitted. He took Jude's hand, blinking the picture away.

Inside, a throng stood between them and the concert hall. He could hear drums beating over a human roar, and a guitar wailing in a way he'd never heard before. The air was humid with smoke, sweat and weed, the queue a tangle of bare legs and straggling hair. The man next to Salim had taken his shirt off; a peace symbol was tattooed on his back under the words *hell no we wont go*. A girl leaned against him, dark curls falling slick onto his shoulder.

Jude stood still as water beside him, while Salim waved his tickets at the doorman. The music inside had stopped, and a rising tide of shrieking had taken its place. The doors were barred shut, two burly men standing in front of them, arms folded.

'There must be a problem or something,' Salim said, desperate. He looked down at Jude. 'I guess this isn't really your kind of thing, is it?' She glanced away, as if the question embarrassed her.

'I had a friend who liked this kind of music.' Her hand rose to touch the chain hidden under her dress. 'Back in Sunderland. It always reminds me of her. We liked to play it after school, and dance and things like that. We gave each other nicknames, like we were famous. My parents didn't approve.'

'And so? What happened?'

She shrugged. 'We're not friends any more. Sorry, Sal. Can you wait? I need the toilet.'

He watched her push through the sweating crowd towards the cloakroom. She looked so out of place that it moved him, a bitter-sweet echo of indefinable kinship. *We're not friends any more.* He found himself thinking of Elia and Mazen and even little Rafan, the brother who used to cling to his legs at night. *Maybe they feel sad about losing me too.* It felt strange to imagine someone else paying a price he'd thought was his alone to bear.

The bare-chested man in front of him was kissing his girlfriend when Jude came back, his face pushing wetly into hers. His wandering arm knocked into Jude as she pressed her body back into the line; his girlfriend stumbled as the couple lost their balance. 'Watch out, man,' he protested, and the girl rounded on Jude and Salim, her lips still shiny with saliva, hair tousled under a red bandana. 'Hey, step off,' she said, her voice loud enough to turn heads all around them. 'What's the fucking rush?'

Jude said, 'I'm sorry,' as she flushed, eyes dropping under the sudden scrutiny of the crowd. Salim was astonished. 'Don't apologize to them,' he told her. 'It was their fault.'

'Yeah, right? Your girlfriend rammed us, man.'

'You were rolling around like animals. She was just standing here.'

The girl laughed, tossing her hair back. 'Get him, eh? Animals. What an arsehole.' She stuck her tongue out at them, pink and round as a painted nail.

'Check it out, babe.' The bare-chested man had oily hair falling across his eyes, and a sneer over his goatee. 'Paki and Square don't like us.'

Salim felt the warmth of Jude's shoulder pressing against the burn of the insult inside his chest. 'Excuse me,' he said, trying for disdain, but the BBC English felt suddenly clumsy on his tongue. 'She's better than a hundred of you idiots.'

'Whatever. Fuck off, Mustapha.'

'You fuck off.' Jude had swung around and her face was red, the words bursting out without warning like steam from a pressure cooker. 'How dare you use that name? How *dare* you? You're not cool, you're horrible, and you don't know anything about us.' She was standing between Salim and the couple, and for the first time he noticed the heaviness of her northern vowels. 'Go on, fuck off!' she shouted, as the bare-chested man took a step back, his sneer becoming an incredulous smile. Then she turned and ran out, Salim following in her wake, leaving the throng behind.

As the fresh night air hit them, she turned back to him, red spots on her cheeks fading back into white. He saw the apology surge to her lips again, and he said, 'Don't. Don't say it.' He reached out to her and she froze at the gesture, her arms hugging the trembling rise and fall of her chest. 'Jude. You were amazing. A real fighter. Like a lion.' Standing there under the white brilliance of the streetlamps she could have been a knight, one of the Christian kings from the Frères' tales he'd loved, from the games they'd mocked him for playing. 'Jude the Lionheart,' he said without thinking. He saw her eyes soften, heard her laughter, and it came bubbling up inside him too as the sound released his heart.

They walked down Seven Sisters Road to Finsbury Park, leaving the roar of the road behind in the dark green and the silence of grass. Winter had left the park trees bare; Jude saw their empty arms reaching up to the blackness, their new buds just points of shadow on the boughs. London's night walkers passed them by — some of them arm in arm, others with dogs, their faces neither old nor young but a universal blank in the half-light. It was the opposite of loneliness, Jude thought, as if they were all peaceful planets travelling on their own course, feeling the comforting tug of each other's presence.

Salim's arm was around her shoulders; he leaned on her as if she were his protector, as she'd leaned on Rebecca and maybe even Dora. His arm pressed her down but strength seemed to flow through it into her. Something had vanished between them, some fundamental human separateness. She was no longer just Jude; her body was filling up with a stranger that only Salim recognized.

A light filtered through the trees ahead, carrying reedy singing with it. Someone had made a campfire of dry twigs and a group of people had gathered around it, shadows flickering over their faces. Stopping just outside the circle, she began to recognize the song – and from the vibration of Salim's chest she saw that he, too, was singing the words under his breath. *If you should ever leave me, though life would still go on believe me, the world could show nothing to me, so what good would living do me?* He broke off to look down at her and said, 'Now this is more your kind of music, isn't it?'

'One of my favourites,' she told him. The old Jude would have given a reason, but now she felt too full for explanations. The guitar player was harmonizing with two other newcomers; it was sweet – as good as the Beach Boys ever were, and the fire transported her out of London to somewhere warm and kind. He was still leaning into her, and she felt herself strengthening with his weight, as if finally pushing roots deep into the ground. The words of the chorus came into her mouth, reminding her of a phrase Rebecca loved to use – her grandmother's answer to all of life's mysteries. And she whispered it to herself along with all the other voices, *God only knows, God only knows*, clasping Salim's hand as the sleeping wood breathed around them.

*

Hassan came back from Nazareth in May. The skies had cleared; warmth was trickling back into England over the wide Atlantic – a faint ghost of the heat filling the orchards of the southern Mediterranean.

Salim dreaded this early touch of summer – it meant final exams, the end of study and the start of difficult choices men must make if they want to eat.

But it was easy to drown his anxiety in Jude. They spent the spring walking along the marble-grey Thames under the blossoming trees of the south bank, the stories pouring out of them. They did not call each other boyfriend and girlfriend. They still were not lovers, no more than a kiss. They were innocents on a boat floating down a river, dipping their toes into unknown currents and gazing up together at the limitless sky.

At first she talked about Paris and Flaubert and Voltaire and he talked about the harvest season and the desert dances of the Nabi Ruben festivals. But then came the other stories: the tale of Kath and Peggy at the door and Elia and Mazen in Clock Tower Square, of the slam of the gates in Jaffa and the knives above the cellar in Kishinev, the empty room in Nazareth and the sirens in the street in Ryhope Road. Salim had never known anything like it – this sharing of souls, this unburdening of griefs and shames. He knew the Christians received absolution from God or their priests; once Hassan had dared him to sneak into a confession box – it was lined in red and smelt of sweat and humid wood. *Let them keep their forgiving God.* Jude was human and imperfect, but she understood him without judgement. And that was better than any kind of divine justice.

Eventually, Salim dragged himself down to see his brother. Hassan had become one of history's simple soldiers, achieving exactly what he'd always promised, no more and no less. Now nearing thirty, he ran a profitable car repair shop in one of the capital's outer suburbs. He'd married a big-breasted Palestinian girl who had immediately started producing children. Two were already in nursery, speaking more Arabic than English, and another one was on the way. Their house smelt of rosewater, allspice and salted nuts. They fasted at Ramadan, although Hassan refused to stop smoking, and sometimes talked about going to the local mosque. Their friends were all cut from the same cloth. But Shireen made an exception for her contingent of long-nailed, blonde girlfriends from the nearby salon – women Salim had heard Hassan complaining about and seen him flirting with.

He was grateful when Hassan asked to meet at his garage. It was where his brother was at his most cheerful, and least likely to give Salim a hard time. The smell of oil and grease was pleasantly relaxing after the relentless hardness of the lecture hall desk and the sharpness of ink on his fingers.

'Abu Saeed!' He called Hassan's honorific out over the groan of the faulty engines. Hassan had, most predictably, named his eldest boy after his own father.

'Abu Mushkila,' a voice shouted back. Salim grinned despite himself. Hassan's way to protest that Salim had not yet married at twenty-six was to call him *father of trouble*. Hassan always milked every available ounce of humour out of his own jokes, often far beyond the cow running dry.

'Come over here, old man,' Hassan shouted again, from his office behind the mass of cars, doors open and engine parts spread indecently over the ground. Salim stepped gingerly over them, wishing he'd changed the good shirt he wore to see Jude that morning. Hassan came out of the office door to meet him, and slapped him on the back with oily hands. 'What the hell have you been doing for the last week? I expected you every day.'

'Studying,' said Salim, pretending to look at the red Beetle being dismantled over Hassan's right shoulder. 'I came as soon as I could, big brother.'

'You study too much. Anyone would think you were bloody Einstein. You'll end up with big brains and no balls like he did.'

'Where do you get these ideas?' Salim pushed his brother's shoulder with a smile. 'It's my final year, I have to study. One day when I'm a rich accountant living in Mayfair I'll send my Jaguar to you to fix, don't worry.'

Hassan bellowed with laughter. 'Okay, so I'll wait for your bloody Jag. Now, let's have a beer and I'll tell you about the disaster in Nazareth.'

They cracked open a beer from the office fridge and Salim listened with half an ear as Hassan complained about everything from the Nazarene imam to the relatives. The only person who stirred his emotions in any way was Nadia. *It's not fair. We never gave you anything in life, and we left you with all the shit.* He wondered what Nadia would make of Jude. How could she not like her? They were two gentle souls set in different shades.

Sharing a beer with Hassan always reminded Salim of his first day in London, on that mouldering brown sofa. He'd worked so hard since that day to fulfil his promise. Those first years he'd laboured like a *fellah*, Hassan's garage by day and school at night, to qualify for university. He'd a head for numbers and a way with Englishmen that impressed them while reminding them they were the master race. When his passport application came through at last, he remembered walking home with it in a daze of triumph, the hard black book weighing in his pocket like a loaded gun.

'So what's up with you, *ya habibi*?' Hassan was bored with Nazareth, and now wanted details of Salim's love life. 'Still seeing that crazy woman, that Margaret?'

'Not any more.' Salim wondered how to bring it up with his brother. 'She found someone who didn't mind getting his eyes scratched out every other day.' Hassan laughed.

'Too bad I'm married,' he hooted. 'I could do with my eyes scratching sometimes. And my arse too, if she's not busy!'

'Well, she's all yours,' Salim said. 'I met someone else.'

'Yes? Who, who?'

'It's nothing.' Salim suddenly felt his palms getting sweaty. 'She's at university too. She studies literature. She reads Russian and French poems.'

'*W'Allah?*' Really? Hassan thought this was hilarious. 'With her clothes off or with them on? Please tell me with her clothes off.'

'It's not like that. She's a decent girl.'

Hassan nudged Salim in the ribs. 'Oh, my poor brother's too in love to use his dick. What's he going to do?'

'I'm not in love.' Salim pushed himself off Hassan's dusty desk. 'It's just… something. She's a *Yehuda*, actually.'

Hassan's eyes widened. 'Wow, Abu Mushkila. You know how to cause a stir, eh? Thank God Baba is dead. He'd have your balls on a plate.'

Suddenly Salim was sick of Hassan. 'Your mouth is as foul as your office, you know that? Clean this place up, for God's sake.' He spoke in English, and Hassan snorted.

'Oh Mister Salim,' he replied in the same tongue. 'So sorry for offending you, sir. You think you're too clean for my workshop then fuck off. You weren't too good for it when you had nowhere else to go.'

'Okay, I'm sorry.' Salim felt the loving despair that was the hallmark of his relationship with Hassan. They called each other one blood, but their veins were strangers – Abu Hassan's dark red against their mother's royal blue. They reached out for each other but were foiled by a wall of confusion and mistranslation.

'I'm trying to tell you that this one is different,' he said. 'She's not a Zionist. She understands us. She understands *me*.'

Hassan looked at him dubiously. 'You've always been looking for someone to understand you, Salim. But you don't even understand yourself. Don't shake your head, just listen to me. I have no problem with Jews. I had a Jewish girl too, a couple of times. But, please, screw them, don't love them. No matter what you think, they can't understand an Arab. It's not in their nature.'

'You don't know her.'

Hassan hauled himself to his feet and got another beer out of the fridge.

'You know what's happening in Palestine now? The Jews want Syria and the Sinai too. They've been sending soldiers across the border. But Nasser is standing up to the fucking Knesset. He'll close the Red Sea to them and cut the Israelis off from the oceans. No more trade for the Jews, eh? Then all hell is going to break loose, by God. This time the Catastrophe will come to *them*.'

Salim remembered how Hassan had clung to the radio after they left Jaffa, and how long and truly he believed in the great myth of Arab liberation by Arabs. But for all Hassan's bluster about Palestine, he would never trade his cosy garage to live there. Salim was the only one who still dreamed about orange blossoms and the sea.

'It's just more talk,' he said to Hassan. 'They can't do a thing for us. Our lives are here now. Your children will grow up here, not in the Sinai.'

'For now,' Hassan said, clapping him on the shoulder again. 'But who knows? Anyway, so it's not a good time to be bringing home a Jew, that's all I'm saying.' Salim nodded. It seemed the easiest way.

As they said their goodbyes, Hassan said, 'Oh by the way – there's something else for you. Nadia thought I shouldn't give it to you, but she still thinks you're a little crybaby.'

He pulled a folded envelope out of his back pocket, grubby from a month of heat and pressing. Salim knew what it was instantly. The postage mark was from Lebanon, a stamp of green cedars against a red field.

It sent a memory through him like a knife, of his mother standing on the balcony in Nazareth with her letter and her secrets. *You died to me then, Mama. I mourned you years ago.* Seeing evidence of her now, alive somewhere, was like watching a ghost rise.

Through the roaring of blood in his ears, he heard Hassan talking. 'They heard about Baba's passing. Rafan writes that he couldn't come either – busy just like his clever brother Salim. But he sends his address and phone number and says you should pay him a visit. Plenty of girls in Beirut, you know. The sun is warmer there, and so are the women. Mama says hello too. For what it's worth.'

A week later, Jude turned nineteen – and Tony boasted he'd cajoled Alex into hosting a birthday dinner for her. The southern Golds, as Alex called them, could usually only stomach one Jewish gathering per season.

'I told him you could be getting up to no end of trouble in this big *goy* world, bring shame upon the family unless we reined you in,' Tony said. 'Besides, can you imagine your mama calling up and squalling that her *schmendrik* brother-in-law was ignoring her little *tchatzkah* and letting her run riot around town?' His voice rose to a pitch of horror.

'Dora would never call me a treasure,' Jude grinned.

'Aye aye. She knows you too well.'

The prospect of this birthday dinner cast the first shadow over her time with Sal. They had talked, briefly, about meeting each other's families. But she could not imagine marching into Alex's Regency home in Portland Place and introducing him as her... what? She didn't even know what he was.

'So he's not your boyfriend?' Ruth Michaels had asked her at the Jewish Society that day. Sal dropped her off on the way to see his brother, his lean arm over her shoulders and those dark eyes so alive and aware like a rich splash of colour on a dirty white page. He'd kissed her goodbye on the steps of the little flat in Manchester Square where the Jewish Society met. The place belonged to the chairperson, Ruth – a Jewish debutante who Tony insisted on calling *Bec* as he did with every Jew north of the river; he liked to claim, 'I've never met a Hampstead Jew without being *shidduched* with his virgin daughter Rebecca.'

'He's a friend,' she'd answered Ruth, and inside she'd thought with secret scorn: *my best friend – better than you, better than any of you.*

Salim returned from Hassan's with his face full of unshed tears. She thought it must be because of his father, or because of talking about home. Or because of her. 'Is it because I went to the Jewish Society meeting?' she asked him, her chest tight with worry and remorse. She'd gone partly to see how he'd react. But he'd not even blinked – just kissed her goodbye saying, 'Have a good time.'

Now he looked at her in astonishment, and said, 'No, no. Not you. I had some unexpected news, but it's nothing.'

Then he sat back down and took her hand in his, cold and rough after the day. 'My Jude,' he said, raising her hand to his eyes as if they hurt him. 'My Jude,' he said again. 'I don't care where you go, as long as you come back to me.'

How, then, was she going to break the news of the birthday party to which he was not invited? She waited until the last minute, on her birthday morning.

Blissfully unaware, he met her that morning in the coffee shop with a bunch of roses and a small box. The necklace inside was gold, broken by some curling letters that he said represented her name spelled out in Arabic. 'Judith can mean *God be praised*,' he said, 'I looked it up. This is *God be praised* in Arabic, because it's how I feel from knowing you.'

Jude was deeply moved – as he was, she could tell, by the flaws in his usually perfect English.

'It's beautiful,' she said, holding it to her neck.

'I know you love your grandmother's chain. But I hope there's a place for this one too.'

'There is,' she said, swamped by the backwash of emotions.

Then, while the tide was still in full flood, she said, 'Sal, my uncle has invited me for a birthday dinner this evening. I can't get out of it. It's just the family.'

He looked taken aback, but then resigned. 'And I guess I don't qualify as family, right?'

'You're not missing anything, believe me,' she said, grasping his hand. 'Tomorrow we can go out together.'

'Right, but…' He took his hand out from under hers, and sat back in the chair. 'How long does this go on for? Are we pretending to our families, or pretending to ourselves?'

'What do you mean?' Jude asked, even though she knew exactly.

'You don't tell your family you have an Arab boyfriend. I don't tell mine I have a Jewish girlfriend. We don't sleep with each other, to make it all true. Where does this go, in the end?'

Jude felt helpless. She could hear Rebecca scolding her. *Be brave. Be a mensch.* She raised her eyes to his in appeal and he straightened up in exasperation.

'Okay, okay, you goose,' he said. 'Forget it for today. Go to your party and have a great birthday. I'm sure you'll have *so* much fun without me.' His voice was light but his smile was strained, and as Jude leaned over to kiss her reassurance, her eyes closed, shutting it out.

The party was a nightmare. Alex had not thought to ask any of Jude's friends. Instead, it was a Pesach reprieve – silverware, candelabras and diamonds pinching the folds of ageing white necks.

The conversation veered away from Jude's age, her studies and her father's health within a matter of minutes. It then plunged straight into a spitting rant about the coming war with the Arab world.

'What Mr Eshkol needs is a bomb, like Truman had,' one said, his lips wobbling in indignation. 'He's *putzing* around on the phone with President Johnson and the United Nations,' he continued, spitting over his left shoulder, 'while the Arabs are talking about blood this and annihilation that, cutting off our shipping and shooting over our borders… if we had the bomb, believe me, it wouldn't go this way.'

'There goes Stanley,' Alex smiled, his freckled scalp gleaming under thin silver hair. 'Always wanting to put the bigger boot in.'

'Oh come on, Alex.' Stanley's wife was deftly stabbing the other side of the chopped liver. 'You know it's the same old story. They couldn't kill us in 'forty-eight. They tried again in 'fifty-six. Now they think Nasser is giving them another chance. When does it end?'

'I don't buy this rivers of blood business,' Alex replied, raising a forkful of chicken breast to his mouth and chewing thoughtfully. 'I mean, what are the Arab leaders going to say to the peasants? Okay, blood, blood – blood, but no *beystsim*, no balls.' He winked at Jude. 'They haven't got the armies to wipe us out. It's all banging on the table.'

'Four Arab armies against Israel, and you don't think it's a threat? Not to mention the Arabs inside Israel, the fifth column. We'll be fighting outside and inside unless we take the first step. We'll never be safe without the Sinai and the West Bank, and the Arabs inside under control.'

Jude shifted uncomfortably in her chair. The Arabs inside. That was Sal. She thought of his sadness, the many things he'd told her and the silences that hid other stories he couldn't bear to tell. What could these people possibly know about him?

She sat up and took a breath. 'Maybe there are other things we could do instead to protect Israel,' she said. 'Like – if only the Arabs inside Israel were treated fairly, if there was real justice for them, maybe that would be something. It could help for making peace with the rest of the Arabs.' Her voice came out louder than she expected.

The rest of the table looked at her – even Tony. Someone laughed. The woman whose name she couldn't remember pointed her fork at

Jude. Yellow pearls dangled from her drooping earlobes, as if her ears were melting and dripping down her shoulders.

'Is this communism, young lady?' she said. 'Alex, your niece is a communist. It's all free love and peace for you young people today, isn't it?'

'I'm not a communist,' Jude retorted. 'You don't have to be a communist to believe in fairness. Not all Arabs want Israel to vanish. They were hurt too, they lost their homes and their families.'

'You kids don't know from Moses,' Stanley boomed. 'I'm very sorry for the poor bloody Arabs but they brought it on themselves. They had every chance for peace, again and again. Half the country, their own government – they could have had it all. Every time their leaders threw it back in our faces. We turned that desert into a garden, gave them proper water, hospitals, schools, roads! In return they shoot at innocent people, cut our trade off and threaten to annihilate us, to finish what the Nazis started. So tell me who's being unfair now?'

'They kicked the United Nations peace force out of the Sinai so that no one would be there to witness it,' his wife said, her words tumbling smoothly out over his. 'And when the Egyptians and their Nasser close the Red Sea to us, we'll be bottled up like fish in a jar.'

'It was our land to begin with,' another elegant, eager voice said at the back of the room – a lawyer, Jude remembered. 'Our ancestral land, a gift from God. At the end of the day the man who doesn't believe in that can't really call himself a Jew.'

Fury filled her, beyond anything she'd known since the moment she'd turned her back on Peggy's front door. She knew they were wrong in her heart, from her time with Sal, from his human doubts against their diamond-hard certainties. But she couldn't find the words to tell them exactly *how* they were wrong, and what the truth might be.

As the conversation spun beyond her again, she caught Tony's eye at the end of the table. He gave her a reassuring smile but all she could think was *you never said a word. You're happy to be one of them. You're clever but you're not a mensch.* And she gave him her sweetest smile back.

The BBC World Service woke Jude up on the morning of the fifth of June, to prove Alex's friends exactly right about one thing at least. The Israelis would strike first. Egypt had an even ruder awakening, when the boys and girls of the Israeli Air Force flew their Dassault Mirages over the border and dropped tarmac-penetrating tonnage on the heads of sleeping Egyptian planes.

A few hours later, Jude heard that Jordan had shelled Israel and Israeli bombs were now falling on Jordanian airstrips. The Arabs in the Old City of Jerusalem were rising. Israeli troops were poised on the border of the West Bank. Blood was being shed in the streets – Arab against Jew.

They'd only spoken twice since her birthday party, each conversation a hurried set of excuses, a mere shadow of the closeness she'd thought they had. But that day she stayed in her room and waited for him, her windows closed against the world outside.

The smells of the student halls crept through the cracks under her door – brown, dirty notes of burned toast, wet clothes and cheap beer filling her nostrils. She'd never noticed them before, but now they were hateful, the stink of the smallness of ordinary lives.

She waited – for Salim to come to her, to rage and shout like Stanley about the blood-hungry Jews and their murderous guns. And she tried to remember what they'd said at the party about having no choice, having tried for peace again and again, about Arabs bringing it on themselves.

He didn't come that day, nor the next. She began to imagine that their time together had been a fantasy. Each evening, the corridor was full of footsteps and laughter, the shrieks of people on their way out to bars, to the pictures. The sounds turned into an ache inside her. She tried to call him; the telephone rang and rang, until she hung up. For the first time she tasted the sourness of jealousy burning in her stomach.

But on the fourth day of fighting he came.

Jude had arrived home from class, switched on the radio and prepared to shut out another day. Turning on the tap, she brought a handful of lukewarm water to her face, pressing her eyes and feeling the wasteful patter of drops onto the rug. The BBC's monotone filtered through her wet fingers. Israeli soldiers were nearly victorious – they were rolling through Palestinian streets in the newly conquered West Bank and Gaza; the burning desert of the Egyptian Sinai was theirs, and the stony hills of the Syrian Golan.

She heard the words *proactive self-defence* – and then another voice, shouting over the first, said *cynical expansionist policy*. The World Service langour became a symphony of competing sounds, the wrongs suffered and the wrongs done. Who on earth could tell them apart?

There was banging behind her, urgent and fierce. Water splashed onto the floor as she turned, her hands dripping. *Let it be him. Let it be him, or else I'll let the water spill over onto the floor and it can wash all of this away.*

The reckless bargain raced through her, as she ran to the door and dragged it open, the radio and the rushing water drowned into silence by the pounding in her ears. Salim's eyes were red and his hands white from clenching the frame.

'I wanted to come before,' he said, his voice hoarse, as if he hadn't used it in days. 'Is this really possible? Are we mad?'

Yes was all she could think as she drew him in with her wet hands, so clumsy against the firmness of his arms. *We're all mad, everything is mad in this world.* The sound of water became a song as she reached up to his face, pulling him downwards, kissing him. 'Stay here tonight,' she whispered. 'It's not our fault, any of it. You have to stay here with me, for as long as you want.' And she felt the

warmth pulsing through him as he pushed her backwards towards
the bed.

They promised that they would tell their families on the same day.

Jude arranged to meet Tony for dinner at his north London flat,
and Salim planned to call Hassan that evening.

'Why don't you go and see him?' she asked. But he smiled at her
and shook his head. 'Never give an Arab bad news in a mechanic's
shop with wrenches to hand,' he said.

Jude knew she was avoiding the issue too, in her own way. She
couldn't imagine how she might tell her parents. The very thought
of it turned her stomach into a writhing mass. But Tony... Tony was
another thing. He would surely understand. He would tell her how
to make it all right.

She dressed in clothes Salim liked, to give her courage – tight blue
bell-bottoms with a loose blouse and a beret on her blonde hair. On
the bus to Camden she pressed her forehead to the window, watching
the soft shades of people flicker by in the faint dusk of early summer,
caught up in a world of carefree happiness beyond her reach.

Tony's flat was a modest size for the son of a rich man. But
everywhere she looked it whispered wealth. The bookshelf was
heavy oak and the old leather bindings of the books said *first edi-
tion* rather than *second-hand*. There was art on the wall where
students would put posters. A sleek turntable in the corner was
playing Ella Fitzgerald.

Over dinner they talked about the family. Tony had recently taken
a job at his father's law offices. He showed Jude a picture of a young
paralegal he was interested in, a Jewish intern from Switzerland. Her
face beamed out of the image, all white teeth and rich brown hair.

She felt oddly deceived by Tony. He talked like a rebel but he'd
slipped into his father's life like a hand into a silken glove. *You
joined your father's company, you'll marry this Bec from Switzerland*

and you'll move to Regent's Park and set your table with crystal. And you'll go to Shul and wear the yarmulke and host your own Passovers with that twinkle in your eye that says it's all a joke to you. But it isn't a joke. It's you, it's who you are and who you always have been.

At last they took their coffee over to the soft leather sofa, and Jude knew that the moment had come. So she told him, in halting words, what she had come to say.

It was easier than she'd imagined. He was an Israeli and a British citizen, nothing like the dangerous men of Uncle Max's nightmares. He had many Jewish friends, in Israel and here. He was destined for great things, one of the best students in his class. He understood more about Jews than most English *goyim* ever could. He spoke Hebrew. And he loved her. He loved her more than anything, and she loved him.

Tony sat as still as stone in his chair, until she'd finished. After the first silence fell, he put his head to one side and looked at her as if seeing her for the first time. Jude waited, her throat tightening.

Finally he asked, 'So what about Jack and Dora? I take it you haven't told them?' She shook her head, looking down at her hands. He blew air out of his mouth in a slow whistle. 'I'm not sure they're going to go for all this Israeli citizen stuff,' he told her, his voice measured and steady. 'You know they think Max is one step above a savage anyway. What does middle-class England want with Israel?' Judith felt a little block of hope slide out from underneath her.

'So what do you suggest, then?' she said, keeping her voice calm. 'I have to tell them something.'

Tony shrugged. 'Tell them he's Jewish.'

'I can't tell them that!' Jude was horrified.

'Why not? He's Israeli. He knows Hebrew. He's a Semite. According to you, he's virtually Moses.'

'I can't do that, Tony. They'd know. And he'd know, too. He'd think I was ashamed of him.'

'Aren't you? You come here like you're coming to an execution. You want me to – what? Give you a blessing? I'm not a Rebbe, you know.' He gave her a weak smile.

'I wanted you to help me break the news to my parents. To…' she hesitated. 'To help me figure out what to do. I just want to help them understand him like I do. I know it's going to be hard.'

'Hard.' Tony leaned back into the cushions and cupped his chin in his hands. 'Darling Jude, you have no idea how hard this is going to be. Never mind Jack and Dora. It's you I'm thinking about, little one. It's going to be impossible, I promise you. You want my advice. Wait a while before you tell anyone else. Just wait, until you're sure.'

'Why should I wait?' Jude was angry now, getting to her feet in agitation and walking to the other end of the sofa. Outside, the lights of darkening London shone dazzling in through the window. 'I know I'm never going to marry a Jew, Tony. Never. I tried for Dad, for you all, but I never met a single person I even liked, never mind loved. Now I have, and he happens to be an Arab. Too bad for you, and Jack and Dora, but why shouldn't it be good for me? Why shouldn't he be as good for me as that Swiss girl of yours and her rich father?'

She saw Tony flinch. He stood up too, set his coffee down and walked over to the bookcase – the communist manifesto, as Alex liked to call it. A signed picture of Sunderland FC was framed above it, one of Tony's most treasured possessions. Jude wanted to apologize, to rage at him. *You're supposed to be on my side. Tell me this is going to be okay. Help me make it good.*

He took a breath. 'I always hated Hebrew school too,' he said. 'You know, the droning Rebbes with their greasy yarmulkes going on about the destiny of the Jewish people. Whole weekends lost to Jewish destiny! When I could have been at the football.' He gave an exaggerated shudder, and Jude smiled despite herself.

'Most of that stuff seemed psychopathic to me, the kind of thing people would get locked up for if they did it in Newcastle. Do you remember the foundation story, not the Moses one – the first one?'

Jude felt lost. 'Abraham?'

'Him, yes. It's one of the worst ones. Truly. I mean, first he marries an eighty-year-old woman and tells her she's supposed to be a mother to a whole people. She frets herself into a frenzy because – surprise, surprise – she can't conceive. So he has sex with a servant girl called Hagar and the two of them take the baby away from her. Then when the old woman finally has a kid of her own, what does he do? Tries to sacrifice it on the mountain, because he hears voices from God telling him to do it. What a great story! No wonder we're so proud of it.' He smiled again, but this time Jude had to force herself to laugh. That old guilt, the horror of rejecting daily bread everybody else finds so delicious, stirred in her stomach.

'They sent her packing, that Arab girl who had the first boy. Ishmael they called him. Abraham's original heir. Sarah was jealous and wanted all of God's goodness for her little Isaac. So they tell us that Hagar and Ishmael went out into the desert. Just a girl and a kid, all alone in the heat, sent to their deaths by his papa like a used rag.

'The Rebbes would tell you it was all part of God's will, to make way for the chosen nation. And Ishmael had a nation of his own in the end, so no harm done, right? But I tell you, there isn't an Arab on earth that doesn't carry a little bit of Ishmael around with him. Who can blame them? They were always the ones to get kicked, first by God and then by everyone else. And they'll never be finished kicking back.'

He turned around to face her, grey in the cold reflection of the window.

'*Bubbellah*, I can see you love this one. And if you say he loves you too, I don't doubt it. But believe me, he'll never forgive you.'

'Forgive me for what?' she whispered.

He walked over to her and took her hand. 'For being on the winning team, darling.'

Salim waited anxiously for Jude to get back that night. He cleaned the two rooms of his flat, made stacks of sandwiches and turned on the old television he'd traded from his neighbour in exchange for some bookkeeping. He flicked from channel to channel through the hiss of the broken aerial, his stomach closed. The room reeked of washing and damp wood. Was he more worried for her or for himself? They would give her a hard time, he knew it. It was always harder for women than for men.

Hassan had proved the truth of that. He'd called Salim a *majnoon* donkey, a born troublemaker, a man without pride in his people, a boy who forgot his own history. But at the back of his outraged insults was that calm certainty that all Arab men have, that their women could be tamed or dropped at will, and that any trouble they brought into a man's life would soon blow over.

When Jude eventually came back, she sounded cheerful and told Salim that Tony would like to meet him one day. But her face was pale and she threw herself into his arms as if he was the only boat floating in an empty sea.

'Was he angry?' Salim asked. 'Did he say he'd talk to your parents?' At the back of his mind the question hovered: *did he turn you against me? Did he make you change your mind?*

'He wasn't angry,' she said, hugging him. 'He was surprised. He said it would be hard for us. But we know that.'

'We know that,' he agreed, kissing her forehead. She was so small to be so brave. 'You're worth everything that comes. You're the most courageous person I know.'

'A *mensch*.' She had tears in her eyes, but she smiled up at him. 'That's what my grandmother would have said. A person has to be brave before they can be worthy. I know she would have loved you, Sal. She would have seen through all of it, seen who you really are.'

He believed her, he had faith in her, more faith than he realized was still left inside him. She'd stood up to her family for his sake. She saw him as worth the risk.

That summer he slaved to get the best possible mark in his finals. Jude would sit up with him late into the night, making little index cards to help him remember equations and theories. And when her head finally drooped in sleep he would lie beside her and watch her breathing, wondering at her choice. Her hair was the soft yellow of candlelight, and her skin felt like still water. He would do anything to justify her faith in him, to become the man she saw through those blue eyes. She knew he was made for better things. She knew what it was to dream of another, forbidden life.

He tried to soften the way for her. He took tea with the sour, fascinated Ruth Michaels of the Jewish Society and even attended the local synagogue. He'd put on the yarmulke and smiled at his neighbours, and anyone would have sworn he was a Jew. *Even me.* And in that lofty room, filled with the rustle of lambswool suits and the rich smell of embroidery, he could almost imagine it himself. That he, Salim Al-Ishmaeli, was not really an Arab, forever predestined to hold losing cards – but one of the chosen ones, the masters, who always seemed to come out on top of the game.

A week after finals, Salim took Jude back to Finsbury Park, 'the scene of the crime', as he called it. Summer had burst through the bareness he remembered; the dark green was now soft and the trees a remote rustling of leaves. He spread out a picnic of cheese sandwiches and early season strawberries on the lawn and she presented him with a bottle of champagne. When she brushed his hair from his forehead he could see the July sunlight shining through drops on her lips, and when she pushed her mouth onto his he could taste it, a mix of sour and sweet.

Two plastic cups later she told him again how proud she was of him, beautiful in her sincerity. He jumped on the moment. He'd been planning it for days, and had waited all morning for this opportunity to confront her.

Despite her promise, Jude had still not told her parents about them. To her family, he didn't exist. Her pride in him was only a half-truth, a self-deception – otherwise why the secrecy? Her face fell as he spoke, the words tumbling out of him.

'You'll feel better after you tell them,' he argued. 'They deserve to know. What are you waiting for?'

He saw her blue eyes shift towards the trees, like birds startled into flight. 'I *will* tell them, but it has to be the right time,' she floundered, nonsensically defensive. 'I need Tony to help me, and he's been away in Geneva all summer.' Then came the counter. 'You haven't even told your sister. Or your mother.'

'My mother hasn't seen me in more than ten years,' he said. 'She doesn't care if I'm alive or dead. And my sister hasn't seen me in nearly as long. They're not part of my life now.'

'You told me about that letter your brother sent you. From Lebanon. She does want to see you, you said. She wrote to you. Why don't you go and see them? It might make *you* feel better.' A child's ploy, easy to see through but hard to deflect.

'Why are we talking about my family and Lebanon? This is about *your* family in Sunderland, the people you don't want to know you're living with an Arab.'

'For God's sake, Sal.'

'No, not for God's sake. For *our* sake, Jude. Isn't there something special here? Something worth the risk?'

'Worth shouting from the rooftops,' she said, but her face was troubled.

'So? What are you afraid of?' She shook her head, her hand coming up to touch his cheek. *Nothing*, the gesture said. But he felt a deep disquiet as he watched her hand fall from his face, retreating to pull at the two gold chains twisted around her neck.

Finally, Salim arranged a coffee with Hassan. It was his last attempt to manipulate her innate sense of fairness, to play on her strongly knotted strings of guilt.

In truth he had been almost as reluctant to get Jude and Hassan together as Jude was to make that long-dreaded phone call to Sunderland. Hassan was an unvarnished Arab, proud to be so, rejecting the English niceties Salim had been so keen to learn. How would he appear to a sheltered Jewish girl whose idea of foreign exoticism was the Parisian Left Bank?

They met at Hassan's house on a Sunday afternoon. Hassan's wife had cooked a greasy feast: cooked soft rolled cabbage leaves stuffed with meat and rice, chicken on a bed of oily potatoes, imitations of *manquish* pastries full of heavy English lamb, and a rich dessert of *kanafi*, buttered vermicelli swimming on top of a bed of sugared white cheese.

They sat on the old, brown twin sofas while Hassan smoked and Salim sipped his beer. Salim could see Jude looking around at the strangeness of the house. Like other Arabs, Hassan and Shireen preferred electricity to sunlight inside their living room. The curtains were partially drawn and the daylight gave way to the glare of cheap ceiling lights. A spicy, greasy smell came from the kitchen, mingling with the ashy haze of cigarettes. Bronze plates and wall hangings with *hadiths* from the Qur'an were placed around plastic flower arrangements. The desperate thought came – *this is not her world.*

Perhaps Hassan sensed his thoughts. Whether or not, he became increasingly irritable and irritating. First, he started berating Salim for not going back to the Middle East after graduating. 'You have no gratitude,' he scoffed. 'Tareq and Nadia put you through university, and you can't even give them five minutes. And what about Rafan? He says you never wrote back to him. Is that what brothers do?'

'Is it what brothers do to be silent for ten years?' Salim shot back, heat rising into his face. 'After one letter you want me to go running to Lebanon. I'm too busy for this nonsense.'

Hassan poked his finger at Jude, a sneer on his face. He had been drinking, Salim saw. 'This big man here, he never forgets an insult, believe me. He can't let anything go. You'll see. Not even with his own family. He's too proud for us. I hope he doesn't get too proud for his English family too.'

'Leave her be, Hassan,' Salim said, in Arabic. He could tell the effort of speaking in English all the time was affronting his brother, making him more provocative.

'Why, then?' Hassan said, refusing to switch from English. 'She comes to my house, she's a grown woman. Let her hear the truth, why not?'

'Sal wants to go back to see his family,' Jude said quickly. Her expression said, all too plainly, *how could this man and mine be brothers?* 'But he has a new job starting in a few weeks. When he's settled, maybe we'll go together?' The last words were framed as a question. He caught her eyes, and she smiled. Salim was startled. Did she think he was going to the Middle East with her?

'You and he are going to Palestine together?' Hassan said, his eyes widening. '*Ya* Salim, what have you been telling this girl? Doesn't she watch the news?'

Salim felt like pebbles were rumbling under his feet, the beginning of the avalanche. 'Stop it, Hassan.'

'No,' said Hassan, his voice rising. 'You want to do this thing together, this peace and love thing? In England, okay. In Palestine there's no peace, no love. If you go together, you won't get flowers, you'll get stones. How can Salim take a Jew back to his family? I'm sorry, but you're crazy, both of you.'

He saw Jude go white, and set her half-tasted cup of Turkish coffee down on the glass table. Her mouth, usually so gentle, narrowed into a hard, thin line.

'Sal and I both belong there,' she said, her voice trembling with anger he'd rarely sensed in her. 'We both have family there. Not everyone throws stones, only the people who want to fight more than they want anything else.'

'You don't belong there,' Hassan said flatly. 'The Zionists think God gave them my house, but it isn't written in the Qur'an or any other book I know. Salim said you weren't a Zionist but what does he know? I say, scratch a Jew and you get Ben-Gurion.'

Jude got to her feet. Salim saw that she was near tears and hating herself for it. He was on his feet too, saying, 'Jude, come on, sit down,' grasping her with one hand and Hassan with another.

'I think we should go home now,' she said, her voice cracking. Hassan threw his hands up in the air and said, in a more subdued voice, to Shireen, 'Someone has to tell them, *yani*.'

Salim could have punched him, could have screamed retaliations at him, but it was too late. As he got Jude's coat and tried to make light of it with small talk, he knew a deeper damage had already been done.

The journey from London's suburban south-east to its busy north-west was achingly long and slow. At Piccadilly Circus, Jude's patience ran out. She told Salim she was going back to her room in the student halls, and she would see him later. His protests were weak. They both wanted to be alone.

She walked through Soho as if she was dreaming, past dark avenues of sex shops and young faces with wildly coloured hair falling over thin shoulders. She pushed through a crowd of them as they laughed, breathing in clouds of smoke from the stub ends of their thin cigarettes and the fruity smell of beer splashing on her shoes.

Different songs floated through the evening air in a faint dissonance, arms of sound grasping at her as she went by. It was late summer and the skies were still emptying like a glass of water, preparing for a pale and star-strewn darkness to set in.

She was still trembling, from the scorn she'd heard in Hassan's voice and the hateful wave of anger she'd felt breaking over her. The scorching bitterness of the Turkish coffee lingered in her mouth, a strong, overpowering taste that mocked her weak palate. She remembered looking up at Hassan from the blackness of the cup and seeing the same colour in his eyes.

She should not blame Salim for his brother, and yet in that moment she felt angry with him – angry he was an Arab, angry he'd pursued her in the first place, furious with herself for becoming so entwined with him that she could not imagine letting go. *Is this how our lives will be? Resentment from all sides, no place to call home?*

She turned onto Warwick Street and walked past the Our Lady of Assumption Chapel, where one of her Polish Catholic classmates used to go for Mass.

It had amazed Judith when she learned that church doors are always unlocked. It spoke of a welcome she could not imagine in her own faith, a world of open arms where no one was an outsider. The heavy brown door of the chapel swung inwards at a touch, drawing Jude across a glowing threshold into the clasp of warmth and candlelight.

Inside, the room was filled with a cloying calm. Candles flickered in the half-light, and rosy-stained windows showed saints reaching out to figures robed in blue and gold. To Jude they looked strangely antiseptic; their impassive white faces gazed down on the penitents huddled in the red pews below.

She edged into one of the rows and sat on the worn cushion. What would Jack and Dora say if they could see her now, their precious daughter and only blood sitting before a statue of the Virgin Mary?

Dora had always reserved a special disdain for Christ's mother; she insisted that Jesus was a product of young Mary's sleepwalking in a Roman military encampment and an unintended encounter with a foot soldier. 'She used to walk in her sleep all the time,' she'd told Jude during a dismissal of her friend Kath's religious beliefs. 'She was known for it.'

This Mary did indeed look sleepy, her eyes half-closed and a sad curl to her lips, nearer to a wince than a smile. The cowls over her head made Jude think of a woman in mourning, of hidden sorrows.

Jude felt those unshed tears come back to her eyes again – the traitor tears that always seemed to come when she wanted to scream instead of weep. Now she did not try to stop them flowing down her cheeks. *Tell me what to do.*

She pushed the thought up towards the ageless Mary in her blue shawl, her skin so white and clear, her hands reaching out to Jude with comfort. Around her the murmur of sorrow and thanksgiving filled the air. It grew around her like waves on the shore at sunset, after the storms of the day have passed.

She asked him to meet her at Virginia's the next morning.

When she arrived he was already sitting there, his face downcast. Her heart went out to him, but she steeled herself.

'How are you?' he said as she sat down.

She nodded quickly, and said, 'I'm okay.' *What a stupid answer.* But he was too distracted to notice.

'I'm sorry for yesterday,' he said, a slight hint of belligerence in his voice. 'You know it wasn't my fault. There's just no point in arguing with Hassan. You should have left it alone.'

She fingered Rebecca's chain for courage.

'But that's just it, Sal,' she said, taking his hand. 'They won't leave us alone. Our families will never accept us like this. I thought yours might, but I don't think so any more.'

He bit his lip, and threw his hands up.

'Jude, you have to understand Hassan. He's an idiot, a peasant. Please, please don't do anything because of him. We can fix all of that, in time.'

'It's not just Hassan,' she said firmly. 'It's all of them. My family hears *Arab* and all they see is angry people killing Jews. And yours think I'm just another Israeli. I can only think of one way to prove them wrong.'

He looked dubious. 'How?'

'Do what Hassan says we can't,' she answered. 'Take me home with you. To Israel. Palestine – you know what I mean. It's the best way to show we don't stand with one side or the other. We can stay with my uncle on his kibbutz and see how things work there. Then we can stay in Nazareth, with your sister. I want to see Jaffa and the place you grew up.'

'We?' He looked at her in such blank disbelief that she felt her certainties shudder. She'd been up half the night thinking about it, turning their lives around like a broken picture, trying to make the pieces fit.

'We have to show them,' she pleaded. 'That Hassan and my uncles are all wrong.' *He has to understand.* 'I've had Israel rammed down my throat all my life. My parents wanted me to go, Max – everyone. But I *never* wanted to. It was meaningless to me. Until now. When you talked about your home, it changed how I felt. I want to see this place through your eyes. And if we can convince our families over *there*, no one *here* could argue – and all of this hiding would be done forever.'

She felt him pull his hand away from hers, the table suddenly cold beneath her fingers. 'How could you even think this, Jude?' The words came out like a slap. 'I was driven out of my home. I never went back. Now you tell me that the first time I should go back, I should go with a Jew? To stay with Zionists? Are you mad?'

She was frozen to the spot, her palms cold with sweat. 'Not with a Jew,' she said, her voice quiet. 'With me.'

He pointed to the chain around her neck. 'You can't hide that thing there. You don't even try. Here, together, maybe something's possible. If we go back there, it's just you and a Palestinian traitor.' He pushed his chair back from the table.

'Is that what you care about?' she said. 'What these people you've always laughed at think of you?'

'They're my people,' he said, his black eyes furious. '*You* care more about your family's approval, about this Jewish thing, than you do about me. You want to take me to your uncle's kibbutz, to prove I'm a tame Arab. I see. Hassan was right. We don't understand each other at all.'

As if in a dream she saw him stand up and begin to walk away. For a moment he slowed – the door was just in front of him, and a tiny, lost thought came to her: *he will come back.*

But then he walked on, and when he passed her in the window she might have been a stranger sitting there, still as a statue, just an empty blur beyond the dirty glass.

BEIRUT

He felt as if his legs did the thinking for him that day, walking him away from the sight of her, pounding down a tunnelled vision of Soho's gloomy streets, and driving him two weeks later to the very place he'd sworn never to go: the airport and a journey to reawaken the dead.

Even the letter he'd eventually opened and the telephone call with Rafan were foggy recollections. He'd wanted to bury the image of Jude in his mother's touch, in the embrace of a brother who used to curl up next to him. As he read Rafan's cheerful prose he pictured them both, waiting for him in a warmer world.

Rafan himself was all enthusiasm. 'Just let me take care of everything, big brother.' Down the hissing line his voice sounded deep and eager. 'I promise, you'll never want to leave.'

Salim replayed that voice many times during the five-hour flight, trying to read the man from his buried memories of the boy – the face he'd last seen smiling in a dark basement in Nazareth. How would they even recognize each other? It was a bitter idea. From take-off to touchdown at Beirut's *Aéroport International*, he tried to wrestle his memories into submission, letting them go to make space for new ones. *I will have a brother again. A mother again. That's all that matters.*

But when he saw the stranger waving from the humid arrivals hall, for a moment his disappointment was sharp as a knife in the ribs. 'Big brother,' the tall stranger said, moving towards him with open arms.

Everything about this Rafan was jarringly familiar, like a favourite tune in a different key. The green eyes were still wide and guileless. And the mouth turned up at the corners in the way that Salim remembered – the tantalizing secret smile. But above his silk shirt the full baby cheeks had thinned and shaped a face as striking as his mother's. His jaw was dark with stubble and expensive sunglasses rested on his fair head.

He greeted Salim with an easy laugh. 'My big brother,' he said again, kissing him lightly on both cheeks. 'I never thought I would see the day.' His lips had become as full and smooth as a girl's.

'Rafan.' Salim found his voice choked with an emotion he did not expect. 'I can't believe you're here.' *Why did it take so long for you to look for me?* That was what he longed to ask.

'Everything happens in its own time, big brother,' Rafan said, his hand tight on Salim's back. 'Now you're here, you'll see. Come on, the car's waiting.'

They headed towards Beirut's white skyscrapers, listening to the radio in Rafan's new Mercedes. The airport was a dwindling speck in the distance, vanishing in a blaze of light. Outside, the southern highway whipped by under dark blue skies. A woman was singing, a sound full of strange memories. *I know that voice.* Umm Kulthum, the mother of music, had been a legend since his mother was a girl. Once the whole Arab world had stopped to listen to her. Now – maybe there was no one left to hear.

The sadness of the song infected him too, as he leaned his forehead against the warm glass.

> *My heart, don't ask where love has gone,*
> *It was a citadel of my imagination that fell,*
> *Pour me a drink, let's drink to the ruins,*
> *And tell the story for me, while I cry*

Rafan was talking over the music; he rhapsodized about the warm seas, about Jounieh's white beaches and champagne at the Saint-Georges Yacht Club. Salim let him talk. This was why he came, to wash the pale English dust off his body and float in carefree Arabian waters.

Tantalizing glimpses of the Mediterranean sparkled out of the window, looking left and west into the falling sun. Ahead of them, the glamorous curve of the city stretched out in a wide embrace.

Beirut! *Warm sun and warmer women*, Hassan had said. That suited him perfectly.

The scenery had changed to their right; Rafan had turned off the highway, and now the Mercedes was crawling past a dirty sprawl of low corrugated roofs, spreading out as far as Salim could see – a filthy brown rug at the white feet of the city. *The refugee camps*. Tens of thousands of Palestinians sheltered there, or so he'd read. More were coming every day, fleeing Israeli tanks in the West Bank. Salim imagined them closing their front doors for the last time, wondering what the future might hold. *It was supposed to be just for a short while*, he thought, remembering the slam of the gate in Jaffa. *And then it turned into the rest of our lives.*

It put a sharp edge on his mood; the view out of the windscreen darkened as Umm Kulthum wailed over the roar of the engine. Beirut's tall skyline loomed ahead.

Rafan paid the camps no attention. 'Change of plan, big brother,' he said. 'It's too early for the house. I don't know about you, but I fancy a drink.' Salim found his accent strange, almost French, with husky, slithering syllables. 'We'll go to Hamra later. Now I want to show you the real Beirut.'

Hamra was the richest part of the city, the home of old Arabic money. When Salim first heard that Rafan was living there, he said, 'How come?' before remembering that he didn't really want to know. Rafan's grin had been audible even over the telephone. 'Hey, big brother. What can I say? Mama did well for herself.'

Beirut had done well for itself too. The jammed road into town gradually unfolded into wide, white boulevards lined with palm trees, brilliantly green in the sunshine.

Everywhere, Salim heard the throaty, thrilling snarl of expensive cars and saw the flash of bronzed legs striding smoothly through the traffic. Around the Place des Martyrs, in between its circulating buses, parked sedans and brand new motorbikes, people moved to the pulse of life in all its fullness, on their way to meetings, to trysts, to coffee houses and shops. Salim's eyes followed them. *Going to dance, to play, to love.*

Beyond the city centre, the Corniche swept the brothers out to the vast blue playground of the Med. New hotels were springing up on the Promenade, and fairgrounds on the beach. Out on the sea waterskiers floated back and forth as silent as a dream, sending white wisps of spray up into the air. A green-capped mountain rose above the shimmering haze. Below the road, on the long sands, Salim could see men and women rushing headlong into the sea together, their bodies warm and lithe in the heat. It reminded him of Tel Aviv, all those years ago – the same brown limbs, the same heedless dance.

They pulled up outside one of the smaller hotels. Salim followed Rafan out onto the patio overlooking the Corniche. They sat quietly, sipping their drinks under a picture of the Virgin Mary. Salim could see the notorious Hotel Saint-Georges on the tip of the bay, glowing roundly in its pink and white shell.

'Look at that,' Rafan said to him. 'It's just like a nipple begging to be sucked.' Salim laughed. How could they be the same person, the little boy who wet the bed and this worldly man? Salim felt strangely elated by his brother's transformation. He sat back in the chair and relaxed. *The sun is warm and the women are warmer*, he thought. Jude was cold. Here he could be himself.

'The Frenchies built this place, you know. The Christians.' Rafan gestured out to the Saint-Georges. 'They're the ones with the money round here. Muslims have never been smart with money, unless they had oil to play with.'

'The Muslims seem to be doing okay too,' Salim said, looking at his brother's silk shirt and heavy gold watch. 'Hassan told me this place was an Arab paradise.'

'A fool's paradise,' Rafan said. 'Although you might say they are one and the same thing. In Israel it's the Jews over the Arabs. Here it's the Christians over the Muslims, with the Druze stirring the pot. One day it will all boil over. But until then…' He picked up his drink, raised it. '*Sahtein*,' he said – good health.

'The English think all Arabs are either emirs or beggars,' Salim said, as the sour cocktail slipped down his throat and warmed his stomach. 'They can't get used to the idea that I'm just an accountant.' Although he'd been a beggar when he'd arrived there. He would never forget that.

Rafan laughed. 'I can't get used to it either. Salim Al-Ishmaeli, counting English pounds? But I guess it's better than being Tareq in Nazareth, counting up his master's shekels.'

'And what kind of money do you count, then?' Rafan had never told Salim what he did for a living. He had a Lebanese passport through their mother, which allowed him to work or study – whichever he wanted. But Rafan didn't dress like a student. Nor did he carry himself like a businessman.

His brother ran one neatly buffed fingernail over the rim of his glass.

'There's only one kind of currency worth counting, big brother,' he said. 'And I don't think they deal it out at the bank.' Behind his head, a waterskier sent a white plume up into the sky; Salim heard a tiny shriek of joy or fear come drifting across the water. He wondered again what he wanted from Rafan. An apology? An explanation? He looked at him, trying to see the boy who'd needed him so, the one fed on secrets and false hopes. The son their mother had chosen to keep.

'Is that why Mama left?' he asked suddenly, pushing his glass to one side. 'Because our father's money wasn't enough for her? Come on, she must have told you. Was that it?'

Rafan leaned back in his seat. He stretched his arms behind his head and regarded his older brother.

'You know, Salim, Mama always says the past is the past. Why do you want to sit here, in this nice place with your nice drink, and talk about all the sad shit we've been through? Does it really matter now?'

'I have a right to know,' Salim said, a spark of anger flaring inside him. 'I looked after you every day for eight years, remember? All this time, and never a word. So why now? What made you write? Don't tell me it was Baba's death, because I know that's bullshit.'

Rafan wagged his finger at Salim. 'What you want to know, I can't give you, Salim. I was only a kid. I don't remember anything about that time, just a bed that stank and bad dreams.' His eyes were impossible to read behind their amber glass, but his words stung nonetheless. After all that love and care, hadn't Salim earned a place in Rafan's memory?

Rafan leaned forward and slid Salim's drink back in front of him. 'But I *can* tell you what I learned after we came here, big brother. The Arabs in Palestine are living like rats. Tareq and Nadia were mice, our father was a rat and we were his little baby rats picking up crumbs from the Israeli table. Is that a way to live? Isn't it better to be a free man among the Arabs than a *fellah* on a white master's farm?' He lifted his glasses onto his forehead and looked calmly at Salim, green eyes narrowed against the sun.

'Free?' Salim said. 'I saw those camps. It looked like there were plenty of rats living there.'

Rafan shrugged his shoulders.

'You can't see everything there is to see from the roadside, big brother,' he said. 'It's like in your English forests. The wolves may

161

hide. But their teeth are still sharp and in the end they rule the other beasts.'

'Wolves, rats,' Salim laughed. 'What are you trying to tell me? That you joined the PLO?' The Palestine Liberation Organization had reached the English news recently. Once Salim had thought it was a joke, another faint-hearted Arab struggle. But Nadia had written to say that young people in the occupied West Bank were joining up after the latest war, and she worried what the future might bring for them.

Rafan laughed too, his mouth opening wide. '*Ya* Salim,' he shook his head. 'Life is too short for politics, old bean.' He spoke in English now, and Salim had heard him conversing with the barman in French. But then his voice became serious. 'I can't explain it all now, big brother. You have to see for yourself. You should know that I never forgot you all these years, not for a minute. I've always wanted you to come here. Yes, to repay you. Whatever happened before, we are family still, the same blood. So come on, drink up. One day the dogs will eat us all.'

When the first glasses had been drained to their rattling ice cubes, and the second, and the third, the sun had dipped under the horizon. The sea turned a violent red and sucked at the shore.

They went into Hamra for dinner. Two smiling girls calling themselves Leila and Dalia joined them, and Rafan ordered for all of them: grilled steak, rich red tomatoes, hot bread and spicy peppers. Later, a young man arrived in a white suit and soft cream car to take them to a club downtown.

They sped down the Rue de Phénicie with open windows, the night air screaming into the car. Salim felt either Leila or Dalia put a warm hand on his leg. Rafan's friend wanted to gamble, and the girls were shrieking 'Crazy Horse! Crazy Horse!' as the lights sped by.

Salim remembered tumbling into a red room, dim with velvet and soft crystal chandeliers. The floor was spinning, it seemed, spinning in a blur of laughter and dark lace. He swayed in time with the pulse of it, stumbling into one of the black pillars beside him. Rafan was in one corner, talking to a blonde girl; his head bent close to her cheek, his hand slipping into hers.

The music reeled across the floor. Leila wanted to dance, and she pulled him into the crowd. Rafan had vanished. Salim leaned forward into Leila's arms, closing his eyes and letting their bodies move together in the hot and close darkness.

He felt as if he could just drift away – away from himself, from memories of Jude, from the person he'd tried to become. The music changed, its beat harder than before, and Leila was pressed up against him. Now he was alone, on an untroubled sea and there were soft hands pulling him, pulling him gently out into the void.

He didn't remember going to bed. When he woke, his head was filled with nails and straw. Light was already blazing in through drawn curtains.

He reached out his hand into the grey space, and hit something hard – a wall. On the other side of him, a person stirred. He looked around. She still had her knickers on, and his shirt. She reminded him of Margaret, lying there on her stomach. Her dark hair tumbled over her back and her nails stretched bloodily out over the sheets.

Voices sounded dimly outside the door. Pushing himself slowly to his feet, he winced with the forgotten pain of a hangover. He found his jeans on the floor, pulled them over his legs and staggered to his feet.

The bedroom door opened into a small living room – dark doors leading directly off it. The late afternoon sun came trickling down through a glass panel in the ceiling, dancing with the dust in the air.

At the central table, four men were sitting. Salim could smell hashish burning somewhere, over the acrid stink of cigarette ash. Rafan was in the same clothes he'd been wearing last night. His eyes were shadowed; they looked black under the faint, filtered skylight.

'Salim, big brother.' Rafan waved him over. 'Come and say hello to the guys.' Salim walked forward and nodded at the rest of the table. These men looked very different to the suave friend of last night. They were darker skinned, heavier, and they did not smile when they saw him. The one closest to him looked up; something was bulging from his belt, black like the butt of a handgun.

'*Keefak, keefak,*' he said to each politely, shaking their hands. *How is this life?* Their accents were familiar, a poorer version of his father's. Their hands were calloused. *Before they came here, they must have been fellahin*, Salim thought. Farmers and street workers, now big men with guns.

'So,' he said, sitting down and taking the joint out of Rafan's hand to fill his own lungs. 'Are you from Palestine?'

'We are, *habibi*,' the man with the bulging belt said. Salim sensed that the greeting, *my beloved friend*, was both welcome and warning. 'My brothers and I are down from Tripoli. Farouk here is visiting from Jordan, from Karameh.' Salim nodded silently. The Jordanian border town was the headquarters of the Palestine Liberation Organization.

The big man called Farouk looked at him with pitted eyes. 'You Al-Ishmaelis are from Jaffa, I hear. God bless you all. I came from there too, from Manshiyya. I worked in the fields, picking the fruit back then, with my father, may Allah bless his eyes.'

'*Ahlan wa sahlan*,' Salim said, automatically. This was a man his father might have employed. The *ay'an* put food in their mouths, but when the *ay'an* fled they were left with nothing to eat and no one to lead them. Now the *ay'an* were living comfortably in Europe and the *fellahin* were left here, taking the fight to the Jews.

'God bless you,' the man said again. 'We have a base in Tripoli now, with our brothers in Fatah. I think our brothers in Jordan may be joining us soon, if the hammer falls there. Jordan is a traitor bitch. Hussein is the Jew's bitch. We'll fuck her like a dog.' His voice was grim. Even Salim knew, from listening to the BBC Arabic Service, that wily King Hussein would one day throw all the Palestinians out again – starting with men like Farouk.

'How did you come here, Farouk?' Salim asked carefully. He felt like the stranger he'd once been in England, afraid to put a foot wrong. Rafan, he saw, was watching him carefully.

'I came to the camps in Tripoli with my family during the *Nakba*. The Irgun drove their tanks through my house in Manshiyya. My wife died, my father died. My youngest son died here in the camps, from the blood in his guts. My oldest son is a soldier with me, may Allah protect him. That's my story, the same as many.' He paused to take a deep draw on the joint.

'But you're in London, Rafan tells us,' he went on, coughing as the strong smoke came streaming out. 'That's a good place to be. Bullets can't drive out the Zionists. We need educated men, big heads. There are men like that now. Arafat. Abbas. Young men, but clever. We need them in Europe too. What do you do in London?'

Rafan answered, 'He's planning to be a rich man, Farouk. Right, big brother? And marry a blonde girl with big tits.'

Salim ignored him and spoke directly to Farouk. 'I studied economics. Now I need to get my first job. I'm not a big man like my brother here, but I haven't forgotten the struggle.' He put his hand over his heart and felt the empty beating there, the hollowness that said *you did forget, you made yourself forget*. Salim wanted no part of the struggle. It never seemed to end, but it never seemed to go anywhere either.

The men stopped talking when Leila came swaying out of the bedroom, kissed Rafan and started to make Turkish coffee. As the sun began to sink again and the room darkened, Salim saw Rafan and Farouk disappear into the bedroom together and come out ten minutes later. Farouk was carrying a duffel bag, black and scarred. There were hard outlines that looked like bricks bulging out of the leather. *Hashish, or money maybe?* A prickle of adrenaline crept like ice down his back. If this was the nature of the struggle, then what was Rafan? And what did this stranger-brother want from him?

Once the men had left, they changed their clothes and went out alone for dinner. Salim had little appetite. He pushed his food back and forth on his plate, trying to understand what he wanted to say. Eventually, Rafan kicked him under the table.

'What did you expect, big brother?' he said. 'A student waving petitions? The Knights of the Round Table? You've been with the *Angleezi* too long. You forgot how to be a Palestinian.'

'I *am* a Palestinian,' Salim protested angrily. 'How dare you judge me? It takes more than hashish and guns to make you a Palestinian. I was the only one that cared about our house, the only one who ever wanted to go back. You, Mama, Hassan – you couldn't get away fast enough.'

'You're wrong, big brother,' Rafan said. 'You're not Palestinians any more. None of you. So you have your British passport and your degree. Good for you. But I never wanted those things, Salim.' He took a mouthful of kebab. 'Hmm, it's good. Try it.' When Salim shook his head, Rafan went on.

'What's special about this place? I'll tell you. Palestine is still alive here, in the camps and with men like Farouk. We have brothers in every other house, from Amman to Tripoli. The PLO is ready to come across the Jordanian border and run the south. The Shia will come on board. Those old chickens over there,' he pointed towards the Christian Maronite sectors east of the city, 'will just lie down. It's coming, you'll see.' Salim sat there, transfixed. Rafan leaned over towards him.

'Why don't you get that clever head of yours to work with your own people?' he said. 'What else do you have to do in London?'

Jude. Her name leapt to his lips, but he pushed it away.

'Why me?' he asked. 'I'm a stranger here.'

'Because you're my brother,' Rafan said, and his green eyes were so compelling that Salim felt his heart lurch. 'Who else do I have but you? All these years we were apart, can you say you were happy? Isn't that why you came looking for me now? To get home to your family, where you belong?'

Salim felt a surge of something somewhere between hope and anger, a swift tide filling his chest. *This is my brother, my real family.* The idea of coming home, of undoing past wrongs – it was so sweet. A true home, not the house of cards he'd been building with Jude. 'And what happens if we win?' he said eventually, knowing what he hoped to hear. 'What do you want in the end, Rafan? Are you saying we can go back?'

Rafan threw back his head and howled with laughter, like a dog out on the beach.

'*Ya* Salim,' he gasped. 'Mama was right. You're a *fellah* like Father. You're obsessed with that pile of bricks and leaves.' He wiped his eyes and his face twisted into a smile. 'No, big brother, there's no going back in our lifetime. But we bring them the bill for the past. And we can make them pay.'

That night, Rafan drove them to his mother's apartment in Hamra. They walked past the guard at the front entrance into a marble lobby full of light. A lift took them up to the top floor, and opened to a long, dark corridor. Translucent lights studded the walls, sculpted in the shape of women's sleeping faces. Salim felt his chest tighten at the sight of them, so serene and so very cold.

As Rafan opened the door, he heard music, faint but soothing – Fairouz, the new Lebanese obsession, singing a song by Umm Kulthum. Beirut's distant nightlife shimmered in through the great arched windows in waves of red, blue and green. Two lamps lit up the room's opposing corners, identical horses rearing up with glowing balls between their hooves. A dark Persian carpet muffled their footsteps.

'Mama,' Rafan called, throwing his keys down onto the lacquered table. 'Mama, come on. Salim is here.'

She came out of her room wearing a flowing green dress, adjusting an earring. Her hair swept up in an auburn tower, plaited over her brow like a crown. As she came towards them, her perfume surrounded Salim like the scent of heated bronze.

'Hi Mama,' he said, amazed to find his eyes full of tears. It was a moment he'd rehearsed so many times in different shades of anger or forgiveness. But the tears shamed him, reducing him into the little boy left behind.

She walked over to him, put her white hand on one cheek and laid her lips against his other. She was not as tall as he remembered, and the light touch of her face felt powdery.

'Salim,' she said, stepping back to look at him, her green eyes dark as the sea. 'You got tall, *ya'eini*. I knew you would.'

'It's been a long time,' he said, trembling. 'I missed you.'

She moved away from him, towards a desk in the corner, and lifted a cigarette out of a silver box. Rafan took a light over to her, and Salim watched her neck rise as she drew the smoke in. He could see the bones moving loosely under the skin. *She got old*, he thought in shock. *Or was she always like this?*

'Some things are too complicated for boys to understand,' she said, walking over to the glimmering window. 'I know it was hard for you, but it was better that way. Now you're a success in England. I have a man who looks after me properly. Everyone's happy.' She stubbed out her cigarette and said, 'There's beer in the kitchen, Rafan. Get some for your brother.'

Seating herself on the edge of the sofa, she patted the cushion beside her. Salim sat slowly down. 'So tell me, *ya'eini*,' she said, her voice edged with hoarseness, 'what's it like in London? You have a degree now, and a good job? I'm so proud of you. I knew you would be a big man.'

They sat there quietly together, while she smoked and gazed at a point over his head. He told her about London, the restaurants and theatres, and the new job he would start next month. *Everything but Jude.* He imagined Jude sitting there beside him, her pale light draining out into the pit of his mother's expression.

After ten minutes the telephone rang. 'I'm coming,' she said into the mouthpiece. Rafan brought over a fur stole, and she pulled it around her shoulders. 'We'll talk more later, *ya'eini*,' she said. Salim thought her eyes looked dead. He'd dreamed of an apology, of her arms around his neck and tears against his face. But as she kissed him goodbye and walked to the door, he found he no longer wanted her arms near him.

The night crawled by, and Salim lay sleepless on his brother's bedroom floor. When morning came, he woke Rafan and said, 'Let's go out.' The door to his mother's room was open. She had not come home.

They drove south along the old Damascus road, before turning west to Shatila refugee camp. The camp outskirts had two barricades. The Lebanese Army held the first. Salim saw an older man in a plain suit watching as the soldier called them to a halt. '*Deuxième Bureau*,' Rafan said, as they were waved through after showing papers and passports. 'Military intelligence. Those bastards will be the first ones to go.'

Camp residents ran the second checkpoint. A man in a black and white checked *keffiyeh* flagged the car down. Rafan greeted him by name and asked after his father. Salim shook his hand through the window.

They drove through into a wall of noise and stench. An open sewer ran beside them, under the tangle of wires linking shack to shack and tenement to tenement. Washing dripped in the dirty air. An old man sat on the ground, a pile of old shoes beside him. One cheek was sunken into toothless gums and fluid from an infected eye ran down the other.

Children ran ahead of the car, cheering them along. He felt something stir inside him, watching them skip past them, yelling in the exuberance of young life. Fifteen years later, after the massacre that left dozens of small bodies red and limp on the ground here, he would think of those children again and wonder if they had vanished in the slaughter.

Abu Ziad, Rafan's friend, was playing backgammon on a plastic chair outside a stall selling falafel. His belly spilled over his knees like the worry beads tumbling over his fist. Parcels stamped with the United Nations logo were being carried into a block behind them. A sticker on the door said *Filastinuna*, with a Palestinian flag sketched next to it.

They drank a short coffee while Abu Ziad bemoaned the Lebanese government and its Christian leadership. Palestinian Muslims couldn't get work permits, he said, while their Christian brothers and the rich could easily buy a passport. 'We are less than dogs to these Beirutis,' he growled. 'But one day dogs bite back.' They talked about the corruption of the official camp supervisors, the slowness of the UN and the prospects for Fatah out of Tripoli. Salim was asked about life in London, and the possibility of the British rejoining the fight on Palestine's side.

Before they left, Rafan handed Abu Ziad some money in an envelope. A contribution, he said, to his children's charity. He was thanked and blessed, and the envelope disappeared into the old man's pocket.

On their way out, Salim breathed the air deeply, wanting to taste the stench of the place fully, to carry it out with him. His life in London – the accountancy job waiting for him – what did it mean, compared to this sink of human misery? At that moment he felt dirty, guilty for courting the supercilious *Angleezi* and for cherishing his British passport. Rafan had it right – he did not deserve to call himself a Palestinian. He had not yet paid the price.

He looked towards Rafan. His brother was unusually silent. Salim saw his mouth was a thin line and his knuckles white on the wheel.

After a moment, Rafan said, 'You know that this is where we lived first, when we left Nazareth?'

Salim was astonished. 'In one of those houses?'

'In worse.'

She left us for that pit? Salim could not fathom it. How could Rafan have survived here at just eight years old, with all his thousand fears?

'But she's Lebanese.'

'She's Lebanese but she came without papers. Israeli passports are no good here. Someone had to bring her in, to fix it for her. So we waited here.'

'Who fixed it? Her family?'

Rafan shrugged. 'A running woman has no family. Someone. Some man.'

The telegram crushed in her palm. He remembered it, a yellow smudge against the dark sky above Nazareth. A name must have been hidden inside, a name worth leaving them for, worth waiting alone in a refugee camp while Salim wept for her, staring out northwards to the hills. *I hope it made you happy, Mama.* And yet last night she'd seemed alone still. Locked in a tower circled by marble and glass, like a captured queen from the old stories.

'Why did she do it?' He spoke aloud, and the sound surprised him. 'It makes no sense.'

'That's what I told her,' Rafan said, answering a different question. Behind the sunglasses his face was stone. 'God knows. Maybe she felt she had some debt to pay.'

The very next day, after a night in Leila's apartment, Rafan woke him up by shaking his shoulder. 'Good news, big brother,' he said, his unwashed face dark with bristle and his green eyes suavely gleaming again. Yesterday had been spat away with his toothpaste. 'We're on our way to Tripoli.'

Salim raised himself on his elbows, shaking off the fog of sleep. 'Why Tripoli?' But of course he already knew.

'Farouk wants you to come. He wants you to meet some people.'

'Brothers.'

Rafan shrugged. 'Brothers. Friends. Interesting people. And you get to see Tripoli. Okay, it's not as lively as here.' Salim saw a flash of Leila's dark hair and golden legs walking into the kitchen behind the open door. 'But it's worth seeing even so. Particularly for you.'

By the time Salim was dressed and in the kitchen, Leila's Turkish coffee was bubbling on the stove. She poured him a cup and rubbed her eyes. 'Have you ever been to Tripoli?' he asked her, sitting down at the table and swirling the thick liquid in its chipped golden cup. She shook her head. 'I'm not a *Filastiniya*,' she said. 'Although we support them here in West Beirut, not like the Christians.' She waved her hands. 'But those people Rafan sees – they're something else. Tripoli is a crazy place, for crazy religious people.'

This is a crazy place, he thought, but stirred his coffee silently. The bubbles went round and round, popping like his thoughts – this one the camps, this one Rafan's face as a child pale in sleep, this one his mother's cold eyes, this one Jude, always Jude and her faith in his dreams.

When Rafan came in, he kissed Leila and whispered something in her ear. She looked at Salim, and went out of the kitchen. Rafan came to sit next to his brother and pulled out a cigarette.

'You took me to meet Abu Ziad,' Salim said to his brother. 'And I already met Farouk. So, I guess they must have liked me. Or is it because I'm your brother?'

'They liked you. What's not to like? You're smart, educated. You speak English like a native. You have an *Angleezi* passport. You could do great things for them.'

'For us,' Salim said softly. Rafan smiled. 'For us, then. For our family.'

'So this Tripoli business, is for what? To see my new offices?'

Rafan laughed again. 'Something like that, yes. Just a conversation, for now.' He leaned forward and handed Salim a cigarette. Salim took it in and felt the heat inside him. Rafan tilted that attractive face of his to one side, just like a hungry bird. He looked at Salim through narrow eyes.

'Think about it, Salim. Why do you want to be an accountant? The *Angleezi* might give you a passport, but in the end they'll spit on you just like all the other Arabs and Indians and Africans they've fucked. You're too dark for their clubs.'

Salim pushed his coffee back across the table. 'You know nothing about my life, *little brother*.'

'I know enough to see you aren't being true to yourself. Israel, England – it's all the same. You're just Arabs working for a white boss.'

'You're wrong,' Salim said softly. All night he'd lain wrestling with it – two futures, one of them drawn by the brother sitting opposite him. But within, someone was whispering – *this is not the boy you knew*. The sweetness and the mischief were gone; somewhere between Nazareth and the camps and his mother's penthouse, Rafan had become something else.

'I had a life in England,' he said. 'I built it myself. Education, respect. Prospects.' *Love, too.* He thought of Jude. She'd loved him, and perhaps still did. A clean love, offering everything and expecting nothing in return. 'You're asking me to give that up, to help you.'

'You say you helped me when we were children, Salim,' Rafan said, getting to his feet. 'Now let me return the favour. Hassan is happy running his garage and humping his fat little wife. But Mama always said you had ambition. What we could do together – it's more than just revenge.' He tapped the table with one finger. 'It's up to you, big brother. All these years they kept us apart. Now you must decide where you belong – with them, or with me?'

He straightened up, and looked at his watch. 'I have to go and finish some business,' he said. 'I'm coming back at six. If you're with me, big brother, we'll go together.' He walked around the table, and Salim stood up as Rafan pulled him into a tight embrace. He heard the words brush against his ear: 'I'll see you later, *Insha'Allah.*' And then his brother was gone down the dark hall, and Salim heard the slam of the door.

After Rafan left, Salim washed his face, pulled on his clothes, said goodbye to Leila and walked out of the building.

The drab little flat was hidden in a maze of old streets that coiled away from the glitz and dazzle of central Beirut. He walked with the sun pounding on his head, like a hammer. By the time he came to the open sea, the sun had tilted into the western skies.

He looked up along the northern coastline, where the sea and land vanished together in the haze. Out there, the modern world waited. He imagined the shore racing up to Turkey and Greece, reaching the Riviera coasts of Europe. Behind him, the sea would sweep past Beirut, Tyre and Israel to the great deserts of North Africa. They really were at the crossroads of the world.

Where do I go from here? To Tripoli and the brothers? Did that road lead back to Jaffa one day? But Rafan had laughed at that idea. His brother neither had a home nor wanted one. He moved through Beirut's streets like sparks from a fire, consuming everything he came across.

Once Salim had thought home could only ever mean Jaffa. But when he closed his eyes he saw something unexpected: blue eyes, open arms and a sweet, frank face.

He pressed his hands over his eyes, trying to make sense of it all. The towering palm trees above him leaned out west, their green dates ripe for harvest and clustering thickly, and a trickle of sorrow ran through him. *I never took in my harvest. I left the fruit on the bough, and it probably rotted and fell.*

It was five o'clock. He hailed a taxi and drove to Hamra. His mother's apartment building was sleepy in the late afternoon; even the concierge was nodding off at his desk.

As he rang the doorbell his chest felt light, his heart weightless. She answered, in her dressing gown. Her face was bare and dull in the sticky evening light, and her forehead wrinkled in surprise.

Salim kissed her cheek and walked inside. She followed him slowly and stood at the top of the stairs, as if hoping he might leave again.

He turned towards her and took a breath. 'Mama, you never apologized to me. You left your son and never sent him a single word. Then I turn up here, and you don't say you're sorry. Nothing. Why? Do I mean so little to you?'

Her face hardened, and her chin went up in that old gesture of scorn. But he could see it now for what it was – guilt masquerading as defiance.

'I have finished apologizing – even to you, my clever son,' she said. 'I learned long ago – we are all alone in this world and we don't care about each other.' She moved to stand in front of him and he saw the loose skin around her mouth and eyes. 'Your father cared only for his pride. You cared only for the house. Rafan cares only for his games. The Jews for their flag, the Palestinians for their acres of dirt.' She threw her hands up in the air and clenched her fists. 'Should I be the only one? To care about the others, and sacrifice myself?'

In the background he could hear a turntable playing – a woman's voice filling the hollow space, echoing into dissonance between the marble walls. He took his mother's thin hand and held it hard when she tried to pull it away. 'Did you ever love us at all?' he asked. This time, there were no tears.

'How could I not?' she said. 'But love brings nothing to people like us. Our roads are set and there's no escape.' He saw her eyes laced with age; they looked through him in fury, the present accusing the past. 'I followed my road, and I don't ask for forgiveness. Now you go follow yours, as you must. Please, *ya'eini*. Run now, and stop wishing for things that could never have been.'

Run now. Salim left her apartment before sunset and took a taxi back to Leila's flat. He packed his clothes into a duffel bag and left Rafan a note. *I'm sorry, but my road is not here.*

The taxi to the airport took two hours and cost him the rest of his Lebanese pounds. He waited in the airport overnight for the first flight to London.

Arriving at Heathrow in the gentle light of a late summer's afternoon, he took the fastest train he could find into the city. The chill of autumn was far away. All around him, people were sitting back in their seats after a long day's work; he imagined them thinking of home and a sweet night to rest with their loves.

He reached her door as the sun was starting its earthward fall, dousing the evening air in thick, yellow light. His heart raced as he knocked. And when the door finally opened, he thought for a second his legs might give way.

Yet, faster than thought, her arms were around his neck and she was crying in his shoulder as he hugged her, held her to him so tightly and felt her heart through her shirt. She was saying, 'Whatever you wanted, I should have given it to you. I should have been brave, I should have taken you home.'

'No,' he said, taking her beautiful face and kissing it over and over. 'You're my home,' he said, through his own joyful tears. 'You're the only place I'm at peace.'

'Our families.' Her fists pressed against his chest, half clinging on, half pushing away. 'Those things you said…'

'I was wrong.' His forehead was against hers, his senses full of the smell of her – her salt skin, her hair, the warmth of her breath. 'Please. None of that matters any more. Nothing else matters, do you hear me? This is a miracle, what we've found.'

Her mouth was pressed to his, clumsily, and he spoke his promise to her lips. 'Jude. My Jude. I'll make you happy, I swear, my love. Whatever else comes, I swear it. I've come home now to you.'

3

RECKONING

He that troubles his own house shall inherit the winds, and the fool shall be servant to the wise.

DOUAY–RHEIMS BIBLE

Peace is more important than land.

ANWAR SADAT, TO THE ISRAELI KNESSET
AFTER THE YOM KIPPUR WAR

1976

KUWAIT

'Can I have an ice-cream? You said I could, remember? Not a lolly, a big *dahab* one, with nuts.'

By the seashore, the birds wheeled and circled in the gasping heat. The Kuwaiti sun was approaching its zenith in a roaring blaze and not a ghost of a breeze lifted from the oily water.

Jude fished in her pocket for change. *Even the coins are hot.* Once, she'd told Marc that their car at midday was hot enough to fry eggs on. The next hour, she had come outside to find him standing by the car bonnet, eggshell in hand, watching the hardening white drip slowly onto the melting tarmac.

'Wait a moment, pet,' she said. 'Daddy will be here soon.'

'Daddy doesn't like ice-cream,' said Sophie solemnly, leaning into the slim shade of her mother's skirt. Marc stood in front of her, feet planted apart. The light turned his hair an aching white and his skin transparent. Fierce blue eyes looked up at her and his lips pressed together in tight disapproval. 'But I want one *now*,' he said firmly. 'Before Daddy comes. He always says no.'

Jude silently willed Salim to hurry. He'd left the house this morning in his best suit and tie, eyes full of anxiety. Jude's heart went out to him, even though she desperately hoped his mission would fail. If he failed, then they could all go home.

She bent down and pinched Marc's chin. He was both old and young for his six years. Sophie, the elder twin, was her mother reprised in olive tones. Within her brown skin and almond eyes was a quiet, meticulous child, gentle and ready to love.

But Marc – goodness knows where Marc came from, Salim used to say. Salim had taken Marc's stubborn paleness to heart – almost as if it were a deliberate affront. Jude understood his incredulous annoyance. *Your Arab friends here were already suspicious of your blonde wife. And now they look at your white son and wonder – whose is he?*

Jude loved Marc's skin, but the feelings that bubbled inside it troubled her. Her little boy had a mind like a bird, full of fever and flight. He did not listen, he could not be still, soaring and plunging through feelings like the desperate gulls behind her skimming the Arabian Gulf.

'Be patient, pet,' she said. 'We have to wait here until Daddy comes to tell us about his job, remember?' Marc dropped his eyes and kicked the ground with his feet. Behind her, Jude heard Sophie shout, 'Daddy!' She pushed herself up, her heart leaping in her chest.

Salim was beaming, kneeling on the dusty ground, his arms open for Sophie as she ran into them. He pulled her up over one shoulder, where she giggled and kicked her legs.

Jude took Marc's hand and hurried towards him. He turned to her and kissed her hard and long on her upturned palm – the most he could legally do in Kuwait's puritan public spaces. 'It's okay, my love,' he said, his voice surging with new confidence. Over the past month, she'd been afraid his courage was leaving him. 'They agreed to give me a trial. For six months at least, we're safe. And if it works out – you're looking at the new Managing Director of Expansion for the Gulf Region.' He stood taller and slapped Sophie on the backside, making her squeal with laughter. 'What do you say to that, you pair of pickles?' he shouted to the children, ruffling Marc's hair.

What do I say? Jude squeezed his hand and smiled at him. 'I'm so proud of you, my love. You deserve it. I hope they're really sorry about what they did to you.'

Salim's face fell slightly, but then he shrugged.

'I suppose they did what they had to. The company has to think of its bottom line, and that division wasn't making so much money.' It was almost word for word what his American mentor had said when they'd let him go the month before.

Three years ago Jude would never have dreamed they'd be living in this empty desert. Their road in England had just started to smooth, the birth of their perfect twins reconciling doubters on both sides. Marc and Sophie had been wondrous, glorious affirmation of their courage. Those first days in the hospital Jude and Salim had been transfixed by them, these two unlikely beings clutching each other, their twined limbs formed by love.

Everything before had been so hard. Dora nearly had a heart attack when Jude told her of the engagement. It was Jack's actual heart attack that finally opened the door to tenuous acceptance. Dora stood grimacing at their tiny wedding at Chelsea Register Office as Tony gave her away, and Hassan loomed woodenly by Salim's side as best man.

Two years later, Salim came home with a strange look on his face. He'd sat on their white and brown spiral carpet and played with the twins, tickling their bellies to make them wriggle with joy.

Once the toddlers were in bed, he gave Jude the news that would set them all on an unknown course. A recruitment company had called to ask if he would consider relocating to Kuwait.

'Where?' was the first thing that Jude could find to say. Salim explained. Kuwait was a small desert nation on the shores of the

Arabian Gulf, sandwiched in between Iraq and Saudi Arabia. 'Small but very rich,' he said, 'and getting richer every day.' An American company was peddling new technologies to the sheiks in their rising business districts. And they wanted someone who knew the region. 'Although that just goes to show how much Americans know about Arabs,' he'd laughed. A Palestinian doesn't even speak the same language as the Kuwaitis.'

'So why go there?' Jude found herself holding on to the edge of the table, a lump in her throat. She'd been planning to return to her master's degree once the children turned three, taking all the old books out of the attic and putting them back on the shelf. 'How could *I* go there?'

He'd looked at her thoughtfully, but she could already see the fires of excitement in his eyes burning away reason. 'You don't look anything other than English,' he'd said. 'There are twice as many foreigners in Kuwait than Arabs – they'd never notice you. We wouldn't need to say anything, my love.'

'And what about you?' she'd countered – later, after his first interview had gone so well. On the sofa that evening, in his arms, she'd played her last card. 'You said you never wanted to go back. You wanted to be free of it, to be your own man.'

She remembered how he'd taken her hand and kissed it. There'd been tears in his eyes, but his voice was wild with happiness.

'Don't you see?' he'd said. 'That's the point of all of this. I have a British passport. I'm not a poor Palestinian any more, being pushed around. I'm British, a westerner. They'll *have* to respect me.' He was looking up at the white ceiling, smiling at the invisible future he saw gathering there. 'Just a few years, and we'll be rich, my love. We will never have to struggle again.'

And a few days later, Douglas Friend, Managing Director of Odell Enterprises Gulf Division, was buying them dinner at Le Gavroche.

She remembered – it had been the Jewish holy day of Yom Kippur in 'seventy-three. Bombs were once again falling around Israel; Arab forces were surging across the deserts and mountains towards Jerusalem. They were calling to take back their stolen lands and Jude despaired of knowing if they were right or wrong.

Salim had persuaded Jude to miss Uncle Alex's uptown breaking-of-the-fast to come with him instead. How could she refuse, when their peoples were killing each other half a world away? So she left the twins with a babysitter and ached for them throughout the meal. As they ate and Salim talked, she watched the pale orange candlelight stream through their empty champagne glasses, painting ghostly pictures on the mirrors behind their heads. Later that night, she took Salim's face in her hands and said, 'One condition, Sal. If we go, we don't change who we are. We protect this family. Even in an Arab country... I want the children to grow up with nothing to hide.'

They'd arrived at the time of the oil embargo that looked set to make Kuwait even richer. Now three years later – three years of diplomatic dinners, weekends at the Equestrian Club, cheap maids and aching loneliness for Jude – the dreams of wealth were slipping away.

That same Doug Friend, the one promising so much, took Salim into his office to tell him he was out of a job. The division he worked for would be shutting down, and Salim's contract would not be renewed. Salim had come home crushed, dazed – like the dockyardman Jude once saw knocked over by a swinging crane catching him from behind.

One thin branch of hope remained – a promise to put Salim forward for a trial position in another part of the company. The weight of Salim's anxiety had been crushing; he *had* to impress, or it was all over.

Now, with Sophie in one hand and Jude in the other, her husband stepped lightly as he led them into the restaurant beside the waterfront. Behind them stood the triple pillars of the new Kuwait

Towers. Their sea-blue globes were raised hundreds of feet into the sky, pierced by long white needles like rockets aimed at the heavens.

Marc was ordering his ice-cream, arguing with Sophie about whether the chocolate or the strawberry *dahab* cone was tastier.

Salim put his arm around Jude's waist. 'I'm so relieved,' he said in a low voice. 'But I know you must feel a little sad, my love. It's just for a while longer. A short while, to secure the rest of our lives.' She smiled up at him, loving him for his awkward attempt at reassurance.

Marc came up beside her and tugged on her arm. 'Mummy, can we go and buy the plants now? I waited all week.' It took a moment before she remembered it: the garden and Marc's obsession. It had started as a notion of their paper-skinned English headmistress; dreaming of cool summer roses under the Arabian sun, she decided to challenge the children to make English gardens at home. They'd each worked for a month, finding plants and flowers that would grow in the gasping air.

Marc's garden had been a fantastical and elaborate construction – flowers, stone towers and a spiral of wires taken from a hoard of trash outside the house.

But the very night before the class visited, Salim destroyed it by accident. Coming home late from the office, he'd stepped on it blindly in the near dark. She'd heard the thin sounds of Marc crying the next day, seen his small hands frantically repositioning his plot in the early morning glare.

The prize went to a girl whose mother had planted a circle of geraniums. Marc pushed all of his disappointment into a ball of belief that they could be persuaded to change their mind if only he could make his garden better.

'Let's take the children to the Friday market,' she said to Salim. 'We did promise Marc last week.'

Salim frowned, and looked at his son. 'Is this about the garden again?' She sensed irritation seeping around the corners of his words.

'It needs to be brighter,' Marc said, blue eyes staring fearlessly into brown. 'Dina's had lots of colours, and that's why she won.'

Salim shrugged. 'Sure, let's go. But this is the last time, Marc. I've had enough of the fuss around this garden. It's not like a man to cry about flowers.' He chucked Marc under the chin as he spoke.

Marc jerked his head away. *This one knows how to carry a grudge.* Jude suddenly thought back to Hassan's words to her, about Salim. *He can't let anything go. You'll see.*

The Friday Market was Kuwait's largest. Jude could always hear it before she saw it – a vast river of sound springing from a thousand throats, animal and human, conjuring camels and bronze pots, the shriek of dealers and beggars wailing. The market itself sprawled under the noonday sun like a disrobed woman with her entrails open in the heat. Flies crowded them as they walked through row upon row of people lying in the dirt, a legion of the armless, eyeless and legless. Hundreds of palms reached out to them as they passed. Those fingers tore into Jude's conscience until she felt blooded with guilt; every time she came, she dreaded it more. Her husband, though, had never given the beggars a second glance. Marc and Sophie, she saw with sadness, did not notice them either.

Under a low tarpaulin sheet ahead of them, the stench from the animal market rose off chokingly small cages. Sophie grabbed her mother's hand and pulled it as they walked past a box full of baby chicks popping over each other with soft cheeping sounds. Each one was dyed a startling pink, green or blue. She heard the tinny rattle of little claws batting against cages and the desperate screech of birds calling for the sky.

Sophie touched the bars as they passed. 'Mummy, can we take another one?' Jude shook her head and said, 'Sorry pet, you know what we said last time.' There was a limit to how many times a child could bring home an animal and wake up to find it dead the next morning.

Marc had raced ahead to a stall of trees and plant pots. He began pulling small tubs of bright, shrub-like flowers to one side. Then he pointed to a small, slender tree with sweet-smelling white blossoms. 'That one can go in the middle,' he said, brimming with excitement. 'The others can go round the edge.'

'The others, fine,' Salim said, coming to stand beside him and motioning the stallholder to put the pots on the back of a wheelbarrow shuttling backwards and forwards between the stall and the cars. 'But not the tree. It's a lime. They don't grow here, not in this heat. In one week it will be dead. He's trying to rob you.' He gave the stallholder a sarcastic smile, while the dark man flashed his yellow teeth back.

Marc shook his head. 'It won't die. I won't let it. I'll water it every day.'

Jude saw Salim wipe his forehead and then bend down to the boy. 'Listen, Marc. I was a farmer once. I know about citrus trees. I can tell you this isn't going to work. You should listen to me. Now don't cry,' he said hastily, as tears started to flow down Marc's cheeks. 'Oh come on now,' he said, straightening up in embarrassment. 'What is it? Shall I get you a bucket?'

Jude stepped up to the two of them. She had to fight the urge to hug Marc to her chest, knowing that it would inflame Salim. He would say *why can't you let him learn to be a man?* And she would answer *he's only six – he's hardly learned how to be a child.*

'What's the harm in taking this tree home?' she said. 'He'll learn something from it, even if it dies. You could help him look after it. It might be good for both of you.' She whispered this last to Salim, lightly pinching his arm.

Salim looked at them both, and then threw his hands up in defeat. 'You're too soft with him,' he said. She watched with sorrow and irritation as his hands found Sophie's head and rubbed her soft dark hair while Marc stood aside, his white arms crossed.

'Let's go home, us and all the plants,' she said, forcing a smile. 'Let's make the best garden in Kuwait.' She took Marc's hand in her own and reached for Salim with the other.

For a second Salim's face looked just as pained as Marc's. But then he rolled his eyes, paid the stallholder and followed his family back to the broiling car.

They planted the tree in the centre of Marc's garden, back at the villa. Long after Jude and Sophie had gone inside to make dinner, Salim saw Marc sitting on the steps outside the glass front door. The white sky had cooled to pink and violet, and the little lime tree fluttered in the rising night breeze.

The boy looked up as Salim came to sit beside him. Marc's eyes were red from the dust of planting. Around them, the hoarse song of the muezzin filled the dusk.

'Are you happy with your tree, then?' he asked his son. Marc nodded. Salim felt the boy's weariness drift over him, like a cloud of dust.

'Did you know that when I was a boy, I had a tree too?' The blond head shook slightly. 'My parents planted it when I was born, and I used to look after it and pick the fruit off it every year. You and I can do that together, if you want.'

Marc looked up again, eyes suddenly wide. 'Okay.' Then suddenly he slid along the stoop until he touched his father's leg. Salim put his arm around him, and they sat in silence, letting the sunset bleed through the air from the wasteland outside. He felt the wind pull through Marc's white hair, as insubstantial as thistledown. The boy's fingers were on his leg, clutching through the fabric. There was a weakness to him that terrified Salim. What chance would he have against the Mazens of this world?

Marc stirred, and he heard the small voice say, 'It's too hot to grow things here, you said.'

189

'That's right.' Salim's eyes were drawn to the garden, the wet dust and the lime tree planted with an anxious tilt. 'It's the desert here. Trees and fruit like that one need water and cool air. That's why I told you to leave it, *habibi*. So I don't want you to be disappointed when it dies. You have to learn to face facts.'

There was a pause while Salim watched Marc contemplating this truth. Then the boy squeezed his hands together and said, 'Things grow in England. I wish we lived there. Then my garden would be amazing.'

'But we live here, Marc. This is our home.' Above the surprise Salim felt something colder settling on him. 'You're an Arab too. You belong here, not there.'

'I wish I was there,' said Marc again. He got to his feet, turned around and went back into the house, leaving Salim alone in the gathering dark.

They spent the evening at a party in the desert, with friends and men who called themselves family. Kuwait was full of *family*, Palestinian *ay'an* who'd travelled to this honeypot where the black wealth oozed out of the ground for anyone to scoop up. Round their dinner tables and at their desert feasts, they'd talk about the brothers dying in Beirut and the camps. And then they'd sigh, wipe their hands and drive back to their villas with their jewelled wives and their plump children.

The family car pulled up in a valley between two high dunes – a place they called *Il-Saraj*, the Saddle. It was famous for its monthly rallies beloved by westerners and Kuwaitis alike. Salim's heart would swell as he filmed Sophie and Marc with his Super 8mm camera, their faces red with cheering from the height of the dunes, exhilarated by the echoing roar of engines and the squeal of tyres ripping up the ground into red strips of dust.

On this evening, the Saddle was quiet. High tent walls were

swaying slowly in the breeze of the valley floor. A goat and a sheep bleated sadly on the back of a pickup truck, their legs tied together. 'Oh no,' wailed Sophie, pressing her face to the car window as Salim turned off the engine. 'Are they going to kill them?'

'That's right,' her brother shot back. Salim could feel his feet kicking the back of the seat. 'They're going to pull their heads off and then we're going to eat them.' Sophie screamed, 'No, we won't, you're so horrible!' and started to cry.

Salim shook his head and left Jude to sort it out. As he closed the car door on their voices, he saw a bedou wrapped in a red-checked *keffiyeh* hoist the sheep onto his shoulders, and carry it slowly away towards the stake and the knife.

Inside the red-fringed tent, the burned smell of Turkish coffee lay thick on the men sprawling on their low cushions. Adnan Al-Khadra was in the corner; he saw Salim and waved him over. Drums drifted in, and the wailing of a fiddle as a bedou raised his thin voice to the sunset sky.

Adnan had been the first name on a list provided by Nadia for their arrival in Kuwait – more cousins of cousins, linked by a fragile trail of bloodlines to Abu Hassan and his long-dead first wife. He'd clapped Salim on the back, kissed him on both cheeks and called him *nephew*. Adnan honoured tradition by referring to Abu Hassan as *my brother* but his other habits screamed *modernist*: he liked to be called by his first name, and his youngest son – a keen gun of twenty-five – was a company man in Salim's new division at Odell.

Tonight he was cracking nuts with his teeth, in a finely tailored open-necked shirt and light linen trousers. His combed silver hair and deep black eyes made Salim think of a big, sleek American car.

'So tell me,' Adnan spat out a shell. 'Everything's good with you? You start work tomorrow, right?'

'*Insha'Allah*,' Salim replied. Adnan grinned. 'That's right, that's right! Never trust the *Americani* until you get your first paycheque.

They messed my Omar around on his salary like he was a dog begging for dinner. But now you and he will be working together. That's very good. He's a young man, still wild, you know? He needs someone with experience to show him how to ride the horse.'

Salim had heard it before. *Riding the horse* in Kuwait City meant clinging onto the mane of the American beast as it galloped through the Arab world. Adnan was saying: *look after my boy, he's one of your own.* He wasn't so modern that he expected his son to get by purely on his own skills.

Salim fantasized about telling Adnan he would happily pass his son's papers on to Human Resources. But the ropes of guilt and duty were wound too tight.

He nodded at Adnan. 'I'll be happy to keep my eye on Omar,' he said as courteously as he could. 'He seems talented enough.'

Adnan hooted with laughter. 'Talented! Yes, for sure he thinks he is. And what can his old father say? We're as useless as old cars to your generation, isn't that it? Let me tell you something. In your father's day and mine, people took different measures of a man. A successful man wasn't just rich – he was – how shall I say it?' He sucked the salt off his fingers and tapped his fist to his chest. 'Generous. He shared his money, his wisdom if he had any. Or even if he didn't! Your father was no genius, you know that. But he was generous in his way. He had an open hand. These days, it's all about how well you did in school, how smart you dress and how much you can cram onto your own plate. My son thinks he's a genius because I sent him to school in the States and the *Americani* gave him a job. He thinks that's all there is to life. And what about you, eh, Salim? Are you an old fellow or a new?' He beamed a white smile.

Jude came into the tent, her blonde hair glorious in the lamplight. A wave of cool air followed her in from the clear darkness outside. She smiled as she came up to him and his heart melted as it always did. Adnan rose to kiss her on the cheek. 'The lovely Jude. You look splendid. How are you, my lady?'

'Hot as the devil in this tent,' Jude said, with a smiling sideways glance at Salim. 'Why don't you all come outside? The children are playing round the fire and the women say they won't dance without an audience.'

'What are we waiting for, then?' Salim took her hand and followed his wife out of the tent. Night had come down like a knife, and the desert cold sliced into him. The fire played underneath the bodies of the sheep and goat, their fat dripping in faint sizzles onto the crackling wood. Inside the tent, bedouin had laid large oval plates of rice with vermicelli, balls of cracked wheat and spiced lamb, cabbage leaves cooked in yoghurt and fragrant salads of cucumber and parsley.

Salim sat down on a rug in the sand next to Adnan. A young man came rushing up out of the firelight, his face flushed, all the absurdity of youth in his tight t-shirt and gulping Adam's apple. *The famous Omar.* He bent to shake Salim's hand. 'Wow, Salim Al-Ishmaeli! Right? So good to see you again. I can't believe we'll be working together!' Enthusiasm blazed from every syllable. *Working under me, not with me.* Salim bit back the words as he returned the handshake.

The women had started dancing around the flames. Jude was among them; he saw her, the sequins in her skirt flying like sparks, her feet bare and her hair around her shoulders darkening to deep gold. The secret of her heritage – their secret – sometimes made him love her even more. It was a hidden part of herself, visible only to him – like those Kuwaiti wives in their long black shrouds filled with the seductive power of the unseen.

She'd tried her best to blend in, taking Arabic lessons and imitating Arabic dancing. But her feet betrayed her roots. She was a northern girl skipping under a cloudy blue sky, to the light rhythms of dockyard shanties. There was nothing of the swaying, sliding east in her. Perhaps that was why he'd wanted her so much.

Marc and Sophie joined her in the dance, their skin and hair turned to bronze against the fire. Sophie followed her mother, but Marc whirled and spun like the dervishes at Nabi Ruben. That was the last time Salim had seen his mother dance, on a night like this one in another world.

'Such beautiful children.' It was Adnan, beside him. 'You're blessed to get two at once.'

'I know I am,' Salim said quietly. He watched them dance around and around in the golden haze. Ashes from the blaze were falling. They brushed his cheek like tears. It was bewitching to see his family so apart from him; like visions on a screen, their radiant happiness vanishing like sparks from the fire into the night sky.

'Your wife is a brave woman to come here,' Adnan continued. Salim looked at him sharply. 'Why so?' he said.

The older man shifted, his eyes fixed on the dancing children. 'It's hard for a western woman to bring up Arabic children. In the Arab way, I mean. Look at your ones. They can't speak to my grandchildren in Arabic. They don't know the Qur'an.'

'Wait there, Adnan,' Salim said, trying to laugh. 'You can't tell me you know the Qur'an. I don't know it either – I went to Catholic school, remember?'

'But you learned it, Salim. We all did and we all do now. So what if you're a believer? Who cares? It's the thing we share. It's what binds us together in this divided world.'

'My children know their heritage,' Salim said. He tried to keep emotion out of his voice. 'They know where they come from.'

Adnan smiled and put his hand on Salim's shoulder. 'My son – you could be my son, you know – you forget something. Men don't raise children. Women do. What those children learn, what they take into their hearts, will come from her. That's why I say she's taken on a big challenge. I hope you can guide her with it, or your kids will be as much of an Arab as she is.'

194

Salim searched for a protest – but suddenly there were plates of rice and dripping meat in front of them, and Adnan was seizing the first eager mouthful as the children danced on and on.

The twins fell asleep in the back of the car on the way home. Salim looked at them, their closed eyes shadowed and pale under the hard brilliance of the street lights, their faces dark with soot. Fingers of unbearable love took his heart and squeezed it. Jude rested against the window, eyes half-closed.

'I want the children to have Arabic lessons,' he said suddenly. The words surprised him, racing ahead of his thoughts.

He saw her raise her head, startled out of sleepiness.

'All right,' she said slowly. 'They can join my lessons if you like. Or you could do it yourself?'

The thought of speaking Arabic to his children disturbed Salim in a way he could not explain.

'I'll teach them too, but you have to make sure they learn,' he said. 'I always listened to my mother more than my father. No reason ours should be any different.'

'All right,' Jude said again. But he could see she was puzzled. 'Why now, though? You never seemed to care much about it before.'

He struggled for an answer. The road reeled out ahead of him, a blur of neon. 'They're getting older. We don't know how long we'll be here. I want them to understand that they're Palestinians, before it's too late.'

Jude was sitting up now, and looking at him blankly. 'They're not just Palestinians, Sal,' she said, her voice steady over the hum of the engine. 'They have two cultures, yours and mine.'

Some people don't feel they belong anywhere. It had been his mother's warning, on the balcony in Nazareth before she ran. Her face floated in his memory, white as a ceramic glaze over an empty hole. *Not my children. Abadan. Never.*

'You can't live in two cultures any more than you can have two hearts,' he said to her. 'They have to know who they are.'

Her face was flushed now. 'This wasn't what we agreed. You said they would never be torn.'

'Never being torn means choosing one.' Salim was angry now. 'My family already lost everything else. What happens if even our children forget where they come from?'

Jude put her hand on his arm. 'We promised not to do this, remember?' she said, her voice urgent. 'We promised not to make it our fight.' He heard her anxiety, but something stronger than compassion had started to gallop inside him.

'Please, for me, arrange the Arabic lessons.' He pushed a plea into his voice. 'We can talk about the rest later.' Jude looked at him for a moment, puzzled, as if seeing a stranger. Then she turned away, pressing her forehead to the window again. He did not challenge her. *She will do it.* He knew his wife, the loving girl, the peacemaker. As the blue lights flashed through the window, he glanced at the children through the rearview mirror. They looked eerie, still, like bodies pulled cold out of the sea. And to his surprise, he saw Marc's eyes open, unfocused, two small mirrors reflecting the flickering lights of the road.

The Vice President of Odell Enterprises, Expansion and Strategy Division, had skyline offices in Kuwait City. They looked out over the hot and heaving markets to the windy Gulf waters and the distant rigs. The air in the room was dry as a desert-bleached bone, and Salim felt it pouring into his throat like sand.

Here he was, lifted above the clamouring Arab heap – but even standing in front of Meyer's secretary this morning he'd felt as if the privilege might be snatched back at any time. Her black hair was curled laboriously around her shoulders and her eyes were suspicious. He thought she might be from Jordan or Palestine, and that in his new suit and confident stride he might be deemed worth a sisterly smile. But her red lips pursed like the bruise in an over-ripe apple. *Hey habibti*, he thought. *Aren't I white enough for you to show me those teeth?*

'Can I help you?' she'd asked coolly. Her neck craned in the most peculiar way – as if to indicate that, although she had no intention of standing up, she was still capable of looking down on him.

Now he was sitting in the Vice President's suite, and Meyer was indeed looking down at him from the corner of his desk.

'So that's where we are, Sal,' he was saying. 'Expansion is always a gamble, but that's what we're here for. Nothing ventured, nothing gained.'

Meyer had a lean patrician face on a heavy-shouldered boxer's body. His first words to Salim that morning had been, 'Hey, Sal. Heard great things, man. No – please, forget the mister. John's fine.' It reminded Salim of what Doug Friend said to him, at the letting go last month. 'Johnny's a good guy. He'll give you a shot and before you know it you'll be on your way up again.'

Meyer went on now. 'I know Doug gave you the basic lowdown on this Baghdad gig, but you have to know, I think it's the biggest thing in construction right now. We need to nail that contract, before the others roll in.' He waggled his fingers in a walking gesture, and Salim imagined hordes of white men with briefcases marching across the Iraqi desert. 'I envy you, seriously, I do. Baghdad is insane. What a place to visit. You're going to have a crazy few months.'

'I'm absolutely ready,' Salim said, brushing his palms on his suit trousers. 'I know how to deal with the Iraqis. I was on Doug's team handling their visit here last year.'

'He said you did a good job on that one.' Meyer took two cigarettes out of a silver box on the table and tossed one to Salim. As he pulled in the smoke he caught a glimpse of the sea behind the American's head, a foamy sweep of grey and white under the noonday haze.

'You can pick your own team,' Meyer said. 'You'll need someone who knows the tech side, how our teams and the local outfits might work together. You need a marketing man and a project assistant. I can give you a few names – or maybe you have some people in mind?'

Salim thought of Omar and his promise to Adnan. 'I might, but I'd be happy to have names as well.' Meyer nodded.

'The expansion business is never the easy place to be, Sal. This market was like a virgin bride a few years ago. Now it's an expensive whore and every man with a dick is queueing up. We're not the only people talking to the Al-Sabahs, the Al-Sauds, the Husseins… you know what I mean? We have to be faster and quicker to keep our market share. Hussein is a big dreamer. He wants Baghdad to be the next Cairo. Okay, so let's help him build it. And if we do a good job, if we nail it, then this temporary position could turn into something a little less temporary.'

Salim stood up and shook the hand held out to him. Behind Meyer's head, the gulls were wheeling and shrieking over the limitless sea. Something inside Salim soared with them, and he clasped Meyer's cushioned palm fiercely. The gold souk was just next door. If he finished early, he could find earrings for Jude, to go with the Arabic necklace she had taken to wearing in place of her grandmother's chain.

As they were walking out of the door together, Meyer said, 'Hey, just wondering – Sal – that sounds like an Italian name. But you're from this neck of the woods, aren't you?'

'Not exactly from here,' Salim said, cautiously. 'I'm Palestinian. From Israel, maybe you would say.'

'Right, right.' Meyer looked at him curiously. 'And your real name is…'

'Salim.' He hadn't been called that even once in his working life, and he hoped he wasn't about to start now.

'Salim.' Meyer pronounced it *Sleem*, in a beautiful drawl that Salim had to stop himself from unconsciously imitating. 'Slim,' he said again, laughing. 'That's what they should call you, you're so god-damn skinny. I wish I had your metabolism.'

'Squash three times a week,' Salim smiled. 'And my wife can't cook.' Meyer laughed out loud, the ease of a man whose voice is the most important in earshot.

'Okay, Slim,' he said. 'It's better than *Sal*, anyway. That one makes you sound like a gangster – at least, where I come from.'

Salim thought for a second to ask him if he was Jewish. Meyer was just that kind of name. Then Salim could share the secret of his Jewish wife, and their families would be friends... and who knows where it would lead? But before he could decide Meyer leapt away to corner another company director, and Salim was following the assistant's heaving backside to his new offices.

Meyer was as good as his word, leaving the names of several project assistants, managers and technicians for Salim to review. His team selection was critical. The Iraqis wanted someone to fill their skies with modern steel; a winning bid would be worth millions to Odell, and more, so much more, to Salim.

As he sat night after night, making lists and interviewing candidates, he sometimes found himself wondering at how earnest these Americans were, how disturbingly professional. *We should just go with a few cases of single malt, some beautiful women and an offer to refund a portion of their payments into their Swiss accounts.* He joked about it later to Meyer, who just fixed him with his grey eyes and said, 'If that's what it takes.'

But the fly in the ointment was Omar. He made good on his father's hints during Ramadan, while everyone else in the office was fading away with pious hunger.

Salim had no interest in going all day without food and drink, particularly not while temperatures outside soared to fifty degrees. 'Does God really care what you have for breakfast?' he'd said to Jude.

Even so, he felt a tinge of sympathy for the fainting fasters at work, and tried his best to hide his afternoon snacks from them.

Not so Omar. He was determined to be a sleek young racehorse, not an old donkey dragging a cart full of religious obligations. He came into Salim's office that day, holding two big Pepsis and a chicken sandwich from the kitchen. 'What are you doing?' Salim asked him, pushing the door shut.

'Sorry!' Omar said, genuinely surprised. 'I thought you'd be hungry. I didn't see you go for lunch. It's okay,' he said, jerking his head back towards the office conspiratorially. 'They know you don't fast. You don't have to care, anyway – Boss! Right?' He sat down at the desk and began to chew on his sandwich, crumbs dabbling his neat pink shirt collar.

It turned out that Omar wanted to talk about the Baghdad project. 'It's going to be an amazing experience,' he said. 'The biggest expansion we've had. I hope one day I get to do what you do. It's so great. How many trips do you think we'll have to do, before it's done? Two or three? They're tough, the Iraqis. I've dealt with them before.'

Salim watched Omar talk with a kind of weary envy. He even sounded like Meyer, a younger version forged in Jordan and America, in marble rooms and private schools. When he talked to Salim about the struggle and his ancestry, it was like Marc or Sophie drawing stick figures in primary colours – images without meaning, fire without heat.

'Omar, you know I haven't chosen my team yet,' he said. 'I have to get approval for every name. I want to take you, but I just can't be sure.'

Omar looked up at him, shocked. 'Why not? I'm very well qualified. I'm the best project assistant on the floor. I'm even an engineer – I can help the technical team. Why on earth wouldn't you pick me?'

Salim wanted to shake him, to drive some understanding into that suave, unlined face. 'It's not about your skills. You're very good, I know – but so are many others. I have to justify every choice, Omar. I can't just pick my friends straight out of the hat. What would it look like?'

Omar put down his Pepsi, resentment in his long-lashed eyes. 'Of course, you have to make the right choice for the team, I understand. But I'm very well qualified,' he repeated. 'No one could blame you for choosing a well-qualified Arab for the job, just like when you got your break.'

Salim flushed. He remembered all those dark hours in London, rising before the sun to sweep the floor in Hassan's garage and studying late into the night after coming off bar shifts. Slipping out of Jude's warm bed in the cold light, to trek into the office and be patronized by wealthy English boys younger than this one.

'I decide who's qualified,' he said coldly. 'There's nothing more to say about it until I've made my review.' Omar's hopeful smile faded and his face fell. For the first time, Salim saw the genuine upset behind the display of petulance. *If we don't help each other, we're nothing.*

'Look. I know you're a brother.' He found himself saying the word, just as Rafan had said it of Farouk so long ago. 'I'll do what I can. Just trust me.'

'I trust you,' Omar said, and that was the end of it.

'Why, why, why can't they just leave me?' he said later to Jude, slumped into the sofa while the children slept. 'Everywhere I go, all these expectations and demands. My life isn't my own – I have to give a piece to Nadia, and a piece to Hassan, to this distant relative, on and on and on. It's like being sucked dry every day.'

He felt Jude run her hand over his neck and her cool palm cover his eyes. He breathed in the smell of her, a soft saltiness like baked bread or sea air.

'Maybe it's not what you think, Sal,' he heard her say. 'Some of these people really love you. Maybe they're just trying to keep you close.'

Salim laughed. 'Omar doesn't love me. He's not my family, not for all of Adnan's bullshit about sharing blood.' He shook his head. 'A mosquito shares my blood, but I don't have to call it *cousin*. And he'll love me less if I don't deliver this thing for him. Wait and see.'

After an autumn and winter of laborious preparation, Salim took his proposal for the bid structure and the Baghdad project team into Meyer's office.

The big visit to the Iraqi capital was set for early spring. The team would make an initial presentation; if it went well, it would secure the Iraqi go-ahead to make a preferential bid for the contract of technical supplier to their construction projects. Within weeks, a fortune might change hands to see Odell lifts in every new Iraqi government-financed building for a decade to come. Or the prize – and Salim's new job – could go to someone else.

He'd lain awake the previous night, hallucinations of failure dancing across the ceiling. In the dead pre-morning hours, Mazen's face had bloomed from the dark ceiling. His black hair had curled tightly around his plump head and his eyes were vicious and merry. *Salim, you donkey*, his voice said, before fading away into the dawn.

In Meyer's air-conditioned office, the chill helped him focus. He outlined his choices one by one. He knew they were all smart. It was a balanced team, and it included nearly all of Meyer's personal recommendations. Nearly all. He had sweated about this too. Choose them all, and he might look like he had no mind of his own. Choose too few, and he would be a rebel, a cowboy. Leave out the wrong one, and he'd be the man who couldn't take a hint.

Meyer sat down and listened courteously. When Salim's pitch ended, he picked the carefully prepared files and leafed through them slowly. Salim's palms moistened and he wiped them unconsciously on his trousers.

'I think you have it here, Slim,' Meyer said at last. 'It's a nice balance. These guys from tech look very impressive. I can't believe they weren't on my radar.'

'They were on Doug's team and they were fantastic on the Qatar project,' Salim said quickly. 'They lost their jobs in the closedown, but I guarantee they can deliver more on this team than anyone else. Not that the team here isn't great, but I thought why lose a skillset this strong to a competitor?'

Meyer smiled. 'Smart, *and* a humanitarian! I love it when we can cover both bases. I'm excited about this.' Relief was flooding Salim.

Meyer turned over another page. 'I see you passed on Eric for the project assistant position.'

'It was very tight. Eric is an excellent planner and I know he's been on the team here for a while.'

'So he has.' Meyer's hand was poised over the page. Salim prayed he would move on to the next section, but the hand hovered there, a platinum wedding ring glinting against a ridge of thick knuckles and a light brush of silver hair.

'I thought that Omar Al-Khadra was a more rounded choice,' Salim said at last, drawn to plunge into the gulf of silence. 'He's an engineer by training. It would be an excellent way to improve liaison with the tech team. He is pretty familiar with Baghdad. You've always given him great performance reviews.' He paused.

Meyer turned the page. 'It's your call of course,' he said. 'But maybe there are a couple of things worth considering, if I might be so bold. This is a very delicate project. There are other Arab teams going in there, I'm sure. Everyone wants to look like a local – local knowledge, local relationships – and so on.' He sat back in his chair and regarded Salim, his heavy body surging up into the long neck and the grey, patrician face.

'See – the thing is, local doesn't really swing it. These guys want us because we're an international, an *American* firm bringing that kind of expertise. And glamour, sorry to say it. That's what they like, even if they don't know it themselves. You know what I mean?' Salim nodded. 'It's pretty unusual for us to have a local man running the team, as I guess you know.'

'I'm British.'

'Sure, I know. But, the question is, does it work against us in the long run to have a local guy doing the liaison too? Does it undermine the subliminal messaging? Nothing against Omar, nothing at all. But do you see my point?'

It's a shitty, unfair point. 'I do, for sure,' Salim said carefully. 'I'll think about it. Rethink, if necessary.'

'That's all I ask.' Meyer leaned over and shook Salim's hand. 'You did great on this. Look forward to the next update on the trip.'

When Salim walked through the door that night, he heard the children shouting in the bedroom. Unusually, the television was on in the family room. He saw Jude in there, pale in the gloom, sitting as the images flickered over her face. She stood up hastily as he came in and shut off the set.

'What's the matter?' he asked, as she walked over to kiss him. 'Nothing,' she replied, but her eyes were guilty. 'The twins are going crazy, I just needed a break. I'm making chicken for dinner.' He watched her slip past him, into the orange-tiled kitchen. Marc came tumbling down the hall shouting 'Mummy!' at the top of his lungs, stopping dead when he saw Salim.

'You came home early,' he said. 'Are you cross?'

Salim shook his head. He did not have the energy for Marc tonight. 'What kind of a question is that, Marc? Who told you I'm cross? I'm not cross.'

'Mummy says you're cross sometimes, when you come home from the office.'

Sophie had joined him, and at that she elbowed him in the chest and whispered, 'Marc, shush.' Salim felt a revitalizing rush of bitterness. *Even here in my own home, I'm misunderstood.*

He walked away from the children, into the family room with the television and the drawn blinds. He flicked the set back on and sat down to watch the news. In the kitchen, Jude was clattering the pans with unnecessary energy, just like her mother the one time they'd met for dinner before their awkward London marriage.

The set came on in a blaze of crackling gunfire and screams. It took a moment for his eyes to adjust, but then he recognized the place – a town in the Galilee, not far from Nadia's flat. The camera panned over a restless, surging mass of people, young men with dark faces. They had sticks in their hands, and they were shouting *Ardna! Damna!* Salim felt their voices go right through him. Our land! Our blood! Tanks were jerking along the rough roads to the villages in lower Galilee, as men in jeans and *keffiyaat* charged rows of young Israeli soldiers.

The commentator's voice rolled over the scenes – an English voice filled with Arab emotions striking Salim strangely. The Israelis were seizing new holdings of Arab land around Nazareth. They cut to the Israeli Prime Minister, Yitzhak Rabin, talking about Israel's need for security and new settlement. And then there was a fuzzy video of a man – some poet, called Ziad – calling on Palestinians to stand up and revolt. *Ziad – like the man in Shatila.* They'd declared a national strike and called it Land Day. *Yom Al-Ard.*

The commentary moved onto tensions in Iran, and Salim flicked it off. He had to face Omar in the morning, to give him the bad news. Now he felt dirty, as dirty as a traitor, sick of the whole thing.

In the kitchen, Jude, Sophie and Marc were already at the table. Sophie was attacking a chicken leg with both hands and Marc was peeling the flesh off the bone and arranging it on his plate in a neat circle. In the corner Sophie's birdcage rattled as its wounded inhabitants, rescued from cats and car windscreens, clambered nervously along the bars.

Jude looked up as he came in. He recognized the expression of unhappy defiance. Salim's senses were still surging on the bitter flood of memory; she looked more than ever like Lili Yashuv, standing behind her husband at the gates of their house. Jude and Lili – their two images overlaid like two transparencies, coming together in striking clarity in the lines of their long noses, their high foreheads and blue eyes.

He pulled up a chair and took a plate of rice from her hands. Shovelling it into his mouth despite his closed stomach, he tried to push the anger away. *I'm British*, he had pathetically pleaded to Meyer that afternoon. Pleaded like a boy, while more of his true home was being leached away by men like Meyer, women like Jude.

'Was it okay at work today?' Jude was asking. 'Was Meyer pleased?'

'Mostly.' He looked over at Marc, who was steadily looking back at him from over a large, flayed chicken leg. 'What about you, Marc? Did you have your Arabic lesson today?'

'It was yesterday,' Sophie said cheerfully. 'Mr Shakir came to the house.'

Salim kept looking at Marc. How could he have such blue eyes? The child who would take his name forward had nothing of his nature. It was so unfair, as if Jude's genes and his mother's had conspired to remind him that he had no real power, nothing left worth passing on.

'What did you learn in your lesson then?' he asked the boy. Marc's eyes flickered back down to his plate.

'We learned how to name all the animals.'

'Really? So you can tell me what you're eating for dinner.' Marc's brow furrowed as he examined his deconstructed chicken. Looking back up at his father, the blue eyes were ruffled with a hint of worry. 'I forgot,' he said.

'*I* know!' Sophie squealed, but Salim put his hand up to silence her.

'I asked Marc. Come on, Marc. Try to remember.'

'I forgot, I told you.'

'That's not good enough. It was only yesterday you learned it. You can't really have forgotten, can you? Weren't you listening in the first place?'

Marc looked at his mother for reassurance, but that sidelong glance infuriated Salim. He hit the table with his hand, and Marc's eyes snapped back to him, his body jerking in shock. Jude said, 'Sal, please, don't.'

'Stay out of this,' he said heatedly. 'They're supposed to be learning and *you're* supposed to be helping them. So Marc, tell me something in Arabic. Tell me anything, so I can see that you're taking this seriously, like a little man. Come on.' He leaned over and pulled Marc's plate from his hands, to leave nothing between the boy and him.

Marc started to cry in that painful way he had, his lip wobbling like a girl's and tears trickling down his nose. Salim saw Jude's face – it was white. 'Sal, for God's sake, enough,' she said, her voice low. Something inside him reached out of the blaze of anger and self-pity to comfort her, to apologize. But the image of those Israeli tanks rolled over it, slamming it down.

'If you had done your job, he wouldn't be so fragile,' he heard himself saying. 'But I guess you don't want him to be like one of these crazy Arabs, right?'

He could see Sophie starting to cry now, her dark almond eyes swimming. *Where do these terrible words come from? What kind of man are you?* Angry with them all, horrified at himself, he got up from the table and went into the bedroom. As he shut the door, he felt the comfort of silence slide over him, blanketing the maelstrom within.

Meyer's wife invited them to the beach that weekend. Jude arrived with a warm smile and all the essential facts ready for new friendships:

Mrs Meyer's name was Anne; she was secretary of the International Women's Club and had three grown children all doing something in New York.

Out on the blazing sands of the Creek, Anne Meyer gave her a fainting handshake from under a drooping sunhat, a butterfly exhausted in the shimmering air. She complimented Jude's 'sweet kids', and complained about the 'god-awful heat'. Then she turned away to her other guests.

Sophie ran off to join the mêlée of sandy little bodies at the edge of the water. 'Be careful, pet,' Jude called out, but her daughter just waved her arm, a brown glimmer of delight. Marc lay down under the umbrella, tracing stick figures in the sand. Out in the haze a tiny sandbank lay white against the blue. *Not more than a hundred yards away*, she thought. *Once I would have swum there without thinking*.

The rush of the water and the children brought back distant echoes of memory, the clamour of Wearside, the Junior Team Tryouts, the brightness of those friendships. *Another life, another road not taken*. She hugged her knees to her chest against the sudden ache, and turned to Salim.

He stood tall above her with the Super 8 camera in his hand, trained on Sophie's leaping form. As their eyes met he knelt down, his body brown as the darkening sand, and slid a hand onto her shoulder. Since that inexplicable fight he'd been contrite and defiant by turn. The pressure of the bid – that's all it was, she told herself. So much pressure on him to prove everyone wrong, to succeed in their hare-brained venture.

'Okay, my love?' She saw the concern in his eyes, and it moved her – these precious reminders that they were still uniquely attuned to each other, that each soul could still resonate with the other's needs.

'Perfect.' She smiled up at him and pointed to the shoreline. 'Look at our Sophie.' Their daughter was skipping with another nameless girl, splashing joyously across the warm sand. 'She's never afraid, is she?'

'Just like her mother,' Salim said, squeezing Jude's shoulder. Inexplicable tears rose to her eyes. Beside her, the sound of Marc's humming mixed with the rush of the waves. It washed old memories over her – rain soaking her forehead when Salim had first kissed her, the flood of her waters breaking and the perfect emptiness of her being when Marc was finally dragged out of her body, hours after Sophie slipped into the doctor's hands. Salim had rejoiced in his son and daughter, taking them from the bassinet and holding them up to the light, his face shining in pure happiness.

Even their names had been precious, a flag in the earth, staking their claim to their own choices. They named Sophie after Safiya, the Prophet's fiery Jewish wife who converted a nation of doubters. Marc's name had been harder to choose. Tradition would force *Saeed* on them, after Salim's father. But they'd buried it behind Marc – in memory of the unknown grandfather who saved Rebecca's life. They were so cherished, those secret truths hidden inside their children, linking their old lives to this new one they were building together.

'Did you talk to Anne?' Salim's eyes were fixed on Meyer's friends, handing out Pepsis under a large umbrella.

Jude forced herself back to the present. 'A little.'

'I really hope you can be friends. Tell you what, I'll get you a drink,' he said, standing up and strolling over to the coolbox.

She watched him, two Pepsis in hand, hovering outside the knot of laughing men. His face was fixed in happy attention, betraying the strain of matching them smile for smile as they ignored him.

Over on the other side of the beach, a large Arab family sprawled out on mats, the scent of cardamom tea drifting on the rising breeze. Every now and again Salim's eyes would be drawn to them. She knew what he was feeling, the unspoken question, the search for a ready embrace.

She left Marc and went over to stand by him, lifting her Pepsi out of his hand. His dark eyes found hers; she saw he was embarrassed. In answer, she called over to Anne, lying in a low deckchair reading a magazine. 'Hi Anne – can I get you something?'

'No thanks.' Only the thin hand moved, a restless fanning of super-heated air. Salim tried again. 'Anne, you know you and Jude are both into teaching? Jude's going to work at the Kuwait International School – she was doing her master's in literature before we came here. I hear you did some teaching too.'

Mrs Meyer made a noise from her throat, halfway between agreement and dismissal. Her head settled back as if to sleep. Salim stood waiting with his Pepsi. His stance was hopeful, poised for an answer, and Jude tasted a raw hatred. *You scrawny bitch.* She wondered where Peggy was now, which beach she was lying on, whose shoulder her pale pink nails were gripping.

Twisting away from Salim, she marched over to the shoreline, fixing her gaze on the sandbank. A lonely gull had landed on the brilliant white, the image of remote perfection. Her fury turned to Salim – these repeated humiliations were his fault, the price of his endless thirst for acceptance. She'd given up her country for him, locked her family's traditions away in the box with Rebecca's menorah, but her love alone didn't satisfy him. A jealous part of her wanted him to run, to throw rejection back in their laughing faces – but would that be any better? Had it made her happy, running from her own humiliation once, leaving all her dreams at Peggy's front door? *I was the best, the best in my year. I should have made the team.*

She stepped out into the water, feeling it stroke her. The salty warmth was far from the cool, green smell of Wearside – but she could imagine Mr Hicks yelling at her, 'Go Judith! Go on, go!' She wanted to stand on that sandbank and look at them all from far away. She wanted to be a girl again, with everything still before her.

The sea was gentle, cooling above the steep drop-off, the waves calm. Her arms slipped through it. As she kicked she felt the glorious, familiar stretch of her body, the ache of muscles long disused, the exultation of resistance and speed.

Halfway across, the current grabbed her.

At first it was a tug at her legs. Then she saw the sandbank slipping away, sliding suddenly to the right.

Now the water gripped her; her arms grappled to make headway. She fought, incredulous, instinct commanding her to *try harder*. Her legs and arms beat the water – but soon her kicks turned to flails as the strength leaked out of her into the running sea.

I can make it. But she no longer knew where the sandbank was and the sun was burning into her head. She was being carried faster now, a forced surrender to the power of the rip.

Swim diagonally. The thought filled her brain. But the swell was on her now, walls of water on all sides. Water was in her mouth and she breathed it into her lungs. She couldn't get enough oxygen, she had to get to land – she lunged out towards nothing and then she was submerged, directionless, her arms weaker, moving in frantic circles.

For a moment she rose, to see the children in sharp relief on the shoreline, like pictures from a book, a girl with her arm pointing outwards laughing or calling.

Then someone else's arms were around her. They raised her head, and she felt them anchor her. The shoreline was there, an unimaginably small distance to safety. And as she put her hand on the man's chest to steady herself, she felt Salim's heart pounding with her own as he pulled them towards the beach.

They were out of the water and she fell on her knees in the sand. He fell next to her, dripping, his arms tight around her. He was crying the words, almost incoherent: 'What were you doing, what were you thinking?' Marc was there too, he clung to their legs and

Sophie pressed between them, a tangle of limbs, of sand-streaked faces and hot tears.

She tried to reach out to them but her arms didn't belong to her any more. And theirs were all around her, safer and stronger than her own. 'I'm so sorry,' was all she could whisper into Salim's shoulder, his sweat sharp in her mouth.

'Doesn't matter,' he choked, as they clung together, fused into one being. 'We're all here now. We're safe.' The words rose around her with the beat of the waves, drowning out everything else. *We're all here now. We're safe, we're safe, we're safe.*

Everything changed a week before the Baghdad trip.

First, Marc's tree died. Lingering just a few months through the cooler Kuwaiti winter, it finally gave up, its light green leaves curling into yellowed scraps and drifting helplessly to the ground. Salim wanted to dig it up, but Marc wept at the suggestion. In the end Sophie set stones around the base of the thin trunk, giving it an ominous aspect. To Salim it was a hateful object as he left the house every morning, something between a shrine and a grave.

On the day they booked the Baghdad tickets, Eric came into Salim's office. Meyer's selection for project assistant was paler than usual, his forehead creased in a puzzled frown.

'What's up?' Salim asked. Eric had bright red hair, allergy-wet eyes and a nose that looked like it was dripping off his face. Meyer's secretary said he was like the fire and the hosepipe in one body.

'A call is coming through to this phone,' he said, significantly, pointing to the handset on Salim's desk. 'I think you should hear it yourself.'

Salim picked up the phone and pushed the flashing red button that indicated a call on hold. The line instantly began to crackle. 'Hello?' he shouted into the long-distance buzzing.

'Mr Al-Ishmaeli, *schlonak!*' An Iraqi greeting from Abdel-Rahman, their man on the ground in Baghdad. 'I wanted to tell you something I heard today, it's very important.' The line screeched and Salim held the phone away from his ear. It had been the siren of a car. Abdel-Rahman had clearly thought it wiser to call from a street phone.

'What is it?' He spoke in English for Eric's benefit.

'I went to the Al-Rashid, to check our bookings,' Abdel shouted. The Al-Rashid was one of Baghdad's most prestigious hotels, close to the Presidential Palaces. 'I wanted to take one room a few days early, for preparation, you know. But the girl at the desk told me no. They have another group coming, some Americans from Bahrain. I got her to show me the name. It's Curran, *habibi*. The men are coming from Curran to Iraq, in three days' time. I called the Minister's office and it's true. That bastard, that *kahlet*, he got ahead of us. Curran will negotiate with the Minister, pay his bribes, get the deal and you will come here in time for a handshake and goodbye.'

Salim felt dizzy. 'Are you sure?'

'Sure, *habibi*, sure. They screwed us. What do you want to do?'

I have no idea. 'I'll call you back in ten minutes, Aboudy. Give me the number you're on, and stay there.'

As he hung up, he looked at Eric, wondering what the young man saw. Another failed Arab leader, no doubt. The world was full enough of them.

'Should we tell Meyer?' Eric asked him, hugging his thin arms around his chest.

God, no. 'Not yet,' Salim said. 'Just give me five minutes.' Eric nodded, and walked slowly out of the door. Salim was left to himself.

Panic raced through him, carrying bitter thoughts. They had not been careful enough – they had got the timing wrong, and someone else would get there first. He would be the man who presided over a disaster, a corporate humiliation.

He stood up and walked over to the window, looking out onto the haze of the city and the long, empty desert beyond. Light glinted off the limousines sliding through the streets below. They reminded him of silver fish, circling above the desert's waiting maw, just a finger's width from oblivion.

A picture of Jude and the children sat on the shelf beside him. Her hair caught his eye, and a memory stirred – the Yiddish phrase she liked to use – *be a mensch*. Be bold. It was fine for her to say, and Meyer. They were born to be masters. The rules worked for them, so they never had to find the backhand way.

And that's when he saw it, clear as the noonday sun, the glint of a hidden road. Meyer would never get it, but any Arab would instantly understand. It was the only possible way.

He walked across the floor to Eric's desk, heart pumping with every step. 'Listen,' he said, throwing Abdel-Rahman's phone number at him. 'I want you to call him back and get every single room in Al-Rashid for tomorrow night. We are going to meet the Minister in Baghdad. Book the flights and tell the team.'

Eric went grey under his freckles, and a drop of sweat trickled off the end of his nose.

'There's no way… I mean, we are so far from being ready. And we haven't even got an appointment with Ramadan. It sounded like they have no interest in seeing us.'

'So what?' Salim said, feeling a glorious wave of superior knowledge for the first time on this project. 'Was your girlfriend interested in seeing you, the first time you met? My wife certainly wasn't. Between now and tomorrow, I'll make them interested.'

He left Eric and walked over to the furthest part of the floor. To his relief, Omar was at his desk.

The young man had hardly spoken a word to him after learning of Salim's decision. Adnan had met Salim at a dinner a week later and the coolness could not have been clearer. He was polite enough, the old man, shaking his head and saying, 'It's a shame that you and

Omar couldn't have been working together.' And later he'd patted Salim on the arm when they were talking about politics or travel, and said, 'We have to watch our backs with these *Americani*, right, Salim? You think they're your friends, you sell yourself, but they will remember who you are in the end.'

Omar's eyes widened as he saw Salim coming. 'Salim! This is a surprise. Are you well?'

'Not the best, to tell you the truth.' Salim sat down on the corner of Omar's desk. 'When you went to Baghdad last time, you hung out with that singer – what's her name?'

'Hanan.'

'That's right. You said she was a close friend of Ramadan.' Taha Ramadan was the Minister of Industry in Iraq – the man who'd promised so much and was now poised to deliver it all into other hands.

'She is,' Omar replied, looking completely lost. 'So what?'

'So I need you to get on the phone to her now,' Salim said. 'I don't care how. She needs to give me Taha's private number. I have to speak to him today, or this entire project is dead.' He saw Omar's face harden.

'I see,' he said sarcastically. 'So now I can do something for you, Salim, for your future.'

Salim shook his head, trying to stay ahead of desperation. 'I can't change what happened,' he said, 'but if this works, Omar, I will personally walk you into Meyer's office and tell him you saved us.' He saw Omar's struggle, the fight between ambition, shame and resentment that he knew so well. When Omar's hand twitched towards the phone, he knew ambition had won. He breathed a sigh of relief and went back to his desk, to comfort a frantic Eric and marshal the bewildered technical team.

He made the phone call at night, just ten hours before their flight was due to depart. Omar's contact had come through, and Salim had the secret phone number in his hand. Throat dry, he picked up the phone.

It did not go well at first. 'How did you get this number?' Ramadan demanded, his voice a furious bass.

'From your girlfriend, Excellency,' Salim replied in his best Iraqi dialect. 'She wants me to check whether you're seeing anyone else.' *All or nothing.*

There was a silence at the end of the phone, and then a raw belly laugh. 'These Americans – so serious,' the deep voice said. 'I can't believe I have to deal with you twice in one week.'

'You may have to deal with us sooner than you think, Excellency,' Salim replied. 'We're coming to see you tomorrow. I can't wait to have some *masgouf* with you beside the Tigris.' He had read somewhere that the Iraqi national dish was Ramadan's favourite – a river-caught carp split in half down its backbone into a flat circle, rubbed with olive and tamarind and slow-cooked on a wood fire.

Ramadan coughed over the phone. '*Yani*, I wish I could. But my schedule is very busy tomorrow. Why the rush?'

Salim needed all of his courage to keep going. 'It's for you I'm coming earlier. We can pay more than Curran. We can do a better deal. But if they come first, it's like a man going to his wedding knowing another man's already been there. My bosses will never allow it. And you'll be stuck with the lowest price.'

The other end of the phone was silent except for the wheeze of Ramadan's hefty breath.

'Why should I care which American I do business with?' he said eventually. 'Aren't you all the same?'

'I'm not an American, Excellency.' Salim took another breath. 'And if you don't meet with me, you'll never know how different I am.' Ramadan snorted, but he stayed quiet – a good sign.

'We can call it a friend's visit,' Salim went on. 'We don't have to make it in the offices. I can arrange something better, something more entertaining.'

Another cough came from the end of the line. 'You say you're coming, so okay, I can't stop you.' Ramadan seemed to be choosing his words carefully, so Salim did the same.

'We arrive tomorrow, at eleven in the morning. I hope I'll see you at the airport, Excellency.'

'*Yallah*, it's late,' Ramadan said. 'Goodnight, Mr Al-Ishmaeli.' He hung up the phone, and the dial tone rang long and loud in Salim's ear.

That night he dreamed of the Orange House.

It was behind him, at the end of a long, bright street. The sun above was as white as Marc's hair, streaming in tendrils down to the ground and obscuring the air.

Ahead of him, a boy kicked a football. Salim squinted into the light; he recognized Mazen. But then somehow Mazen changed into Hassan and Rafan, as tall as men, and the ball was driving towards him so fast, too fast to catch. It flew past him as they laughed, but he couldn't turn around to find it again. The Orange House was whispering at his back, and his mother was calling him.

He looked over the heads of the boy-men standing like shadows on the road, searching for the sea, but it was as dark and still as glass.

A terror rose inside him, and he pulled himself away from it, turning and turning until his hand hit the floor. Then he woke tangled in the sheets, neither in bed nor out of it, halfway to the ground.

The plane touched the tarmac in the furnace of Baghdad the next morning, the languorous palms of Mesopotamia beckoning them down. As the wheels screamed their protest, Salim would have prayed if there were any gods left to believe in.

The team had not slept, had not eaten, and could hardly look at each other. *If I've led them here on a fool's chase, they'll never forgive me.*

There'd been a time for faith, for belief in fairness, and Salim tried to reach back to it. He'd tried so hard, risked so much. Those waving palms, their green fronds so blithely welcoming – were they a sign? The trees were laden with dates close to ripening. They were smaller than oranges, but no less sweet. Had he lost his first harvest to be rewarded with a better one here?

Passing through customs, they emerged into the arrivals hall. Women and children flocked around them, old and young men hugged each other. Not a dignitary in sight. Salim's heart, so full of hope, finally sank. It was over.

Then, Eric clutched his arm and gasped. The doors slid open, and walking in on a wave of summer heat came Ramadan, his deputy and a delegation to greet them. The Iraqis had come. And at that moment Salim knew that he was finally the man he'd dreamed of being – a winner of the race, a master of his fate.

The touchdown in Kuwait three days later was his first taste of pure triumph. From the company car he looked out at the boundless blue of the Arabian Gulf and felt the cresting surge of victory. He'd pulled off a miracle, he knew. His thrusting young executives were awed to a man. Abdel-Rahman, a gnarled Baghdadi seared to hard leather by years in the crucible of Iraqi politics, had shaken his hand with a wicked smile and said *mabrouk* – an Arab's most sincere congratulations. In his briefcase, he carried the signed contract that only a few days before had been destined for another company. Meyer would bask in the glory, take most of the credit and officially confirm Salim as his Managing Director.

The lift that took him to Meyer's floor was the same model as the many they would install in Baghdad's expanding government and business district. It whirred softly upwards, and Salim pushed his hands to its smooth metal walls. *Such a strange, boxy thing to carry a man's life.* He closed his eyes and felt the gentle tug of gravity releasing him as Odell's technology pushed through it.

Meyer was every bit as delighted as Salim had imagined and replayed many times on the flight from Baghdad. 'That was one ballsy move, Slim. There's not a man in a thousand could have pulled it off.'

'The team was amazing,' Salim said, relaxing back in the leather chair. 'They all did their part, put together the pitch and delivered it on no sleep.'

'They should get a bonus, don't you think?' Meyer walked back over to his desk and made a note. He seemed to prefer talking to Salim perched on the corner of his desk.

'I certainly do.' He remembered his promise to Omar; now he could finally shake the clinging guilt off his back. 'You should know, I couldn't have done it without Omar Al Khadra. He had the inside track to Ramadan. Thank God he has a busy social life, is all I can say.'

'Well, maybe we should give him a closer look. Maybe something in liaison and oversight, when the ball gets rolling in Baghdad. Right?'

Salim had a fleeting memory of Mazen's scorn, his father's constant dismissals and the superiority of his first colleagues, those mighty Englishmen. 'The Iraqis will want us to hire one of their own as well,' he said, hiding his delight. 'It was part of our unofficial deal with Ramadan.'

'You're the boss,' Meyer said. He stood up again, and sat on the desk, a file in hand. 'Slim, it's time we confirmed you in the job. You've exceeded expectations, you know. I'm thrilled Doug passed you on to us. I drew up the contract. You can look it over if you like, but I'm happy for you to sign here and now.' He held the file out to Salim, grey eyes impassively looking down.

Salim took it, his own hands shaking. As he read the first page, the beating of his heart rose as thunder in his ears, drowning Meyer's smooth drawl: 'Of course there'll be a signing bonus, and well deserved.'

Salim's fingers were cold. He looked up at Meyer, trying to sound cheerful. 'There's a mistake here, John. This contract says Associate Director. The agreement was full Managing Director.'

The American shifted his weight on the desk, his eyes still as mirrors. 'I'm surprised you would think that, Slim. We talked about a number of positions currently open, including the Managing Director and Associate Director roles. You've been filling in for all of them – doing an incredible job, for which I intend to recognize you. This offer is part of that recognition.'

Salim stood up now, his eyes level with Meyer. 'I remember our conversation very clearly. You said I would be reporting directly to you, your second in command.'

'As you have been. Now Houston is sending someone, a very talented and experienced man with more than ten years of service to the company. He's a great guy and I know you'll love working with him.'

'But it's my job.' Salim felt the pain spreading inside him like the kick of a horse to the stomach – breathlessness and dullness giving way to a searing ache. 'I did everything to earn it. You promised it to me.'

Meyer was eye-to-eye with Salim now, and he could have been etched from granite, a carving from Andromeda's rocks. 'I'm so sorry you feel this way, Slim.' His voice floated into Salim's ears. 'I feel terrible if there was a misunderstanding, that your expectations were raised.' Behind Meyer's head, Salim could see waves breaking white on the limitless sea.

'If it makes any difference, I can tell you that we've never had a non-American Managing Director here. Wrong, maybe, but that's how it is. So this is still a great chance for you. You'll have a fantastic life with your family and get rich just as quickly. If it's not good enough for you, well, I wish you the very best of luck.'

Meyer reached his hand out to Salim, who took it by instinct, heart thudding as the dry palm slid into his own.

'You're a fantastic guy, Slim. You'll go far in any organization, I'm sure.' Meyer dropped the hand and motioned at the door. 'Now, why don't you go home, take a rest and think about it. You've had a long few days.'

Salim had to force his body to move, force himself not to break out in any more humiliating arguments. *If only I had a hat to hold out, I could ask him for some spare change.* He walked out of the office like an old man, past the bored secretary, towards the steel of the lift doors that opened for him as if he was expected.

Once inside, he felt a disorienting lightness. It was a moment before he realized they had begun their descent towards the ground, surrendering to the grip that only closes once you try to escape.

Jude heard Salim's car pull into the drive earlier than expected that day. She stood up, *The Brothers Karamazov* sliding to the floor. Her interview with the Kuwait International School was scheduled for the following morning. She'd spent hours that day brushing up on college reading, taking out her old books and clearing the shelves joyfully in preparation for more.

Through the glass-fronted door she saw her husband walk in past the villa gate. The sun was setting over the heap of tyres and rubble in the wasteland across the dirt road. His jacket and tie were off and he carried a box under his arm.

He stopped beside Marc's beloved, dead lime tree and slowly reached out to touch it. The tiny, bare branches reached into the dry air like atrophied hands.

At first she couldn't work out why Salim was standing there, the debris of his office around him. But then, to her horror, he picked up the shovel that stood by the gate and drove it into the ground.

She barely knew she was running by the time she reached the front door and pulled it open. 'Sal, don't!' she shouted from the porch, her bare feet slipping on the dusty stone. Dirt from the parched ground was swirling around him in a yellow cloud.

The tree's little roots were already exposed; Salim dropped the spade, took hold of the trunk and wrenched it loose. Clinging fibres rose and tore, streaming dirt into the deepening hole. Jude felt something pierce the underside of her foot as she scrambled down the steps. Reaching out, she tried to drag Salim's arm away with all her strength, the choking warmth of dust filling her lungs.

At that moment Jude heard a wail behind her, a high, savage note, and felt something rush past her and crash into Salim, throwing them both off balance.

The little boy was crying and thrashing, his hands grappling for the tree falling from Salim's hand, dirt from the ground covering his face. 'No, no, no, it's mine!' he was shouting.

Salim gripped Marc by the shoulders and shouted back, 'It's dead, do you understand me! It's dead!' Jude felt lost in confusion as she saw Salim's own tears begin to stream down; now he was trying to hug the boy but furious fists pushed him away.

Marc crouched on the ground and tried to lift his tree, to set it back in its space, only to see it fall down. He tried again, and again, weeping over the brittle branches as they broke and scratched him, leaving red and brown welts on his arms.

Salim stood up and looked over at Jude, his eyes full of sorrow and something that felt much colder – a kind of disgust. Then he turned around and walked into the house, past her and Sophie standing at the door with wide brown eyes.

Her first thought was her interview in the morning. Everything was a shambles, all her careful preparation. The neat little patio was a squalid earthy mess; Marc was covered in branches, tears and dirt. And when she leaned down to say 'Let it go, pet,' his eyes flicked up to hers, swollen and filled with blue rage.

It was Sophie who persuaded him to lay the tree on the ground and cover it with a blanket. Sophie whose arms he huddled in, submissive and empty, while Jude put antiseptic on his cuts. Eventually she laid them both in bed, cuddled up against each other. Marc was white and drained and Sophie subdued. 'Why is Daddy so sad?'

she'd asked her mother. Marc turned his face to the wall. 'I suppose he had some bad news at work, pet,' Jude answered, trying to keep the fear from her voice.

As they lay with their arms wrapped round each other, Jude had the strangest sensation that they were two alien creatures, belonging to each other and not to her at all. She sat with them until their breath slowed and their faces relaxed. The pale and the dark foreheads were inches apart, heartbreaking in their sweetness.

As night fell, she stood hesitant outside her bedroom door. It opened at the faintest touch of her fingers, and she stepped warily inside.

He was sitting on the bed in a clean t-shirt and shorts. In his hand he held the picture that lived on their mantelpiece, that fading image of his old house and the baby boy in front of it. His shoulder blades jutted out as he hunched over, the teenager showing through the man. In the middle of her anger, she felt her heart ache for him.

'You didn't get the job?' She sat down beside him, a finger's width away.

Without raising his head, he passed her the picture. She took it automatically, running her fingers over the baby's sweet, upturned face, yellowing now in its frame.

'They were right when I was a boy.' His voice was hoarse. 'Mazen, I mean, about my father and me. He said we were stupid, just *fellahin* with a little money and big ideas. I used to think he was wrong. But then my father was tricked by Abu Mazen, and now these Americans have shown me I'm just as stupid.'

'What's happened, Sal?' He wouldn't look at her. 'I thought it went so well.'

'What's happened is I've failed,' he told her. 'You and the kids. Everyone.'

'That's not true.' She reached for the right words. 'It doesn't matter to us.'

'It matters.' He looked up and laughed. 'I've come all this way for nothing.'

The picture frame felt heavy in her hands – a leaden weight of memory pushing him back to a past they couldn't share.

'I'm something, aren't I?' Her fingers dug into the glass. 'Your children are something. We might be the only people like us in the world. Shouldn't we be proud of that?'

'Proud.' She saw the black head shake. 'The twins can watch your tanks crushing my people on the news and wonder who to cheer on.'

Jude froze. 'They're not my tanks, Sal. And now *we're* your people. Your family.'

They sat in silence for a moment, and she wondered if he'd even heard her. Then he said, 'You saw how it was, that day on the beach. An Arab with pretensions. Maybe it's all I'll ever be.' She remembered Peggy smiling over Kathleen's shoulder, the closing oak door, and her stomach clenched.

'Let's just go back to England,' she pleaded. 'You'd find a good job there. For God's sake, Salim, you don't have to prove anything to anyone.'

He snatched the picture back from her hand. 'What do you know about having to prove yourself? You want me to go crawling back to England for some other white man to fuck me over? Or to work in Hassan's garage? You know, if it wasn't for your people, for the Jews, I would already be somebody.' His voice was trembling. 'A landowner in my own right. Not this.' He hit his own chest, the flat of his hand slamming down.

She got to her feet, her own tears coming in an angry rush. 'Look at me, Sal. Please, look at me. It's Jude. Your wife. Am I the enemy?'

As his head turned towards her, she could see a boy's longing in his face. It was every inch as sad and lost as Marc's, clinging onto his dead tree.

'Maybe I'm just sick of being the *fellah* who everyone pushes around,' he said. He turned away from her to lie on his side. 'Now let me sleep, please.'

Jude felt the brush of air as the bedroom door shut, and the warm brown carpet beneath her feet. It was an easy house to be quiet in, each footfall cushioned and the air conditioners ironing out the noises. But whenever Salim went into his room, silence seemed to lie heavier on the house, an oppressive presence impossible to escape.

Stepping quickly into their dressing room, she closed the door lightly and turned on the small light by the mirror. Her fingers reached behind a painting of the Kuwait Towers Sophie had made at nursery and pulled out a small key. It unlocked the bottom drawer near her feet, the one with all her jewellery and a small, brown box right at the back. It rattled as she dragged it out into the light.

Silver glinted as the lid came off. The shape of it was so familiar in her hands: the menorah that she used to light at Hanukkah, Rebecca's gift to her, carried on her long journey out of the ashes of Kishinev. She almost laughed at the thought of her Arab husband lying next door. *Who would have thought that road could lead here?*

She closed her eyes, but, try as she might, she could not see her grandmother's hands. Tears came into her eyes. *Bubby. I'm so lonely.* She had not been able to put a name to the cold feeling inside her, as cold as the moment she'd walked into Rebecca's room and watched her life seeping away.

And then other memories came – of countless Sabbaths when the Gold family would light their solitary little candlesticks and sing the Friday night prayers. Dora had offered the Sabbath candlesticks to her as a parting gift, but Jude had politely declined.

She remembered how she used to let the candles dazzle her in the dark rooms, the rich smell of the wax and the high wail of her mother's voice. It was a sound that seemed to come from across oceans and miles, a great tidal surge of millions of other voices sweeping over the earth. How often had she been thinking of school, or Kath, or Peggy, and wanting to be somewhere else, or someone else?

Taking two half-melted candles from the bottom of the box, she pushed them into the two furthest holes of the menorah. *They would tell me that it's not done, that it's forbidden. But they are far away and I'm here, alone, in the dark.* Striking a match from the box, she lit the flames and saw her face reflected in the mirror.

It was a stranger's face she saw; the young woman had gone, and the old one inside was beginning to flower. Shadows dug into her cheeks, but the flickering light made her eyes burn, an inner flame she did not recognize. Leaning over the candles, she put her hands to her face and very quietly started to sing.

1982

In the twins' twelfth autumn, Jude was on her way back from the Kuwait International School when she heard about the bombs.

'Hush,' she said, over the twins' chatter in the back seat. She reached over to turn up the radio. *Was it bombs I heard today?* It had sounded like thunder, a deep thud and the rattle of windows. A wind had picked up afterwards and she'd seen dark clouds in the sky. *Sandstorm.* That was her first instinct. She'd long learned to dread them. Every window in the house was taped shut, every crack and crevice covered. But when the storms came, the howling desert would test their defences with insidious fingers. It would always find a way in.

But today it was bombs, not sand. Six bombs, the announcer said, hitting the French and American embassies, an oil refinery and other places. More would have died, but the bombers had not learned their trade well. The war between Iran and Iraq had finally come to Kuwait, the little country placed so precariously between them. Salim's friend Adnan had described it as two giants wrestling over an oily dwarf.

'What's that, Mum?' Sophie asked. 'What's happened?'

'Nothing, pet,' Jude said. 'They're just talking about the war.' She saw Sophie's eyes narrow at her mother's transparency.

Jude's hands gripped the wheel. Ever since Israel's invasion of Lebanon that summer, war had cast a shadow over all their old routines. Everything felt precarious – from conversation at the dinner table to the drive home past Kuwait's army posts, bristling with suspicious eyes.

For years she'd brought the twins home from the International School after her classes. The primary school finished early so they'd wait for her on the playground trampoline. It was there she'd first learned that Marc was a spectacular and daring sky dancer. He had something extraordinary, something gravity-defying in his legs. He leapt as if the sky could be breached by will alone, arms stretched above his head, hair like a white halo. Now he was the star of Kuwait's annual school theatrical, run by a group of ancient headmasters with aristocratic vowels and imperial pasts.

'It's not fair,' Sophie had complained earlier in the car, for the hundredth time. 'He makes me wait on the side all the time. It's boring enough being there, if I'm not allowed to have a go.'

In the rearview mirror, Jude saw Marc make a face at his twin, and Sophie lash out with one elegant brown arm saying, 'Stop it, idiot.'

'No fighting in the car,' Jude said, without much heat. They goaded each other for amusement, but she knew their love was as solid as the days they used to sleep clenched tight in each other's arms.

'Okay, Mum, we can wait till we get home to fight.' Marc's voice was still a boy's – high and quick, to match his slender white body, as perfect as a chrysalis. But it would not be long before the man in him awoke, and Jude sometimes wondered what would emerge from the shell.

They pulled up into the drive and Sophie said, 'Oh, Daddy's home early.' His white Chevrolet was in the drive, and the front door was open.

Jude's heart sank. Since Salim had turned down the job at Odell, he'd taken four other jobs, each with less enticing prospects than the last. She never asked why, because in her heart she knew the truth of it: he felt perennially undervalued, he fought with management and his wounded spirit was quick to suspect slights.

Strangely, as Salim's world shrank, Jude's own career had started to blossom. At the end of her three-month trial at the school, the headmaster told her she had a gift for storytelling. Slowly, over the last six years, the shelves of the house had filled up with books sent by Tony from England or salvaged from the market and houses of others. Teaching had become a home of a different kind; she loved the smell of the classroom and the round eyes of her pupils as she walked them through worlds they would never see, lives stranger than their own.

Salim always said he was proud of her. But more and more these days, those words tasted of envy. And now – if Salim was back before the end of the working day, it could mean only one thing: another resignation, another few weeks frustrated at home, before another job pulled him into an ever-narrowing circle of possibilities.

She got out of the family car, her once white arms flecked from the relentless Arabian sun. Salim was in the doorway and she tried to smile at him. *I've become so wary. Once I would have run and thrown my arms around his neck.* Now it was Sophie who took that role.

Then she noticed another figure beside him – shorter, but the same lean shape and sliced cheekbones raking up to almond eyes. The strange man grinned, and rubbed his hand across the stubble on his chin. 'My sister,' he called out, walking casually down the steps into the dusty front garden. 'So sorry to drop in on you like this, without an invitation.'

His accent sounded American, with a trace of something thicker, almost like French. He reached her, and she saw his eyes were a deep green, slanted like Salim's but guileless as a child's. He smiled, and it chilled her to the bone.

Her husband stood sheepishly behind him, like a taller shadow. 'My love, this is Rafan,' he said. 'My younger brother.' From the awkward tone, she knew Salim had no part in this sudden appearance – that he was probably as surprised as she was.

'Hello,' she said, holding out her hand. 'I'm so glad to meet you at last.' He clasped her hand in both of his, as if they'd been meeting every year. 'Of course,' he said. 'It's such a shame we never got the chance until now. But we'll make up for it, don't worry.' He raised his hands in a gesture of greeting to the twins, who hovered mystified on the edge of the conversation.

As they went into the house, Jude felt her heart jump like a rabbit bolting across the downs. Salim had rarely spoken of his brother. Jude knew that he lived in Lebanon, and never asked more. He was part of that other world – the one that Salim left behind to marry her.

They sat at dinner, the twins polite and quiet, waiting for the stranger to speak. Rafan tucked into his meal, all smiles and compliments. Salim pushed his food around the plate. *He knows why Rafan is here, and doesn't want to say.* Some secret conversation on the way back from the airport had put that guilty, angry look on Salim's drawn face.

It was Marc who finally broke the silence. 'Did you know that Uncle Rafan was visiting, Dad?' Marc had stopped calling his father *Daddy* many years ago. In fact, she could hardly remember if he'd ever done it.

Rafan waved a fork of lamb at Marc.

'I surprised your father, little man. It's very bad manners. But he's such a good brother, that he doesn't mind. Of course, in England it's not so polite to drop in like this. In Arab families, though, it's different. Our homes are always open to each other, did you know that?' Marc raised his eyebrows. 'Particularly if a brother or sister really needs help.'

'Do you need help?' Sophie asked.

'A little bit, beauty. You know I live in Beirut, right? You know where that is?' The twins nodded. 'Well, there are many other Palestinians who live there. They don't have houses like this one.

They live in camps, all piled together, and very poor and dirty. I'm sure your father has told you.'

'Mr Shakir told us,' Sophie said. 'He's our Arabic teacher.' Rafan laughed and nudged Salim in the ribs. 'You got them a teacher for their own language, big brother,' he said to Salim in Arabic. Jude's own learning had sped far ahead of her children's. She could understand much more than Salim ever had cause to know.

Marc pushed his elbows onto the table, looking at Rafan with his head on one side. He asked, 'So, do you live in those camps, then?' Rafan shook his head and said, 'No, I was lucky to have a Lebanese passport, so I didn't have to. But I had many friends who did. In one camp, called Shatila, there were many of my friends trying to make a better life for the Palestinian people.' His green eyes found Jude's and held them. 'Trying to take back the lands that were ours before they were stolen.'

'The Jews were in Israel thousands of years ago. They were always there,' Marc said casually, and Jude felt fear snap inside her. 'Doesn't that make Israel the Jews' land as well as yours?'

Rafan slowly turned back to Marc and smiled that feline grin. 'Well, that's what they say, Marc. That's what the Jews would say. But the Jews left the land a very long time ago. If you leave something precious on the floor and someone else comes along and cares for it – let's say, for two thousand years – do you have the right to come back and just take it away?' Marc opened his mouth to argue, but he saw his mother's face and closed it again.

Salim leaned forward, incredulous, and said, 'Where did this come from, Marc?' But Rafan tapped him on the arm, and went on.

'So, my friends in this camp, they were protecting their Lebanese brothers from the civil war. But the Israelis knew that the bravest Palestinians were there in the camp. And they decided to get rid of those Palestinians for once and for all. So the Jews came into Lebanon with their armies. Then they made a deal with the Christians.' He paused to swallow a mouthful of lamb. The children sat rapt, their forks at their sides.

'In the morning, just a few days ago, the Israelis and the Christians drove their tanks to the edge of the camp, where the children and women were still sleeping in their beds. The Israelis stood guard outside, while the Phalangists went in with guns and knives.' Rafan took his knife off the plate and slowly slid it across his throat, the blade a hair's breadth from the skin. Jude's mouth was too dry to swallow.

Rafan went on. 'By the time they were finished, thousands were dead, even the little babies and the old people. You could hear the screaming across the city.' He shovelled a forkful of meat into his mouth and chewed.

Marc's cheeks were flushed red. 'That can't be true,' he said, his voice young and pained. *It's my fault,* she thought. *I told him both sides, I told him not to judge. He doesn't want either of us to be monsters.*

'Yes, little man, I don't blame you. But it's true. I went in afterwards and saw what happened. And I thought if this can happen to my friends it could just as easily happen to me. So I decided to come here for a while, to see my dear brother and get to know my English family.' Another smile, this time to Jude. But she could not smile back. She'd heard about the massacre of Palestinians in Lebanon but had pushed it out of her mind. And now here it was in her kitchen, pointing a bloody finger at her and at Dora, Max and Rebecca – all those she loved. And if it was true, they were all bloodstained, every single one of them.

The table was silent for a moment, until Salim spoke up. 'Rafan will be staying for as long as he likes. He can have the spare room.' He spoke to Rafan. 'My wife will arrange it for you.'

Rafan turned to Jude and gave her a nod of apparent gratitude. She returned it with a smile and a stilted 'You're welcome'. But inside she heard drums beating, the distant thunder of an enemy on the march.

*

She skipped work the next morning and drove Rafan to the local market to buy some clothes. He'd come with only one duffel bag, and he said he needed to stock up. He had a contact, he said, and asked Jude with exaggerated gallantry if she would accompany him.

In the car, she cast around for something to say. All night she'd dreamed of the screams of children chasing her down narrow, red streets. This morning, the autumn heat was oppressive and her face was moist with sweat. Her heart ached for the dead and for the others still to die as the wheel of retaliation turned.

'I am so sorry about what happened,' she said finally. 'I can't believe anyone would be so cruel.'

He turned towards her, seeming surprised.

'Why would you be sorry, my sister? You didn't kill anyone.'

'You know what I mean,' she said.

Rafan's smile crept across his face. Today his green eyes were shaded behind dark glasses, and his t-shirt clung to a wiry body.

'I do know what you mean, dear Jude,' he paused, looking out of the window as the streets of Kuwait's urban outskirts reeled by, landscaped flowers wilting in the morning heat. 'I must say, I think you are a very brave woman.'

That surprised her. 'Brave? Why am I brave?'

He took off his glasses, and turned to face her. She felt his gaze like prickles of heat on her skin.

'I admire anyone willing to keep fighting a losing battle,' he said. 'Anyone can see it. Even your kids can see it. That Marc, he's trying to fight your battle for you. And you're letting him.'

'What do you mean?' She nearly took her hands off the wheel in shock. 'I don't want anyone to fight. That's why...' She paused to rethink. 'Sal and I always knew it would be difficult. But we just want the children to be happy – not to feel pressured or forced to choose.' She remembered Marc's argument at the dinner table, his innocent defence of her. She hadn't meant to influence him, but she'd been so afraid of what he was learning from the news that Salim now insisted on watching every night. While Sophie went straight to her room to read, Marc would go and hover by the flickering light of the screen, his young body bathing in the ceaseless colours of rage.

'You're dreaming, my sister,' Rafan said. 'You can't live in both worlds. I know, I tried it. I am either Palestinian or Lebanese. You are either Salim's wife, or a Jew. I have nothing against Jews, truly. Believe me. I'm just telling you this for your own sake. Here, here – on the left.' He wound down the window and pointed to the side of the road.

They pulled up outside a shop that looked as if it sold gold, not clothes. But Rafan jumped out quickly and said, 'Five minutes, I promise.'

As she waited, Jude rested her head on her arm. Outside the car, a man herded goats across the busy road, cars roaring their complaints.

She'd married Salim knowing they could make one home out of two: each brick an act of courage – Jude confronting Dora's rage, Salim defying Arab disapproval. But Rafan was right – something had changed. Over the years Salim had turned his 'betrayal' at work into something more destructive – a reliving of all the betrayals of his past, a fear that he himself was a traitor – to his own heritage. All those disapproving Arab faces, all those miserable nights in front of the television watching their peoples tear each other apart. The doors of their home had slowly opened to the world outside, and something dangerous had entered – ghosts of loss and disappointment.

When Rafan came back into the car empty handed, she asked in surprise, 'Where are the clothes?'

'Don't worry,' he said. 'They'll be delivered in the next few days. I have very exacting specifications.' He winked, and she smiled despite herself.

'Why are you so sure that what Sal and I have isn't possible?' she said, as they set off for home. 'Isn't this what everyone says they want? Peace, happiness, an end to the violence?'

Rafan shook his head. 'You're so naïve, you English. Who wants peace? Let me tell you a truth. The goal of fighting is to keep fighting. Once you win, you get less money and more responsibilities.' He laughed. 'That's what the Jews are finding out now.'

'I don't believe you,' Jude retorted. 'Last night you told us you escaped from a massacre – who could possibly want more bloodshed like that?'

He pushed his glasses back on. 'Peace may be sweet, dear Jude. But other things will always be sweeter. That's why I say I admire you. When you pick peace, you pick the losing side.'

Rafan's clothes, several black duffel bags of them, were delivered two weeks later by a narrow-faced man driving a brown pickup.

Salim helped him load the bags into the disused maid's quarters at the back of the villa. Jude watched from the back door, her skin prickling.

Afterwards, Rafan came sauntering into the kitchen with a satisfied smile. He pinched Sophie's cheek, took a glass of water from the filter and yawned, saying he needed a nap. 'A long day, beauty.' Then he vanished into the dark of his bedroom.

Salim said he was going to buy some cans and yeast; Rafan had fired him up about the idea of brewing homemade wine in the storage room. 'I can't believe you let these bedouin whoremongers tell you what to drink,' he'd scoffed.

As Jude waved the car out of the drive, the song of the muezzin came rolling in behind it across the darkening wasteland. Once it had been an alien sound, a painful reminder of her loneliness. But her ears had changed with the passage of time; now its sadness spoke to her of familiar things, and resonated with her own losses. It was a drift from hate to love so gentle she could not say when she'd crossed the line between.

Sophie appeared at her side. 'He sounds cross today, doesn't he?' Her daughter at twelve was nearly as tall as Jude, a slim shadow against the falling dusk.

'Who? Your father?' Salim had been on edge since the morning; the trip to the supermarket was probably another ruse to avoid them.

'No, not Daddy. The mosque.' One hand pulled through her long hair, a habit carried out of her childhood.

Jude touched the twisting fingers and asked, 'What's bothering you, pet?'

Sophie rubbed her foot on the ground. 'Nothing. Only – Uncle Rafan... do you like him?'

Jude's chest tightened. 'Why? Did he say something to you?'

'No. He's okay. He's funny. I mean... not funny ha-ha.' Sophie looked out into the desert, thoughtful. 'He looks like Daddy but he isn't like him at all.'

Jude pulled her daughter towards her, feeling the strong smoothness of Sophie's skin. 'I could say the same about you and Daddy,' she said. Sophie's brown tones were the mirror of her father's. She had his look but only Marc had inherited the restless heat of his nature. Her daughter's colours conjured different things for Jude – cool earth and dark lakes, and Rebecca's sturdy pine trees.

'Daddy's been unhappy since Uncle Rafan came,' Sophie said, resting against her mother's shoulder. *So intuitive, my daughter.* The confusion in Salim's mind had been more visible than ever that morning, from the defiant hunch of his shoulders as he hoisted Rafan's bags onto his back.

Suddenly, Sophie hugged her arm. 'Hey, it's Friday night, you know.'

'You want to light the candles?'

'If you'd like. Daddy won't be back for a while.'

'Get Marc then,' Jude said, through the familiar rush of guilt and pleasure. 'I'll meet you in there.'

As Jude pulled the menorah out of the dressing room drawer, her fingers fumbled. When she'd first shown the children how to pray, how to light the Sabbath and Hanukkah candles, it was meant to be just once. She'd told herself: *I have to pass on the knowledge.* But they'd enjoyed it. And it had touched her, those whispered prayers and hidden lights while the muezzin rang through the air outside, so much more than the grand festivities in the open daylight of her childhood.

But that evening, her prayers came hard. In the light of the struck match she could see their distraction. Marc's eyes were tracing the ceiling, and she found herself wanting to shake him into the present. *This is how his father feels sometimes.* But even Sophie's face was thoughtful, her mind elsewhere.

When Jude finished the song and lifted her hands from her face, she heard Sophie say, 'That thing about the place in Lebanon? Where Uncle Rafan said the Jews helped kill all those people? It's true, you know. I heard about it at school. They really did do that.' Marc's gaze swung round towards her and Jude felt the cold bite of shame.

'I know.' Her throat was full. She sensed Sophie looking at her, and Marc too, searching for an explanation. But there was none to give.

'No wonder he hates them,' she heard Sophie whisper to her brother. *Hates us*, Jude wanted to say. But in the semi-darkness she felt the back of her neck prickle, as if unfriendly eyes were on them, an invisible witness judging every word.

'What's your brother really doing here?' she asked Salim later, lying in bed. 'Hiding from Israeli assassins,' he said, rolling over and pretending to fall asleep. She lay there in the warm darkness listening to the unhappy rhythm of his breathing and trying to calm the buzzing of her mind.

The next morning she took Marc to his rehearsals. He was waiting in the car, dressed in the long, blue leotard he would wear on stage in just a month's time. A pair of wire wings lay on the seat next to him. He gave her his most gleeful smile as she opened the car door, saying, 'Come on, Mum, the star can't be late.'

'Who says you're a star, you cheeky monkey,' she said, feeling love reach deep into her heart. She stretched over the seat to touch his face.

'Mr Trevellian says I am,' he said, very seriously. 'There's no one better than me, not even in the year above. He says I have strength and flexibility. That's why they gave me Puck, even though the older boys wanted it.'

'I know, pet. I'm very proud of you.'

After the tree catastrophe all those years ago, Marc's enthusiasm for life had dimmed to a dull glow. Jude had worried for a time that this strange, fragile child might not recover.

It was the Theatrical Society's *Midsummer Night's Dream* that saved him. It had young dancers, a tumbling Puck and a talking donkey. Marc had sat in enthralled silence for the whole two hours and had to be prised from his seat after the house lights came up. The next day at primary school he'd marched to the teacher to demand enrolment in the next production. Jude had received a sympathetic phone call saying no child under twelve was allowed to perform: but after Marc mastered his profound disappointment and grasped the concept of waiting, he once again had something to live for. For six years, he'd punished his body in relentless after-school gymnastics and dance training while Sophie was at Brownies, to be ready for his chance.

And at last it had come. The Society had made the serendipitous decision to restage *A Midsummer Night's Dream* for the 1982 October production, after Marc's twelfth birthday. Marc would finally play Puck on stage this year. *My son is about to find out what it's like to realize a dream.*

They pulled up outside the dance school, a long, whitewashed building surrounded by old palms and watered by a deep well. Jude always felt strangely soothed under the gentle shadow of those palms, dappling the world with swashes of green and white. And the milk-and-biscuit smell of the wooden halls reminded her of Bede's Grammar and those first bittersweet steps out of childhood.

The hall was a scrum of other children and parents. Marc vanished quickly into the crowd, and Jude heard someone shout her name. A tall woman approached her, beads of sweat dappling a brown chignon with grey hairs threaded through it like wires. She held two glasses above her head, as children scurried around her.

'Hey, Miss Jude. Want some lemonade? It's cold as all hell.'

Jude took the glass and smiled. Helen was one of the few American Embassy wives who didn't think it beneath her to mix without a diplomatic passport. Her daughter was in Jude's class at school. 'I could never get her to read a damn thing and now she's giving me Dickens over breakfast,' she'd said to Jude one parents' evening. 'I would kiss you, but imagine the scandal!'

Today Helen's eyes narrowed as she looked down at her, and Jude flinched under the scrutiny.

'Now, none of that, honey. What's up? Man or money?'

Jude shrugged. 'I'm okay. Sal's... okay. But his brother just arrived out of the blue from Beirut, to stay with us. And I get the feeling he's in a lot of trouble.'

'How so?'

'I don't know exactly.' All of her suspicions came surging onto the tip of her tongue under Helen's attentive eye. 'He's from Beirut, I think involved in the war somehow. He's...' she suddenly stopped, biting down her words. Helen's husband was the big, jovial Chargé d'Affaires at the Embassy. 'Look at him,' Salim had whispered the first time they met at the Club. 'Way too old for that job. CIA for sure.'

Helen sipped her drink. 'Divine,' she said. Jude took a swallow; the false sweetness of the lemon left a strange taste in her mouth. 'That's the thing about Arabs, honey,' Helen went on, wiping her forehead. 'Family here, family there. People can't get away from them. If I had to live with my family I swear I'd go crazy. Well, crazier. No disrespect to your man, but just tell him it's not on, if you don't like it.'

If only it were that simple. 'I'm going to.' Jude put her drink down on the table. 'I am. But I just have to find the right way. Sal feels like he owes his brother somehow. But we come first with him, I know it.'

'Just say the word if you need a hand. We're pretty good at getting rid of unwanted pests, you know.'

Suddenly, Marc rounded the corner, breathless and red-faced. 'Mum!'

'What's the matter?'

'I left one shoe behind, on my bed.'

'Can't you dance barefoot today?'

'No way.' Marc's voice was pained. 'The floor's all uneven – some places you stick, some places you slip. We have to go back.'

'Oh, for God's sake,' Jude said, half-laughing, half-scolding. 'I'll throw a party when you learn how to drive yourself. Just go into the rehearsal, and I'll go back for the shoe. Go on!'

She reached over and squeezed Helen's hand. 'I'll speak to you later, Helen. Thanks for the talk.'

'Any time, honey. Remember what I said.'

She took the dirt road back – harder on the car but a shorter round trip. Leaving the car with the engine turning over outside the gate, she rushed into the house through the kitchen door, and into Marc's bedroom. The beige dancing slipper was there, curled up on the pillow like a dead mouse. She put it in the back pocket of her trousers, and was walking towards the front door when she heard Rafan in the family room. He said the word *Jude*.

She stopped dead, holding her breath. *Was he talking to me?* But then she heard Salim reply, and she inched closer to listen.

'Jude hates what happened in Shatila as much as I do. As much as you do. She would never tell the children anything else,' she heard her husband say.

Rafan's voice followed. 'You're blind and she's blind. What do you know about Shatila anyway – either of you? They stood guard over the camp until even the children were dead. Do you know what three thousand dead people smell like, Salim?' There was a brief silence, and Jude imagined how Salim would see it in his mind – the bodies of Marc and Sophie lying red on the ground, while a man of stone with a Star of David on his gun stood with his back to them, shutting out the world.

'I don't know what you want from me,' Salim said, in English again. 'I have a family now. I have children. I can't come to Lebanon, even if I wanted to.'

'There's no need to come to Lebanon. There are things to be done everywhere. Even here.' Rafan used the word *mumkin*, meaning all things are possible. 'Where do you think our brothers get their money?' She heard another sound, a metallic clinking, and Salim said fiercely, 'Where did you get that?'

'From your bedroom, big brother. It's hers. She lights it when you're not here, to pray to the children in Hebrew. Sophie told me by mistake.'

Ice crept down her spine and her heart seemed to freeze. *My menorah?* As she groped for how and when he'd found it, a memory washed through her of the last *Shabbas* night with Sophie and Marc, and the feeling of being watched.

A creak of a chair startled her into movement. Turning on the soft carpet, she tiptoed as fast as she dared into the kitchen and ran down the garden to the running car, panic at her heels. She slammed the door and pushed the car into gear, kicking up dust until she was safely around the corner. *Running like a rat.* She remembered Rebecca's letter, the rats hiding in the cellar, afraid of the axes, barely human. Slamming her foot on the brake, she pulled up. *Where is my courage?* Jude leaned her head forward on the steering wheel, and wept.

*

241

That night at dinner, the storm broke. *I've done nothing wrong*, she kept reminding herself. *I will not hide.*

Rafan turned up for the evening meal, as excruciatingly friendly as ever. She loathed him – his insolence, his cynicism, his infectious falseness. And what was worse, she could not escape the sickening knowledge that she was partly to blame for him. The Jews had helped to forge this dark soul flying into her kitchen on the wings of bloody slaughter.

Salim came to the table late, his eyes shadowed and sad. They ate in silence for a while. At last, Marc turned to Jude and said, 'Mr Trevellian told me that there are dance schools in England where I can learn properly. Could I go to one next year? He said he was going to talk to you about it.'

Jude looked over at Salim, who in turn had raised his head to look at his son.

'So you want to live in England, Marc?' he said quietly. Marc nodded, blindly unwary in his excitement. 'I want to be a professional dancer.' Rafan laughed and said, 'Good for you, little man. Speak up for what you want.'

Salim said, 'Did your mother suggest this to you? I know she loves dancing.' His eyes were wet, but his face was pinched in a way they had all learned to dread – the strain of the volcano before the eruption.

Marc caught the tone, and fell silent for a moment. Then, boldly, he said, 'Well, why not? We can't stay here forever.'

Salim's eyes widened. 'Really? Is that what you talk about, when you're saying your Jewish prayers? How to get away from here, and from your people and your father too?'

Jude's eyes met his, defiant blue against the deep black. 'You know that's not true. How could you even think it?'

'How can I think it?' He flushed. 'I ask you to give the children Arabic lessons. Now they're twelve, nearly adults, and they can hardly speak a word. You fill them with stories of England, even though this is their home. And you teach them Jewish prayers? My children, with my name?' His voice choked, and through the blur of her own emotions Jude saw her husband struggling under the weight of pain.

Marc sat with his mouth open; Jude tried to speak but Sophie jumped ahead of her. '*I* asked to light the candles, Daddy,' she said. 'It was just for fun.' Jude marvelled at her daughter's courage; she was fearless in the face of anger, like an ocean soaking up a storm.

'You?' Salim was incredulous. 'I don't believe you, Sophie. What's fun about this? What were you thinking?'

'Leave her alone,' Marc shouted, jumping to his feet. 'That's not how it was. It's not just about *your* side of things.'

'No, Marc,' Jude said, pulling him back. 'I should have told you, Sal. But they have the right to learn something about my culture too.'

'Not if it means they turn against me,' he said, his face white. 'Not if it makes them more Jew than Arab. You've made them into foreigners, into Zionists – like you.'

Marc yelled back, 'Why are you so horrible all the time? You're the one turning us against you. You don't care about us, about anything except the stupid Arabic lessons!'

Jude gasped as Salim leapt to his feet and slapped Marc across the face. His hand left a red welt on the white cheek already losing its baby softness to the harder person underneath.

The boy put his hand up in shock. Jude saw Sophie raise hers in echoed pain. And then, into the silence, Marc spat, 'I hate you,' before running out of the kitchen and slamming his bedroom door.

Salim had pointed his finger at Jude and said, 'No more dancing for him. He has to learn a lesson.' Then the two brothers went out. She watched them from the back window, carrying Rafan's bulky black bags from his room and hoisting them into the boot of the family car before screeching out of the drive without explanations.

She left Sophie with the dishes and found Marc in his room doing handstands against the wall. It was still covered with the story of Mowgli – the parentless boy who learned to leap like a monkey and hunt like a tiger.

Upside down, his face was bright purple. She saw tears on his forehead, nearly dried.

'I can't do anything right for him,' he croaked, his arms shaking to hold him up. 'He hates me and I hate him.'

'It only feels like that,' she said. 'Love and hate feel very similar sometimes.'

Marc glanced dubiously at her. He swung his legs down and sat up flushed.

'He never asks me anything any more, except to tell me that I'm not good enough at something.'

'Your father had a very hard life. So many people let him down. He's wrong to behave this way, but that doesn't mean you should hate him.'

She saw Marc's unconvinced face, and took his chin in her hand. 'You two are just like each other. You both only see your side of things. When he comes back, I'm going to talk to him.' Marc's pale blue eyes filled with tears, and she ached to see the need there. He nodded quietly.

When she left his room, she went to the telephone and dialled Tony's number. They spoke infrequently, because it was expensive and the lines were bad. The last time she'd seen him, the summer before on a holiday to England, his wife had been expecting their third child – and Tony had acquired a belly plus a partnership in his father's firm.

'This is madness,' he said to her, after she sketched the outline of her fears. 'You need to come home, and now. It sounds like this Rafan is in the PLO or something. Remember Munich, those Israeli athletes. These maniacs don't know the innocent from the guilty.' Tony and his wife had gone to Munich's Olympiad on their honeymoon; they flew home with their tickets unused as images of the eleven slaughtered athletes filled the world's television screens.

'Sal will never agree to leave Kuwait now,' she said, gripping the telephone. 'It's his brother, and he's been through things we can't imagine, Tony. But I need to start making a plan.'

'What do you mean?' Behind Tony's voice she could hear his children chattering.

'I need you to look for schools, good schools for the twins,' she said. 'Someone prepared to take them after the start of the school year. If I can convince him it's best for the children, perhaps he'll consider it.'

'I'll do anything for you, *bubbellah*, you know that.' Tony sounded earnest. 'But honestly, it worries me that you have to resort to all this cloak and dagger stuff. The Jude I knew would just have stood up for herself. Remember the *Knedlach* Incident!' She laughed, but a part of her wanted to weep.

'Just please let me know soon, Tony,' she said. When he hung up the phone she listened to the dial tone for a few seconds before she could bear to set it down too.

When she turned on the light in Rafan's room, it was empty as an open grave – only scuffs on the floor where the black duffel bags had been sitting.

By the time Salim and Rafan returned, light was creeping back over the desert wasteland, its pink fingers touching the house. She was lying on the sofa in the family room, and heard them coming up the steps to the front door.

Rafan was saying, 'Our Iraqi friends will take the money to the border tonight. By morning it will be in Syria. The Americans are always watching. So we meet in a different place every time. The sheikh arranges it all.' A key turned in the lock.

245

Salim said in Arabic, 'How many times are you going to do this?' His brother said something indistinct; Jude thought it was *ma baraf* – who knows?

They walked straight past her and Rafan headed for his room. When she heard the door close, she crept out of the room and said softly, 'Salim.' The name sounded strange on her tongue, and she tasted a moment of regret that she'd never called him that before.

He came back out of the bedroom, a dark outline against the open door.

'Why are you awake?' He looked guilty, like a boy caught in a prank gone wrong.

'I couldn't sleep,' she said, coming to stand opposite him. 'Where have you been? I was worried.'

'Nowhere,' he said. 'Don't be silly. There's nothing wrong. I was only helping him to run an errand. It's nothing.' But his face was drawn and his eyes slick as marbles. She heard the lie in his voice.

'An errand.' Fury was so close to the surface, but she swallowed it down. *That's not the way to reach him.* 'Bags of money leaving our house in the middle of the night, where our children sleep. To buy what, Sal?' He didn't answer. 'You know what, don't you? Guns to kill other children, in other houses. Is that what you want?'

He shook his head. 'You've got it wrong, Jude. Rafan's into politics, that's all. We're helping the refugees.' His voice was defiant, but he passed his hand over his eyes in a gesture of weary futility.

'You can't do this,' she said, reaching inside herself for courage. 'I know he's your brother, and for whatever reason you love him. But if you go this way you're abandoning us.'

He stood still for a moment, then said, 'I'm the abandoned one, Jude. First my home. Then my mother. Then the rewards they promised me for all my hard work here. My relatives think I'm a traitor. Now my son tells me he hates me, that my family wants to leave me and that he'd rather learn a Jewish prayer than an Arabic greeting. So what do you care what I do now?'

She took his hand and pressed it to the groove between her breasts, where his head had lain and his mouth kissed so many times.

'Remember the day you asked me to marry you?' she said, feeling her heart beat under his palm. 'You hadn't even unpacked your suitcases. You held my hand and promised me you'd buy me a ring the next day. That we would be happy, we would make our own way. You kept every promise. Until today.' His face was white and drawn, his eyes wet.

'I know what I promised.' His voice was full of sorrow. 'But it got too hard. You can pretend there's no war if you like, but it's everywhere, all around us. And look what I became, closing my eyes and chasing my big dreams. Not an Englishman, but not a real Arab either. You changed too.' His eyes found hers. 'You used to understand me without even speaking. Now look at us.' He opened his palm and showed it to her, pale and empty.

Jude put one hand on Salim's cheek. 'I still love you just as much,' she said, but the words sounded tired, worn. 'We were children back then. So defiant, just like Marc. All of these things now, they're just... growing up.'

'You heard Marc. He doesn't even want to be my son.'

'He's a child,' she argued, exhausted. 'He's like your shadow. He needs you desperately. Please, tell Rafan to go. If you want to fight for something, fight for us. It's a fight you can win, Sal.'

She felt the warmth of his hand, and her heart beating in response. He looked down at her and shook his head. But he said, 'I'll talk to Marc. God knows my father never talked to me.' She saw tears in his eyes and knew what he was thinking. *Why does history only ever repeat its sorrows, and not its joys?*

'He wants you to care about the things that are important to him too,' she said. 'His play, his dancing. He needs to know you value him for more than his last name.'

He gave a bitter laugh, squeezed her hand and released it. 'Okay,' he said – a capitulation, but whether to love or weariness she didn't know. 'Rafan... I'll deal with him. Go to bed now.' She opened her mouth to reply, but he cut her off. 'Go, please, don't worry. I'll be there in a moment.' He walked around her towards the kitchen, back hunched like a beast of burden. And she slowly retreated into the dark bedroom where the picture of the orange tree was catching the faintest rays of morning.

Salim waited until he heard the quiet click of the door that signalled the end of Jude's vigil. He turned on the kitchen tap and splashed his face with the tepid water. The drops shone between his fingers in the early light.

The kitchen window looked over the compound wall, wreathed in drying vines from their neighbour's villa. The other house itself looked asleep, still and silent. He had a sudden mad fantasy: if he just went next door and lay there under that quiet roof he too might wake into the day bright and untroubled.

Jude was sleeping when he crept into their room to take the picture of the Orange House down from the mantelpiece.

Holding it in gentle hands, he walked over to the children's bedroom. *They should have their own rooms*, he thought as he pushed open the door. It was time. They were nearly adults. *We can paint it whatever colour he wants. We can do it together.*

Their heads peeped out from the blankets, dark hair and white falling over their round cheeks, and mouths pursed like babies. The covers shifted with the soft beat of their breath – these two miracles, these unlikely survivors of cruel tides that had ripped so many apart.

Love swept back his hurt, like the deep undertow after a violent wave. He sat down next to Marc's curled body. Under the covers he looked tiny, drained of defiance. As the bed creaked, the boy opened his eyes. They were glazed and the room's shadows made them soft and dark as Salim's own.

'What's the matter?' he said, his voice high with morning hoarseness. He sat up, hugging his knees, and Salim saw his features start to re-form and re-settle into the wariness he knew so well.

'Nothing.' As Salim sat there, he felt lost, robbed of direction. He looked at the boy's flushed face, the arrogance of manhood struggling against a child's uncertainty.

'I wanted to talk to you,' he said quickly, before the words could eat themselves. 'To... to say sorry. For slapping you. That was wrong.' Marc's eyes widened, and his hands clutched his knees more tightly. Salim waited for him to say something. *Help me do this.*

'You're always angry with me.' It was a tiny voice, a little boy's voice, and it reached around Salim's throat like clenching fingers of guilt.

'I know,' he said. He felt tears on his eyelids as he blinked. 'It must seem that way. But it's not your fault. I just want you to understand your history, that's all. It hurts when it feels like you don't want to know.'

'But you don't talk to us about anything,' Marc said, his own eyes wet. 'You never tell us things. You just expect us to be on your side no matter what. It's not fair to be like that.'

'I know,' Salim said. He handed Marc the photograph, and saw his son's eyes widen like the baby in the frame. 'You talk about going home sometimes. But I wanted to show you *my* home. The one that was stolen when I was a boy, even younger than you. It was a very beautiful place, can you see? The sea is just behind it, and it was always warm. And this orange tree here was planted when I was born. Jaffa oranges are the sweetest in the world.' He felt his voice catching. 'You're what I have now, instead of my home, you and Sophie. And so I guess I expect a lot from you. Maybe too much.'

Marc ran his fingers along the picture, fascinated.

'It looks nice,' he said.

'It was.' Grief rose up, catching him unawares.

'I don't want to be a Palestinian or a Jew,' Marc went on, flexing his legs onto the bed. 'Sophie and me, we're not like that. We don't want to get involved in all that fighting. You never ask us what *we* want, who *we* want to be.'

'All right,' Salim said. 'Who do you want to be?'

Marc paused, his face such an innocent blend of scepticism and hope that Salim almost laughed.

'A dancer,' he finally said, pointing his toes. 'I'm really, really good. You never came to one rehearsal for my play. Mum's coming next week to the Parents' Performance but I bet you don't even know that it's happening.'

I did, but I was too angry to care. 'I told your mother I'd try to come. We aren't communicating properly, that's all. Your mother isn't a great communicator. Maybe I'm not so great either.'

'So will you come?' Marc said. 'It's just two weeks until the opening night and this is just to see what we need to work on.' Sophie was stirring in the other bed. Salim looked up at the closed curtains and the white light now streaming in.

'I'll be there, I promise,' he said. 'We'll talk more afterwards. I want that. I really do.'

He saw a ghost of a smile touch Marc's face, a ripple of warmth crossing the white. Then his son nodded and said, 'Okay, deal.' Salim leaned forward and kissed his cheek. It was smooth as marble wrapped in the sweet mustiness of sleep.

'So, a dancer?' he said, getting to his feet as Sophie sat up and stretched her arms.

'That's right.' Marc's voice held the hint of a challenge, a cat ready to spring.

'Whatever you like,' Salim said. 'As long as you're my son.'

*

The Parents' Performance was scheduled for Wednesday night – the last school night of the week.

Salim put the invitation on the bedroom shelf, next to the picture of the Orange House. It was a gold card imprinted with a picture of a winged boy. *It's an absurd thing*, Salim thought, *so very English-abroad*. That child, a winged spirit lifted from a fairytale – it wasn't Marc but it had Marc's essence. Its eyes looked through Salim to some wonderful world beyond.

His attendance had been a solemn promise, and Marc was lifted by it into a cheerfulness Jude and Salim had rarely seen. He practised furiously in his room after school. Sophie was his eager helper, encouraging him, propping up his confidence and managing the music on her new boom box – a present from Rafan.

For the next four nights Marc ate voraciously at dinner and chatted to Rafan about the difficulty of the dance moves and how he was the youngest person ever to play such an important role. 'One of the leading roles,' he said, between mouthfuls of cinnamon lamb cooked over rice and vermicelli.

Rafan patted him on the back and laughed. 'This one will keep you in your old age,' he said to Jude. 'He has his eyes on the stars.' Salim saw Jude smile politely, the half-smile that had moved into her eyes and taken possession of her face these past weeks.

The night before Marc's show, Salim planned to speak to Rafan and set a limit on his stay. Hassan approved; when Salim called him to wish him happy Eid that morning he'd sniffed to hear that their youngest brother was still around. '*W'Allah*, you're more generous than I would be, Salim,' he said down the telephone. 'I tell you something for nothing – that boy has always been trouble and he'll always be trouble. Your wife is right for once. Send him packing.'

As he put the receiver down, Salim noticed a scrap of sticky paper pushed under the phone base. Two words jumped out. *England school.*

He pulled it out and held it up to the light. It was in Sophie's neat print. *Mum*, it said, *Uncle Tony called about England school plans. Good news call him quickly.* Cold fingers touched the back of his neck.

He looked back towards the kitchen, seeing the flash of Jude's blonde hair as she set the table, vanishing behind the door. *England school plans.* What plans were these? Cold fingers of anxiety pressed into him, constricting his chest.

'Dad!' Marc was calling, asking for an opinion on his routine. He grabbed Salim's arm, pulling him out onto the patio with giddy excitement, lit from within. 'You mother said you're perfect,' Salim told him with a smile. 'Why do you need my vote?'

'Mum always says I'm perfect,' Marc replied, pressing play on the cassette deck as the sun dipped. 'But you'll tell me the truth.'

As Salim watched his son leaping into the night air his heart leapt too, the confused vertigo of flying without a net. The note in his pocket was like a stone pulling him towards earth. *England school plans. Call quickly.* Never. Jude would never make plans to leave without telling him, never betray him like that. He tried to scramble the possibilities into a more reassuring shape as Marc spun and leapt in front of him. But his mouth was dry, and finally he had to ask his son to stop for a break.

He was drinking their homebrewed wine on the patio, swallowing down his fears, when he saw Rafan's face coming out of the dark. His brother came to stand beside him, leaning over the low wall into the night. The thin sounds of darkness whispered around the edge of hearing – the squeak of crickets and the faint whine of mosquitoes. Salim felt silence drawing out like a wire between them. *I'll deal with Rafan*, he'd promised her. His mouth opened, but doubts lay heavy on him – about Jude, love and loyalty – each one a stone in his chest.

'I had a message today,' Rafan said at last. Salim could only see the outline of his features, the hooked nose under a narrow brow. 'From the Iraqis.' His words brought that night back – their car on an empty desert road, the blank faces of the men hoisting Rafan's bags out of the trunk, sweat trickling down Salim's face in the driver's seat.

Rafan turned to look at him. 'We need to make another trip to the border tomorrow. A last time.'

Weariness filled Salim as his brother went on. 'This location is further than before. I think at least five hours' driving. It's better to start in the early evening. We can leave from here after your work.'

'I promised Marc I'd go with him tomorrow night,' Salim said. The air around him seemed to be moving, racing through him like seconds – the future streaming into the past.

'*Ma'alish.*' Never mind. 'He's a boy, you're a man. There'll be another time for that. But not for this.'

Salim bent his head to his hands. He was tired of these decisions – at every step, another test of who he wanted to be. 'You can take the car. Go by yourself.'

'I can't. I have no identity here. If anyone stops me, I'm lost, big brother. You're the only one I can trust. The only one I have.'

Salim turned his back to the wall, looking at his brother, trying to see the little boy who used to lie next to him at night, who cried in his sleep. *This is not the same person. That boy is gone, and this man is using you.*

'Fuck you, Rafan.' He threw the words out, but they seemed to rebound on him. 'Fuck these bullshit hints. You chose your own way – leave me to choose mine.'

Rafan snorted. 'You know the trouble with you, Salim? You're clever but you're not smart. You think because you got qualifications and a British passport that the white boys would open up to you? Well, they didn't. You think that your Jewish wife can forget her heritage and raise Arabic children? She didn't. You think that you can forget all the shit you came from by living somewhere else? You can't. You know what I see when I look at you? A man who doesn't know who he is.'

Salim pressed his hands to his eyes. In the blackness, the words he had written to Rafan on the day he left Lebanon burned fierce and white. *I'm sorry, but my road is not here.* Would he feel better, freer, less lost, if he had never written it?

'I know who I am,' he said, to Rafan, to himself. 'I have a family to think about.'

'You're fooling yourself. You know it, brother. She's a lovely girl and all that, but she'll make her own plans in the end. They always do, these people. That's why they always win, and we always lose.'

He felt Rafan's hand on his shoulder. *England school plans. Call quickly.* A dam was cracking inside him, anger leaking out in a cold flood. Her hand on his chest the other night, telling him to choose her, talking about love. And all the time, had she been keeping her own secrets? Planning a life without him, a world in which he had no place?

His brother's voice said, 'This isn't bullshit, Salim. *I* know who you are. You're my brother. One blood. These men we're helping – they're our blood too. Forget this *white husband* game you're playing, Salim. If they really love you they won't stand in your way. You want to take back what's yours? It's time to pay the price.'

Salim closed his eyes. Nothing about him was real; he felt like a ghost haunting the present, while Rafan and Jude loomed before him, terrifying and solid. Behind them he saw blood seeping into Clock Tower Square and the mortars falling over the sea, children skipping in Shatila while the tanks rolled in. He saw the shadow of the new settlements dwarfing Nadia's tiny home. *Our land, our blood*, the words shouted over the crackle of gunfire. Meyer, coolly brushing Omar's name into the bin. And Jude, his wife, letting the flames of the enemy burn in their children's eyes.

He touched the note in his pocket. *England schools. Call quickly.* How much he'd loved her, all those years and miles ago, her face turned up to his under the cold London sun. That memory still lived in him, the sweetness of her, the thrill of entering an unknown room and suddenly recognizing it as your own. But now their house was full of strangers. The doors had closed and nothing was familiar any more.

'One time.' The words were out before he realized it, born of doubt rather than conviction. 'One time, for Jaffa.' He felt a corrosive satisfaction at turning Jude's ultimatum back on her, at calling her bluff. Did she really love him, or just an idea of him? This was the only way to tell.

But as Rafan nodded, he felt it again, the inexplicable paralysis of his dreams. Home was somewhere close by, but his feet were frozen, fixed into the dust. *Here I am, rooted helpless as a tree trunk.* And there was no way to move forward without tearing up the ground.

At six o'clock on the performance night, Jude put Marc in the car and went back into the house to get Sophie. The girl was in her bedroom, carefully spreading a rose pink lipstick onto her upper lip. Jude gave her a mock pat on the head and said, 'Come on, mademoiselle. It's not a fashion show, you know.'

'I don't know why we're hurrying,' Sophie said casually, smudging the pink smear with her finger. 'Dad's not even here yet.'

'I know, pet.' Jude felt her stomach turn again. *He cannot miss this. He promised Marc.*

The conversation with Tony had set her mind flying today. He'd rung in the middle of the afternoon with a simple message – brutally simple, as it turned out. There were three schools, right next to their old home in east London, willing to consider the children for placement after the official start of the school year. Each one required an entrance exam, to be sat in November. *Less than a month.* Otherwise, they would be waiting another year.

'Think about it very, very carefully,' Tony had said. 'I can help you if you decide to come. I'll do anything you need.'

'I just don't know, Tony,' she'd told him, filled with confusion.

'He promised to send his brother away. If he does that, how can I leave?'

There was a long pause on the end of the line, and then Tony said, 'It sounds like you're at a crossroads, *bubbellah*. Only you know the right way to go. Just know that I'm waiting for you once you take the next step.'

The sound of another car pulling into the drive sent a flood of relief through her. 'Come on,' she said, tugging Sophie's arm. 'Daddy's finally turned up, so let's get going.'

She tumbled out into the fading light of day with Sophie just behind her. She saw Marc get out of the back seat of their car, his face alight.

Something's wrong. Rafan was striding towards them from the maid's quarters. One bulky black duffel bag was slung over his shoulder. He gave Jude a sidelong flick of his eyes as he passed her. There was a tear in the thick black leather, showing pale green notes underneath. In an instant her heart froze.

Salim was standing by their car in shirtsleeves, his dark eyes hesitant. Rafan called out to him – '*Yallah*, Salim. Let's go. We'll get the other ones later.'

Jude's hand went up to her mouth, and she said to Salim, 'You can't.' His head shot up and he looked her straight in the eyes. For the first time in their married life she saw nothing – nothing at all – that she recognized. Marc's voice drifted over them, a high cry of 'What's happening? Where are you going?'

'I'm sorry,' she heard Salim say to his son. 'I have to do something very important. I'll come to your play another time.'

'You said you would tonight. You said.' She heard the tears before she saw them fall. Her young man, reduced to a crying child once again. Even as her heart ached she found herself moving towards Salim and taking his arm in her hand. She felt as if her fingers could tear through the skin of this stranger, to find the man she'd married underneath.

'Don't, Salim,' she said, only the third time she had ever used his real name, she realized. The first was on the day of their marriage, when she took him for her own.

She felt something stir in him – a constriction of guilt. But he pulled his hand away from her, and turned and walked towards the gate. The last thing she saw was the blackness of his hair as he turned the corner, framed by the cheerful wave of Rafan's hand as he turned to take him away.

Marc flew like a bird that night on stage, his wings a rainbow of sparkling colour over the paint on his face. His eyes were wild and his body seemed too light for the ground. She felt her heart pause every time she saw him; every movement was a vice in her chest, and she had to fight the impulse to reach out and grab him, to hold him to the earth.

They didn't stay afterwards, not even to share a drink with Helen or hear Mr Trevellian's praise. They drove back in silence. Sophie leaned her forehead against the rear window and Marc slumped in his seat. Jude knew that once Salim came home again later that night or the next, they would be living in a different world. If he came back at all.

The house was empty when they pulled into the drive, covered in the silent darkness of a desert night. Marc went quietly into the twins' room and closed the door. Sophie watched his back, and then turned to her mother. Through the dim light Jude saw the faintest shimmer of pink still clinging to her daughter's lips in faded patches.

'Where did they go tonight?' Sophie said, her voice firm. 'Dad and Uncle Rafan. You know, don't you?'

Seeing her there, so beautiful in the dying moments of childhood, Jude felt a memory stir of her Batmitzvah at the very same age. *The day you can stop being afraid, the day you take your place as a woman among your people.* Rebecca's day had arrived on a broken cart, Jude's at her grandmother's bedside. Now it was Sophie's turn, here in the desert, thousands of miles down the road.

'They're taking money to Rafan's friends,' Jude said. A grown woman deserved the truth. 'The Palestinian fighters.' Sophie nodded, her arms reaching up to hug herself as if in a cold wind.

'We can't go on like this,' she said, dropping her eyes to the ground. 'You know we can't, Mummy.' And then she turned to follow her brother into the bedroom, her skirt fluttering in the still air.

When the children were finally in bed, Jude went to lie down in her room. She felt as if she were floating away from her body, into a dream in which she hovered over a vast road spanning winter fields. Other roads forked and splintered off from it in every direction.

Along one, a horse-drawn cart came creaking, a girl inside it nodding her head with every step of the horse. Jude was seized with the absolute conviction that she must follow it. She raced forward, heart leaping – but then in the panic of nightmares realized the cart had already passed by. And though she tried and tried, running until her lungs burst, she could not see which of the many roads it had taken.

She woke into the light before dawn. Jumping out of bed, she pulled open the drawer where Rebecca's menorah had been hidden. Rafan had taken it to show Salim – and she had never thought to ask if it had been put back.

The old hiding place was empty. She threw open drawer after drawer – tearing down clothes and old boxes like a madwoman.

She finally found it under the bed. Clutching it to her, she almost wept – from relief and from wonder that he'd saved it after all. For all these months it had been underneath her while she slept, keeping its silent watch.

Suddenly, she felt her desperation harden into resolution. *Be brave. Be a mensch.* The whistle had blown; it was time for the fearless leap into the air.

In the darkness of the maid's quarters, only two black bags were left. She dragged them into the garden and emptied them over the sand, every cell of her body listening for the sound of returning wheels.

Bricks of green bills wrapped in cord flopped out, more and more as if from a bottomless pit. She watched them fall until they lay in a heap, tens of thousands of dollars stinking in the warm air.

When you choose peace, you choose the losing side. Maybe it was true. But she would not let Rafan win either.

Walking into the kitchen she pulled the can of kerosene out from under the sink. A box of matches stood on the side, by the gas hob. The door swung as she carried it back into the garden where the banknotes trembled in the breeze. Their flickering became rapid, helpless as the fuel drenched them.

Stepping back, she lit the match and looked into the tiny flame. The heat wavered at the tips of her fingers.

A hundred times she'd used that flame to celebrate life on birthdays, to kindle the lights during their secret Sabbath prayers. Now she would use it to set them all free.

Her fingers let the match go; it floated down and the fire seemed to roar up to meet it. She was mesmerized; there were voices in the flames. *Go, Judith, go! For God's sake, girl.*

Turning her back on the blaze she ran into the children's bedroom.

'What's happening?' Sophie said, as Jude shook their shoulders and pushed them to their feet. Marc was already up, his face shining in the gloom.

'Get your clothes packed,' she said, pulling their suitcases down from the top of the cupboard. 'We're going to the airport. Uncle Tony has found you schools, and you'll sit the exam for places next month.'

Sophie put her hand over her mouth, her face white. Jude reached over to take her daughter's hand. 'You were right,' she said, squeezing it tight. 'It's time to find a happy place – for all of us.' Tears fell as Sophie nodded, one hand clutching her blanket painted with leaping horses.

Marc said instantly, 'But what about Daddy?' The plea in his voice, the wild panic, almost derailed her. She knelt down beside him and took his face in her hands.

'Your father needs to make an important decision,' she said. 'Until he does, we need to go somewhere safe. I'll explain in the car, but now we must hurry.'

'And my play?' His hands caught her shoulders, clutching helplessly at her. 'What about my play?'

She pulled him into her arms. 'I'm so sorry, Marc. Sometimes life is so hard, I know. But I promise, there are other things waiting for you, wonderful, exciting things. Do you trust me?'

Marc nodded but his whole body wilted, like the lime tree he'd so carefully tended. He must have known, she thought, when his father walked out of the gate today, that his grand moment was like Puck himself – only ever a dream.

By the time their bags were packed and in the car, morning had arrived. The quiet of the desert surrounded them, as Jude drove to Kuwait's airport for the last time.

The world slept, and somewhere out there Salim might be making his way back to an empty house. As if reading her mind, Sophie whispered from the back seat, 'Will he ever forgive us?'

'He will,' Jude said. *I know who he is, even if he has forgotten.* 'He loves us more than anything. He just needs to remember how that feels.'

As she drove, she wound down the window to let in the cool wind. It rang in her ears like the gusts down the Wear when she was a little girl, like the call of the crowd at the swimming championships she'd imagined in the silence of her room.

And then she felt it, somewhere between a memory and a wish:

her toes on the edge of the pool, the water dazzling beneath her, waiting for the whistle, poised to spring.

It unfolded in a perfect moment, just as it should have happened – the glorious blue of the water, the falling light, the thrill of the cheering and the bubbles of anticipation rising within her, carrying her forward into the race. On the other side was safety, the exultation of arms linked with hers as they ran home under the boundless northern sky.

As the world blurred and the road whipped by she saw them all running beside her, clear as day – Kath and Peggy, Jack and Dora, Marc and Sophie, even Salim and Rafan – all hurtling homewards as the clouds streamed above them, chasing each other into an unknown future. Silence followed them, an emptiness slowly filling with another presence, flooding Jude with joy and relief. *You are here.* Rebecca was here, walking beside her, and she suddenly understood that *here* was the place they were supposed to meet, that she'd been waiting here all this time for Jude to find her on the long road. And so Jude reached up with love to grasp her grandmother's hand, finally ready to guide them both home.

4

HOMECOMING

If you wish to inherit the land of your birth,
Buckle on the sword and take up the bow.

NAPHTALI HERZ IMBER

And we walked the moonlit path, joy skipping ahead of us,
And we laughed like two children together,
And we ran and raced our shadows,
And we became aware after the euphoria, and woke up.
If only we did not awaken.

IBRAHIM NAGI, 'THE RUINS',
SUNG BY UMM KULTHUM

1987

LONDON

He came back to silence, to a smouldering pile of embers in the driveway, scattered clothes in the bedroom and a letter from Jude. As he held it in numb fingers, he watched Rafan walk away from the remains of the fire, ashes drifting from his hands. A black bag lay crumpled like an empty skin on the porch. Rafan picked it up and shook it, his forearms black with burned paper.

Sal, you broke your promise, Jude's note said. *I'm doing this to save our family. I'm taking us home. How could you be so blind, Sal? Jews or Arabs, what does it matter who we are? How dare you make our children part of a war they didn't start?*

But the ending was kinder, the loving heart that had once opened for him. *You're still my husband,* she wrote. *I know you, I believe in you, in the man I married. You belong to us, Sal, to Sophie and Marc and me, not to your brother or to the past. It's your choice. Please, come home. It's not too late. Come home to us.* The last line said she would call when she got to England, from Tony's house.

He felt Rafan's hand on his shoulder, and his brother's voice came to him, as if from down a long tunnel.

'I told you, big brother,' it said. 'They take everything. Home, money, history. Even your children. Everything. There's only one thing they can't take.'

Salim turned slowly to face him, the letter tight in his fist.

'And what's that?' he said, over the roar of blood.

'Our revenge.' And Rafan reached over to lift Jude's letter out of his hand.

Later, Rafan dragged her clothes out of the house and threw them into the wasteland. Salim watched his face, working with effort and rage, as he heaved the summer dresses onto piles of tyres.

'I have to get out of here,' Rafan told him later in the shadow of the porch, holding one of his empty bags. 'Today. They won't believe I lost the money. That bitch.' The genial mask was gone; his face was an ugly blur of rage. 'I can catch a flight to Amman. There are brothers there too. We can still be in touch, Salim, don't worry.' His hand closed on Salim's wrist, the fingers tight.

In the quiet house after Rafan's departure, Salim took the picture of the Orange House and curled up with it on their bed. And as he slept he dreamed that the oranges were ripening and there was food waiting for him on the table. He and Hassan looked just like Marc and Sophie, and his mother was laughing at Abu Hassan's jokes as they sat together and ate. He woke into an almost unbearable yearning.

Two days later, she called him.

'What did you expect?' She sounded calm over the miles. He'd been counting on remorse, on tears, but her voice was a smooth wall leaving him no purchase.

'Rafan's gone,' he said. He heard her intake of breath.

'I knew you would do the right thing.' Now life spread back into her tone.

She went on, 'Wait – someone wants to talk to you.' The line went dead for a moment, and then he heard breath coming quick and anxious. 'Dad?'

'Marc.' He'd been expecting Sophie, and in the spin of his thoughts he couldn't find words.

'Are you angry with us?' the boy asked. Salim felt his own throat catch. Yes, he wanted to say. Yes yes yes.

'No, I'm not angry.'

'Are you coming to England?'

'I don't know.'

Marc fell silent. Salim looked out into the garden, over the dark spot where Jude's fire had sat. Marc had danced there only three days before. In the half-light Salim could still see his leaping form, a ghost of joy.

'When will you know?' Marc's voice was girlish and urgent. It pricked Salim with slivers of guilt.

'You're too young to understand, you and Sophie,' he said. 'Maybe it's better for us to be apart for a while.'

'But...' and now the tears came. 'But you said we'd get better at talking to each other.' The boy's voice was still nowhere near breaking into manhood. 'And it's really good here. I'm going to audition for White Lodge. It's the best ballet school in England. If I get in, I'll be famous one day.' Salim laughed aloud. This was how it was going to be – the flowering of their lives happening away from him, snatching something precious away before he had the chance to claim it.

'You have to come back,' Marc was saying. 'Mum and Sophie want you to. I do too.'

Salim gripped the telephone. Marc. Rafan. Palestine. The Orange House. It was too much for one mind to measure. Out of nowhere a ridiculous memory surfaced, the discussion with Jude at Virginia's all those lifetimes ago. *Who could you be*, she'd asked, *if you didn't mind giving up everything you are now?* And he'd told her it was impossible to weigh the value of things past against the price of those things yet to come.

'We'll work something out,' he told the boy at last. 'You're right, we should be together.'

But the words that seemed so true for Marc on the telephone later began to fester. In the days that followed, every morning brought a rush of new anger, pitiless as the rising sun. The unfairness of it all rankled. Jude had forced his hand. If he refused to return, she would say *he* had chosen to leave them.

'You can't force me to live in England,' he told her when they discussed the arrangements. 'But while the children are young I'll make sure I come often to visit.' She sounded taken aback. *What did you expect?* he wanted to throw at her.

He moved into a small apartment in Kuwait City and took part-time work so he could come back to see them for a few months a year. The first time he touched down at Heathrow, Jude and the children met him at the airport. They came hurtling into his arms and for a while it was like those first years of their infancy, when all they knew was love. That night he lay next to Jude in their first marriage bed, the warm smell of sweat and bare skin surrounding them, and watched her sleeping face.

By the third year of their separation, he'd moved into the spare room. And the children no longer came to the airport to meet him. Only Sophie still hugged him when he came through the door. And Marc, caught in the cruel pinch of adolescence, asked him to sign a piece of paper promising not to fight while he was there.

But the arguments came despite it all. No matter how many times he was driven to accuse her – of coldness, of betrayal, of rejection – she refused to bend. She was not sorry. She had done the right thing. In that house, everyone had a purpose. Jude had found her place teaching English, telling old stories to London's multicoloured classrooms. Jews and Arabs and all the rest, she liked to say. Sophie was one of her eager young students. And Marc was still caught in his dreams. Soon he would join the Royal Ballet School, and leave them all behind. The brightness of their lives cast a shadow over the failures of his. He brooded on them, until the steps onto the flight to Heathrow felt covered with nails.

One day Salim came from the airport to find the house empty. Jude was not back from work. The twins' bedrooms were dark. He stood for a moment, remembering that desolate morning in the desert four years earlier – the blank rooms, the closed doors.

Dropping his bag on the floor, he unzipped the front pocket and pulled out his picture of the Orange House. One by one, he picked every one of Jude's photographs off their mantelpiece in the living room – carelessly arranged snaps of their family picnics in Il-Saraj, of Marc in his ballet shoes and Sophie riding. Once the shelf was bare, he settled the picture of the Orange House reverently on the dusty wood. He'd bought a new gold frame for it in Kuwait, but the shine off the rim made the photograph look even more ghostly, the faintest imprint of yellow and brown.

When Jude came back an hour later with Marc she apologized for being late.

'I had to take Marc to the doctor for more tests,' she said. 'They think he needs help concentrating and keeping calm. Right, pet?' Marc shrugged thin shoulders, his eyes downcast. 'The teachers are stupid,' he said. 'Dancers aren't supposed to be calm.'

Then the empty shelf and its lonely picture caught Marc's fleeting eye. 'What's that doing there?' he asked.

'It's our house in Palestine,' Salim said. He saw Marc's brow furrow and waited for the protests to start. But the boy just looked from the picture to his father. 'I remember,' was all he said.

One year later, on Salim's forty-fifth birthday, the picture vanished. He was due to leave for Kuwait the following day. Jude was at work and Sophie was home with a cold, cheerfully helping him pack.

In the chaos of the spare bedroom he handed her clothes and she folded them with arms as sandy brown as Jaffa's beaches. He had to remind himself that the little girl he'd once thrown in the air would soon leave secondary school, a year ahead of her peers. Her blossoming intelligence left him awed and fearful, the child of his memory drifting out of his reach.

She was lecturing him now. 'Don't you get tired of all this going back and forth?' she said, draping a shirt into the suitcase. 'Whatever happened to the plan to move back here for good?'

'You'd soon get tired of me if I did,' he said lightly, but she flicked him a questioning glance.

'Is that the best excuse you can come up with?'

He looked away from her. It confounded him that despite her Arab colouring she was still Jude in essence – the same stubborn steadfastness. 'You don't understand, Sophie.'

'That you and Mum have problems? That Marc is difficult? I grew up in this family too, you know. I remember.'

'You only remember what you want to,' he said, feeling defensive. 'Or what your mother told you. It's not always the truth.'

'You blame us for wanting to come back here. You always have.' Salim knew she was right even as he opened his mouth to protest. 'We just wanted a place to settle down and be happy. You of all people should understand. I mean, after all those family stories about people running from one place to another – you, Uncle Rafan, Mum's family. Maybe you didn't have a choice about it then – but now we do.'

'That's what you think,' he said automatically. She rolled her eyes, took the shirt into her hands and started back into the bedroom. As she disappeared, she called back, 'Dad, did you already pack the picture? I couldn't see it.'

He turned to the mantelpiece, alarmed. Jude's pictures were back – restored after another fierce argument. But in the centre was a hollow space where the Orange House usually stood.

Panic flooded him. Jude must have finally thrown it away. How could she? Ripping through the dustbins, and then the cupboards in her room, he tasted the sourness of fear. His picture was nowhere to be found.

In desperation, he pushed open the door to Marc's room. The bed was neat and the wall papered with images of male dancers, their bodies arched in hidden pain.

On the table lay the pills Marc was supposed to take when he got what he called his angry headaches. Jude had insisted after the Royal Ballet sent a warning letter: Marc had tried to start a fire in the car park – next to a car owned by a teacher with whom he was at odds.

Beside the bottle was the Orange House, lying out of its frame. Next to it lay another photograph, a replica of Salim's blown up to twice its normal size. But this one had been defaced, Salim saw with horror. Marc had drawn other pictures over it in bold colours. Jude and Sophie stood by his tree with books in their arms. Marc was next to them in a dancer's pose, coloured with a red tutu and gold ballet shoes. On the edge stood Salim holding an orange. A Star of David was painted over the door, above the heads of Jude and Sophie. Marc's fingers pointed up to it, and another stretched out to his father.

As Salim lifted it in astonishment, he heard the click of the door. He turned to see Marc framed in the door with his ballet gear, poised like a bird ready to flee.

'I was making it for your birthday,' the boy said eventually. 'It's better than looking at that old picture all the time. You should have a picture of us to take with you.'

Salim held out the photograph. 'You put a Star of David on my house.' Marc rubbed his forehead and cast his head down, his foot tracing a jagged path on the floor.

'Sort of. But that's not what it means.'

'What? What do you think it means?' Salim's relief at finding his precious picture was draining away, turning to anger.

'I thought you'd understand!' Marc threw back, defiant. 'It's all of us and the house together. You said it was *our* house. That means Mum too, and the star's for her.'

'And what about you?' Salim saw fear enter Marc's blue eyes. He pointed to the boy in the tutu. 'Do you want to be Jewish, like those boys at your school? Is that why you dressed yourself like this? To remind me you can't be an Arab? You think I'd let a Jew inherit anything of mine?'

'I'm not a *Jew*. I'm just a dancer.'

'There are no Arab ballet dancers, Marc.'

'Then I'll be the first.'

Salim looked down at Marc's picture, the pointed toes and girl's dress, and felt rage subside into anxious pity.

'No, you won't,' he said. *Better he understand quickly, before it's too late.* 'You're not like the English boys in your class. You're an Al-Ishmaeli, even if you don't want to be. You can look like them and act like them. And they'll accept you as long as I pay the fees. But you'll never be one of them. That's the reason there are no other Arabs at your ballet school, Marc. They know better than to try.' Marc had started wiping his eyes.

'You're lying,' the boy said, his eyes down. 'You don't know anything about it.'

'Once you said I told you the truth,' Salim said, dropping the picture and moving forward to grip Marc's shoulders. 'I'm telling you now. It won't work.' His throat constricted, and he tossed Marc's creation on the floor. 'A white Arab in a dress – you're probably just a joke to them. And you'll fail every time, like I did, if you keep pretending to be something you're not.'

'I know who I am!' Marc shouted.

'Who then?' Salim was yelling too. 'Tell me! Not Arab, not Jew. Not man, not woman. So who?'

The echoing silence was shocking. Marc's eyes were red as they found his. His son whispered, 'I know who I am.' And suddenly he wrenched away, a blur of white, leaving nothing behind but the echo of the slammed front door.

School was out that summer's afternoon, and the twins were home. Salim sat in Jude's lounge on a soft, cream armchair, a new, unsigned contract in his hand. An American construction company in Kuwait needed an accountant for a year. The title was 'Financial Assistant'. Each page seemed to laugh at him as he turned it. *I was a Managing Director once*, he wanted to scream back.

Jude had replaced the brown spiral carpet with apricot, and the walls were a grassy green. The late afternoon sun played across the furniture. It could almost have been an orchard – a very English one, full of light summer fruits and berries and the song of birds.

Sophie was sitting at the table cutting something out of the newspaper. Jude was busy in the kitchen; the door was open and as he looked up he heard the click of her heels and saw a flash of legs. For the first time in many months he remembered she was still a beautiful woman.

Then Sophie was walking over to him, holding something out. 'Here, Dad,' she'd said. 'It's a story from *The Times*. About Jaffa.'

He took it from her hand and scanned it. Something only *The Times* would cover, a piece about how the Jews and the Arabs were finally working together to save the old city. There was a black and white picture of the Clock Tower halfway down the article. For an instant he was back in the Square – remembering its grandeur before the days of blood, rubble and decay.

He pushed it back at her, saying, 'Very interesting.' Her face fell, and he felt a sharp tug of guilt. But then, as Jude walked back into the room, he was flooded with a new idea.

'Why don't you go?' he asked his daughter. 'Your exams are finished. You should pay a visit. Aunt Nadia and Uncle Tareq will look

273

after you. You can see for yourself what all this is about.' He indicated the limp newspaper cutting she held in her hand.

It was just one movement that undid him – the brief second when Sophie spun her brown head to the side and looked at Jude with her eyebrows raised.

Marc walked into the room just as Sophie was saying carefully, 'That might be great! Could I bring a friend? I promised to go away with the girls this summer.'

'Marc,' Salim said, ignoring her. 'Why don't you go to Jaffa with Sophie this summer?' Marc turned to Sophie with a puzzled frown. Salim saw her give her brother a wink, as she said, 'Come on, Markey, it'll be fun!'

Marc's eyes did not meet his. They'd barely spoken since that afternoon in his bedroom. When he'd arrived back, Salim had found Marc's picture waiting on the spare room bed – cut into neat shreds.

'I've got auditions this summer at the School,' the boy muttered. 'I can't make any plans.'

'If they won't wait for you a week or two, they're not interested in you,' Salim said, feeling the familiar clench of his jaw. 'Or are you just making excuses?'

Marc flushed as Jude put a restraining hand on his arm.

'That's not how it works!' he spat, and Salim could almost see the wires of tension stringing Marc's thin body together. 'Do you have any idea how hard you have to slog to make it as a dancer? If I miss the auditions, that's it for me.'

'You don't think your history is important?' Salim stood up, the contract pages scattering on the floor.

'That's not what I said. Why do you always twist everything?'

'Because the only reason I'm not in Jaffa right now is for you, Marc. Remember? When your mother ran away with you – and you begged me to come back?'

'That's fucking rich, blaming me!' Marc yelled, his face livid.

'*You* ditched us in Kuwait! *You* told me I wasn't a real man! *You* said I would be a failure! So why should I go to fucking Jaffa?' He stepped closer to his father, hands balled into fists at his side. For one second, Salim realized in amazement that this boy was trying to deliver a man's challenge.

He heard Jude cry somewhere in the background, 'No, Marc!' But it was Sophie who stepped between them, her arms raised, saying, 'Stop it, both of you. Please. Please.'

Salim pulled her out of the way. That was the moment he thought Marc might actually hit him. But as the seconds passed he saw the boy's courage fail him as he'd known it would, saw the fear pushing rage out of those pale blue eyes. His son's stance altered, his weight shifted nervously towards the back foot. Salim's head was reeling; no blow could have been more powerful than the force of his hurt and disappointment.

He heard Marc clear his throat and say, coldly, 'I don't know why you keep on about that stupid house. It's not like it even belongs to you any more.'

It doesn't belong to you any more. Suddenly he realized the insanity of it. It had all been for nothing, the visits and the compromises. He'd lost his family years ago.

He tore up the new contract with the American firm that same night. When Jude came in and found him packing his bags, she said, 'But you're not going back to Kuwait today?'

'Not to Kuwait,' he'd told her. 'To Palestine.'

At the last minute, as he opened the door, Marc came charging out of his bedroom. He looked wild, his face white.

'Where are you going?' he demanded, his voice coming in harsh pants. Jude was standing at the back of the room, her arms helplessly by her side. The Star of David was lying on her chest wrapped around the Arabic chain he'd given her when they met. She made an effort to wear it when he was around. Looking straight past Marc, Salim pointed at her neck.

'You should take one of those off,' he said, hearing the venom in his voice.

She looked back, her face calm but weary. 'They're both part of me,' was her quiet reply. He shook his head. Marc opened his mouth, but nothing came out. And then there was nothing left to do but close the door.

JAFFA

His homecoming started at the end of the long Mediterranean summer.

Standing on Nadia's balcony looking west, the music of evening drifted up from the street. The song of the mosque, street hawkers and car engines mingled with the scratch and wail of a record spinning on her ancient turntable. Fingers of shadow crept from the lofty Jewish settlement of Nazareth Illit down over the old city and the long slopes of the Galilee. Once, only the hills and the sky had stood above this refuge. *Watch out, you monkey*, Nadia used to say. *Up here, Allah has an unobstructed view.*

Now Salim could hear her calling him inside. She didn't like him sitting alone out here. *Brooding*, she called it. But he wasn't brooding. He was planning.

'It's nearly dinner time, *ya* Salim,' she sang. 'The food will get cold.'

'One minute,' he called back. Tareq's voice filtered through the kitchen, shouting down the telephone in Hebrew. The deeds to the Orange House were spread out in front of him.

Nadia's music troubled him. It was the same song he'd heard in the car that day in Beirut – the green time of his youth when he'd chosen to follow his love. But, like so many other things, that had turned out to be a false hope.

277

At dinner, Nadia spooned thick helpings of spiced cabbage and lamb onto their plates. Tareq lectured Salim about what Hassan had called 'this crazy scheme of yours'.

'What I am trying to tell you, Salim, like I said before,' Tareq's glasses were misty and the once black hair white at the temples, 'taking back Arab property is a very complicated thing. People don't win these cases against the State. And the process is agonizing.' Tareq shook his head, took off his glasses and wiped them on the corner of his jacket. 'Agonizing.' He looked straight at Salim with his small eyes and kind face.

'It seems very simple to me,' Salim said. The table was piled high with papers, including records of other property cases Tareq had pinched from a connection at the Magistrates' Court. 'The Jews bought our house from a man who did not own it. A child could see that the deeds were faked. It was an outright fraud. They owe us. There are precedents for this – I've read about them.' Since he'd left Jude and Marc standing at the door, he'd read about little else.

Tareq's hands spread out. 'You would be right, in any other country. Here, you are fighting against an agenda. The Jews made these laws to take the land for themselves – to be sure the Arabs could never return. Security, they called it. Or God's promise. Now you think you can persuade them to change their minds – you, Salim Al-Ishmaeli? You may have a British passport, but when all is said and done, you're still an Arab.'

Salim slammed his hand on the table. 'Fuck the Israelis,' he shouted. 'It was a war – everyone was running. Didn't the Jews run too, when the Nazis came? And when the Nazis stole what they left behind, did the Jews call *that* justice?'

'Listen, Salim,' Tareq was saying, 'I am not an expert at this. I'm a family lawyer. You need a man who can help you. I have some ideas. But I think you must moderate your expectations.'

Salim knew Tareq and Nadia did not approve of any of this. They were just like Hassan, happy to sympathize with his difficulties, to rage at fate and join in sad reminiscences. But they did not see the value in any pointless struggles.

Rafan understood, though. He knew why Salim was here. 'Don't bother with the cup of tears these people sell you,' he'd said the day he left Kuwait. 'There are sweeter things to drink in this world.'

Salim put his hand on Tareq's arm. 'I know you want nothing but the best for me. You and Nadia were more than my own mother and father. But don't ask me to moderate my expectations. I'm sick of living like a beggar, thanking the men who robbed me for the pennies they throw. Nothing is more important to me than this.'

Tareq looked down at his papers, fiddling with the corners. Salim could sense the rebuke.

'"Nothing" is a big word, Salim,' the older man said eventually. 'For a man with a family to care for.'

'They don't care for me and they don't need me,' he retorted instantly. 'They left me.'

'You know that's not true.'

'You weren't there,' Salim said, the bitter sting of it radiating through his body. 'You don't have any idea how it was, so please don't tell me.' Tareq shrugged his shoulders and sighed. 'As you say. I'll go and make some calls then, if you're sure.'

'I'm sure.'

Tareq sighed and nodded. Salim watched him walk away towards the television, his frame still lean, but bent. He'd always thought of Tareq as a tall man; he recalled looking up to talk to him, waiting for his answers, his approval and his guidance. But memories were tricky. He'd found himself looking down at this Tareq, just like the tall Jewish settlements looked down on old, shackled Nazareth.

The news was full of boys in the occupied streets of Jerusalem's West Bank throwing burning bottles at Israeli tanks. They were just

Marc's age, black bands around their heads and the same wild defiance in their eyes.

Salim escaped to the balcony to watch the sunset. There, with the skies of the Galilee sweeping out before him, he whispered the words again to himself. *I'm sure.* In the silence of evening it sounded weak, like a plea.

It occurred to him that his mother might have said the very same thing in this place, all those years ago, as she took her wish and tossed it out in this endless sky. *I'm just following your footsteps, Mama. Would you be proud of me?* He tried to remember her face, but all he could see was Jude, her blue eyes hard as ice. But then her image blurred like the western hills as the sunset swallowed them into darkness.

The next day, Tareq drove to Tel Aviv to file a petition with the Magistrates' Court.

This motion, he explained, was to set aside the legal limitation period on land claims. 'Normally you would only have twenty-five years to make a complaint against the State,' he said. 'After forty years you wouldn't have a hope. But in this case, you might have me to thank! Let me explain.'

The very year Salim had left for England, Tareq had persuaded Abu Hassan to lodge a claim contesting seizure of his house. 'Just in case there was any chance, you know. Not that he had the heart for it, mind you.'

Soon afterwards, his father had become unwell with a series of strokes. Tareq would now be able to argue that the years in which Abu Hassan could hardly hold a spoon should not be counted against his heir's right to claim.

With Tareq away, Salim paced the room to calm his nerves.

In the kitchen, he could see Nadia shaping *labneh* balls – thick clumps of strained yoghurt rolled into palm-sized ovals and dropped into a jar of olive oil and salt. The sour smell of the buttermilk drifted from the kitchen, as he watched her hands slapping over and over each other, squeezing and moulding in a silent dance.

Moving to the telephone, he dialled the number of Rafan's friend, the man his brother said could help him. Rafan was in Jordan now. 'Living a quiet life, big brother,' he'd said. 'There's nothing to do here but raise sheep and eat them. I'll be fat next time you see me.' Somehow, Salim doubted it.

The name written next to the phone number was *Jamil*. Rafan called him Jimmy. 'Jimmy is a good man to know. He's from Haifa originally, but he moved to Tel Aviv after the war. He writes for everyone. Even for that liberal Jew paper, *Haaretz*. They love him. He's a man with more than one face, you know what I mean?' Salim knew exactly what he meant. *With so many masks to wear, how do you remember who you are?*

Jimmy's voice on the end of the phone was a commanding, cheerful bass.

'Salim Al-Ishmaeli,' he boomed, rolling the words around on his tongue. 'Yes, I know your brother. He's been a good friend. He's done me some favours, given me some interesting stories. And now maybe you have another one for me?'

Salim explained his mission, as Jimmy made encouraging noises.

'*W'Allah, habibi*,' he said, at the end. 'That's quite the tale. I know this guy, this Abu Mazen. He passed away a while ago, God rest him. Or perhaps I shouldn't say that!' The laugh was full and throaty. 'But his boy is still around somewhere, making trouble.'

Salim pictured the fat face and the black curls. 'I don't want to see him,' he said.

'Sure,' Jimmy was saying. 'You have bigger fruit to pick. Rafan asked me to help you out, so let me. First we should meet. Why don't you come to Jaffa tomorrow? We can have a coffee and talk things over.'

*

Tareq returned from Tel Aviv that afternoon, pink with effort and oddly pleased with himself. He'd filed two motions: one with the Magistrates' Court to challenge the Statute of Limitations on Salim's case, one to sue Amidar, the government housing corporation that had swallowed their land.

'It's actually better than I thought,' he said to Salim over dinner. 'In fact, I have a surprise for you.' But he wouldn't budge when Nadia and Salim pressed him. He just shook his spectacled head and smiled. 'Later, later. I promised.'

Salim told him about Jimmy – leaving out the part about Rafan. Tareq was hesitant. But he agreed that the Palestinian press might be useful. 'The Arabs here still have many papers and radio stations, not that the Israelis care about those. But *Haaretz* might help. They cover many Arab stories. And I might have something else helpful for you in Tel Aviv. Wait and see.'

They set off the next day in Tareq's Nissan, down the rocky shoulders of the Galilee to the wide maritime plains. Salim leaned his forehead on the window, looking ahead as the land grew smooth and broad.

Car after car rolled by them, glinting in the blue daylight. The road wound down before them like a silver stream through dark fields. Petrol stations and compounds whipped past them, steel and glass where once was only green. *The land has been eaten*, he thought. *Eaten by the Jews, and here am I begging them to regurgitate a mouthful.*

As they reached Tel Aviv, row upon row of white apartment blocks blazed in the bright air, hundreds of windows like blank eyes gazing out over the sea. Ahead of him, the sky was spiked with high towers just like the ones rising over the Gulf sheikhs' waterfront.

But not everything was perfect. As they skirted the business district to older parts of town, signs of wear came creeping in through the window. Tel Aviv's Bauhaus buildings were once the envy of

Jaffa. Even Mayor Heikal had praised them, with their sweeping curves and strange angles, white as the foam on the sea. Now tired awnings draped from their balcony rails, and salt had scored brown and yellow marks into the walls. The sight of them touched Salim with a strange sense of sorrow.

They came to the crossing from Tel Aviv into Jaffa. Salim could not breathe out, holding the air down in his lungs against the sudden sting of memory. *I'm here*, he told himself. *Home.*

The road rolled on, past buildings he did not recognize into an area that seemed designed for tourists. Someone had lifted out Jaffa's crumbling yellow brickwork, soaked with the smells of nargile and coffee, and replaced it with new stones buffed to a neat sandstone shine.

Salim wound down the window, searching, desperate for Tareq to slow down until he could find something familiar, some point to anchor all his hopes. His eyes slid along the strange streets, watching old couples with cameras and girls with tanned legs flocking along the pavements. They left him feeling ridiculous, like a child waiting arms-open for an embrace that could never come.

Then he saw it at last. The Jaffa Clock Tower, still beautiful, now sitting apologetically in the middle of a busy traffic intersection. Relief surged through him as he traced its unyielding lines. It was smaller than he remembered, but how could that matter? Here they'd sat to lick *kanafi* from Souk Attarin off their fingers; here he'd played pebblestones through the din of the Mahmoudiya mosque. Here the nargile smokers had kicked his ankles when Mazen dared him to upset their backgammon tables. And here he'd pulled out pieces of rubble after the Irgun's bomb, never realizing that a bigger disaster was coming for all of them.

Now tourists, white and plump, stood around taking pictures. Others sat at the cafés, relaxing in the autumn sun.

They were to meet Jimmy at a nearby coffee shop called Beitna. Jimmy himself suggested it. He'd thought it was funny – the name meant *our house* in Arabic and Hebrew. 'It's a Jewish place, but don't worry,' he said. 'I know them, they're progressives. And the girl who runs it is a beauty.' He was right. Girls with short sleeves and long legs were serving coffee to laughing boys with dark eyes.

A whale of a man stood up as they walked in. His belly bumped the cup of Turkish coffee in front of him, spilling dark liquid into an overflowing ashtray. His bearlike arms reached out as Salim approached, seizing him with cushioned hands. 'Salim Al-Ishmaeli,' he roared, as half the café turned to look at them. 'But don't you look like your brother!'

Jimmy insisted on buying coffee and cakes before getting down to business. 'These Europeans all have bad digestion,' he said. 'Their bowels are hard, like their brains. They keep their mouths closed while they eat, like it's a shame to be hungry. But an Arab does his best work at the table and in the bedroom. Right?' Tareq shifted in his seat and cleared his throat. Salim caught his brother-in-law's sideways glance, the quizzical look that said *who is this animal?*

True to his word, Jimmy could eat and talk at the same time. 'I'm no lawyer,' he said, wiping the crumbs of a honey cake from his mouth after Salim outlined where they stood. 'So I'll leave that side of the business to you.' He nodded at Tareq, who nodded warily back. 'But I have a few friends, a little organization, you might say, very interested in property rights here. You know the authorities are still moving people out of the old Arab buildings. Slums, they call them. It's a political issue. Mayor Shlomo's initiative.' He flicked a cigarette into the ashtray.

'We have a number of people who have come to us for help, but your story is – how shall I say it?' He smiled up at Salim. 'Poetic. I don't know anyone who can still make a claim from 'forty-eight. No one dares.'

'Rafan said you could help me,' Salim said, caution ticking in his brain. 'What kind of help does your organization provide?'

Jimmy sat back in his chair. His hands rested on the ridge of his stomach. 'We provide moral support,' he said. Salim looked blank. *Does he think I need a shoulder to cry on?* 'Public opinion,' Jimmy went on. 'We rally people to your cause. We get them interested – the press, the local leadership. We make it hard for the courts to ignore you. That's what we do.'

'And in return?' Tareq asked. His coffee was untouched before him.

Jimmy shrugged. 'What's good for you is good for us. We're all brothers here.' Salim's back stiffened at the word. He remembered Farouk, in Beirut, with his black eyes and bag full of bullets. Now there was a new *Najjada*, a boy's army in the occupied areas – *Hamas*, the Eager Ones. It sounded like a youth club. But this youth club sent teenagers with stones and Molotov cocktails to face Israeli soldiers with automatic rifles.

He put down his coffee very carefully, and looked at the man in front of him. 'Just so we're clear, Jamil. Whatever Rafan may have told you, I just want my house back. I'd appreciate your help with the press, anything to support my case. But nothing else.' Jimmy laughed and spread his hands.

'Rafan said you were a clever man! No, nothing else. We support our brothers fighting in the West Bank. But we support them in legal ways, because we are citizens of Israel now. For us, the struggle is for fair treatment and a share of the power. Isn't that right?'

Salim sat back again, still troubled. 'So, what do you want us to do?'

'Just be ready, and keep me informed. I'll write a couple of stories and when you get your first court hearing, then perhaps we can do something bigger. There are lots of people here ready to get behind a cause. Not all of my friends are Arabs, you know. Hey, Osnat!' He yelled across to the counter, making Salim jump. 'This man wants his house back from the State. Shall we help him get it?'

A Jewish girl with cool grey eyes and olive skin looked up. Her black t-shirt was smudged with sugar from the cakes and her hair was tied in a bandana. 'Sure,' she said, a grin sneaking across her face. 'Why not?'

As he watched Jimmy waddle away from the café, Salim felt doubt gnaw at him. Why was this friend of Rafan's so keen to help him? He feared to trust him – but then, he was so tired of fighting his battles alone.

Tareq tapped his watch anxiously. 'Salim, we need to get back to Tel Aviv. There's something I have to show you.'

'I'm not ready to go yet.' Salim shook his head and thrust his hands in his pockets. 'I need some time to myself here.'

Tareq checked his watch again. 'Okay, I'll tell you what. Let's meet here in half an hour. I can make a round trip and come back to get you. It's portable, this surprise I have.' He gave a small smile.

As his brother-in-law walked towards the car, Salim set off down the street – past the Clock Tower and these strange buildings with their fresh, white smell. He headed south by instinct, as if the spirit of his boyhood had stepped quietly into his shoes.

The old city was surrounded by a high wall, a church spire peeping over its top. To his left, the buildings began to get shabbier and the tourists vanished. He swung around the wall, west, towards his memory of the sea.

He began to understand where he was. Passing the old cemetery on his right his feet swung to the south again. Now he could see it – the port and the sea. Once he had walked across the port wall with Mazen, on his way to the Square for sweets. But today the wall was blocked off by long, sharp rows of steel containers. Ahead of him, the end of the sea wall was a modern car park a hundred feet wide. Sea birds flocked above it, lifted by the cold air.

Southwards again, and now he knew he was in old Al-Ajami, or a place that once was Al-Ajami. After the war, the Catastrophe, all the Palestinians in Jaffa had flocked here, making Salim obscurely proud that he'd lived in the Arabs' last stand in Jaffa. Until, that is, he had come to know the truth – it had only ever been the first prison of their defeat.

Now the buildings were crumbling, falling into each other, wires running from one to the other like a string of puppets frozen in a pitiful dance. Most of the land next to the sea had been cleared. Brown strips of scrub still ran downhill, out west into the rushing surf.

Through the haze, the sea was pale and clear – not a sail to be seen on the ruffling waters. There were no boats any more, no reason for them to come. The sharp, bruised sweetness of the harvest season would never fill the air here again. The trucks now took Jaffa's oranges to the modern Israeli port of Ashdod, forty miles south.

The sun was low in the sky, sending waves of blinding light into his eyes. Two small roads headed off towards the shore. He took the second and walked to an intersection. Someone had paved it with tarmac. It felt strange under his feet, and yet he knew it was the right way.

There it is. The gate was still there, black and solid. Behind it, the pale house rose up two storeys. The old bougainvillea was bigger than ever, leaning in bursts of drunken red against the villa's side.

It hit him with a force that threw breath from his body, a violent collision of memory and the physical world. Colours rushed his senses, overwhelming him, the blossoms and the blue sky, the burning white stone. They burned through the fading image he'd cherished so long in his mind's eye, erasing it like a shadow at full noon.

He walked up to the gate and put his palm against the cold iron, imagining he could feel a heartbeat. This is where his dreams had always ended. There was no next step.

Raising his hands, he pressed the bell. A small dog started barking inside, a high, frantic yelping. A Hebrew voice sounded from the speakerphone. He opened his mouth to reply but nothing came out. Eventually the gate rattled, and swung open.

She was young, Jude's age perhaps. Her brown hair was caught in a bun, over slacks and a shirt with the sleeves rolled up. She wore a rubber glove on one hand, and smiled at him through the gap in the gate. Behind her, the trees rustled. Their boughs were heavy with bright orange globes, ready for picking. The evening sun shone through them, dappling the garden with shafts of dark and light green.

He knew she was asking him again for his business here, and he answered in English.

'My name is Salim,' he said. 'Salim Al-Ishmaeli.'

'Yes?' she said again, her English accented and slow, the question in her face. 'I can help you?'

He reached out his hand to the white walls behind her, obscured behind the branches. She stepped back startled, and he felt the words surging to his lips despite himself.

'This is my house. Was my house – once.' He saw her face contract, puzzled, and then her eyes widened in surprise. He shook his head – he did not want her to be frightened. 'It's okay, it's okay.' His throat felt tight. 'I just wanted to see it again.'

She held her hands to her mouth, and her English came through them, carrying the heavy lilt of Europe, like Jude's mother.

'Oh God,' she said. 'When? When did you live here?'

'Before the war,' he said. Tears came to him then, and he put his face in his hands. 'Oh God,' she said again, and he felt her hand tighten on his shoulder.

Instantly he straightened. *What do we do now?* She was holding her rubber glove to her chest, her blue eyes sorrowful. *She doesn't sound Israeli.* 'When did you come here?' he asked her.

'Not so long ago,' she said. 'From Hungary. My parents moved here after the war. I came to be near them.' He realized that when she spoke about the war, she meant a different one. *Their war, with Germany.* For each of their peoples, there would only ever be one war.

She was standing holding the door open now, her face creased in sympathy. 'Do you want to come in? I can show you the house, or make you some tea?'

He felt a sudden disgust at the idea of going inside. Shaking his head he said, 'No, thank you. I just… I have to go.' If he won this case, then she would be the one leaving. Somehow, that did not feel like a victory.

She gave him a rueful smile, and held up her hand to wave him goodbye. He turned to leave, and heard the gate begin to close.

Suddenly he turned back, and said, 'One thing! Please. Could I…' He pointed to the orange tree in the background. One of them was his, but he could no longer remember which. 'Could I take an orange? It was something we used to do, as boys. A… a tradition.'

'I will get you one,' she said, keeping the gate half-shut. He saw her walk to the nearest tree, stretch her long, slim frame up into the boughs and pull until the branches shook. When she came back, an orange lay in her palm, rich and round.

She held it out, at the edge of the gate, and he took it from her. They stood silently for a moment, then she nodded and said, 'Well, goodbye.' The gate shut. Salim stood, rooted to the earth. The orange weighed down his hand, as heavy as all the sorrows he'd carried away from this place. He could smell the sharpness of it, and the sweetness. He bowed his head.

He was still standing there when he heard the car behind him. Turning around, wiping his eyes, he saw Tareq's Nissan pull up, and his brother-in-law leapt out of the door.

'I thought we might find you here,' Tareq said, hurrying towards him and grasping his arm. 'Are you okay? You didn't do anything stupid?'

Salim returned Tareq's grip with his other hand, to reassure him. He was dimly aware of another person standing behind the open car door. Tareq was saying, 'Listen, we should get back. There's much to discuss. And I have your surprise here. Didn't you see him?' He pointed back towards the car.

The stranger came into focus. He was tall and pale, his hair was thinning but his eyes were as dark as a hawk's. He smiled when Salim looked up, and instantly he knew. But now he was a grown man, and he stepped forward to grasp Salim's shoulder. *Elia.*

'Salim, how are you?' he said, in Arabic. 'I couldn't believe it when Tareq said you'd come.'

Salim's hand reached up to Elia's arm and clung on, feeling the strange solidity of bone. The confusion of joys and sorrows made him nauseous, as if all these memories were never meant to walk again.

'Elia.' He tried again, but the name was all that came to him. 'Elia.'

'Salim.' Elia was smiling too, his eyes wet. 'You know, I'm a lawyer now? A long way from the tailor's shop. I handle property cases. If I can, I will help you.' He grasped Salim's other shoulder, steadying them both against the earth. 'I promise, my friend. I will help you get some justice.'

The Al-Ishmaeli initial court hearing was set for the first week of November. Nazareth's mornings were already grey and chill. But Salim knew that down by the sea the skies would be a perfect winter blue.

He pulled on a shirt and a tie and a light wool blazer. The mirror in the spare room was dark and scratched. He stood before it for a moment, wondering at the face that looked back out at his.

Not old yet. The cheeks were thinner than he imagined, and shadowed with stubble. For the first time, he saw flecks of grey at his temple. He touched them with confused reverence.

Elia had promised to meet them at court. He was a family man himself now. His wife did social work for poor families, while her husband tried to tug pieces of Arab land back from Israel's iron fist.

It was an uphill task; Elia said Israel had spent years passing laws to make sure cases like Salim's never came to court. 'It's not enough that the land is theirs now. They want to make it so that it was never yours in the first place.'

Still, there were small reasons to hope in this case. 'Your father's name is recorded on the Ottoman Land Registry. The registry proves that the deeds used to sell the house were false. And that there is a case against the State for negligence, for compensation for what you lost.'

But, as he reminded Salim repeatedly, he was no miracle worker. 'I'll tell you the difference between Arabs and Israelis,' he said. 'Arabs want to be judged by the pure law – the one we learn as children where right follows wrong and punishment follows crime like night follows day. But in Israel we have another kind of law. This one is a matter of articles, clauses and sub-clauses, with many interpretations and a heavy bias against you. God has nothing to do with this kind of law. Nor does justice.'

Salim had struggled with this. *Compensation for what I lost. What could that mean to me now?* He'd lost so much more than money, more than land. Sometimes he imagined opening his old bedroom door and seeing all the might-have-beens that waited there – another self brimming with confidence, a laughing wife and children, his mother with her arms outstretched.

Tel Aviv's courthouse was a grey set of squares and rectangles, conveying just the right mix of officiousness and impenetrability. The courtyard before the Magistrates' Court had been decorated with metal sculptures shaped like nothing recognizable – foreshadowing the myriad confusions waiting inside.

As Salim and Tareq walked to the compound entrance, the older man said, 'Well, that's strange.'

He pointed to a crowd, small but vigorous, held away from the entrance by three security guards. Salim could make out two placards

in Hebrew and Arabic. One read: *Justice for the Al-Ishmaelis!* The
other read: *Justice for Jaffa!*

Jimmy. They had talked the previous day. 'Don't worry, my people
will be there,' he'd said. Salim pushed through the crowd, as they
cheered and slapped him on the back. He wanted to talk to them, but
Tareq pulled him through. He was just about to remonstrate, when
he saw Elia moving towards them.

'Did you see the people at the gate?' Salim said, his delight spilling over into a new confidence.

Elia raised his eyebrows. 'It's nice, but unless they are all law-
yers... Anyway, I hope the judges come in the other entrance.
These riots in the West Bank have given people a poor view of
Arab activism.'

'This isn't a riot,' Salim said, looking back at the placards waving
over the walls. 'It's publicity. What's wrong with that?' Elia shrugged,
dismissive.

The courtroom itself was low and poorly lit. The judge came in
with no ceremony. He was thin, with drooping eyes and chin folds. His
black robes hung loosely over a white shirt and pencil-thin black tie.

The younger men standing on the opposite bench were from
Amidar Housing Corporation. 'They are the administrators of the
property, owned by the State,' Elia whispered. 'The government in
business suits.' Salim looked over at them. *When I lost my house,
these men were boys, barely able to read and write.* He was struck by
the lunacy of it. The children of the war had grown up to fight each
other over things that they scarcely even remembered.

The proceedings were in Hebrew and lasted less than fifteen
minutes. Elia laid out the grounds for allowing the claim originally
filed by Salim's father to continue. Amidar's lawyers contended that
the claim had expired, like old milk left too long in the sun.

The judge sat hunched in his black robes. He spoke only once – to
ask Elia a question and point at Salim. Even when he spoke Salim's

name, his eyes remained fixed on the lawyers. He imagined he heard shouts outside the courthouse. *Justice for Jaffa!*

Suddenly, as quickly as he came in, the judge stood up and walked out. Salim understood that the proceedings were at an end – but how could it be? They had not decided anything. He'd not even been given a chance to speak!

'Don't worry,' Elia said with a smile, seeing Salim's expression. 'Actually, it's good.' This is the preliminary proceeding. I know this judge, and he will move quickly to determine one way or the other whether we can go forward. We'll have a second hearing. Maybe in a few weeks, maybe less.'

Patience. It was a word Salim breathed to himself every morning when he woke. But it was easier to say than to practise.

'Thank you,' he said to Elia, swallowing his hurt pride and reaching over to grasp the man's hand. 'You've done so much for us. I don't know why, but thank you.'

Elia began packing his papers away into his briefcase. Without looking up, he said, 'My mother, God rest her, used to talk about your mother all the time. She would come into the shop and they would chat about things – nothing special, just women's things.' A smile crept across his lips. 'We thought she was the most beautiful woman we had ever seen.'

'She was,' Salim said. 'But it didn't last.'

'Maybe,' Elia said, straightening up. 'Nothing lasts. But for that time, you helped us feel less lonely. The Jews in Tel Aviv treated my father like garbage. Our neighbours in Jaffa didn't trust us. But your mother, and you – you were our friends. We remember.' He laid his hand on Salim's shoulder. 'I'll see you soon.' Salim watched him square his narrow shoulders, and walk out of the court.

The next day, Jimmy called. 'Did you like the crowd at the courthouse?' he asked.

'Fantastic,' Salim laughed. 'Who were they?'

An echoing laugh down the other end of the line turned into a barking cough. 'I told you,' he rasped. 'Our organization has many friends – Arabs, Jews. Buddhists!' The cough came again. 'Now we do some interviews for the press. And I'd like you to speak at some meetings – just a small group of helpful people.'

'And when would this be?' Salim asked. Talking to Jimmy was like the rhyme he used to watch the twins skip to. *Eeny meeny miny moe. Catch a tiger by the toe. If he squeals, let him go!* But he had a feeling that anyone letting this tiger go would quickly become dinner.

'I'll call you,' Jimmy said. 'And by the way, watch the news tomorrow. Maybe there will be something for you there, too.'

As it happened, Salim did not need to watch the news. Tareq delivered it personally, banging fiercely on his bedroom door the next afternoon. He jerked awake from a dream of Jude; she had been young, with her Star of David necklace and the golden lights in her hair.

'Hey, Salim!' Tareq sounded furious.

'What is it?' he called out. The door opened and his brother-in-law stood at the doorway, lips pursed primly.

'It's your friend, this Jimmy.'

'What about him?'

Tareq's nostrils flared and he threw his hands up in the air. 'I got a call from Elia. There's been an incident at the house.'

Salim felt sleepy and stupid. 'What house? What are you talking about?'

'The house, the house!' Tareq looked as if he wanted to shake him. 'There was a protest. It started at the old Clock Tower, with some group making speeches about land rights in Jaffa, and then these people marched over to your father's house and painted the walls with this *Justice for Jaffa* nonsense. The police came and arrested some of them.'

'That's incredible.' Salim had to look at his hands, to hide his secret delight.

Tareq shook his finger. 'Incredible is not good. Remember what Elia said. When people see angry Arabs they don't think activist. They think terrorist.'

'Jimmy is Rafan's friend,' Salim said. 'I'll speak to Rafan. I'll make sure it doesn't get out of hand.'

That night, he watched the protest on television. The Orange House was unrecognizable. Red paint was splattered across its walls and a crowd blocked the gate with young and eager faces. One woman was gesticulating to the camera, speaking in Hebrew. She wore a Palestinian *keffiyeh* around her. Her skin and hair were as olive as Sophie's. The thought caused a stab of pain so vivid that he put his hand over his mouth and closed his eyes.

The telephone rang, and Nadia came bustling in to pick it up. The newscaster had moved on to scenes of the riots they were starting to call the *Intifada*, and new emergency laws being passed in the Knesset. Something was troubling him, something not quite right about Nadia's voice behind him. Then he realized. She was speaking English.

He turned slowly and Nadia's eyes met his. She said, 'Yes, I give you him now.' Slowly, she handed him the telephone.

Her voice was wary, but he leaned into the sound of it. 'I hope it's an okay time,' she was saying.

'It's fine,' he replied. She paused, a catch of breath that he knew so well. They'd not spoken since he'd left for Israel.

'I heard your case is going well,' she said. 'Hassan says you've had your first day in court.'

'I didn't know you were still speaking to Hassan.'

'I'm still speaking to everyone, Sal.'

He closed his eyes. *Why does she call? Do we have anything left to say to each other?*

There was another pause, and then she said, 'Didn't you get my message?' He looked over at Nadia working in the kitchen. There'd been a message about Jude's call, left on his bed a few days ago. But he'd not found the courage to call her back.

'It's been very busy,' he said. 'I'm sorry. What's going on?'

'For God's sake, Sal.' The tears in her voice surprised him. What had happened?

'It's Marc,' she went on. 'He's been expelled from the Royal Ballet School. He got into a fight with one of the students.'

Salim heard himself laughing despite his shock. 'Marc, in a fist fight? I didn't think he had it in him.'

Jude's voice was cold. 'He scratched the boy's face, enough to draw blood, Sal. Actually, I think you had something to do with it. It was a Jewish boy and Marc said he made some crack about the Palestinians. When I picked him up from the infirmary he was raving about how you told him all about how the Arabs were always a joke and that he wouldn't be laughed at. Since then... I don't know.' He heard the strain in her voice. 'I'm worried about him. He says he's taking his medicine but I don't think he is. Then yesterday the police brought him in for setting fire to that horrible old shack down the street. They said he threw a Molotov cocktail at it.'

'Wow,' Salim almost laughed again. 'That place needed to be burned down. Good for him.'

'What's the matter with you?' She was almost shouting now. 'It isn't funny. This expulsion, it's the end of a dream for him. A lifelong dream. God, Sal, don't you remember what it was like to have dreams?'

'I had so many over the years,' Salim retorted, a hot wind sifting the embers of his pain and resentment. 'This is just Marc's first one. Believe me, he'll get over it.'

'Like you got over your losses, you mean?' The sarcasm bit hard. He remembered Marc's eyes filling that day in the bedroom. He'd felt nothing then, but now a trickle of grief for his son began to filter through him.

'I'm sorry for Marc,' he said. 'But what do you want, Jude? He doesn't need anything from me.'

'You're his father,' she replied. 'His future's in the air, and he needs his parents. He's confused, Sal, and ashamed. One day he tells me he's going travelling, the next he's asking me if you're coming back. He wants you back, even if he can't tell you to your face. Shouldn't that make you happy?'

It should. It could be so easy – just to say yes, to jump on a plane and surprise them. But then he heard the newscaster behind him, and remembered the red paint on the walls of the Orange House. *Justice for Jaffa!* He'd made a decision, he had a purpose. He could not give it up – not for Marc, not for anyone.

'If you spoke to Hassan, you know I can't leave now,' he said. The words sounded harsher than he meant. 'We're in the middle of a battle here. If I leave, it will be all for nothing. I have to stay. Do you understand? You have to explain it to Marc.'

She was silent, and he pictured her, the blue eyes wide and her face still so clear, like a glass of water. Then her voice came again, heavy and resigned.

'I'm not sure that I can explain it, because I don't understand it myself. Your son needs you. What could be more important than that?'

'I am doing this for him,' he said, over the guilt and frustration. 'For his future, our legacy. He should care. He should understand.'

'Okay, Sal,' she said. 'You stay and fight your battle.' Her breathing was calm again. 'I hope it brings you joy. You know where we are. Bye.' There was a click and then the steady tone signalled the end of the moment.

As he slowly dropped the receiver into its cradle he saw Nadia standing in the kitchen doorway. Her hands were folded over her plump chest, and her eyes were filled with reproach. 'I don't understand you,' she said, her voice soft with sadness. 'What are you doing here?'

'What do you mean?' He was immediately defensive. 'You of all people – how can you ask that?'

'I mean you should not have come,' she said. 'You know it, in your heart. The brother I knew would not have left his family. He would have protected them, first and before all things.' Her eyes were red and her hands trembling, as if terrified by her sudden courage.

'How could you cry for her?' he shouted, clinging to his rage. 'You don't even know her. You didn't come to our wedding, you hardly spoke to her all the years we were married. You never approved of her. So why cry for her now? Isn't it a bit late?'

'I am not crying for her,' Nadia said, raising her face to his – a worn face of goodness unrewarded. 'What kind of man are you, to care what other people think of your woman, of your choice? It's you I am crying for. Oh, my little brother.' He saw the tears running unchecked down her cheeks. 'So much you had, so many good things. And look at you. You threw them all away.'

Many years ago, as a little child, Salim had been taken out on a fishing boat to learn how the nets brought home the catch. They'd set out in the pre-dawn light, when the sea and the sky were the same colour and the world had yet to draw its first breath. For more than an hour they'd hauled in the empty lines, while the wooden hull swayed. Salim had clung to the gunwale to steady his turning stomach, as the vast quiet rocked him into a nauseous slumber. Then, all at once, there'd been a shout. A net full of silver, flashing madly in the first rays of the sun, poured into the bottom of the boat. The floor at his feet exploded into motion – fish everywhere, leaping, flying, slicing into the air like a hundred little knives. And from above the silent raiders came, gulls plunging towards the deck to steal a morsel away, screaming when the fishermen lashed out with sticks to drive them back.

When Elia called with the news about the court date, he felt it again – the thrill and fear of the mêlée as it washed over him. It drowned out his lingering guilt about Jude's call, and the nameless fears for Marc pricking his conscience.

'The judge will hear both parties again one more time,' Elia said. 'He has promised we will not leave without a judgment.' The date was set; on the twenty-first of December, in two weeks' time, the game would either begin or end.

Jimmy was also busy with his own preparations. His organization was catching fire, he told Salim with delight. 'You're a natural speaker, a natural,' he said, munching into a giant pita sandwich of falafel and pickles. Red harissa sauce spilled over the corners of his mouth and dripped onto his collar. 'Where've you been hiding, *habibi*? If only the municipal elections were now, I would have you standing for one party or the other. But *ma'alish*. At least we have you for now, and anyone we pick for the vote in two years will just have to take a few lessons, *sah*?' He wiped his folded chin, and Salim imagined himself disappearing down that enormous gullet. *The giant of Jaffa. He eats me and shits out a seat on the municipal council.*

Jimmy had worked out a demonstration schedule leading up to the final hearing. 'It's just enough and not too much,' he said in his jovial bass. 'The kids are full of energy, God bless them. I left them in Jaffa, painting tents to tie to the top of their cars when they drive around. Why tents, I asked them? You know what they said? It's a symbol of displacement. After they drive them around for everyone to see the slogans, they untie them and hold what the Americans call a *sit-in*. They plan to camp outside your house! Advertising and protest prop! It's the Jew kids who came up with it. That's the problem with us, Salim. We can't think further than a stone or a bomb. The Jews are more sophisticated – that's why they won in the end.'

Jimmy was as good as his word. The movement in Jaffa was swelling. Every other day, Salim was wheeled down in one of Jimmy's cars to parade his story to his progressives and marvel at how keenly these young Jews and Arabs listened. They looked alike to him in the way that the English say foreigners do – a jumble of tanned faces and lanky limbs, *keffiyaat* slung with equal nonchalance across men and women, the girls in downbeat uniforms of jeans and loose tops, the men's hair either casually long or brutally short. They were all young – but the Jews were both the youngest and the oldest among them. All the eighteen year olds were away on national service, decked in the green colours of the Israel Defence Forces learning to shoot at strange Arabs in the occupied territories.

Salim saw the tents on television one night, wobbling precariously along the streets of Jaffa and Tel Aviv atop a long line of cars. Loudspeakers blared and he saw his name written in Arabic and Hebrew on one out of every three. The programme cut quickly to a sharp interview with Shlomo Lahat, Mayor of Tel Aviv for more than fifteen years. *Hooliganism*, he boomed, his blonde hair sweeping up over his forehead in an indignant quiff and his white eyebrows waggling. He went on to assure the interviewer of the many great things planned for Jaffa and the investments scheduled for the slums of Al-Ajami. His eyelids quivered at the suggestion that Israel's courts were not interested in justice. 'Whoever wants to keep Jaffa in turmoil, these people are not interested in justice,' he said.

The grand finale was planned for a Sunday, the day before the final court judgment. Salim would speak at a press conference in front of the Orange House. 'Trust me, *habibi*,' Jimmy told him, 'it will be the perfect moment.'

On Saturday morning, Rafan called. Nadia handed the telephone to Salim, her nose wrinkled in dislike.

'I'm glad Jimmy is doing such a good job, big brother,' the crackling voice said. 'Even in this big farmyard over here, we are getting some news.'

'Jimmy has been a great help. Thank you for introducing us.'

'No thanks needed, big brother. You help me, I help you. And round and round it goes.'

That's what Salim was afraid of. 'I'm sorry you're not enjoying Jordan more,' he said, casting around for a way to get Rafan off the telephone. 'It's a shame you can't be here.'

'You may not have to be sorry for that much longer.' Salim heard the grin across the hundreds of miles of wire. 'It's my big brother's big day. How could I miss it?'

Salim thought again of the birds, diving from the sky with their claws and beaks. There was nothing he wanted less at this moment than for Rafan to come back. But maybe he was already here in spirit, with Jimmy and his progressives and their secret plans.

'Don't risk coming across the border,' he said, in the reflex of panic. 'You said the Israelis had marked you. Why would you take a chance?'

'For you?' Rafan laughed. 'Anything for you, big brother. You took the first step, getting this thing moving in Jaffa. I'm telling you, there's a lot we can do with it. So don't worry. Jimmy's not the only Palestinian with more than one face. *Insha'Allah*, I'll see you tomorrow.'

As the sun went down that evening, before Jimmy arrived to take him to the last protest meeting, Salim watched his family on Tareq's old projector.

He'd brought all the reels with him from Kuwait to England and now here. Each one was carefully marked. *The Creek. Il-Saraj. Sophie's birthday party. Marc's garden.* He watched them flicker through the years, growing and changing, their faces full of silent laughter. Lines gathered around Jude's eyes, Sophie's hair lengthened, Marc's frail body stretched and filled. And then with a flick of a switch he reversed time, winding them back into childhood and innocence. Jude smiled up at him from the beach, freckles on her cheeks. Sophie skipped around the fire and Marc ran to join her, his arms vanishing into the golden light.

Again and again he played them, searching for some lost truth hidden in their faces. *When did it all turn upside down?* Back then, his only dreams were of oranges and the warm sea. But the oranges had gone and the sea was surrounded by concrete. Now he wanted to dream of Jude's golden hair, of Sophie's eyes, of Marc leaping through the air. But his nights were silent, and when he awoke they left no trace behind.

Jimmy picked Salim up after sunset. The flyer for the night's entertainment read: *Justice for Jaffa.*

Salim sat watching the fields and gas stations roll by, wondering at his deep foreboding. He felt like a man who'd fallen asleep while driving, waking to find his hand no longer on the wheel.

Jimmy cleared his throat. 'Salim. I have a surprise waiting for you tonight.' His huge hands clamped to the wheel. 'An old friend. I think maybe he can be good for us, perhaps for the elections to come.'

Salim was instantly suspicious. 'Who are you talking about?'

'Mazen. The Al-Khalili boy.'

His hair stood up on his arms and his stomach clenched as if an iron fist had punched it. *Surely he's joking.*

'Why would you think I want to see Mazen?' He raised his voice and Jimmy turned to look at him, the eyes unfathomable under his deep cheek folds. 'They were the ones. They betrayed us.'

'Wait a moment there, *habibi.*' Jimmy's voice had a chilly edge to it. 'Let's remember who betrayed who. It was the Jews who made this whole mess. Everyone else just did what they had to. I've spoken to Mazen – he's very sorry about the past. Now that his father's buried, God rest him, he doesn't have a lot of money. It turns out that the Al-Khalilis are not very good businessmen. But he's old Jaffa and once we clean him up, he'll do very well.'

'Do very well for what?'

'For us. For Jaffa, for the elections. We need an old Jaffa man beside you, a man who can get some public opinion behind him. You and Mazen, you're boyhood friends,' Jimmy repeated. 'All they need is to see him next to you. After all,' he looked kindly at Salim, his eyes like pools of black ice, 'I did a favour on this one, for your brother. We should all get something out of this, no?'

They arrived at the hall on the outskirts of Tel Aviv. It was where the old Manshiyya district used to be, before the tanks razed it to the ground. Inside the low doorway, nameless young people shook his hand.

Halfway down the row of faces, there he was. Salim stopped in front of him and Mazen blinked slowly, his feet shifting.

The tight black curls were the same, but the rich rolls of fat hung empty and loose around his stomach and cheeks. The full redness of those curling lips now looked bruised, bitten. His clothes reminded Salim not of the suave Abu Mazen, but of his own father and his shabby suits marked with the sweat of uncertainty.

'Salim Al-Ishmaeli,' Mazen said. He cleared his throat and stuck his hand out in a gesture that smelt of embarrassment. It was a second before Salim, under Jimmy's careful gaze, could bring himself to shake it. Mazen's palm was moist and soft.

'Who would have thought, after so long? I heard you went to be the big man in London.'

'Not a *fellah* these days,' Salim heard himself saying.

Mazen laughed, but his eyes were anxious as they flickered towards Jimmy. '*Ya* Salim, I can't believe you remember all that.'

Salim could not look away from him. 'I remember everything,' he said, the words rising up on the heat of his heart. 'Even that day in Tel Aviv.' He had the satisfaction of seeing Mazen turn a defiant red.

'You don't remember how it really was.' There was a wheedling tone in his voice. 'We were prisoners in Jaffa after the Jews came,

303

like sheep behind barbed wire. While you were living in that nice flat in Nazareth, we had to shit in holes because there were so many of us the drains overflowed. There was nothing to be done, except what they told us to do.' He looked up at Salim. 'The Israelis tried to turn us against each other.' Jimmy nodded in heavy agreement. 'It's right we should stand together now.'

'Okay, enough, it's time,' Jimmy said. 'Finish the reunion later. They're waiting.'

After Salim had finished speaking that night, Jimmy brought Mazen up to spin his own tale. When Mazen held out his hand to Salim, under the eager gaze of their young audience, Salim found himself taking it to the sound of cheers. Mazen smiled through his sweat and Salim felt their hands slide apart, leaving a slick trail of wetness behind. And he remembered how the Frères used to treat the boys to a puppet show every Saturday morning. He would sit by Mazen and Hassan, and laugh at their rictus grins and jerky little dances. For a moment he imagined himself down there among them, looking up at himself with scornful eyes.

It was nearly midnight by the time Jimmy pulled up outside the Nazareth apartment. They'd been silent all the way back. Salim wiped his hands together, but he could still feel Mazen's sweat.

'What's up, Salim?' Jimmy asked him. 'You're nearly home. Every journalist in Tel Aviv is confirmed for the press conference tomorrow. The day after, you'll get your judgment. Then the real work starts. What could be wrong? It's all going to plan.'

What could be wrong? 'All my life I wanted Mazen to pay for what he did,' Salim said slowly. 'But tonight I shook his hand. What does that make me?'

'It makes you smart,' Jimmy said. 'Listen to me, my friend. You don't see wires and checkpoints here like in the West Bank. But we are still a people under siege. We can't afford to fight each other for things in the past. You did the right thing, *habibi*. And tomorrow you will see.'

The long walk up the stairs was full of whispers, reaching out of the darkness to urge things, important things – but they stayed just beyond the edge of hearing.

Weary, he pulled out his key and opened the door to Nadia's flat. A figure rose quickly from the armchair opposite and turned to face him. Salim froze in the doorway. Standing there, gaunt and tense, was Marc.

Salim was dumbfounded. The television was still on and it was as if Marc had stepped out of it, a living fragment of memory come to haunt him.

His son looked almost skeletal. A pair of jeans hung from his hips and a black t-shirt dangled loosely from wire-thin shoulders. His arms were taut and finely muscled and his head tipped upwards on a long neck. The dancer's pose.

'Surprised?' the boy said. He was oddly motionless except for his fingers, long and pale as they closed and flexed repeatedly.

Salim stepped towards him, saying, 'Marc…' But he stopped dead when Marc said, 'Don't. Don't. I didn't come for that.'

Salim tried to take in the sight of this stranger in front of him. The tall bones and wild eyes belonged to a young man he'd never met. There were only traces of the child he remembered from just months before. He flinched at the sight of them, the bitten lips, the frail wrists and the soft whiteness of his hair.

'Then why did you come?' he asked, dreading the answer. 'Does your mother know you're here?'

'She will,' Marc said. 'I had to take some money from her.' His laugh was a bark. 'It doesn't matter what I do now. I guess she told you what happened? I failed. You were right after all. Aren't you happy about that?'

Salim groped for the words. 'That was never what I meant.'

'I did it for you, you know,' Marc went on, his body framed by the refracted light from the stairwell. 'I thought he was my friend, but then he said Arabs were dogs and he had a look on his face, so I *knew* he meant me. I stood up to him, like you told me to. Now I'm fucked. They'll never take me back.'

Salim felt the familiar rise of his hackles. 'Don't blame me for that, Marc. You made your own choice. Maybe it was the right choice, if someone insulted you. There'll be other ballet schools, won't there?'

Marc laughed again, but something happened in his eyes, a plane shift from one emotion to another – perhaps from anger to tears. In the light, it was impossible to tell.

'Mum said you'd come back when it happened. She still thinks you care. She's deluded. I told her. You don't care at all, you never have. But I'd like to know why.'

'You don't know what you're talking about.'

'Come on, you can admit it now. You were never happy with us. Was it because of the Arabic lessons? Or because you couldn't hold down a job for five minutes? Or were you just too angry about everything to love us? Poor old Dad, and his poor old house that the wicked Jews took.' Marc's voice was hoarse.

'You're crazy,' Salim said, half in worry and half in anger. 'Marc, you're not well. You should go home. There's nothing for you here.'

Marc lifted his head as the light from Nadia's doorway seemed to shine around his throat. His eyes were closed, but his fingers still flickered.

'Nothing, I know. You're right. But I wanted to see you. To tell you something.' His words were so rapid that they seemed to spill from him. 'After they expelled me I was trying to work it out – why I was never happy. I just can't remember that feeling. I think, it was only when I danced – then it was like nothing could catch me. But now I know why. Shall I tell you? Do you care?' Salim heard his voice catch.

'Tell me then,' he said. 'If it means so much to you.' In the dim room his son's blue eyes were darker than his own, black as the void.

'It was because of you,' Marc said, and a hollow place inside Salim ached in sympathy. 'You never wanted us to be a happy family. You always wanted to be somewhere else. I tried to make up for it. But it wasn't enough for you. Of course you were right, Dad. I wasn't nearly enough.'

A moment of silence passed between them. Then the boy lifted a large backpack off the floor and hoisted it onto one shoulder. Its shadow merged into his on the wall behind him, a trick of the light at once monstrous and threatening.

'They said you have a press conference tomorrow,' he said. 'At the famous house.'

'That's right,' Salim said. 'I'd say come, but I guess you don't want to.'

Marc shrugged. 'Maybe I'd like to see this place. What did you call it? Your legacy. That's perfect. It was always more your child than I was.'

Somewhere deep in the recesses of memory Salim heard his voice screaming, heard the words he'd thrown at his own father in that same apartment. *It's your fault. You made us miserable. You did everything wrong.* They rang in his head as Marc pushed past him in the same haze of pain and bravado.

It was instinct that made him seize his son's arm, the sudden overwhelming urge to throw everything else away, to convince his son that he was loved, that they were all loved, that they could find a new place to begin. Marc's face was half-turned towards him, half in the shadows, and he paused for the briefest moment. But it was too quick; the surface of Salim's mind was still full of press conferences and plans, and the words he needed were buried so deep they could not find their way out.

Marc wrenched his arm away and walked through the door. The last thing Salim saw was his hand, clutching his bag as he disappeared into the dark of the stairwell. ''Bye, Dad,' he heard. And then, like a dream, Marc was gone.

The last day bloomed bright as a rose in Jaffa. By noon the Orange House was wrapped in a blaze of light under a radiant winter sky.

Salim stood at the end of the track. It was like looking through a frame, as if the house lived only in a picture, set apart from the racing world.

Creepers tumbled over the closed garden walls, moving softly with the sway and fall of the cool December air. The arching windows of the top floor were wide eyes looking out to sea. Their gaze sped over the top of the dirty new Jaffa, through the softening light of the harbour over to the glorious old city.

Around the house, it was pandemonium. Mobile tents painted by Jimmy' progressives swelled on the scrubland like unripe melons. The front gate was guarded by two police officers. More stood beside police cars blocking the street. Their sirens waved silently, flashing white and blue into the air.

A crowd was arriving for the spectacle. They came in huddles, people with nothing to do on a Sunday morning. Most kept their distance, standing linked arm to arm behind the cordon of police cars, whispering to each other. Others, the bolder ones, came laughing into the arena of tents, pointing at the placards and taking pictures.

Across the wreck of fallen Al-Ajami, the bells were ringing for the Christian Sabbath. Salim saw, to his amazement, a light burning in the upper window of the house. *A menorah.* Then he remembered. It was the twentieth of December, the sixth day of Hanukkah. The day after tomorrow, someone's hand would light the eighth flame to celebrate the day the Jews rose in rebellion and took back the Temple. *How ironic.*

'She moved out, you know.' It was Jimmy, suddenly standing behind him. A half-eaten piece of *manquish* was in his hand, rich and cheesy.

'Who moved out?'

'Her.' Jimmy waved the *manquish* towards the light in the window. 'The woman who lived here, and her kid. Just for today, I heard. I guess she didn't want to get her face in the papers. I don't blame her.'

Salim remembered her puzzled smile, and her hand on his shoulder. Regret touched him – for another soul infected with the pain of loss.

'Not to worry about it now, *habibi*. We have work to do today. Let's talk again later. *Yallah*, I'll go get Mazen. You boys look so good together. I want him in the pictures.'

The crowd and the noise were building together. Salim walked over to the podium. One of Jimmy's progressives was wrapping it carefully in the Palestinian flag. Watching, Salim remembered that the flag had actually been designed by a British diplomat called Sykes in the days of the Arab Revolt against the Turks. Tareq called it a joke, another trick of the British Empire, to fool Arabs into believing they were one people.

It was Mazen he thought of, who'd once showed him how to strangle a chicken from the market. 'They're stupid,' he'd said, as the bird gabbled around with a rope around its neck. 'They try to run and run and they don't notice the knot is getting tighter.' Salim rubbed his throat, feeling the constriction of an invisible noose. Maybe Rafan, or Jimmy, was pulling on the other end. Worse, maybe he'd been pulling it himself. *I'm more stupid than the chicken*, he thought. *I didn't notice it for forty years*. The whole performance suddenly felt as hollow as the flag-draped podium. *I turned my son away for this?*

He saw Elia pushing his way through the throng. His friend's face was furrowed, as he squinted over Salim's shoulder into the glare of the lights.

'Quite a turnout,' he said, shaking his head. 'I hope it does you good, Salim. But I told you before, I don't think this is the way.'

'I know,' Salim replied, feeling the weight of sadness hush his voice. 'It's gone far enough – too far.' Elia looked at him in concern. 'What's the matter? You look terrible. Did something happen?'

The words came into his mouth automatically. *My son came to me, and I failed him.* But what was the point of telling Elia? When this was over, after the judgment tomorrow, he would make it right.

He looked at the house, at the light burning in its window. For a moment he wished he believed in God, in something more sacred than a pile of bricks that could hold him to his promise.

Elia pinched his arm, nodding at Jimmy walking towards him with Mazen alongside. Tareq followed unhappily behind them. Mazen caught Elia's eye, and Salim saw his face shift from a puzzled frown to resentful recognition.

'Elia, by God,' he said, 'always taking up with the Arabs.'

Elia turned away, his body instinctively shielding itself as he did when they were boys. 'We're on the same side now, Mazen. It's not about politics. This is for Salim.'

Mazen snorted. 'Yes, we're on the same side,' he said, his shoulders squaring. 'A master and his dogs.'

'Boys, boys,' Jimmy said, pushing between them. 'Give me one moment. I have to talk to the star of the show.' His chin wobbled as he jerked his head and pulled Salim to the edge of the crowd.

'There's a message just arrived from Jerusalem,' he said, his voice low. 'Your brother needs you.' He held out a piece of paper, folded in the middle. Salim had no choice but to take it, but his heart revolted. It was half-open, like a door, and Salim knew where it led. *I don't have to walk through.*

'He crossed the border okay. But then we were betrayed. They raided the safe house in the West Bank this morning and took everyone inside.'

Salim touched his throat and felt the tug of the rope again. Once it had been Rafan's arms around his neck, the love of a frightened little brother. And he grieved for Rafan, for Marc, for himself, for all the little boys consumed by this ever-hungry land.

Jimmy slapped Salim on the cheek, a light warning. 'Hey, wake up. This is very serious. This could mean Mossad, and your brother's life maybe.' He bent towards Salim. 'He told them he's here for you, just visiting family. He's using British papers. After this, we go to the station. You need to back up his story.'

Salim slowly opened the note. It read, in English: *Big brother – remember, I help you and you help me. Come as soon as you can. I'm waiting here for you, Rafan.*

Salim turned his head and looked out west, over the crowds towards the sea. It was only an instant, but he thought he saw Marc's face at the edge of the scene, pale and bright as the day. He whipped his body around, but the face had vanished – if it had ever been there at all.

He turned back to Jimmy. 'When this is finished, I have to find my son,' he said. He thrust the note back into the fat hand and walked back towards the podium.

Tareq, Elia and Mazen were beside it still locked in their argument. The crowds had gathered in an arc around them, grinning as they shouted. Mazen was laughing at Elia. 'You want to be an Arab, go ask your mama. Maybe the white *Yehuda* got bored of fucking a tailor, maybe she was spreading her legs for a dark one in Manshiyya.'

Jimmy caught his shoulder, panting. 'You're joking, Salim.'

Ignoring him, Salim pushed in front of Mazen. He saw the rage there, dug deep by the years of disappointment.

'Be careful what you say to these people, Mazen,' he said. 'They're my family.' He felt Tareq and Elia standing close against his right shoulder, breathing hard, and saw Mazen back away in surprise.

'Your family?' Jimmy put his arm round Mazen's shoulder, the contempt unleashed in his voice. 'Your family is sitting in a prison cell, Salim, waiting for you to finish this fucking speech. So *yallah*, let's go. Both of you. It's time to get you in the pictures.'

'Don't listen, Salim,' Tareq said quietly. 'Some dogs never change their bark.'

Mazen's heavy eyes swivelled wildly from Salim's face to Jimmy's and back again. But then he seemed to gather himself; he leaned forward, his breath warm on Salim's cheeks. The ghost of the smile that once haunted Salim, the taunting boyhood sneer, crept onto his lips. 'Better a dog than a donkey,' he said, and he gave Salim a wink. Behind Mazen, Salim heard Jimmy snort with laughter.

Salim took Mazen's head in his hands, and pulled his face close. It was almost an embrace, and he could see Mazen's confusion as their eyes met for a long second. In the background he saw Jimmy's features blur into his father's, into Rafan's, into the Irgun and their bloody bombs and all the faceless men to whom he'd handed the reins of his life.

'Not your donkey any more,' Salim whispered. Then he pushed Mazen backwards, with that same sudden relief he'd known long ago watching their football fly high across the wasteland.

There was a moment of impact. Mazen stumbled and slammed into Jimmy. And then the big man was rolling in the dirt with a red mess trickling out of his nose.

Someone screamed and cameras flashed. Jimmy grabbed someone's sleeve to hoist himself up, turning it bloody. As he staggered to his feet his eyes met Salim's in reproachful amazement.

'Put that in your pictures,' Salim said to him. Turning away, he took the microphone from an outstretched hand and stepped onto the podium.

His first instinct was to look around for Marc. But there was no sign of his son. It must have been a trick of the light, a mirage made of wishes. He sensed the Orange House behind him, a looming presence.

Even the light was like his dreams, an over-brightness that hurt the eyes, the distant calling of voices over a profound, expectant silence.

He felt that silence, a well to fall into. *I know what they want me to say.* He could tell them the same old story, that peace will never come until all the homes are restored and we are all back at our own tables. But that was only one truth.

The other was much harder to say, harder to hear. If only Marc were in front of him, he could find the words for it. He'd lost his first home despite all he could do. But that loss wasn't as painful, as terrible to accept as the home he'd built and then destroyed himself.

He opened his mouth to speak. But suddenly there was another sound rising around, sweeping away his words before they could take shape.

In that instant of confusion he could not make it out. It started as a shriek from someone in the crowd, or from a bird sailing above them, and then a high *woomf* of heat and light.

Now he could hear it, an angry roar, as the sea of people screamed and surged. Turning, he saw the flames falling like leaves over the wall, the smoke creeping like a silent hand over the windows.

Then there was a deeper sound, a flash of wind and energy and a bone-shaking wail that blew silence into his ears and dust over his eyes. His mind felt light as a bird as his legs gave way and the podium crumbled. He was falling slowly into space, and as he reached out the ground of Jaffa groaned and opened to take him inside.

THE SEA

They found Marc's body inside what used to be the kitchen. According to the police, he'd scaled the back wall of the compound, climbed down through the trees and broken into the kitchen. Then he'd thrown his arsenal of Molotov cocktails one by one into the downstairs rooms. The last three had been left to burn beside him, with the gas stove turned up.

No one knew if he'd meant to die. The newspapers called it a suicidal act, but Salim refused to believe it. Marc had booked a return ticket to London on a flight leaving that same night. Then he saw a letter to Sophie, posted before the press conference. It started: *I don't expect you to forgive me*, and ended: *I love you always*. At the bottom of the page Marc had drawn a small figure. It was leaping forward into the sky, its arms held up in rapturous greeting.

The magnificent crescendo of Marc's revenge took many months to die into silence. He passed into the hands of the press, who fought over his story – the tragic figure taking revenge for his lost inheritance, or the would-be terrorist who misjudged the moment and was able to kill only himself. Much was made of his psychological disorder – and the influence of his uncle, long-wanted by Mossad and now finally in their hands.

314

Then there was the question of liabilities and claims and compensations. The forty-year-old case of Saeed Al-Ishmaeli and sons was put aside by the courts. The owner of the house wept on television as the bulldozers moved in to clear away the rubble. 'God saved us,' the woman cried to the cameras, her hand clasping her little son's arm. 'We should have been in that house.' Watching her, Salim prayed, for the first time in his adult life, that Marc had known the house was empty before he sent death inside.

He saw Jude once that year, across the room of the inquest. When the judge pronounced death by misadventure, she raised her bowed head. Her blue eyes turned to him, dark with pain. And when the court rose he watched Nadia pull her close as she tried to move towards him. But he saw her eyes and read the words rather than heard them, as if she'd burned them into the air. *You. You killed him. You killed our boy.*

And then finally, there was silence. The newspapers moved on, the payments were made. The site of the Orange House was cleared and left for the sea to claim. Green shoots and saplings began to grow again under the wheeling gulls. By the time the authorities decided what to do with the land, they would be young trees just ready to fruit.

A year to the day after Marc's death, Salim stood across a rising path, leading up from the sea. The sun was high and the wind blew cold and fresh from the west. Dry stalks of grass rattled around him, as feathered white seeds drifted through the shining air. They would find a place to land, not too far away, to grow again with the first breath of spring.

In the soft haze he watched a small knot of people gathered on the highest point of the land. They stood around a young tree, slim and green with the earth newly dug at its base.

They are all here. He saw Sophie, taller than Jude with her crown of dark hair. A man stood next to her, just as young and slender, black haired and fair skinned. He put his arms round her waist, and pulled her to him with love. Pale Gertie was there, and Uncle Max, and Tony, soberly dressed in a black suit alongside his wife and children. Dora, thin and bent, held onto her brother-in-law Alex's arm. Her other arm held Nadia's, who patted the old woman's hand. Tareq stood beside Jude, and Elia beside him. Even Hassan was there, his wife and children huddled around and three little grandchildren kicking up dirt behind the group.

Then he saw Jude, her golden head high. She knelt down on the land and scooped up some of Jaffa's soil in one hand. Reaching into her pocket with her other hand, she brought out a bound cloth.

As he watched, she poured dark and crumbling English earth from the scarf into the lighter, warmer soil in her palm. Dust sprinkled away from her in glittering flakes, as she placed the mixed soils at the foot of the tree.

He stood there, listening to the wind catch and blow through the scrubland. It sang to him, a sweet, wordless song he'd always loved to hear.

Sophie walked to stand beside her mother, tipping a pitcher, one Nadia used to make yoghurt. Water streamed down, clear as the sky, onto the hard ground. The tree drank it like a baby at the breast, its soil turning dark with life.

The ceremony was over, and the people started to move away. Sophie took Jude's arm and they both looked towards him. She kissed her daughter and Sophie's hand dropped. Then, Jude was coming down the slope, unbuttoning her dark blue coat.

The light caught the chains around her neck. His gift to her was there, tangled with Rebecca's star. *My other gift to her is lying under the earth.* Marc was part of the land now.

Finally, they stood opposite each other, across the path. The wind blew around them, catching at their clothes. He saw it then – a third chain in white gold. A child with butterfly wings, leaping for the sky.

Jude tried to absorb the stranger opposite, the remains of the boy she'd loved for his sweetness, his easy warmth. Her husband was hunched, lifeless. A grey figure etched in pain. Part of her mourned, even as another part rejoiced it was so.

'Remember we once talked about coming here together,' she said, forcing herself to break the silence.

He nodded. 'I told you it was impossible.'

'And yet, here we are.' Her eyes went out to the billowing sea. 'I guess you never know how things will turn out.'

Behind her the crowd was moving towards the cars. Sophie was standing at the brow of the hill, her lover's hand in hers. Marc's tree stood on its own, a delicate sliver of life, its green arms waving in the sunshine. Beyond it, the two cities, old and new, rose into the distance.

'I don't blame you for hating me,' he said. There were claws in his throat. 'You were right. I killed him.'

Her eyes were dry. 'I did hate you, Sal. I would still hate you until my last breath, if it could bring Marc back. But he wouldn't want that.' Her hand touched the hollow of her throat, where the leaping boy lay still. 'You know what he was like. He'd want us to say goodbye.'

'I know.' His voice was soft. Reaching into his coat pocket, he pulled out a slim rectangle wrapped in white silk, the colour of innocence.

'What's this?' she asked, wary.

'I was going to bury it,' he replied. 'There, where he's resting. But I thought he wouldn't want me to come. I failed him.' Tears came at last, the first he'd cried. They burned his face as they fell. 'He came to me for help, but I didn't understand. I missed my chance.'

She pulled off the silk, and held up the picture of the Orange House. The little boy's eyes stared up at them both out of the golden frame in sweet bewilderment. The tree seemed so fragile behind him, just like the one fluttering lightly above Marc's ashes.

She laughed at the sight of it, unlocking her own tears. 'Wow, Sal,' she said. 'After all this time, you can still surprise me.' She hugged the picture to her chest. In the bitterness of her grief, her one consolation had been that the Orange House had also burned – that it, too, had felt the searing pain of the flames. *Gone forever, like my child.* But from her hands the baby looked straight into her, back through the years of her life to her own girlhood. That face was Marc, was Salim, was herself in Rebecca's arms. It freed something inside her, an old weight – she felt it floating away from them, up to the sky.

Salim saw her tears falling onto the frame. *My Jude. I'm so sorry. I don't deserve to weep.*

'Take it,' he said. 'It belongs to you now. You and Sophie. You're the only things I want to remember.'

Her hand traced the child. Salim's last glimpse of the Orange House was through her fingers, as she slipped it quietly into her pocket.

'I learned a strange thing from Nadia today,' she said, recovering. 'She says Muslims believe it was Ishmael, not Isaac, who Abraham nearly sacrificed. That Ishmael was his true heir.'

'We learned it at school,' he said. 'Around the time of the Eid. I was never really paying attention.'

'What a thing for us to argue over.' She wiped her nose on her sleeve. 'Which son to sacrifice.' He saw the white winter sun pouring through her fingers.

'I was so in love with you once,' she went on. Not the words she'd planned, but they came flooding out like water. 'Such an unlikely love, but it was amazing, wasn't it? That's what made our children. What made Marc.'

'It was.' He pictured them through the light, the twins when they were little, the glory and the wonder of them as he held them in his arms.

'And when Nadia was telling me that story, I thought – all these old, hateful tales that we can't forget, they're the real enemy, aren't they?' She looked out to sea. 'So whatever you've done, Sal, whoever's to blame – I don't want to be angry any more.'

He heard Sophie's voice calling from the hillside, and the rumble of car engines. Jude looked up; but she didn't turn to leave. Salim felt a wave of hope break in him, in time with the crash of the surf.

'So... what now?' he asked her. 'Where should we go from here?'

Her eyes closed, and his heart sank – but he dared not look away; he sensed a turning coming fast for both of them, approaching with terrifying speed. *I missed so many, because I was always looking behind me. I lost her because I could not find my own way.*

And then, to his wonder, her eyes met his. They were open as the day he'd first seen her, alone in a crowd at the party.

'You used to tell us about the sea by your house,' she said, and he remembered. *Those days lying side by side like Marc and Sophie in a boat on the English river, sharing stories of home.* 'Why don't you show me, since we're here?'

He laughed. 'It's cold. It's winter, in case you hadn't noticed.'

She bit her lip in the ghost of a smile. 'So you swim, and I'll wave.'

Her fingers were still covered with soil. He wanted to reach out and take them, but shame held him back, just as grief held her. Away to the south, the muezzin began to call the noon prayer. *Maybe there are no roads left to try.* She sighed and started to turn away.

'Come on then, Judith Rebecca Al-Ishmaeli,' he said. 'One walk with your husband. Before they send the search party out.' Her head came up, and he saw Marc's smile on her face.

She set off ahead, towards the beach. He heard her calling, '*Yallah*, slow coach. Are you coming?' She was a small beacon in the wasteland, a boy chasing a football hurled up into the blue, carried onwards by the winds to who knows where.

He answered – *I'm coming* – and he followed, turning away from the land and its fruits, running to her through the blowing seeds, the watching world vanishing behind. As he reached her she turned, and he saw it stretching out ahead of them – the long-forgotten way. They set a course through the empty space, a single outline blurred against the light. And at the edge of the shore the winding path met them, carrying them downwards to the sea.

ACKNOWLEDGEMENTS

So many thanks are due.

First, with deepest gratitude and love, to those who gave me their blessing and everything else besides – my family Rowan, Leila, and especially my beautiful mother. Her life tells a tale more extraordinary than fiction; she gave me – and this novel – a starting point.

To those already gone ahead – Ethel, Nouhad, Sayed, Max, Trudy, Gerald, Anne, Marwan, the Book sisters and brothers – and to those still with us on the road – Abla, Blanche, Polly, Mahmoud, Haj, Sam and my cousins, the generation born along the way – for carrying both tribes' precious stories forward to new worlds.

To my agent Gordon Wise, for his faith. To Juliet at Oneworld for rolling the dice and to my editors Ros, Eléonore and Jenny for helping me bring a long-sleeping story to life.

To Paolo Hewitt, the Don of north London, for that all-important introduction, and to Jenny Fairfax for opening the door.

To Adam LeBor, for his kindness to a stranger and the wonderful *Jaffa, City of Oranges*.

To William Goodlad, for taking the first look.

To Stephen Vizinczey, for his friendship, for letting me steal that line from *An Innocent Millionaire* and for every other word he's written – which still dazzle me as they've dazzled millions before me.

Finally and above all, to my husband – who, while saving the world, gave me the space and the love to take this long journey. Thank you, sweetheart. You know what it meant. And to my daughter, who at last gave me the reason. Delilah, my love. Here is your story.